Spotligh

Also by Ilana Fox

The Making of Mia

Spotlight

ILANA FOX

First published in Great Britain in 2010 by Orion Books,
an imprint of The Orion Publishing Group Ltd
Orion House, 5 Upper Saint Martin's Lane
London WC2H 9EA

An Hachette UK Company

3 5 7 9 10 8 6 4 2

A CIP catalogue record for this book is
available from the British Library.

ISBN (Hardback) 978 1 4091 1451 2
ISBN (Trade Paperback) 978 1 4091 1452 9

Typeset at The Spartan Press Ltd,
Lymington, Hants

Printed and bound in Great Britain by
Clays Ltd, St Ives plc

The Orion Publishing Group's policy is to use papers
that are natural, renewable and recyclable products and
made from wood grown in sustainable forests. The logging
and manufacturing processes are expected to conform to
the environmental regulations of the country of origin.

www.orionbooks.co.uk

For Naomi and Abigail Stern xxx

Acknowledgements

Thank you so much to Michael Sissons and Fiona Petheram at PFD. I'm so lucky to have such lovely agents.

At Orion I'd like to thank Kate Mills, Jade Chandler, Genevieve Pegg, Ruth Sharvell, Gaby Young, and Sidonie Beresford-Browne.

Family and friends, thank you: Harry and Nan, Peter and Magda, Naomi and Christian, Abi and Ben, George and Isabella. Ben Harvey, Sarah Graham, Holly Seddon, James Seddon, Hannah Weimers, Andre Litwin, Justin Myers, Jamie Griffin, Ian Strachan, Di James, Helen Nicholson, Anouska Graham, Chris Chivrall, Natalie Wall, Claudia Dutson, Kirsty Greenwood, and all my mates at The Sun (Cobras especially) and ASOS.com. You know who you are.

Finally, thanks to Sean Griffin, who never let go of my hand during the ride.

Chapter One

America

Madison stood at the top of the filthy staircase. There was only one way to go — and that was down.

'You know, being a waitress really wasn't that bad,' she pleaded, trying to think of a way out of the situation without losing face. 'And I was getting by on the cash I was making . . . just about.'

'Are you nuts?' Leesa said incredulously. 'You were getting two-dollar tips compared to the two-*hundred*-dollar ones you could be taking home. If you want to make it in Manhattan and really be *someone*, this is how do you do it. And fast.'

The two friends walked down the metal stairs to the basement club, which was just around the corner from the neon lights of Times Square. Leesa led the way up front in her hot-pink cowboy boots, and Madison followed tentatively behind in the patent black stilettos, white micro-mini and cheap red boob tube Leesa had lent her. Together they pushed open the heavy door at the bottom. A security guard sat inside. and he looked them up and down. He was big, butch and bored.

'She's here to audition,' Leesa said breathlessly in a sugar-sweet voice. She pushed Madison in front of her, and while the security guard was checking out Madison's legs, Leesa yanked the boob tube down even further. 'She wants to be a star.'

The guard's eyes lingered on Madison's breasts and hips. The girl had long chestnut hair, bright blue eyes, and incredible soft, pouty lips. She was young – but not too young – with killer curves and a fresh face. When she smiled he felt his balls ache. She was stunning.

'We're not auditioning today,' he said, struggling to sound uninterested, his voice gruff from a hangover. 'Not her, anyway.'

Leesa put her hand on her hip and grinned. She'd expected this – it was the famous first stage of getting a dancing gig, and she'd been through it herself. 'Oh, come on, honey,' she whined softly, before trying out one of her sticky lip-gloss pouts. 'My friend can really move . . . I've been giving her special one-on-one lessons . . . if you know what I mean.'

Madison felt a blush rising, and told herself to ignore it. If she was really going to go through with this she'd have to get used to being talked about like a whore. This was how it was. If you were working as a 'dancer' in New York you were always in the spotlight. That was the point.

'Look, if you let her audition I'll slip you fifty dollars, and my pal here will dance her socks off . . . along with other things, too,' Leesa added, and the security guard sighed. He was used to girls begging, but this one clearly knew the rules, what to say . . . And she worked here already. How could he say no?

'Go straight through,' he relented. 'And ladies? Don't let me down . . . I'm quality control in this dive.'

Madison felt her heart beating hard. She slithered past the security guard as sexily as she could in such high heels. She was nearly on her way . . . Although to what, she still wasn't sure.

When Madison Miller graduated from high school several months earlier, she hadn't a clue what she was going to do with her life. Since she was a tiny girl, all she'd wanted to do was sing, and from the age of five she'd spent all her time performing in local competitions and pageants. Her mom – who'd dreamt of being a singer herself, but had fallen pregnant and married young – had coached her, taught her to dance and sing as best she could, and was determined to make her the next big thing.

But as soon as Madison turned fifteen and started noticing boys, she'd put her ambition on hold . . . at least in public. She suddenly became shy – she'd developed some scary, sexy curves – and rather than loving being the centre of attention, she wanted out of the spotlight. She felt gawky and awkward, and even though her mom said she had a body to kill for, Madison was way too reserved to show it off. She still sung in her bedroom (naively leaving the window open in case a record producer just happened to be passing their house in Walkertown, Ohio), still spent her free time making up dance routines, but none of the other kids in school had the same burning ambition, and she didn't want to stand out as someone who would do anything to get ahead. Besides, didn't everyone fantasise about being a singer, and wasn't it time she grew up?

'What do you want to do with your life, Madison?' the career adviser had asked during the mandatory 'chat' in her senior year. She encouraged ambition, and had a friendly, open face. She was someone you could confide in.

'I want to be a singer,' Madison replied, remembering how she used to tell people that this was what she was going to do when she 'grew up'. She'd not voiced it out loud for a while, and it felt kind of awkward, but the moment she said it she remembered just how much she wanted it. It was performing or bust for her.

The career adviser looked over her steel-rimmed glasses at the teenager in front of her, and sighed. That morning she'd seen four wannabe actors, a weedy boy who was determined to be a wrestler, and three girls who were all convinced they'd make millions by being reality TV stars.

'And if the singing doesn't work out?' she asked gently. 'Madison, we need to work out what you can do if you *don't* become a singer. We need to give you some options.'

Madison looked at her as if she were mad. If she couldn't be a singer then she wouldn't do anything else. She'd just settle down in Walkertown and sing as a hobby instead, just as her mom had done. Besides, if being a singer didn't work out she still had Kyle, and so long as he was her boyfriend, she was happy.

Madison had been going steady with Kyle Brockway for just over three years, and he'd changed her life – or at least her reputation. When she'd first started at Walkertown High, Madison had been one of those girls the other kids were only aware of because they'd been at junior high together. She wasn't *known*.

A quiet girl who didn't excel at school, and only really came alive on stage, Madison blended into the crowd. She used to stare at the popular girls in her class with the kind of admiration people normally reserve for movie stars. They were all confident and sexy, and Madison didn't have the balls even to try joining their set. What was the point?

Her mom, as usual, had different ideas for her.

'Honey, if you're not going to sing, what *are* you going to do?' she asked her daughter one day after school. Madison was in a slump – she missed singing in talent competitions, but she just couldn't stand up there by herself and open her mouth. Not at the moment. Not while she felt like a little girl in a woman's body.

She shrugged and helped herself to an Oreo. 'My homework?' she muttered, separating the top half of the cookie from the bottom and scraping the cream off with her front teeth.

Jeanie Miller sighed. 'You're going to put your name down to be a cheerleader, and you're going to get your confidence back. Being part of a squad will make you less self-conscious. Trust me.'

Madison did as she was told. To her surprise (but not her mother's), she passed with flying colours, and after the cheer squad's initiation ceremony she had a new bunch of friends: the cutest and most popular girls in school, including head cheerleader Leesa Harland. Then it was only a matter of time before the guys in the football team checked her out in her tight, short cheer uniform, and it was after the third game of the season that Kyle asked her on a date. For Madison, it was love as soon as he kissed her in the back seat of his truck.

From that point on, high school was all about making sure everything she did was 'right', and screw her grades or singing. She took her cue from Leesa and the other cheerleaders, and started wearing short skirts and make-up, and spending more time making sure she was popular than on her homework. Sometimes she worried about not applying herself properly, but Madison was on a high from being part of the popular set – and although she didn't like it when the others tripped up the nerdy girl in recess, or laughed at the computer geek with pimples, she didn't say anything. She kept her mouth shut, or, more appealingly, attached it to Kyle's in a cutesy kiss to show everyone that if he loved her, she really was good enough to be part of the cool gang.

After Prom – where Madison and Kyle were naturally made Homecoming King and Queen, and Madison drunkenly and predictably lost her virginity in a motel room – things started to go downhill. It was their last summer together before Kyle went to Ohio State University (safe in the knowledge that he had a job waiting for him at his father's law firm), and Madison tried to work out her next move.

'Baby,' she began one afternoon late in the summer, when the sun was streaming through his bedroom window, 'I'm going to miss you so, so much.' She'd been watching Kyle folding sweaters to take to college, and every time he put one in his case she wanted to grab it and steal it back. It seemed as though he was slowly packing up his whole life and taking it away from her.

Kyle turned to her and grinned. 'Gonna miss you, too, but we're not going to be that far away from each other, and we can still date.'

Madison felt a stab of fear run through her. Dating wasn't the same as going steady, and she couldn't stand the thought of Kyle seeing other girls, however casually.

'I don't think I can face Walkertown without you. How would you feel if I came to Ohio State and hung with you instead?'

A shadow passed over Kyle's face, and he turned away from her. Kyle had been the broadest and tallest linebacker the Wildcats football team had ever seen, and he was a legend at school. Madison stared at his back and realised he no longer looked like a football-playing teenager, but a man.

'What would you study, Madison? The only things you're good at are singing, cheerleading and being my girlfriend. And I don't think the college would let you major in any of those.'

Madison bit her lip and thought hard. She was desperate. 'They have a vet school. I always liked animals . . .'

'Yeah, but you flunked biology, and besides, you've missed admissions.' Kyle sighed and sat down on his bed. 'I thought we agreed you'd stay here and raise some cash for singing lessons, since the only thing you ever said you wanted to do was be a *popstar*' – he said the word distastefully – 'and it's not like you're ever going to be good at anything else.'

Madison froze. She couldn't believe that Kyle could ever be so cruel. And only a few hours after they'd woken in each other's arms. 'What?'

'You know, one of the things I'm really looking forward to

most at college is meeting girls with ambition. Girls who want a career as well as a husband. Girls with brains as well as beauty.' Kyle looked at Madison properly but ignored the tears streaming down her face.

'You don't love me because I don't have ambition?' Madison asked disbelievingly. 'Because I *have* ambition . . .' Her voice trailed off as she realised Kyle was right. She'd fallen so in love with him that she'd forgotten how much she wanted to sing.

'Madison, your "ambition" amounts to either wanting to marry me and picking out Pottery Barn pieces for "our house", or singing in front of a mirror pretending to be Britney or Tori Catrino. They're little girl daydreams, and neither are going to happen.

'I'm not saying I don't love you, Madison, because I do, really, in a high school kind of way, but there's more to life than Walkertown, and there's gotta be more to relationships than going to the movies and making out in the back seat.'

'You don't want to marry me?' Madison asked in a quiet voice. It choked her to even get the words out, and she felt that with every breath she was being stabbed. She'd never hurt so much.

'You're kidding, right?' Kyle looked at Madison in horror. 'Sure, we can go out when I'm home from school, but you didn't really think we'd end up as Mr and Mrs Brockway, did you?'

Madison did, but she wasn't going to let Kyle know that. 'No, of course not,' she said quietly, wishing she could stop herself from crying, wishing she could hold it together. 'Not at all.'

Madison walked out of his bedroom, feeling as though the best part of her life had ended and she'd never be happy again.

*

'God, he's a bastard,' Leesa muttered down the phone to Madison that night after she'd heard what Kyle had done. 'Are you okay?'

Madison shook her head and took a deep breath. She couldn't stop crying, and it made it hard to speak. She'd only kept in touch with Leesa via Facebook the past year – it had been hard, as Madison had been so busy with Kyle and cheerleading, and Leesa had left Walkertown the previous year and was living a frantically fun life in New York – but she was glad her best friend was there for her now.

'No,' Madison whispered, struggling to get a hold of herself.

The girls had bonded the moment Madison joined the cheer squad. Leesa was a year older, and Madison had hero-worshipped her from the moment they'd met. She thought of her as a big sister. With long, strawberry-blonde hair, huge blue eyes, a Cupid-bow mouth, and a year-round tan, Leesa had been the sexiest girl at school, and therefore the most popular. She was the 'Girl Most Likely To', and although the Brains and the Emo kids muttered that that meant she was most likely to go all the way, Leesa was the golden girl. She got straight As, had been a child model, and was always the lead part in the school plays. When she graduated, nobody was surprised that she planned to go to New York to make it on Broadway. If anyone was going to put Walkertown, Ohio, on the map, it was Leesa Harland.

'And he said he didn't want to be with you because you don't have ambition?' Leesa asked incredulously, cracking her gum in irritation. Madison winced. She still felt raw. 'What a load of shit. All he aspires to is sleeping his way around his new campus and then working for Pop in his law firm when he comes back. He's full of it.'

Fresh tears sprang to Madison's eyes when she thought about Kyle sleeping with other girls, but Leesa had made her smile, too. She was right; he wasn't the most ambitious guy on the planet, and compared to Leesa, who was actually in New York City making something of herself, he was small town.

'Why don't you come out and visit me for a vacation?' Leesa continued. 'Even better, why don't you move out here? I've got space in my new apartment, and now you've graduated and ditched that awful meathead there's nothing stopping you. We can be the New York Wildcats. It'll be fun! I'll become an actress, you'll become a singer, and when we're rich and famous we'll tell everyone we met as cheerleaders. It will be so cool!'

Madison smiled. 'I thought you were already an actress?' she teased, but this was met with an awkward silence.

'I've put the acting on hold, and I'm an exotic dancer now, Mads,' Leesa said breezily, as if it didn't matter. Madison could tell it did. 'It's easy money, and it's real classy, honest. Loads of girls start off this way just to get noticed . . . and yeah, I'm not quite singing and dancing on Broadway yet, but give it time. How could they fail to want me?'

Madison's heart sunk. If Leesa – beautiful Leesa – couldn't make it as an actress, how would Madison become a singer? Leesa had always made everything seem so easy. 'If you want something,' she'd say, 'all you have to do is smile, flirt and fight until you get it.' But what if it wasn't that easy? What if she moved to New York and ended up 'dancing', too?

Although she'd not done anything about it, Madison dreamt about appearing on *American Idol* or *Teen Star USA* and winning over the judges. She knew that becoming a famous singer was just a fantasy – didn't every girl in America want to be the next Christina Aguilera? – but she'd be happy just to make a living out of singing, whether it was in a small dusky blues club or as the headline at Madison Square Garden (which always made her laugh – 'Madison at Madison Square Garden' had such a ring to it). But if Leesa couldn't even get cast in a commercial, how would Madison ever get a singing break?

'I'm not sure me moving to Manhattan is such a good idea, Lees,' Madison said, after thinking about it for a moment. 'I mean, I don't know how to become a singer. It's not like there are job ads for it.'

Madison could hear Leesa's smirk in her voice. 'Babe, there are loads of job ads for singers in the city. You just don't know that because you're not here yet. I know a couple of girls who sing in bands as well as one or two who do the bar circuit – they're always getting approached by people in the industry,' she said, half truthfully, not mentioning that most of the time the girls were approached for sex, not music contracts.

'Plus, think of all the great singing coaches out here. If you want to have singing lessons in Walkertown, the only person who can help you is Mrs Baranowski.'

Madison pictured their old music teacher at Walkertown High, and shuddered. Mrs Baranowski was old, smelt of dog, and had a hairy wart.

'But where will I live?' she said. She wasn't prepared for the fantasy life Leesa seemed to be offering her.

'With me! I told you I got a new place, and there's space for two, if you don't mind a room the size of your mom's pantry. It's in Harlem, and it's cool.'

'But . . . what about my parents?'

Leesa laughed. 'Your mom will practically push you onto the plane. Trust me, your parents will be made up for you. I'll see you soon.'

Chapter Two

Although everyone at school used to say they were just like each other, Madison knew deep down that she and Leesa were very different. Leesa was a bubbly, wholesome blonde, and although Madison acted that way in public to keep up with the popular set, in private she was quieter and a little shy.

But since moving to New York, Leesa had changed. Her strawberry-blonde hair was now peroxide white, and even though she was still gorgeous, her face had developed a hard, cynical edge. She lined her eyes with harsh black pencil, and her eyebrows were plucked into thin, brittle strips. She looked older than nineteen, and could have passed for at least twenty-seven.

Almost as soon as Madison had arrived in Manhattan, Leesa had suggested she start 'dancing' with her. The money and hours were great, she said, and it left the days to go to singing lessons. Madison simply shook her head and said she'd do something a little less energetic, like waitressing or answering phones, while she found her feet.

To Madison, New York was intimidating, fast-paced, crass and dirty. The first time she went to Times Square she felt dizzy and sick from the electric billboards screaming adverts at her, the noise of the traffic, the snarls of the locals pushing at the tourists. Walkertown was sleepy and quiet, a place where everyone knew everyone else, at least by sight. New York was a million miles from that, and when she wasn't running around the city feeling exhilarated, Madison curled up in a ball on Leesa's couch, unsure how she was going to survive.

The first conventional job Madison got was like a slap in the face – a baptism of fire into 'real life'. She'd beaten off the competition to be a waitress in a scummy diner in the Lower East Side purely by being the only female applicant, but the pay was lousy, and the tips even worse. Leesa said she was incredibly lucky to get a server job because they were so scarce, so Madison stuck at it, even though she hated it.

But every weekend Leesa went shopping for outfits in the West Village or Fifth Avenue, while Madison stayed in her tiny room in their apartment, working out that she needed at least $1000 a month to eat and have singing lessons with the legendary Patty Bekessy – a former star in *Cats* – once a week. She was barely making $600.

As a result Madison stopped getting her hair done and stopped going out, and she even started to skip meals so that she could pay her rent and visit Patty in her dramatic uptown apartment. Madison knew it was worth it. Patty made her work hard – she taught Madison how to control her breathing as well as extending her vocal range – and when she saw Patty's eyes sparkle over the piano, Madison knew she was onto a good thing. Her singing lessons were the best part of a difficult life, and the only thing that stopped Madison from packing her bags to go back home. In New York she was invisible, and while the beautiful people whizzed past her in their Lincoln Town Cars, Madison could barely afford the subway.

A few months into her job, Madison felt as though she could serve with her eyes shut. She spent most of the day rushing around and refilling people's coffee cups, and when she wasn't doing that she was taking orders, running to and from the kitchen, and wiping her sweaty hands on her grease-stained apron. Leesa bought her *It Could Happen to You*, an old Nick Cage movie where a cop wins the lottery and shares the ticket with a waitress, and every time her job started to get her down (which was almost every ten minutes), Madison remembered good things could happen. And that was what she was thinking late one night when a dark-haired man walked in and took her breath away.

The first thing Madison noticed – if she was honest with herself – was that he looked just like Kyle. He was broad and tall, and his eyes were a similar, piercing blue. He also smiled at her in that geeky, crooked way Kyle did when he messed up a catch, and that was enough for Madison to apply a touch of lip-gloss to her tired, dry lips before going over to say hi. She didn't miss sex, not really, but she missed the attention and affection Kyle had showered on her.

'Coffee and pancakes,' the guy said, pulling a copy of *Variety* out of his pocket and barely glancing at her. He was gorgeous, and he brought promise and money into the diner along with the lingering scent of his aftershave. Most of her customers were old and poor.

Madison forced a grin that he didn't see. 'Sure,' she said, and as she walked towards the stove to grab some coffee she felt her face flush. The lack of decent food and stupid working hours had sent her crazy, she thought. It must have done – how could she think a movie guy like him (because everyone in New York who read *Variety* seemed to be in the movies) would be interested in a waitress like her? Still, he looked loaded, and Madison always struck up a conversation with the customers even when she couldn't be bothered. If she pretended to be interested in them she was guaranteed a half-decent tip.

The man put down his magazine and gazed at Madison as she poured his coffee and asked him how he was. 'You're new to New York,' he said, ignoring her question. 'You have that look.'

Madison was momentarily startled. Customers only ever talked about themselves.

'How can you tell?' she asked with a flirty grin. Without thinking, she put the coffee jug on the table and sat down. She didn't care that she was meant to stay on her feet regardless of how empty the diner was. She needed a break.

'You have that gleam, that shine. When girls have been here a while they kind of get . . . hard,' he said. 'You look brand new.'

Madison smiled. It was a compliment. 'I've been here a couple of months – I'm from Ohio originally, and I want to be a—'

'A movie star,' the man interrupted. 'You girls always want to be in the movies. Don't you know you're meant to go to Hollywood?'

'Well, you know . . . I really want to be a singer,' Madison confided. 'Only I'm not sure how to do it.'

The man looked at her for a second, and smiled. 'I'm an A and R man,' he said casually. 'I'm normally in LA, but I came out here for a party tonight. Tiny canapés, though, which is why I'm totally craving pancakes.'

Madison blushed, embarrassed she'd forgotten she was meant to be serving him. 'Coming right up,' she said, rising from the table.

The man grabbed her wrist. 'Make sure you sit back down when you bring me my midnight feast,' he said with a grin. 'I bet I know someone who could help you out.'

A stack of pancakes later, the man stood up to leave. He'd given Madison some tips on how to make it in the music business, while she told him about her break-up with Kyle. She suddenly felt sad. This stranger had been the first person, other than Leesa and Patty, to be friendly to her in the city, and he was going back to Hollywood. It wasn't fair.

'Where's the best place to get a cab?' he asked her.

They were the only people left in the diner, so Madison said she'd walk with him up to Grand Street where she normally got the subway home. 'It's only a few blocks away, if you don't mind walking.'

As they strolled along East Broadway the man put his arm casually around Madison's shoulders, and it brought back memories of Kyle looping his body around hers after he'd won games. He'd be tired, and she'd be aching from the cheers, but when they fitted together so easily their pains drifted away. For Madison this friendly, easy gesture from a stranger had the same effect.

'How about you and I share a cab back to your place?' the man asked then, and the spell was broken. Madison panicked. Obviously she wasn't a virgin – in fact, she was nowhere near – but she'd only ever slept with Kyle, and she barely *knew* this guy.

'I don't even know your name,' Madison laughed, as she felt the man's grip tighten around her.

'You don't need to,' he said, and there was something in his voice that Madison didn't like. She pushed his arms off her shoulders and looked at him.

'You know, I'm the kind of girl that does,' she said, and she started walking away from him as quickly as she could. He followed.

'Don't give me that, baby,' he called after her. 'I told you I'd help make you a star . . . and in New York that kind of talk requires payment.'

Madison got to the subway, and before she ran down the steps she spun around and looked at him. 'I'm not a prostitute,' she spat.

The man laughed. 'Not yet, baby, but you soon will be.'

'You know, I get paid big bucks to be hit on every night,' Leesa said conversationally as she leant against the doorway. Madison was in tears, but Leesa couldn't see what the problem was. If men knew they could get away with it, they'd do anything to have sex with you, she thought. The trick was playing them at their own game. And not taking life so seriously.

Madison looked up at Leesa and frowned. 'I hate being hit on. It makes me feel so seedy. I mean, do I look like a slut?'

Leesa rolled her eyes. 'Honey, there are thousands of girls in this city alone who would kill to have a guy pay them attention, and here you are boo-hooing because someone found you attractive. Get over it.'

Leesa was wearing her pre-work clothes – a faded Juicy Couture tracksuit and Nike sneakers – but Madison knew that as soon as she got to the club, Leesa would be strutting around in tiny hotpants, cupless bras and high platform heels. Madison had no idea how she did it.

'I thought he was a nice guy,' she muttered, wiping up the last of her tears with a soggy tissue. 'I thought he liked me for who I am.'

'You know, he probably did, but you can't blame him for making a move – you're hot. Way too hot to be a waitress. Why don't you ditch the job and come and dance with me? I made four hundred dollars last night, and that was a bad night. I'm gonna make three times that tonight because one of my regulars is coming in and he always asks for at least two dances.'

'You sound like a hooker,' Madison said bluntly.

Leesa swung herself onto Madison's hard bed. 'Yeah, I know, but the difference between me and a hooker is that they can't even touch me, let alone fuck me. I shake my thing, and they pay up. That's all there is to it.'

'Yeah, until you do your "private dances" . . .' Madison said softly. What Leesa said sounded too good to be true. A job where you danced and got paid big bucks just for that had to have a catch.

'I told you before, nothing happens. Men come in, pick the girl they want to dance for them, and then we do it. God, I'd be kicked out in a sec if the House Mom thought I was touching a guy. It's totally breaking the rules.'

'The House Mom?'

'Yeah, she, like, looks after us. She's too old to dance herself so she gets a cut of our action. And makes sure the girls aren't getting drunk — which is harder than it looks.'

'You drink on the job?'

Leesa laughed. 'Part of our job is to get customers drinking as much as possible. So they come in, we tell them we want a bottle of pink bubbles — because that's the most expensive — and then we have to somehow drain our glasses without getting drunk. I normally take my glass to the bar and spill it into a bucket behind the counter when the guy's not looking.'

'And he doesn't notice?'

'We take it in turns to distract the men,' Leesa said simply. 'You know, team work.'

'So basically, you sit with men in your underwear, get paid to drink pink champagne, and sometimes do private sexy dances. Even though the guys can't touch you?'

Leesa grinned. 'Sounds about right,' she said.

'And that's it?'

'That's it. So why don't you do it with me? You'd be perfect, you know. You have an incredible body and you've got so skinny since you stopped eating properly.'

Madison looked down at herself. 'I look awful . . .' she began.

Leesa laughed. 'You look chic, like a woman. No more puppy fat, but those huge, perky breasts.'

Madison bit her lip. She wasn't a prude, but she hated talking like this, hated how Leesa had turned from a fun, bubbly girl into someone who could be so cold about working in the sex industry. 'Lees, I didn't move out here to be a stripper . . .' she said.

'So why did you move out here?' Leesa sounded curt.

'You asked, and I thought I could make it as a singer.'

Leesa laughed. 'Like I thought I could make it as an actress? I'm gonna make it, but you have to go through the motions to get there first. You have to survive to get to that point. Madison, it's time to understand the real world and to grow up. Don't you agree?'

Madison sighed. She supposed she was being childish and a bit of a prude . . . And if being an exotic dancer really meant that all you did was dance, she supposed there was no harm in it. Besides, the cash would come in handy . . . She had another five singing lessons with Patty Bekessy booked, and if she made as much money as Leesa did she'd be able eat a couple of decent meals, too.

She didn't look enough like a drag queen, Madison thought, as she sat in front of the dressing table backstage at Spotlight. She'd already applied a layer of thick, dark foundation, but her eyeliner was too light, and her lips needed to pout and sparkle more. Madison picked up her eyeliner and added what felt like an extra inch on top of her lids. The black liquid oozed over the silver, gloopy eyeshadow she'd already smeared on, and when it dried she expertly dotted eyelash glue onto her lids and put her long fake lashes in place.

'Looking good, sister,' Erika lied as she walked past in a thong and stilettos, her fake-tanned ass wobbling. Even though Madison had been working here for nearly six months, she still found it hard to get used to the girls strutting around naked. The dressing room smelt not just of sweat – despite the knock-off perfume all the girls used – but of sadness. They were the clowns, Madison thought. Clowns painting on their smiles.

Madison reached for her purple lip-liner and carefully drew an outline of a bigger, more luscious mouth on top of her own, filling it in with a shimmering, near-black violet. Then she reached for the glitter, which she painted liberally on the top. She thought she looked awful, but the guys liked it . . . and she wanted at least three private dances tonight so she could pay for more singing lessons, and maybe a massage. She'd made nearly $10,000 in the six months she'd worked at Spotlight, but it wasn't enough. It was never enough. Most of her money went on the apartment she rented off Lafayette Street, and any extra went on the essentials: food, clothes and the twice-weekly singing lessons with Patty.

'Showtime, ladies!' the House Mom yelled into the shambolic room, and Madison peeled off her dressing gown and gave herself a cursory look in the mirror. She was wearing one of her best outfits tonight: a hot-pink basque with gold trim, purple thigh-high PVC boots, and a baby-pink garter to set off the tiny black thong. She knew she looked like a hooker from the ghetto, but that was what Spotlight was all about – letting men live the dream, even if their dream involved cheap-looking girls who made them splurge the cash.

'You really don't look like Madison any more,' Leesa whispered as she fluttered past, and Madison recoiled from the sweet smell of booze on her friend's breath. Leesa was drunk again, and had probably taken coke. She was drinking more and more on the job, and sometimes she let guys touch her in the hope of getting extra cash. She'd paid for long blonde extensions, and had lost so much weight she looked scrawny. These days she was jealous of Madison's success at the club. Madison tried to tell her that she was only popular with the guys because she was fresh meat, but they both knew it wasn't true. The men loved Madison because of her glossy hair, her tight curves, and the way she moved her body. Leesa was full of self-loathing, and it showed.

'Are you drunk? Or have you taken drugs again?' Madison had chased after her, and they were standing at the side of the stage. Leesa swayed slightly, and Madison knew it wasn't because of her super-high heels.

'So what if I have?' Leesa said aggressively. 'Sometimes I need to take the edge off it a little.' She started laughing. 'Besides, it helps me move. We can't all pretend we're Madonna when we're on stage. Some of us are *realists*.'

Madison felt herself blush under her make-up. The only way she'd got through those early days of being a 'dancer' was to pretend she was Madonna or Tori Catrino or even Pink – and that the guys in the audience were there to hear her sing. The taking the clothes off bit – well, that was just part of the act . . . and besides, there were worse ways to live.

'I don't do that any more,' Madison hissed, but both girls knew she was lying.

'Sure,' Leesa shrugged. 'Whatever.' She looked as though she was going to say something else, but the music started up, and the girls had to take their places on stage. It was showtime.

During the day Spotlight looked like any other basement club. The dingy black walls were dotted with greasy full-length mirrors, the silver tables were peeling, and the floor was sticky with spilt booze from the night before. But when the crowds surged in at night, and the lights dimmed, Madison felt a rush of energy. Neon striplights cast electric shadows on the girls, and when the DJ started spinning, the club wasn't seedy or sordid. It was exciting.

As Madison moved about on stage she let herself go and imagined she was Mariah Carey – the unstoppable main attraction – while all the other girls were her backing dancers. She watched as Erika turned her back on the crowd and started swishing her ass from side to side, and glanced at Mona who was standing on the spot shaking her shoulders. She didn't need to move any other part of her body – her tits swung in time with the music, and even Madison had to admit it was mesmerising.

Madison did her own thing, dancing around a pole as suggestively as she dared – sometimes shooting flirty looks into the crowd, sometimes ignoring them completely. She loathed being a *stripper* when her parents thought she worked in a bookshop in Union Square, but she couldn't help loving the buzz that she got from performing in front of a paying audience. She imagined the men at the front were her biggest fans, and as she cast her eyes over them she worked out which ones she'd give an autograph to, which ones she'd allow to take her picture. Leesa may have thought she was a stupid little girl for pretending she was a high-class singer rather than a low-rent stripper, but she didn't care. She loved being on stage, even if she hated what she was doing.

As soon as the number finished Madison hopped off the platform and worked the floor, saying hi to the regulars and fixing her gaze on the newer guys, who were trying not to look nervous. Someone pushed a glass of champagne in her hands, and she sipped it as she leant over tables and smiled her special, Spotlight-only sleazy grin. Within ten minutes she had four private dances booked, and it felt great. That was at least $400 – minus the cut she gave the House Mom and DJ.

'Hey,' a voice called out, and Madison turned. A guy was sitting alone at a table – which wasn't unusual – but he was surrounded by some of the other girls, who had flocked to him because he clearly had money to burn. His well-cut designer suit and perfect grooming made him stand out in an instant. 'You're Angel, right?' he said to her as she approached, and Madison nodded. This was her Spotlight name, so she could be whatever fantasy the guys wanted her to be.

'Sit with me,' he directed, and some of the other girls shot her daggers to warn her off.

'Looks like you have your hands full already,' Madison said lightly, but she didn't turn away. He was obviously loaded, and as callous as it seemed, Madison wanted some of his cash.

'Yeah, with girls I don't want,' he said cruelly.

Leesa visibly winced, and Madison felt for her. This wasn't going to help their relationship any.

'Get these ladies away from me and I'm yours all night,' the man remarked.

Madison stared at him. His blue-black hair set off his black eyes, which were flashing with fun. He was gorgeous – and he wanted *her*.

'It will cost you,' she remarked, as she worked out how much. 'Five hundred dollars for me to sit with you, and that's without a dance.'

'Deal,' he said. 'But I don't want a dance.'

The other girls glowered and sullenly stalked away, and Madison slipped smoothly into the booth next to him.

'What kind of man doesn't want a dance from me?' Madison said in her Spotlight baby voice.

He shook his head. 'The same man who wants to talk business, not pleasure,' he replied.

Madison was momentarily stunned. 'You know,' she said slowly, 'I'm not quite sure what you want.'

'Nothing wrong with talking to a pretty girl, is there?' the man said, picking up a glass of champagne and knocking it back.

'No, but why pay for it when you could pick up any girl at Bungalow 8 or Marquee?'

'Because I don't want just any girl. I want you, Madison.'

Hearing her real name said out loud in the club sent a jolt through her. It was as if a balloon had unexpectedly burst and her bones were trying to jump out of her skin. Madison did the only thing she knew: she smiled and gulped her champagne.

'Do I know you?' she laughed nervously.

The man shook his head. 'Not yet, but I'm hoping we can get to know each other *real* well . . .'

Madison relaxed. So that was his game – he thought she was a prostitute. About once a week a guy propositioned her, and promised her the earth if she slept with him. Madison's response was always the same – as much as she'd *love* to, it was against the rules. No matter that she'd never, *ever* wanted to get intimate with her clients. She wouldn't sleep with someone she didn't love, and they were generally unattractive and overweight, but so long as their egos remained intact, they'd almost always come back for another dance.

'Sorry, no can do. Spotlight would sling me out if I even touched you,' Madison laughed.

'I don't want to sleep with you, Madison,' he said slowly, looking at her carefully, as Madison put down her glass of champagne and wondered again how he knew her name. 'I'm

Beau Silverman, and I own Slate Street Records. Patty Bekessy sent me. She tells me you've been having singing lessons with her — and that you're just the kind of girl I've been looking for.'

Chapter Three

'You want to make me a star?' Madison asked disbelievingly.

They were sitting in one of the small rooms off the dance-floor which were more commonly used for private dances, but true to his word, Beau Silverman only wanted to talk.

'That pretty much sums it up,' he commented, and cracked open a bottle of champagne. Madison raised her eyebrows. 'What, don't you believe me?'

Madison laughed and shook her head. 'Things like this just don't *happen*, Mr Silverman. Things like this happen in the movies or in books – a girl is down on her luck and reaching breaking point when a knight on a white stallion rides past and rescues her.'

'You can't be down on your luck if you can afford Patty Bekessy,' Beau remarked.

'Yeah, because she's the best. But I can only afford her by dressing like this.' Madison gestured to the tiny amount of clothing she was wearing, and tried not to feel self-conscious. 'Believe me, if I wasn't down on my luck I wouldn't be a stripper.'

Beau wordlessly slipped off his designer jacket and placed it gently over her shoulders. Madison smiled at him gratefully.

'I can take you away from all of this,' Beau said easily. 'Just do an audition from me, show me you've got what Patty thinks you have, and you're the girl I want.'

'So you keep saying! But . . .'

Beau grinned. 'But what?'

Madison was silent for a moment. 'Is it really that simple? It can't be, surely.'

'Madison, when you've been in the industry all your life as I have, you'll realise that some people are magnets for success. And I think you are one of them.' He let his gaze run over Madison's face.

Madison struggled with what was happening. 'I don't believe you,' she said bluntly. 'I don't know who you are, or how you know my real name, but you can't have just walked in here and told me you want to make me a popstar. You can't have.'

'This is my card,' Beau said, handing her a shiny black business card with his name embossed on the front in tiny silver letters, 'and here's my cell. Call Patty, talk to her.'

Madison took Beau's cell and searched through the contacts until she found Patty Bekessy's name. Her hand started to shake when she saw Patty's number was under Paris Hilton's.

'Beau, darling!' Patty's gravelly voice sung through the phone, and Madison smiled. Even though she wasn't on Broadway any more, Patty still had a touch of the theatrical in everything she did. She wore long silk scarves with bells on the end, and her life was a performance. Every movement she made, every word she uttered was undertaken with melodrama and showmanship, as if she were constantly on stage with a director whispering at her from the wings. Madison adored her.

'Patty? It's . . . Madison Miller. I'm on Beau Silverman's cell, and—'

'Madison, darling!' Patty cried. 'So he found you. Fantastic! I hope you don't mind me sending him down to that shabby little "dancing" place of yours, but he said he simply had to see you!'

'But who is he?' Madison asked quietly, turning her back on Beau.

'Beau Silverman, darling? Everyone knows Beau. He heads up Slate Street Records. Isn't he divine? He's the son of Griffith Silverman. You must have heard of *him*?'

There was an expectant pause while Madison frowned.

'Um, no, I haven't. Who?'

'Griffith Silverman!' Patty bellowed. 'Lead singer of the Jailbaits! I spent *years* getting high with them all in the sixties, and had *quite* the affair with Griffo. Of course, it didn't last as his wife caught us in a tepee, but—'

'Patty,' Madison interrupted urgently, aware that Beau was watching her carefully. 'Why did you send Beau to me?'

Madison heard Patty light a match and inhale deeply. Despite being a professional singer, Patty had never thought to give up smoking cigarettes.

'Because, darling, he asked me who I thought the best young singer was, and I told him about you.'

Madison shot a look at Beau. 'What did you tell him?' she hissed.

'Well, first of all I played him a tape of you singing, and he loved it. *Loved* it! When he asked what you're like I told him you're the most adorable girl, but you pay for your singing lessons by being a *hooker*. That you're bright, funny, gorgeous and would simply *shine* as a superstar!'

'I'm not a hooker, Patty, I'm an exotic dancer.'

Patty laughed. 'Whatever you say, sweetheart,' she remarked airily. 'Beau needs a new act, and I told him you were the girl he wants.'

Madison said goodbye to Patty, and ended the call, then turned to look at Beau again.

27

'Mr Silverman,' she began tentatively, trying to take in everything Patty had just told her. 'You're really serious, aren't you?'

Beau smiled. 'I'm always serious about work. And Madison, when I tell someone I'm going to make them a superstar, I intend to do it.'

Madison gently put his cell on the table and stared at him. 'I can't believe this is happening,' she said in a quiet voice.

Beau leant back in his chair. 'Patty's a feeder for me,' he said with a shrug. 'I've known her since . . . well, for ever, and if I'm in need of a new act I go to her first. She keeps her ear to the ground and sometimes gives lessons to my acts.'

'Like who?'

Beau handed Madison another glass of champagne. 'Like The Pistol Slingers,' he said. 'Ever heard of them?'

Madison gulped and nodded. The Pistol Slingers were the hottest, coolest rock band in the States at the moment, and even though rock wasn't quite Madison's thing she fancied Blake, the lead singer. He was a skinny, edgy bad boy who oozed sex. 'Blake's had singing lessons with Patty?' she asked incredulously.

'Sure,' Beau said. 'And so did Tori Catrino.'

'Oh my God,' Madison said. 'I had no idea Patty was so . . . that she had such . . .' Her voice trailed off.

'That Patty gives singing lessons only to the best? Sure she does.'

'But Tori Catrino!' Tori had been famous since she was seventeen – one of those teeny-bopper, virgin-until-marriage types – who'd recently thrown away her career by disappearing off the face of the planet.

'Didn't Tori get dumped by her record label for getting overweight or something?' Madison asked, and although Beau kept on smiling his black eyes hardened.

'She used to be on Slate Street, yes,' he said. 'But she broke her contract and that was the end of that.' Something in Beau's expression told Madison not to push it.

'And you think I'm good enough to be on Slate Street?'

Beau looked at Madison for a moment. 'I don't know,' he said. 'But your tape was pretty good, and Patty says you're cute . . . Although I can't tell with all that shit on your face.' He paused again, and Madison felt his eyes on her breasts, which were only half-hidden by his jacket. She knew he was checking out her figure and that he liked what he saw.

'I want you to come down to the Slate Street studios and put a demo together for me. How does that sound?'

Madison smiled. It sounded amazing. Even if Beau hated her voice and didn't want to take it further, it would be fantastic just to be in a recording studio, a dream come true.

'That would be great,' Madison said softly, and suddenly she stopped remembering to be careful and allowed herself to fall headlong into her dream.

'So what happened to you?' Leesa had stumbled into Madison's apartment, stinking of alcohol and cigarettes, and smearing her make-up all over Madison's cream sofa. 'Word is you went in the back with that guy, and then you just disappeared.'

'You won't believe what happened to me!' Madison said excitedly.

'Sure I do,' Leesa said, rolling her eyes.

'You do?'

'Uh-huh.' Leesa pulled a tiny bottle of vodka out of her purse. 'Got anything I can mix this with?'

Madison eyed the bottle warily. 'There's some Coke in the fridge. But how do you know?'

'You've only got fat Coke?' her friend called from the kitchen. 'I wanted Diet . . . Guess I'll have it neat.' She swigged the vodka straight from the bottle, then wiped her mouth with the back of her hand. More make-up slid off her face, but if Leesa cared she didn't give any sign of it.

'That guy was from Runway 69, right?'

'What?'

Leesa laughed. 'Madison Miller, don't play dumb with me. That guy was from Runway 69 and he poached you to go dance for them. Hell, I'd do it if I was asked . . .'

'What's Runway 69?' Madison asked, bewildered.

Leesa rolled her eyes again. 'You've never heard of the hottest, most exclusive strip joint in New York City? Yeah, right.'

'No, I'm serious, Lees . . . He wasn't from another strip club; he was a record exec!'

Leesa took another swig of her vodka. 'And what, you sung for him while you did a lap dance?'

Madison beamed. 'No, he didn't want me to dance at all. Patty – Patty Bekessy, you know, my singing teacher – well, she's friends with Beau and she told him I was great and he wants to hear me sing! Properly! And if he likes me . . .' Madison didn't dare say it out loud.

'If he likes you he'll sign you up, make you famous, and you'll never have to dance again?' There was something in Leesa's tone that wasn't quite right. Madison ignored it.

'Yeah! Isn't that the most amazing thing ever?'

Leesa pursed her lips. 'Honey, you're still new to this game and this happens all the time. Remember when Erika was totally upset a few months back? Well, that was because some guy came in and told her he was a glamour photographer and he thought Erika could make it as a model. Turned out he was just a sleaze and when Erika went to his "studio" he tried to have sex with her. Lucky for her she can run in heels, right?'

'But Beau's legit . . . I'm going down to his offices in a couple of days and I'm going to record a demo.'

Leesa finished her vodka, and tossed the bottle onto the floor. She was wasted. 'Sure, honey, whatever you say,' she commented lightly. 'But when he turns out to be after your body and not your voice, don't come running to me.' She stood up and walked towards the door.

'He's not like that, honestly.'

Leesa shrugged. 'Whatever,' she said. 'Are you coming back to Spotlight? Because the House Mom sure is pissed with you for pulling your disappearing act . . . Bet she fines you for that.'

Madison knew she wouldn't be able to perform while her mind was on her audition tape.

'I don't think so, Lees,' she said quietly.

'Your call,' said her friend, staring at her. 'But don't come begging when you find out your little fantasy is just that.' She slammed the front door behind her.

Madison picked up the empty bottle of vodka from the floor. It was smeared with pink lipstick, and Madison resolved to practise her singing every moment she had so she'd never end up like Leesa.

'That was shit – let's go again,' the producer said from the control room.

Madison eyeballed him from the safety of the isolation booth. He was a lanky Texan called Bud, possibly the uncoolest man Madison had ever met. His long, filthy flares dragged against the ground, and his beer belly – hairy with ginger fluff – protruded from underneath an old REM T-shirt. He was as different from Beau as could be – not to mention the guys in Ohio – yet Beau had spoken highly of him, and entrusted her demo to him.

Madison didn't get it. He didn't look like he even knew how to wash, let alone mix a great track.

'You missed a couple of notes near the start,' Bud added, and Madison squeezed her eyes tight and inhaled deeply. She had to concentrate, had to put her soul into the song, and, most importantly, not overthink it. She had to *feel* it. The background music filtered into the vocal booth, and suddenly she had her cue. Madison forgot about Bud, forgot about Beau, and went for it. She sung her heart out.

'And . . . cut,' Bud said, as soon as Madison had breathed the final note of Kelly Clarkson's 'Because of You'. He was jabbing at buttons on what Madison assumed was a mixing desk, and listening intently to her vocals. Madison wished she could hear them, but the room was soundproofed.

'How did I do?' Madison asked tentatively through her microphone, but Bud didn't look up from the other side of the glass. She tried not to feel rejected. She'd given it her all, and that had to be enough.

'Come on through and have a listen.' Bud's voice cut into her thoughts.

Madison put her headphones on the stand and made her way into the control room.

'Is it terrible?' she asked nervously.

Bud grinned at her. 'Awful,' he said, and pressed play.

For a moment Madison wanted to run out of the studio in shame. She'd always thought she was a good singer – everyone at school had always said so, and even Kyle agreed she was good – but finding out she was terrible in a professional recording studio was embarrassing. She bit her lip as the opening bars of the piano filled the room, and then heard her voice overlaid on top.

She sounded beautiful.

'That note there isn't right,' Bud said conversationally, 'and you sound robotic here.'

Madison nodded, and Bud played it again. At the start her voice ribboned around the backing track, darting in and out of the chords of the piano, and reverberating softly against the solemn notes. When the tempo picked up and the drums kicked in, her voice became stronger but tender, passionate and poignant. Madison had never heard her voice played back before, and she couldn't distance herself from it to make a judgement.

'Is it good enough?' she whispered, almost unable to voice her fears. If Beau hated it, she was back at Spotlight dancing for dollars . . . if they allowed her to come back.

'Honey, it's one of the best demos I've ever heard. It's almost *too* great for what Beau's after.'

Madison barely heard him. This scruffy, messy man thought she could sing. And that was good enough for her.

'Let's cut the pleasantries and get down to what I need,' Beau said after they'd ordered their food. He and Madison were in Asia de Cuba at Morgans, and she was feeling uncomfortable. It was the first time she was seeing Beau as herself and not as an 'exotic dancer', and she didn't know how to act. When he told her where they were eating, Madison freaked out. Everyone knew Asia de Cuba was cool, and she didn't think her tacky strip club outfits or her Ohio high school clothes would cut it. A quick shopping trip at Barneys and $300 later, and Madison was wearing a simple black A-line dress. It was boring and way too conservative for her – but Beau wanted to talk *business*, and Madison guessed she needed to look sensible and grown up, as well as fashionable. Even so, she wished she was wearing skin-tight jeans instead. She didn't feel sexy at all.

'Ever heard of *Teen Star*?' Beau asked, and Madison nodded, smiling. *Teen Star USA* was one of the biggest shows on TV in which fresh-faced under-25s auditioned to be crowned the *Teen Star* of the year. It was like *American Idol*, but included acting and dancing, too. Jacy Robins – a budding blonde actress with pillow-plump lips – had won it last year and had landed a part on a new show that was beating all audience records. She was made.

'I love *Teen Star*,' Madison said conversationally. 'I've watched it the past two seasons.'

Beau didn't smile. 'Slate Street owns a controlling portion of the show – we developed it with the network.'

Madison was momentarily dumbstruck. 'Wow . . . so you know Jacy Robins?'

This time Beau did grin. 'Madison, I *own* Jacy Robins. The winner of the show is automatically signed up to the Slate Street Agency.'

When Madison didn't say anything – for she truly didn't know how to respond to that – Beau couldn't help but look satisfied. He was so used to being a big cheese that he forgot just how impressive he could be. And the power it had over people.

'Wanna know a secret?' he asked conspiratorially. 'It's all a fix.'

Madison's baby-blue eyes widened. 'What? You mean the voting?'

Beau raised his eyebrows. 'Well, to put it bluntly, yes. But we also put forward acts we're already aware of. Jacy had been taking acting lessons with a teacher I know, and he suggested we put her on the show. We knew she'd be an instant hit.'

Madison took a slug of her drink and tried not to feel disappointed. She'd voted for Jacy three times. 'So she wasn't an unknown?'

'She was an unknown for sure . . . I mean, the American public didn't know her, did they? No, what I mean is, for every

34

fifty auditions, we only get one or two real talents, and then there's something not quite right about them. Maybe they're twenty pounds too heavy, or they're just not photogenic enough. You need the whole package. So we put people with the whole package into the process. The judges know who they are, they make sure they go through, and as well as being great for ratings, we're guaranteed professionals who will win and can make it in the careers we give them.'

'I had no idea . . .' Madison trailed off. 'I mean, how many people know about this?'

'Only a few people who work on the show. And the teens we put forward, of course. Which is where you come in.'

'You want me to go on *Teen Star USA*?' Madison yelped, and Beau frowned, gesturing for her to lower her voice.

'That's the idea, Madison,' he said, and he raised his eyebrows. 'But how would you feel about winning it, too?'

Luckily for Madison, her roast pork arrived and saved her from completely freaking out. She focused on her plate and took a deep breath.

'Are you serious? Are you really, really serious?'

Beau paused for a second. 'I thought I told you before, I don't make jokes about this stuff.' He pushed his plate of food away and took Madison's hand, which was shaking.

'There are conditions, which you would have to accept if you chose to do it. First, you're not to have any contact with your friends or family, in case you're tempted to let them in on the secret, and second, you trust me. I've been in this game for a while, and I'm successful at what I do. I've taken on too many acts that thought I was wrong, and they paid the price for going against what I knew was best for them.'

Madison thought about not having contact with her family – especially her mom – and her heart sank a little. But then her mom would tell her to take this opportunity and never look back. She knew she would.

Beau eyed Madison thoughtfully. 'I know this is a lot to take in, and it seems kinda whirlwind,' he said softly, 'but I really think that if you stick with me you could be a star.'

Chapter Four

England

'Have you finished bagging up those samples yet?' Faye asked Jess from the doorway of the fashion cupboard.

Jess was sitting on the thinly carpeted floor of the tiny room just off the newsroom. 'Um, not yet,' she replied nervously, pushing her dark blonde hair behind her ears, and wondering if the fashion editor would lose her temper. She was an absolute cow. Jess checked out her one-shouldered gold dress over a hot-pink T-shirt, and wondered if the millions of readers who read Faye's fashion pages realised they were taking fashion advice from someone who dressed like a Z-list celeb. She doubted it.

'So long as it's done by five. And remember to let the couriers know.'

Jess glanced at the clock and tried not to sigh. She was dying to get out of here and have a drink.

'Also, have you been able to . . .' Whatever Faye was about to ask Jess was interrupted by a flurry of activity on the news desk. Jess stood and poked her head out of the door.

'An exchange student's been murdered in Egypt!' Matthew called out.

Jess watched him thoughtfully. Matthew Parker thrived on the rush of breaking news. In comparison the fashion desk only ever got excited about the freebies stacked up in the fashion cupboard

– or what celebrities they'd met the night before – and they didn't seem to care about actual *fashion*. Not like she did.

Matthew turned from the breaking news ticker on *Sky News* to the desk behind him. 'Is there anything on the wires?' he yelled out to nobody in particular, and when a prompt reply wasn't forthcoming he brushed his hands through his light brown hair. He looked furious. Sexy, but furious.

'For fuck's sake, is there anything on the fucking wires?' he roared.

Ryan, the 23-year-old new boy, looked shaken. 'Nothing's on PA yet,' he said, his voice as steady as he could make it.

'As soon as it drops, get on it,' Matthew barked, and he turned back to *Sky News* with interest.

Jess stared at him. Objectively speaking, he was attractive – handsome, even. He was tall, tanned, lean, had broad shoulders that tapered down to a tight bottom, and even though everyone else looked crumpled in cheap suits and shirts stained with ink and tea, he looked impeccable.

'This could be our splash tomorrow,' he said to one of his colleagues, who nodded in agreement. 'This could be the big one for this week. It's got it all – Brit girl abroad, stabbed in the chest by some bloody foreigner, parents with plenty of dosh no doubt . . . Let's just cross our fingers she's pretty, no fucking point covering it if she isn't.'

Jess looked at him with distaste. Sometimes she hated her boyfriend when he was at work.

Faye caught her eye. 'Matthew's on the ball again,' she commented, and Jess nodded, trying hard not to watch him marching around the office telling people to get on the first Cairo flight out of Heathrow. 'Does that mean you won't be going for your romantic dinner on the South Bank after all?'

Jess looked back at the news desk and again at *Sky News*,

which was running the story of the poor murdered girl as their lead.

'Doubt it,' she said, but she wasn't too disappointed. As much as she liked spending time with Matthew, she'd rather go back home to her parents' place in Chelsea and play on her sewing machine.

Faye grinned. 'Good. We've had a last-minute invitation to some designer bash – PPQ, or something like that.'

'And I can go?' Jess said excitedly. She'd been working in the fashion department at the *Daily World* for ages now, and she was desperate to go to some decent events so she could start networking. Maybe this was the one that would start the ball rolling.

Faye laughed cruelly. 'Er, no. As I was saying, before you interrupted me, we absolutely must have all these beauty products cleaned up and filed before we send them back to the cosmetic houses. If you haven't got plans *you* can do it.' Her eyes flashed challengingly, and Jess felt her heart sink – until she had a flash of inspiration.

'Um, I'd love to, but, gosh, I've just remembered my godfather's coming round tonight, and I promised I'd see him,' she lied badly.

Faye stared at Jess for a moment, but she let it pass. Everyone knew Jess's godfather was one of the columnists on the paper, and one of the Editor's trusted and most valuable henchmen. Faye didn't want to put a foot wrong in her career. One mistake – or even one typo – and you were out. Pissing off one of the top men in the newsroom would not be a good move for her, and she knew it.

'Sure,' she said with difficulty, clearly hating the fashion assistant getting one up on her. 'So long as you finish up the bagging, I suppose that would be okay.'

Jess smiled as sweetly as she could. 'Thanks,' she said. 'I'll just finish up and be on my way.'

Back to putting size 0 outfits into Jiffy bags and trying not to think about how she wasn't going to the PPQ party tonight. If only she'd been invited, she might have met some real designers who could have helped her with her career . . . But Faye seemed determined to keep her in the sample cupboard, like some sort of newspaper Cinderella.

'Baby, I'm sorry, I'm going to have to stay late tonight because of that dead girl in Egypt.' Matthew's public-school-educated voice was confident and clear. Jess smiled as she curled up on her bed, her iPhone pressed to her ear. Even though he could be an idiot at work, she couldn't help finding his voice really sexy, especially when he was being sweet like this.

'It's going to be a bit of an all-nighter, unfortunately,' he continued, and Jess bit her lip in confusion. She may not have worked for the paper for long, but even she knew that they concentrated on British stories, and rarely touched anything that happened anywhere else – unless it was about celebs in America.

'Really? Why? Do you think it's going to be a big story?'

Matthew paused, and Jess knew, instantly, she shouldn't have asked that. When you worked on a paper you had to know instinctively what would make a great story, but she just didn't have the knack, not like her boyfriend. Matthew thought it was more important to know about politics and current affairs than anything else, and he often wondered why Jess was more interested in Dior than Downing Street.

'Yes, it's going to be a massive story,' Matthew said, his voice straining as he tried to remain patient. 'Didn't you catch all the buzz in the newsroom today?'

Jess shook her head. 'I was too busy putting clothes in Jiffy bags in the sample cupboard,' she said, annoyed at the self-pity she could hear in her voice. 'Matthew, tell me something, is this all I'm good for?'

'Course not, babes. We all know you're better than that.'

Jess wondered if that was true. All she seemed to be good at was the fashion equivalent of filing, and going on errands for Faye.

'Do you think so?' she asked quietly.

'Of course! I'd wager Faye's going to let you write something soon.'

'Really? Do you think she would? You know I really want to be a designer, and if I could write stuff it would give me the chance to meet people, to be part of that world. It would be amazing to see my name in print. If only she'd give me a chance.'

Matthew chuckled again, and Jess wondered what was so funny.

'I've just had an idea,' he said, his voice filled with laughter. 'Instead of waiting for Faye to ask you to write something, why don't you use your initiative and file something without her permission? I reckon five hundred words on why black's going to be the hottest colour this season would be a winner. After all, the parents of this dead girl in Egypt are going to be wearing nothing but black for months.'

Jess shut her eyes again and told herself that Matthew was only being crass because he was in the newsroom, and that showing off and being a dick was practically part of his job. When you were in a relationship with someone, you accepted someone's flaws as well as their good bits. Didn't you?

'If it's that terrible, why don't you just leave?' Poppy said to Jess as they were sipping pints in a pub off the King's Road later that night. Jess had kissed her godfather hello and goodbye, and now she was relaxing – hard – in her favourite pub. Despite being in Chelsea the pub was down to earth, with old man regulars, dusty bottles of wine, a limited food menu that included scampi and chips, and a brassy barmaid straight out of the *EastEnders* school of casting. Poppy and Jess loved it because it reminded them of the pub they used to go to when they were students in Leeds. In here they could shake off their jobs, their pretensions, and just be themselves.

Jess grimaced. 'Are you talking about the *Daily World* or Matthew?'

'Ha. The *Daily World* primarily, but how's it going with sexy Matthew?'

Poppy loved Matthew almost as much as she adored her fiancé. All girls did. Matthew flirted with and charmed all women as if his life depended on it, and even though Jess found him very good-looking – albeit in an obvious way – it had taken her a while to warm to him. Secretly she thought he looked like an Action Man doll, the complete opposite of the slinky-hipped rocker types she'd gone out with at uni.

'Fine,' she said, desperate to gossip with her best friend, but wanting to stay loyal to her boyfriend. Gossip won. 'Although, he's just such a workaholic sometimes. He's all about the bloody newspaper, and I want to shake him and tell him there's more to life than breaking news and brown-nosing your way up the career ladder.'

'There is?' Poppy exclaimed with mock, wide-eyed innocence. Poppy worked for a website doing something that Jess didn't really understand, but she knew her friend put in long hours at work and even longer hours at the pub. She understood the pressure of working for a national newspaper, even though she had never worked for one herself.

'It's like all he wants to do is live in a little *Daily World*

42

bubble, and if we go out it's always with his – our – colleagues, and if he ever comes round to see me at home it's only when Andy's there so they can talk shop. It drives me mad . . .'

'Speaking of Andy,' Poppy began slowly. 'Your godfather wrote something fucking awful about immigrants the other day. Everyone in the office was talking about it, and it was so embarrassing. They all know I'm friends with you and that he's your godfather. I didn't know what to say.'

Jess grinned. 'But you know he doesn't believe half the stuff he writes, right? It's just for effect. And circulation.'

Poppy shook her head. 'How do you stand it?' she asked. 'Don't you believe in half the stuff the fashion pages print?'

'You know I don't. And that's the problem.'

For as long as she could remember, Jess had wanted to work in fashion. Her earliest memory was of sitting on her mother's lap devouring *Vogue*, drinking in the beautiful women and imagining she was wearing what she called their 'lady clothes'. At the age of twelve, Jess wanted to be a model, although as soon as she turned fourteen she realised she was never going to be tall enough or skinny enough to do the job, despite being breathtakingly pretty with honey-blonde hair, cornflower-blue eyes and a broad, sunny smile.

It wasn't until she was sixteen that Jess realised she wanted to be a designer. The idea had come out of the blue – she'd been rummaging through her old toys when she came across a Barbie wearing skin-tight bronze 'leather' trousers and one red slingback mule. Jess had stared at the trousers for a moment, and then clothed her topless Barbie in a shimmering, midnight-blue vest top from the battered toy wardrobe in the doll's house. Jess ached with longing as she wished she had an adult-sized version of Barbie's outfit, and without really thinking she caught the tube

43

to Soho, bought some material, and started making her own clothes on her mother's sewing machine.

Immediately Jess felt that rush of being in love, only it wasn't with an older boy at school, or a boy-band, but with the glowing certainty that she'd discovered what she wanted to do with her life, that she'd found a passion she knew would never, ever die.

The only problem was the fashion industry didn't seem to love her as much as she loved it.

Throughout university, Jess had had a sideline in customising clothes. It started when one of her friends came to her sobbing because she'd piled on the pounds from drinking too much, and her beloved denim mini-skirt no longer fitted. Jess had expanded the skirt with subtle, gorgeous panels of different denim, and the friend was so pleased she started spreading the word that Jess was hot with a sewing machine. During the three years Jess was in Leeds she became known as the girl who could solve any clothing crisis, and when friends lost weight due to worrying about exams, or ballooned from partying too much, they knew Jess could sort out their wardrobes.

Her fledgling business expanded: as well as altering existing pieces, Jess started buying in cheap T-shirts, and customised them by ripping them to sexy shreds and adding strips of leather and fake fur, sequins and appliqué and vintage lace. She and her friends wore her creations when they went out clubbing. They turned heads – and not just because none of them wore bras.

Soon Jess had so much business that she was cash-rich but time-poor – and it started affecting her grades.

'If you don't start studying properly you're going to fail your degree,' Jess's tutor said to her sternly, the morning after a very late night at Leeds' hottest new club.

Jess stifled a yawn and tried not to rub her eyes, which felt as if they were covered in grit. She'd handed out at least fifty business cards to girls of all ages who said they loved her outfits, and despite the hangover she knew it had been a successful night.

'I'm studying as hard as I can,' Jess said wearily, but the tutor didn't look impressed.

'Forty-three percent on this last paper, and only thirty-nine on the one before. Jessica, if you don't knuckle down you're not even going to get a third.'

Jess heard him, but it felt as though she was underwater. It didn't really touch her . . . All she could think about was where she was going to source the material for a skirt she'd been drawing. It was indigo lace over navy tartan, and she knew it would look perfect teamed with a super-large safety pin.

When Jess walked away from Leeds with a non-honours degree, the reality of what she'd done hit her hard. She was back in London, living with her parents, and suddenly none of her college friends wanted her clothes any more.

'It's too slutty,' one had said, when Jess had suggested she'd look great in a slashed halter-neck with cerise peeping through black cotton. 'The look is great for Leeds, but I'm starting my career in London, and I need to look subtly sexy, not like a prostitute.'

It was the same for everyone else. Now everyone had to start paying back their student loans and needed to look half-respectable, nobody wanted her pieces. Jess sat in her childhood bedroom trying to work out what they *would* buy from her, but nothing worked. Everyone was into office separates from Oasis and Reiss, and the shock of London rent prices had hit home, too. Nobody had any spare cash – and especially not for a style they'd grown out of.

It had been Poppy – darling Poppy, still wearing her Jessica Piper T-shirts with pride – who suggested she ask her godfather for a job. Poppy had been working at a start-up website for several months, and as time went on she was getting more and more worried about her best friend. Jess had practically stopped living. She spent all her time in her bedroom making clothes, and no longer went out with her friends or cared about getting a proper job. She was like a girl obsessed, only her obsession wasn't healthy, and if she didn't sort herself out soon she'd end up still living at home at thirty with nothing to show for it but bin-liners full of clothes.

'Ask Andy for a job,' Poppy had urged one night, after Jess's mother had made them a shepherd's pie for dinner. Andy was coming round for drinks that evening, and Poppy was in awe of him. He was the most famous person she knew, and was legendary as an outspoken right-wing columnist who sometimes appeared on *Newsnight* and current affairs programmes.

'What, as his assistant, you mean?' Jess replied, pulling a face. She couldn't stand her godfather's public views, although she adored him when they were just gossiping and catching up. In private he was softly spoken and kind, but in public he was obnoxious and opinionated.

Poppy laughed. 'Yeah, I can just see you getting into that. No, why don't you see if you can work for the fashion pages of the *Daily World*?'

Jess thought about it. She'd still be working *in* fashion, and even if she wasn't creating her own lines, she could still be part of that world.

'But what would I do for them? I don't know if I'm that good a writer.'

Poppy thought for a moment. 'You could intern at the very least, although they probably wouldn't pay you. But it would get you noticed with the fashion journalists, and they'd probably let you write after a while, if you showed you were keen. Imagine – you could even interview designers and models!'

And so Jess started her career at the *Daily World* as a work experience girl, graduating after a couple of months to become the fashion assistant. It was a fantastic job on paper, and all her friends were deeply envious, but Jess was starting to dislike it. She hated that she got paid peanuts to work twelve-hour days, hated that she had to run around after the fashion editor doing work a five-year-old would find too easy, and hated that even though she probably knew more about fashion than anyone else at the *Daily World*, she wasn't allowed to go to events or even write anything just because Faye had it in for her. It totally sucked.

'Work's rubbish at the moment,' Jess said to Poppy, as they began picking at a greasy bowl of chips and started on their third pints of the evening. 'Faye keeps on getting me to do her personal errands. The other day she even made me go and get her some tampons . . . and then had the nerve to tell me off for getting her supers rather than regulars. Said I'd made her look like she had a really heavy flow.'

Poppy stared at her. 'What's wrong with that?'

Jess shrugged. 'According to Faye, only fat people have heavy periods. Because the thinner you are, the less likely you are to menstruate properly.'

Poppy's mouth dropped open. 'You're joking. Does she really believe that?'

'Apparently. She made me bin the tampons, and I had to go out in the pouring rain *again* to get her some regular ones. Honestly, I could have quit then and there.'

'But you won't, will you?' Poppy said, quickly. 'Faye's just being difficult, and everyone has bad boss days. You need to think about all the good things – remember how you met those girls from ASOS the other week when they asked to see the sample cupboard? Just imagine how handy those contacts will be when you start making clothes again.'

Jess took a large swig of beer, and tried not to think about how long it had been since she'd sat at her sewing machine for a decent amount of time, and how much she missed designing clothes. She felt as if she was in mourning, and nobody, not even Poppy, seemed to get that. The closest she got to designing was poring over her scrapbooks of ink drawings, and daydreaming about Stella McCartney spotting her in the street in a one-off, Jessica Piper outfit and begging to know where she got it.

Jess had the same fantasy every night before she went to bed, and that night was no exception. As she climbed into her single bed – the same one she'd had since she was fifteen – she started thinking about reams of oriental silk and golden threads. She'd be wearing a long, sweeping gown of satin when Stella McCartney saw her on Marylebone High Street. Her high, silver sandals had straps that twisted up her calves, and as she glided across the littered streets the mermaid tail of the dress would rustle against the ground. Every so often the skirt would lift to give a tantalising glimpse of the silver shoes.

Jess was so caught up in her daydream that when her mobile beeped with a sexy text from Matthew, she didn't even stir. But even if she had heard her phone, she wouldn't care. For her, fashion would always come first.

Chapter Five

Jess was on her knees again, this time sorting out all the junk jewellery that the last fashion assistant had haphazardly thrown into stiff cardboard bags and left in a tangle. Faye had asked her to organise it all by type and colour, and Jess was busy filling in a notebook when she spotted a pair of black shiny shoes in front of her. She looked up.

'While you're down there,' Matthew said cheekily, and he gestured to his fly with one hand while the other softly stroked her hair.

Jess watched his cock grow hard through his expensive trousers, and she quickly stood up and pushed him away.

'Hey, we're in the office,' she gently chastised, but Matthew just grinned at her.

'And I got the front page this morning, which always makes me horny . . .' Jess saw his eyes grow lustful, and she knew what was coming next. 'How about taking me into the fashion cupboard and blowing me?'

'What if we get caught?' she hissed, wondering why they had this conversation every week, and why he wouldn't get the hint. She loved having sex with him, but she wasn't prepared to do it – and get sprung – at work. It would be in the *Media Guardian* before they knew it, and Andy would never forgive her.

'Then every fucker here would be even more jealous of me,'

Matthew replied. 'Come on, babes, you're no fun. Everyone's at it. There are so many cheap sluts here, shagging whoever they can after a few drinks and you can barely get into a disabled toilet any more because of all the sex that goes on. What harm would a quick blow job do?'

Jess bit her lip. She wanted to make Matthew happy, but not like this. Not at work.

'You'd get a warning, and I'd lose my job,' she said, hating herself for sounding so prim. She wanted to be wild and wanton, but she just couldn't bring herself to do it. Not at work. She'd feel so cheap.

'It would be worth it,' Matthew winked, and Jess felt herself soften. 'You drive me crazy, you know.'

Jess looked down at Matthew's groin again, and he was unmistakably rock hard. He didn't even bother to try and hide it.

'You walk past the news desk flaunting your tight body, and all I can think about is your ass under your mini-skirt, your long legs wrapping themselves around me, your fantastic, chewable nipples. I just want to grab you by your long blonde hair and pull you towards me.'

Despite herself Jess felt herself weaken, and she put her hand on Matthew's waist. She felt his muscles underneath his shirt, and she knew she was lost to him. He was so fit.

'Why don't I come back to yours tonight?' she asked huskily, hoping he wouldn't suggest going into the fashion cupboard again, because she really wasn't sure she'd be able to say no.

Matthew smiled a slow, sexy smile. It was the one that got her every time, and he knew it.

'We'll go for that dinner we missed last night, and then you can sort this out for me,' he said, gesturing to his cock.

Jess grinned, and the pair shared one final, private look, before Jess returned to her knees, desperately trying to remember where she'd got to with her jewellery organising, and berating herself for finding Matthew just so damn attractive.

'Here's to us,' Matthew said, raising a large glass of Chardonnay – the only wine Jess really liked – and fixing his eyes on her. He'd taken her to E & O, and even though the room was buzzing, they'd managed to bag an intimate table in the corner by getting the Editor's secretary to book it for them. Jess sipped her wine, and beamed at Matthew. For once he wasn't wearing work clothes, but he still looked smart in a white shirt and jeans. The cotton of the shirt stretched across his torso, and Jess could feel herself getting turned on just looking at him. Damn. He was so hot.

'My ginger cheesecake's amazing,' she murmured, trying to distract herself and diffuse the sexual tension between them.

Matthew grinned at her, knowing precisely what she was thinking and feeling. He had her exactly where he wanted her.

'I think *you're* amazing,' he teased, and Jess felt herself blush. She'd always had boyfriends, but none that were this open about their feelings.

'But not as amazing as getting the front page three times this week,' Jess said lightly. Suddenly she didn't care that Matthew was all about his career. She was, too – or would be if she could find a way to design for a living. It was why their relationship worked. They weren't intense, it wasn't serious, and they had fun.

'Yeah, that's pretty fucking cool, too,' he said, with a slight frown. 'But I want to go on the editing rota. I want to be taken seriously.'

'You *are* taken seriously!' Jess exclaimed. 'Everyone at work thinks you're fantastic. You're so close to being on the back bench you must be able to smell it.'

'Jess, I'm just a fucking reporter, and you know it.' Matthew's eyes flashed angrily, even though she knew he wasn't angry with her. But she didn't understand why his job wasn't enough. He was doing what he loved to do *and* getting paid for it – unlike her.

'Everyone on the paper thinks of you as more than a reporter,' she said softly, hoping to calm him down. Their dinner had been going so well up to this point. 'And, if you give it time, the Editor will give you more power. You could be head of news soon. But you have to prove yourself, first.'

'Don't you think I've proven myself already?' His blue eyes were shining in the dim light of the restaurant, and Jess felt sorry for him. He wanted promotion so badly.

'Yes,' she said in a small voice. 'I think you deserve a break. You know I do.'

Matthew eyeballed Jess for a long moment as if he were considering something.

'If you really thought that you'd help me . . .' he began, then stopped and shook his head. 'No, don't worry about it. Forget I said anything.'

'What? How could I help?' Jess was willing to do anything to put her boyfriend in a better mood.

Matthew took a swig of wine. 'No, really, I shouldn't ask.'

'Babes, you know if I could do anything to help I would.'

Matthew put his wine glass down and looked seriously at Jess. He took a deep breath, then groaned. 'Speak to Andy for me. Tell him to put in a good word. Tell him I want the back bench.'

Jess's mouth dropped open. 'Matthew, you know I can't do that.'

Matthew reddened. 'I know, I know,' he said, and for a moment Jess could see the *real* Matthew, and not the one who was so cocksure in the newsroom. 'But I had to ask. I won't again.'

Jess tried not to sigh with relief. A couple of journalists at work had tried to get 'in' with her because of her godfather, and she hated it. What kind of people only wanted to be friends with you because of who you knew?

'Look,' Matthew said gently, as he reached for her hand. 'I'm sorry. I know you get a bit . . . *intimidated* by me when I'm talking about the paper, so I'll stop it. I'm just crazy about you, babes. And you love me, right?'

It was the question she always dreaded. Yes, she fancied Matthew – who wouldn't? – and yes, they had fun, but she wasn't sure she really knew what love was. Was this it? All she knew was that Matthew was the only thing that made working at the *Daily World* bearable.

'I adore you, you know that.'

'And I love you, too,' he smiled back, obviously relieved.

Jess was pleased. His dissatisfaction about not being an editor had waned, and he'd moved off the subject of her godfather. He'd mentioned it once before, when he was drunk, and Jess hated being put in that position. She knew Matthew wouldn't really use her like that, despite his ambition.

'I've been meaning to say this for a while, but work keeps on getting in the way,' Matthew began with a wry smile, and Jess concentrated hard on keeping her face as blank as possible. She wasn't sure she liked where this was going . . .

'Jess, I'm addicted to you. You're the most beautiful, sexy girl in the office, and I can't get enough of you.'

Matthew squeezed her hands hard, and Jess felt herself relax. It was more sex talk, more of the same. Every so often Matthew rhapsodised about how much he fancied her, and that was fine by her. So long as he didn't get serious, she was happy to be with him. She was too young, and had too much to do if she was going to claw back a proper fashion career. Her friends might all be settling down, but she wanted some success before she even thought about that part of her life.

'I'm mad about you, too,' Jess replied over her wine, and Matthew shot her another easy, sexy smile.

'I'm pleased,' he said, and then he narrowed his eyes ever so slightly. Jess had seen that look before, but only in the news-room, and only when he was after something. 'But I'm sick of only seeing you a couple of nights a week.'

Jess laughed. 'We see each other every day at work!'

'Yeah, but that's not proper time. Not quality time.' Matthew took a deep breath, and stared intently into Jess's eyes. 'I want you to move in with me. And then I want you to seriously think about spending the rest of your life with me. I think we make a good team.'

Jess recoiled, and as she pulled her hands back, she acciden-tally knocked her wine glass onto the floor, where it shattered into hundreds of glittering pieces.

'So what did you say?' Poppy asked hesitantly the next day.

They were both in their offices – Jess on her mobile outside the newsroom, and Poppy at her desk – and they knew their conversation had to get straight to the point. Like most of their phone calls, though, this hardly ever went to plan.

'Well, I knocked over my glass of wine, and by the time the waiter had cleared it up, Matthew wasn't being so, you know, hardcore about everything.'

'But what did you *say*?'

Jess sighed and examined her hair for split ends. 'I said I'd think about it. I mean, he didn't think I'd say yes and jump up and down, did he?' Poppy was silent. 'Oh shit, do you think that's what I was meant to do?'

'Look, all I'm saying is that Matthew is pretty much God's gift to women. He's fit, he's kind, he's on an amazing career path, and he's loaded. Oh, and he's obviously madly in love with you. He probably expected you to cry and beg to move in that night.'

'But I didn't.'

'No. You didn't. It's probably why he likes you so much. You're a challenge.'

'What?' Jess was confused.

'Well, think about it,' Poppy began. 'He's Matthew Parker, rising star of the *Daily World*, and he's stunning. He has loads of girls after him – God, it was only last week you told me about that slapper from the features desk who keeps throwing herself at him – but the only one that really interests him is you, and that's probably because you play it so cool.'

'Thanks! And not because I'm pretty and funny and clever?'

Poppy laughed. 'You know what I mean.'

Jess sighed. 'If I was madly in love with him then playing it cool would be the perfect way to act. But I'm not in love with him. I think. I mean, I don't *know*.'

'So you're not going to move in with him?'

Jess thought about it. 'I'd rather move in with you.'

'But I'm living with Joe now, and we're planning our wedding,' Poppy said matter-of-factly, and then she sighed, too. 'Look, if we had room you know I'd take you in. I miss living with you as well.'

Jess smiled. 'I suppose it's time to grow up, isn't it,' she sighed. 'You're engaged, everyone from uni's in serious relationships – and God, Kelly had a baby last month. I'm the only one still living at home, and that's just sad at our age, isn't it?'

'It is a bit,' Poppy agreed as nicely as she could. 'So why don't you do it? Is his flat nice?'

'It's amazing. A little small, but I think it's probably big enough for all my clothes.'

'So you're going to do it? Really?' Poppy was ecstatic.

'I think I might give it a trial run,' Jess said cautiously. 'Just to see how it goes.'

'Er, just how much stuff have you got?' Matthew said, as Jess opened the door of her parents' home to show him all her boxes and bin-liners of clothes.

'Not *that* much,' Jess grinned. 'Just the essentials.'

'I'm not sure this is all going to fit into my car . . . And there's not much space at my place.' Matthew lived in a two-bedroom flat just off Brick Lane, and he loved its minimalist functionality. With all of Jess's bits and bobs it was going to look like a different apartment. It was going to look 'girlie'.

'It will be okay,' Jess said happily. 'It will all fit.' She was going to miss her parents – and the King's Road – but she couldn't wait to move. It was like starting her life again. And this time, she was determined to be more proactive about her career. She was going to make her parents proud of her.

'You know, I don't think it will,' Matthew said simply.

Jess stopped and stared at him. 'You're joking, right?' she asked tentatively.

Matthew sighed. 'Not really. I don't think I've got room for all your stuff in my flat. Do you really need to bring that?' He nodded at Jess's beloved sewing machine, and Jess wanted to rush over to it to protect it from Matthew's glare.

'Yes!' she exclaimed. 'I need it more than I need my books or my photos or anything else. I use it to make my designs into actual clothes – and you know it.'

Matthew stared at it. 'I thought you wanted to be a fashion writer,' he commented.

Jess wanted to scream. How many times had they had this conversation? Why didn't he *listen* to her?

'No,' she began gently. 'I want to be a fashion *designer*.'

Matthew looked at her as if she were mad. 'Well, if you bring that,' he remarked, nodding at the sewing machine, 'you can't bring much else. There's just not enough room.'

Jess looked at all her belongings – the boxes of photos, collections of books, and bags and bags of clothes – and realised that if she was going to live with Matthew she would have to compromise. And that the most important thing she owned was her sewing machine and art pads and pens.

'Help me take everything else back to my bedroom then,' she said. Then she glanced at him with one eyebrow raised. 'I suppose I don't need to bring this many clothes, do I?'

'Not if you're planning on walking around the flat naked, no,' Matthew said with a smirk.

Jess smiled back. Even if she couldn't bring all her belongings with her, living together was definitely the right thing to do.

'Jess! Are you listening to me?' Faye's clipped voice practically echoed throughout the newsroom, and Jess saw Matthew's head turn slightly in their direction. It was a sign he'd overheard Faye's annoyed tones, and Jess didn't want him to hear any more. It was embarrassing enough to be talked to like a dogsbody without her boyfriend listening in.

'Yes, yes, I am,' Jess replied soothingly, hoping Faye would adopt the same quiet tone. 'What's up?'

Faye sighed. 'You are *now*, but only because I've been yelling at you. I need you to do something for me.'

Jess tried not to wince. Her whole body ached from moving

her stuff into Matthew's flat the day before, and her head pounded from the hangover she couldn't shake off. Matthew had bought them a couple of bottles of champagne to celebrate Jess moving in, and even though she hadn't been up for getting drunk, Matthew had insisted. She was paying for being such a doormat now, and while she looked rough, Matthew seemed sprightly and fresh and glowing with health. She hated that he hardly ever got hangovers. It wasn't fair.

'Are you particularly busy?' Faye's voice implied she didn't think Jess was at all occupied, and Jess wondered why she was in such a bad mood.

'I was just familiarising myself with *Vogue*,' Jess said as confidently as she could. She'd been gazing at the latest issue and checking out the Miu Miu collection. If she'd designed the cherry-red cape the model was wearing she'd have made it an inch longer so that it swung more freely, and she'd have teamed it with tight cigarette trousers rather than a mini-skirt. Jess could have stared at pictures of clothes all day long. Especially as she didn't think she had the energy to do anything else.

'Is there something you'd like me to do instead?' she added with a smile, hoping she sounded perky. She remembered the Australian intern who'd worked in the office several months earlier. She'd always been friendly and happy, and at the time Jess had resolved to try to be more like her. It was hard, especially when Faye was being a bitch.

'Find my earring,' Faye said bluntly, and she turned back to her monitor.

Jess hovered by her desk, but Faye pretended not to notice her.

'Um . . . sorry, what?'

Faye scowled aggressively. 'Jess, I'm on deadline. What is it?'

Jess was momentarily stunned. 'Er, did you just ask me to find your earring?'

Faye looked her up and down. Today Jess was wearing a pretty antique lace blouse that had been dyed navy blue, skin-tight black jeans, and her favourite red Louboutins. She knew she looked great, despite the hangover. 'Yes. It fell out somewhere in the newsroom. My husband paid a fortune for them, and I can't afford to lose one. Find it, please.'

Jess didn't move. She knew part of her job description was to assist Faye in any way, but did she really need to get on her hands and knees and crawl about the newsroom looking for an earring? It would be mortifying.

'Jessica . . .' Faye said in a low, warning tone.

Jess turned on her heel, and slowly walked up and down the newsroom, her gaze locked on the carpet in the hope that a tiny, glinting diamond would catch her eye. Everyone stopped and stared at her as she walked past, but Jess refused to look up – not even when she suddenly dropped to the floor after thinking a scrap of a sweet wrapper was the missing earring, and a sports reporter begged her to sit under his desk with an open mouth.

Eventually, Jess gave up. She'd walked around the office for hours, and the more she searched for Faye's missing earring, the more her head throbbed and her legs felt as though they'd buckle beneath her. She crept quietly back to her desk, and was just reaching for her Evian bottle to take a much-needed swig of water when Faye spotted her.

'Why aren't you tidying the fashion cupboard?' she asked evenly, as if she was struggling not to yell at her fashion assistant.

Jess stared at her. 'Because I've been looking for your missing earring.'

'Oh, that,' Faye said airily, waving her hand in the air. 'Found it on my desk hours ago. Must have forgotten to tell you.'

It took all of Jess's strength not to resign then and there.

'Honestly, she was such a bitch today!' Jess exclaimed to Matthew through the bathroom door. God, what was he *doing*? He'd been in there for about two hours already. 'She made me walk up and down the office practically all morning, and then, when I sat down, she had the nerve to ask why I wasn't doing something else. Like I should have *known* she'd found her earring.'

'We all have to start somewhere, babes,' Matthew said, sounding distracted. 'You're lucky to be working with Faye – she's very respected in the industry.'

'Sod the industry. She's a cow.'

Matthew opened the bathroom door, naked but for a towel around his waist. He looked . . . different somehow. 'You're so sexy when you're angry. I love the way you scowl.'

Jess studied him, but she couldn't work out what was different. 'Have you changed your hair or something?' she asked.

'I've just been plucking my eyebrows,' he replied, staring at himself in the mirror. 'They were getting a bit overgrown.'

'You *pluck* your eyebrows?' Jess said in astonishment. 'Really?'

Matthew shrugged. 'I'm a metrosexual man, babes, you know that.'

Jess walked into the bathroom and opened the mirrored cabinet. Her mouth dropped open. In the cabinet were moisturisers and anti-ageing gels, hair products and . . . fake tan. 'Fake tan? You use fake tan?' she said, taking the bottle out of the cabinet and examining it.

Matthew beamed at her. 'You didn't think I was naturally this sun-kissed, did you?' he replied. 'And while you've got it out, I don't suppose you could do my back, could you? It's such a bitch trying to do it myself, and I'm getting it waxed tomorrow so I'd rather do it today so that my pores aren't too visible post-wax.'

'You know, you don't have to use this. You're really sexy already.'

Matthew stared in the mirror. 'Oh, I know that,' he said. 'But every little helps, doesn't it?'

Jess wondered why she hadn't suspected his healthy glow wasn't real. She just hadn't thought he was the type, she supposed. He was such a *man* at work.

'What do you want to do tonight?' Matthew asked her, as she swept the fake tan along the muscles of his back. 'Some of the lads from the office are going to the pub. I said we'd probably join them.'

'You go,' Jess said, after a pause. 'I want to stay in and work on some of my designs.' Since deciding to move in with Matthew, Jess had suddenly found some motivation – and the sights and colours of Brick Lane inspired her to add different twists to her clothes. She was currently dreaming of a taffeta skirt teamed with Indian silk ribbons, and she knew her sketches were some of the best she'd done in ages.

Matthew sighed. 'Jess, it's more important to network with colleagues than draw your silly little pictures. Don't you think you should come to the pub?'

Jess put down the fake tan and began washing her hands vigorously. 'They're not "silly little pictures", they're designs for clothes I want to make and then sell.'

'And how do you plan on selling them?' Matthew smirked. He knew Jess had sold clothes at university, but he'd always thought of it as a hobby, not a career.

'I've been speaking to a girl on Spitalfields Market and she said she'd help me get some space, or maybe even a stall. Loads of designers sell their clothes there, and I thought it would be a good starting point. I can do it around work. If Faye won't give me a break I'll have to make my own.'

Matthew groaned. 'Jess, you work at the *Daily World*. Do you have any idea how embarrassing it will be for the paper if it became known that you were selling scraps of clothes on a market stall? It will look like they don't pay you enough.'

'Well, they don't. But that's not the point. This is what I want to do with my life. This is my *dream*.'

Matthew sighed in exasperation. 'Look, darling, this fashion designing business has got to stop. It's just too messy, and I don't like it in my flat. It's a waste of your time, and I don't think you should be doing it any more.'

Jess took a deep breath. 'I disagree,' she said quietly. 'As I've said to you before, this is my career.'

Matthew laughed. 'But it's not! Your career is researching the clothes that the wannabes are going to be wearing on *Teen Star USA*, not pretending you're Chocolate Chanel or whatever her name is. Look, when I was little I wanted to be a fireman,' he reasoned. 'You need to grow up and accept that some dreams are just fantasies, and that they're never going to come true. I don't know much about fashion, but I'm willing to bet that most people who work as designers were born into the industry. That's how they got there. You were born into the newspaper industry – it's *your* calling.'

Jess bit her lip. 'But nobody in my family's ever worked in the media.'

Matthew stared at her for a moment, wishing Jess was less argumentative. Less *independent*. Most girls worshipped him . . . why couldn't she?

'But your godfather is Andy Shields of the *Daily World*. You are Jessica Piper, currently fashion assistant at the *Daily World* . . . and, well, your fiancé is Matthew Parker of the *Daily World* . . . if you'll have me.'

Jess froze. What did he just say?

Matthew took Jess's shocked expression as a good sign, and he smiled at her like the cat that got the cream. 'Jessica Piper,' he said theatrically, as he dropped to one knee, his body glistening with fake tan, 'Will you marry me?'

Chapter Six

Madison was giving it her all. Silvery, smoky vapours whispered around her gold Manolo Blahnik heels, and twisted up her lean, tanned legs as if in time with the music. The midnight-blue lighting of the stage picked out the subtle highlights in her chestnut hair, and the pearly spotlight enveloping her made her make-up gleam. She was stunning – a delicate, wholesome-looking girl with a powerful, beautiful voice – but her appearance was the last thing on her mind. She was singing, live on stage, in front of 40 million Americans. When Madison sang, it was almost as if she ceased to exist and someone else took over.

As Madison sung the final notes of Whitney Houston's 'I Will Always Love You' she clasped the microphone stand tightly, oblivious to the tiny specks of rainbow glitter falling down on her and sticking to her gold dress and hair. She blinked, and it was if she'd suddenly come to – as if she was only just aware of the 300 people in the auditorium cheering wildly, of the judging panel of *Teen Star USA* leading the standing ovation, of the team of producers and cameramen looking at her in stunned awe.

Madison bit her lip, and as the programme's director ordered a close-up of her nervous, unsure face, America's collective heart gave a lurch. *Teen Star USA* had never found an act like her. She always gave the performance of her life, always hit the right notes, but when she stopped singing she turned back into a shy little girl who looked as though she didn't understand why she was suddenly America's number one sweetheart.

The judges took it in turns to appraise her performance, but Madison barely listened to them. She was naked under her gold dress – it was so sheer the stage lighting would have picked up any lines underneath it – and she felt exposed. It was like she was an awkward teenager on stage at a pageant again, and she felt insecure about how sexy she looked.

Madison's eyes swept across the front row of the audience until she found Beau. She needed reassurance, and even though they'd only known each other for a few months, he was the closest thing she had to a friend on the show. For the first time that evening he wasn't fiddling with his BlackBerry as he had been when the other *Teen Star* contestants performed, but was staring right at her, with an expression she couldn't quite read. She shot him a little grin and raised her eyebrows as if to ask if her performance had been okay.

Beau smiled back, ever so slowly. He knew everything that happened on the show down to the last detail, and with that one look she knew Beau was aware that she was naked under the thin sheath dress, and that he liked it. Madison felt a wave of sexual attraction run through her. It was even better than the rush she got when she sang.

The presenter of *Teen Star USA* put his arms around her, snapping Madison out of the connection between her and Beau, and asked the viewers to vote for her on her *Teen Star USA* contestant phone number. Madison shifted her gaze so she was looking straight at the camera, and gave a bashful smile, as if she didn't really believe she was good enough for anyone to vote for her. But all the while she was thinking about Beau, too, about how he was watching her on the monitor, and how she was as blown away by him as she was by the *Teen Star USA* experience.

She wasn't sure – not one hundred per cent, anyway – but she realised at that moment that she might just be in love with Beau Silverman. And that he clearly had feelings for her, too.

'You know you're gonna win, right?' Beau remarked conversationally. He was visiting Madison in the house where she was living while they filmed *Teen Star USA* at Television City in Hollywood. The other contestants were all staying in a shared house close to Mulholland Drive, and Madison had lived there for a couple of weeks, too, until an actress with fake breasts and a permanent orange tan started flying into jealous rages over Madison's talent. Madison had been removed from the house 'for her own good', but she hadn't really minded. Only she knew she was going to win the competition, and whenever she saw how hard the other contestants were working, it made her feel bad. She was going to crush their dreams of stardom regardless of how much they practised.

Madison refused to think of the other contestants – it was a dog-eat-dog world, right? – and instead grinned back at Beau. He looked so hot today, in light blue jeans and a tight black T-shirt that made his dark hair look almost blue-black. He was thirty-seven – probably too old for her – but he was so sexy. Madison felt as though she could drown in his black eyes for ever.

'I thought that was the point,' she teased, tucking her shiny brown hair behind one ear. 'Isn't that why we've recorded half of my winner's album already?'

Beau took a sip of mineral water and raised his eyebrows. He wasn't used to anyone – let alone girls – being anything but deferential towards him.

'What I mean is, even if we hadn't planned it that you were

66

gonna win, you're gonna win. You got eighty-nine per cent of the votes on the last live show. You'll walk it.'

Madison shivered happily. Knowing that made her feel less guilty about the other contestants. 'So it's turned legit?' she asked with a smile.

Beau took her hand and squeezed it. 'I'd never have said you were going to win if I didn't think you'd do it legitimately.'

She suddenly felt shy. He had the ability to make her feel completely naked, and it unnerved her. She was intoxicated by his power.

'So when do we release my album?' she said, desperately trying to ignore the sexual tension between them. Beau couldn't *really* have a crush on her, could he? He could have any woman he wanted, and if the rumours that floated around Television City were true, he regularly did.

'A couple of months after you win. That gives you two months at the top of the Billboard Hot 100 with the *Teen Star* song, and as soon as your single starts to slide we release the second one and the album. You'll be heading the charts for a year with this album. Maybe even eighteen months, depending on sales.'

Madison's face broke out into a huge grin. She wanted to act blasé, as if what was happening to her wasn't a big deal, but she couldn't help herself. It was so amazing. So! Incredibly! Amazing!

'And then will I be famous?' Madison said in a small voice.

Beau roared with laughter. 'You already are the most famous girl in America, if not the world. Everyone's going crazy about you.'

Madison paused. 'But I mean . . .' She wasn't quite sure how she was going to articulate what she wanted to say. 'Everyone on *Teen Star* is famous *right now*. Like last year, Bud and Tracee and

Judi were all famous because they were on *Teen Star*, but now they're has-beens. When they go to parties and events, magazines, like, mock them. Will that happen to me?'

Beau smoothed a wrinkle line on her forehead and smiled at her. 'No, because you're bigger than all of them. You're going to be a worldwide smash. People in Europe are talking about you. You're already a superstar.'

He reached into his bag and pulled out a file, which he pushed towards her.

'Here are your European cuttings,' he said simply. 'This one's from *Le Monde*, that one's from *Bild* – German, by the way,' he commented when Madison's face remained blank, 'and these are the ones from the UK: the *Sun*, the *Daily Mail*, the *Daily World* . . .'

Madison picked up the cuttings and read one from the *Daily World* which told her that not only was she a superstar singer, but that she also had 'superstar fashion sense'.

'I didn't realise,' she whispered, feeling giddy. How had she not known she was being written about in newspapers across the world?

'And when you do a Google search for your name, there are over half a million results. The web's totally buzzing about you.'

'So I'm famous? Like, properly famous?'

Beau started laughing again. When he'd first seen Madison in Spotlight he'd thought she was streetwise and tough. You had to be if you were working as a stripper. But that had been an act. She truly was an innocent.

'Madison, how many normal girls have the paparazzi following them everywhere they go? How many girls are on the cover of *US Weekly* or being fawned over by Perez Hilton? How many girls are being screamed at in the street when they go to pick up groceries even when I tell them not to, that someone from Slate Street will do all their errands for them?'

Madison sat back in her chair feeling as if the life had just been sucked out of her. It was true – she was famous. She'd just been so busy, in so much of a whirlwind, that she hadn't really noticed. Suddenly it all felt too much, too overwhelming. Madison burst into tears.

'Hey,' Beau said softly, moving to sit next to her. He wiped away a tear from her face, but when fresh tears fell he scooped her up and held her close to him. Madison's body shook, and he squeezed her tightly, pressing her breasts against his torso, and rocking her slightly. Slowly, her tears began to stop, and her breathing steadied. But Madison didn't let go. She didn't want to stop feeling Beau's warm breath on her hair, or his strong hands on her waist.

When she looked up at Beau she saw her feelings for him reflected in his dark eyes. Neither said a word for a moment, then Beau took her hand again, and led her into her bedroom.

It wasn't until the next day that they resurfaced, and Madison knew, with all her heart, that she'd found the greatest love of her life.

Madison stood next to Justin Lewis and fidgeted nervously with the peony corsage on her wrist. Just a few moments earlier Beau had grabbed her and pulled her into a dark corner backstage where nobody could spot them. He'd kissed her so tenderly that Madison felt her heart melt, and then, with a flourish, he'd produced the beautiful corsage. As he fastened it to her wrist he told her that she was incredibly special, and then, without warning, he'd gone – probably back to his front-row seat, or to make small talk with the sponsors.

As Madison remembered the taste of Beau's lips she allowed

herself a tiny smile, then she remembered where she was. She was on TV, and millions of people were holding their breath to see who would be crowned *Teen Star USA*. Despite Beau's assurances, she was nervous about the results of the phone votes, and she shot a look at the other finalist. Justin Lewis was an actor, and gorgeous as well as genuinely talented and funny. All the magazines had been speculating that he was going to win the contest, that as the underdog his success could be the shock of the year. She looked at him again, and when she realised he was more nervous than she was, she reached for his hand as a sign of solidarity. His palms were freezing cold.

'Good luck,' Madison whispered to him, as the presenter took to the podium for the final time that year. Justin began to shake slightly, and Madison started to feel guilty again. Even though she was nervous, too, she *knew* her win was in the bag, and really, she didn't have anything to be worried about. Unscripted, she pulled him over for a hug, and as they squeezed each other tightly, Madison spotted Beau scowling in the front row of the audience. Her heart raced yet again. They'd had to keep their relationship a secret, and she got a little thrill from making him jealous. It proved how much he loved her . . . even though he'd not said it yet.

The presenter cleared his throat, and suddenly the whole of Television City went dark, apart from the three silver spotlights. All eyes were on them as the presenter opened the envelope that contained the name of the winner, and Madison held her breath. She'd been worried that when this moment came she'd look too blasé, that she wouldn't be able to fake ignorance, but the atmosphere in the studio was electric. She was, she realised, genuinely nervous. What if Justin's fans had voted so many times that she couldn't win? She'd die, she thought. She wouldn't be able to stand it.

'And the winner of *Teen Star USA* is . . .'

The presenter paused for what felt like an eternity. Justin's face paled, and Madison concentrated on Beau's black eyes, which were gazing intently at her. When she was with Beau, nothing but their feelings for each other mattered, and it calmed her.

'. . . Madison Miller!'

Behind them an explosion of red, white and blue fireworks lit up the stage, and the *Teen Star USA* theme music blared. Everyone was on their feet cheering, and Madison smiled coyly and let Justin give her a congratulatory hug. This was the defining moment of her life, she thought, and she pictured her parents back home watching this on their television. Kyle Brockway would be sitting in his dorm with his mouth open in shock, and Leesa – poor Leesa – would be alone in her New York apartment with a bottle of vodka, preparing to go to work at Spotlight. Everyone across the country was watching her, and she was determined to give the performance of her life. She burst into tears of joy.

'I don't know what to say,' she sobbed, as the presenter congratulated her. 'This is incredible, I never thought I'd win . . .' Her voice trailed off as emotion consumed her, and she wished she could stop the tiny voice in her head that kept telling her she was a hypocrite. Of *course* she knew she was going to win, it said, over and over. She'd been hand-picked to win months ago.

The presenter thrust a microphone in her hand, and Justin was led from the stage. Before she knew it she had to sing again. The music started and she was singing the *Teen Star USA* song – her first single. A real single! From midnight it would be online and in shops across the country, and within a week she'd have her first Billboard number one. It was mind-blowing. Absolutely mind-blowing.

Madison concentrated hard on her performance, and as she sang, the voices in her head disappeared, drowned out by the melody. She was no longer on *Teen Star USA*, but performing in her bedroom in Walkertown, wishing a record producer would wander past her house and make her famous. As she sang she relaxed, and it was only when she reached the end of the song that she was forced back into reality: she was the winner of *Teen Star USA*, and she was going to be a superstar.

'I'm falling in love with you,' Beau whispered to Madison, as they lay curled up in his bed in his Manhattan penthouse apartment. As soon as they'd got back to New York they'd begun tearing at each other's clothes. Madison hadn't known sex like it – unlike sex with Kyle, it was tender, aggressive, playful . . . meaningful. Madison was addicted to it – and to Beau himself.

Madison felt her breath catch, but she didn't say anything immediately. Instead, she lay there, his body coiled around hers, and felt pure joy consume her. Was this what love was like for everyone? she wondered. How many other people in the city could possibly be as happy as she was? From the bed she could see the rest of the city through the floor-to-ceiling windows, and as she took in the views over Central Park and beyond, she pushed her body even closer to Beau's. She had the start of an amazing, jaw-dropping career, and the love of one of the most incredible men in the record business. And she was only nineteen! It was like something out of a fairytale.

'I love you, too,' Madison murmured eventually, and she rolled over to face Beau. She stared into his black eyes, then kissed him gently on the lips. He tasted salty, of sweat and champagne, and Madison didn't want this moment to end. Ever.

Beau responded with a lazy smile, then padded softly to the shower as Madison drank in his body. His broad shoulders and strong muscles showed that he worked out regularly, and coarse black hair covered his chest. Kyle had been strong, too, but in comparison he looked and acted like a boy. Beau was all man – she was in no doubt about that.

As Madison watched him, Beau gave her a little wink, knowing that she liked what she saw. He was completely unself-conscious when he was naked, unlike her, and that she was shy without clothes on made him laugh. He had no idea how she'd managed to last as a stripper for so long, he often joked, and inside Madison winced. She hated it that the first time they'd met she'd been made-up like a tramp. But, she reasoned to herself, if he knew about that and still adored her, it must really be love. She wished she knew everything there was to know about Beau – and what skeletons were in his closet – but she was sure she had the rest of her life to find out.

'Let's go for a bite to eat,' Beau suggested, as he emerged from the shower with a white towel wrapped around his waist, and his damp hair sticking up. 'Where do you fancy going?'

Madison lay back on the soft pillow and considered it. 'Somewhere amazing,' she said, with a soft sigh. 'Somewhere incredible.'

Beau looked at her for a moment. 'If we go somewhere fancy you know we can't act like a couple,' he said. 'You're the most famous girl in America at the moment, and you need to remain single.'

Madison pouted. 'Why do we have to keep our relationship a secret?' she said, aware that she sounded whiny, but not caring. 'What does it matter?'

Beau's dark eyes flashed. 'It matters because I own Slate Street, and therefore *Teen Star USA* and also you. I can't be seen to be fucking the talent. It would make your win look suspect.'

Madison winced at his description of their relationship, but she knew he didn't mean it, not really.

'So if we go out I can't kiss you, or hold your hand, or anything like that?' she said with a pout.

Beau shook his head.

'Then let's order in,' Madison said, finally. She'd wanted to go somewhere where she could dress up, drink champagne, and be glamorous. But not being able to hold Beau's hand and enjoy it properly would be too hard.

'No, I don't think so,' Beau said bluntly. 'You're Miss *Teen Star USA*, and I want you in the papers tomorrow. We'll go to an exclusive Asian place I know. They don't normally let the paparazzi anywhere near the place, but I'll make a few phone calls. Get dressed.'

He left the bedroom, and Madison obediently went to the wardrobe, where his staff had unpacked her clothes. The producers of *Teen Star USA* had given her all of her stage dresses, and she chose a shimmering black one, cinching in her waist with a glittery black belt. She knew she looked sensational.

'What do you think?' she said proudly, as Beau came back into the bedroom to get his BlackBerry.

He looked Madison up and down. 'Never wear black when you know you're going to be papped. It doesn't look great in photos. Wear the white one, with no bra.'

He stalked back out of the room, and Madison watched him leave, silently. She was hurt by his coldness. Hadn't he just told her he loved her? She sighed, and pulled off the black dress before slithering into the white one, doing as she was told and removing her bra. It must be so hard for him, she thought, as she sat down at the dressing table and began putting on her make-up.

Being her boss but also her boyfriend would mean that some-times he wouldn't know how to treat her – and she would just have to be more accepting of it, and of the inevitable mood swings. As Madison applied nude lip-gloss, just as she'd been taught by the make-up artists on the set of the show, she realised yet again how dream-like life had become. And she wasn't going to let Beau's bossy little outbursts ruin it for her. He was used to getting his own way, but that was only because he knew best. It was why he was so successful. And why she would be, too.

Chapter Seven

Madison swung her legs out of the Lincoln Town Car and gasped. There were about thirty photographers milling around outside the restaurant, and as soon as her feet touched the sidewalk all eyes were upon her, and New York roared into silence. Madison blinked. Then, with a rush, the paparazzi started screaming her name, and all she could see were the disorientating camera flashes. She stumbled.

'I've got you,' she heard Beau murmur into her ear as he put his hand on the small of her back to steady her. 'Tilt your head slightly downwards, put your hand on your hip, and, for God's sake, smile.'

Madison obediently did as she was told, and within seconds she'd transformed from a shy nobody into a superstar. The paparazzi clustered around her, and even though it was terrifying to be surrounded by aggressive men with cameras pointed in her direction, Madison's smile remained and her lip-gloss glittered. She had always wanted to be famous, and this was it. She was beautiful, talented, recognised and, most importantly, desired.

As the cameras flashed, people stopped to see what had caused the commotion, and cars that had been inching slowly up Lexington Avenue ground to a halt so they could get a glimpse of America's brand-new sweetheart. Everyone stared, and some people even had their mouths open in shock. Madison Miller —

the most famous girl on the planet at that moment – was standing in front of them. In the flesh. Some people joined the paparazzi and started taking photos of Madison on their cell phones, but most people just stood in respectful awe. It was Madison Miller!

Beau led Madison into the restaurant, which was probably the hottest place to eat in the city at the moment. As soon as the noise of the paps melted away, Madison was able to take a deep breath, feel her heart rate steady, and take in her surroundings. Slate-grey floor tiles were complemented by a thick red carpet, and the walls were covered with ornate Chinese prints. As Madison slid into a red booth and took in the gorgeous crimson tea-lights on the dark wood table, she knew she shone in her white dress, and was glad Beau had told her to wear it. If she had worn black she'd have slipped away into the shadows. But in white, nobody could fail to notice her, and she knew that every eye in the place was on her, even though it was desperately uncool for trendy New Yorkers to look impressed by any celebrity.

'That was amazing,' Madison breathed to Beau as he passed her a menu with one eyebrow raised. 'I'm really famous, aren't I?'

Beau laughed. 'That's what I've been telling you.'

Madison beamed at him, and moved her hand across the table to his. Beau frowned, and quickly withdrew his hand.

'We're in public,' he said in a low voice. 'And everyone is watching you.'

Madison pouted. 'I'm not trying to make out with you,' she commented as quietly as she could. 'I just wanted to hold your hand for a moment . . . Sometimes I can't resist you.'

Beau stared at her for a second, and then opened his menu. Madison could feel her good mood deflating.

'You know, this is the best Chinese food in the city, if not the world,' he said conversationally, as if he were speaking to any client on his roster. 'The Peking duck is out of the world – I couldn't find better in Hong Kong when I visited last year.'

Madison paled slightly. 'Duck? As in . . . birds?' A memory of feeding the ducks on the large pond in Walkertown came flooding back, and she felt sick.

Beau smiled patronisingly. 'Have you never had it?' he asked. 'It's divine, especially here.'

Madison looked at her menu. There was lots of tofu – which she was not prepared to try as she'd never heard of it – and some crab caviar soup. Just the thought of eating crab eggs made her stomach turn. Madison was more of a hamburger and pizza girl, and she couldn't eat anything that was even vaguely unusual. Besides, she'd never eaten Chinese in her life.

'I think I'll just have the fried chicken with, um, Chinese ponzu,' she said, hoping her meal would be more KFC than some of the exotic dishes she could see on nearby tables. She leant closer to Beau. 'What *is* ponzu?' she asked, feeling dumb.

Beau looked at her condescendingly. 'It's a sauce, kind of spicy but sweet. You'll like it.'

Madison breathed a sigh of relief. That sounded perfect – really, it was just fried chicken with a sweet and sour sauce. She could cope with that.

'And it's low calorie, which is great, as you need to drop a few pounds, especially around your stomach.'

Madison felt as though she'd been punched. Only hours before they'd been in bed, and Beau had whispered how incredible he found her body, and that she turned him on so much. Had he been lying?

'You'll see what I mean when those photos of you end up in the papers tomorrow. Your white dress showed off your pot-belly a bit more than I'd hoped – it's definitely time for you to start working out with Tia. She can start thinking about your moves for your first tour, too. It's never too early to start planning this stuff.'

Tia was Slate Street's choreographer, and Madison had only met her once, briefly, in the label's head office. She knew that Tia had instantly taken a dislike to her, although she wasn't sure why. The thought of working with her filled her with dread.

'Isn't there anyone else I can do the dance moves with?' she asked in a small voice.

Beau smiled, but it was a smooth professional one, rather than the more personal kind that Madison craved.

'No,' he said. 'Tia's the best, and she'll get you into shape. Now, there's a couple of girls standing in the corner, and I think they're about to ask for your autograph.' He watched Madison glance to the other side of the restaurant, and smirked when her face coloured. He loved clients when they were still getting used to fame and fortune. They were so much more pliable, and less demanding.

'When they come over, I want you to be gracious, sign whatever the fuck they have in their hands, and then ask them to excuse you for some privacy.'

Madison bit her lip. 'Isn't that a little rude?'

'Not unless you want them to join us for dinner,' Beau remarked with a swig of mineral water.

'Beau, I don't want to be a bitch,' she began, but Beau put one hand up to silence her.

'Just do as I tell you to,' he said coldly. 'I'm in charge here, not you.'

Madison stared at her boyfriend for a moment, then quickly smiled when the fans came over. They were not much older than her, and couldn't be more excited about meeting her.

'Oh my God, Madison honey, we voted for you, like, a

million times,' one of them said in a Southern drawl. 'We just loved your performance of Madonna's "Live to Tell".'

Madison coloured. The girls were clearly wealthy. If she'd been in Walkertown she'd have been intimidated by their calf-skin Dior handbags, Christian Louboutin heels, and what looked suspiciously like Versace dresses. But she wasn't in Walkertown, and she wasn't the same girl. She was in Manhattan, she was Madison Miller, Miss *Teen Star USA*, she was famous, and she was wearing Jimmy Choos.

'Thank you so much!' she replied, taking the luxury leather notebooks the girls passed to her. She looked at Beau, keen to include him in the moment, but he looked unimpressed at her eagerness. Madison decided to ignore him – why was he in such a bad mood anyway? – and grinned at the girls.

'What are your names? I'll write something personal if you like,' she said, wanting to milk the moment for all it was worth, and not caring if Beau wanted them to be left alone or not. She was the star, not him.

'Madison, you haven't time for that,' Beau interrupted, his voice like ice.

The girls' faces dropped.

'Don't be silly,' Madison remarked breezily, facing Beau square on. 'Our food hasn't arrived, and I can spare a few moments. These girls did vote for me after all.'

Madison turned back to her fans, not noticing Beau's black eyes flashing angrily. It was the first time she'd ever been asked for her autograph, and she wanted to savour it. Beau wasn't going to ruin it for her, no way.

'You mustn't mind my manager. He gets a little crabby sometimes,' Madison said, trying to make light of Beau's rude-ness. But as she began signing the notebooks she didn't see Beau give a little nod to a waiter, and within seconds a security guard stood over their table.

'Ladies, I'm going to have to ask you to leave Miss Miller in peace,' he said, in a deep, quiet voice, and although he looked placid enough, he was heavily built, and could clearly kick anyone's ass.

'Really, it's fine—' Madison began, but again Beau interrupted smoothly.

'Miss Miller thanks you for being fans, but it's time you were moving on,' he said, a note of impatience in his voice.

The girls took in the security guard's heavy frame and Beau's icy tone, and decided not to make a scene. When you were in a hip New York restaurant you behaved. Who knew who was watching you?

'Why did you do that?' Madison asked Beau sadly in a small voice, as the girls returned to their table. 'They were fans, real fans, and they were the ones who put me where I am today. I should be nice to them.'

Beau twisted his lips into a cruel little smile.

'I put you where you are today, Madison,' he hissed quietly. 'And you should be nice to *me*.'

'One, two, three, four, go Wildcats, go!'

Madison finished her cheer routine in the splits, and stood up, awkwardly. Tia Costello – probably the best dancer/ choreographer in America – was watching her silently. Madison wondered if it was because she was out of shape. It didn't feel that long ago that she'd been cheering on the field in front of her classmates, but she felt out of breath by the end of her perform- ance. She shot her keenest smile at Tia. She was determined to make the woman like her, no matter what.

'Not bad,' Tia commented, 'but not great, either. Not like

Tori was. If you're going to learn my routine in time for your tour we're gonna have to go back to basics and get rid of all this baby choreography you picked up at school.'

'You didn't like it?' Madison said, disappointed. She'd devised the routine and had been pretty pleased with it at the time. Kyle had loved it . . . as had Beau when she'd performed it to him one drunken, hazy night when she dressed up in a cheerleading outfit.

'I hated it,' Tia said bluntly, and Madison knew instantly that Tia didn't just dislike her, but despised her. 'Your arm movements are straight out of an eighties Tiffany video, your legs were all over the place, and if that was sexy . . . Girl, you really *can't* move.'

Although everyone was rude in New York, Madison was still shocked. But she knew how to bite, too . . . Being part of the popular clique at school had taught her how to.

'Sure,' she said perkily. 'But tell me, who's Tiffany? I don't think I'd been born when she was famous.'

Tia – who was at least thirty – looked as if she wanted to murder the cute, tight nineteen-year-old in front of her. Madison grinned.

'Why don't you stand in front of the mirror and work on copying what I do,' Tia barked, and she walked over to her iPod and pressed play. Kanye West began to blare out, and Tia performed a few complicated moves.

'Go on,' she directed, and Madison stood there helplessly, her smile wiped off her face.

'Too fast for you?' Tia smirked.

'Let me do it slower,' she said, though she felt like walking out.

Tia did the moves again, only marginally slower, and Madison struggled to keep up.

82

'Listen, honey, if you can't do the moves you ain't gonna be a superstar,' Tia said happily.

'I'm a singer,' Madison said through gritted teeth. 'Not a dancer.'

Tia laughed. 'And you think a pretty voice is gonna be enough? We need to work on your body – you're at least five pounds too heavy, if not more – and we need to get your strength up. You have to be able to move like a pro. Because, according to Beau and the great American public, you are. Just wait till you get on tour. It's like a three-hour spinning class – only in front of thousands of people. I thought Beau said you were a *dancer* anyway,' she said pointedly.

Madison blushed. 'It wasn't that kind of dancing,' she muttered, thinking about the routines she and Leesa had made up in her first few weeks at Spotlight.

Tia's lips curled upwards. 'Oh?' she asked in a tone of voice that suggested she knew exactly what kind of 'dancing' Madison meant.

Madison felt a surge of strength come from nowhere.

'No. It wasn't really dancing – I was a stripper. I stood on stage, moved sexily, and took my clothes off.' She said it as matter-of-factly as she could, hating having to admit it, but suddenly not caring what Tia thought of her. She was standing close to the choreographer, and as they were the same height their stares burned into one another.

Tia broke into a smile. Respect. 'Now that sounds like something we could work with. Why don't you show me exactly what you got up to when you were on stage and we can take it from there.'

As Madison moved around the floor with her eyes shut – for she was too embarrassed to catch Tia's eye in the bright light of the studio and had only ever 'danced' like that in a dark, dirty club – Tia felt a rush of excitement go through her.

The girl really could move.

The dance lessons were just the beginning. Since moving back to New York and into Beau's apartment, Madison's life became a whirlwind of hard work, luxury she had only ever dreamt of, and frantic adoration. Everywhere she went people cried out her name, desperate for a piece of her, and whatever Madison wanted, she could have.

Instead of shopping at the sales at Macy's or Century 21, it was Fifth Avenue all the way, and Bergdorf Goodman even closed the entire store one night so Madison could browse the Zac Posen, Stella McCartney, Emilio Pucci and Alberta Ferretti collections without being mobbed by fans. When she was ushered into Tiffany's – Tiffany's! – Madison was fawned over, and given a diamond and pink sapphire celebration ring. Just for being photographed for going into the store!

The paparazzi followed her everywhere, and although Madison had been adamant in the beginning that she didn't want – or need – security, she soon chose to be accompanied by two burly, smile-free men who went everywhere with her. They kept the photographers and fans at a safe distance, and often came in handy when Madison was weighed down with shopping bags. Beau saw a photo of Madison's bodyguards carrying designer bags in *US Weekly*, and hit the roof, declaring he wasn't paying for the best security in the country to carry her shopping, but Madison ignored him. She spent most of her days with Phil and Jason, and they'd offered to help. They were two friendly faces in a Manhattan that was becoming increasingly scary to her. Being famous wasn't quite what Madison had expected. She hadn't realised you could never escape from it, and that everywhere you went you were always watched, always judged. You couldn't trust anybody.

'Yeah, girl, you've got it bad,' Phil said to her early one morning as they were driven to a New Jersey photographic studio. She was having some more promo photos done, and even though the sun was barely up, the paparazzi were already tailing her. 'I've never had a gig like this before.'

Madison turned in her seat and looked at the two cars following them. In each there was a driver, a guy with a video camera, and another with a SLR. She felt like she was in a zoo – and was half exhilarated, half exhausted by it.

'Other people on Slate Street must have had this kind of attention, though,' Madison replied, still watching the two cars weaving in and out of the lanes as they angled to get the best snaps of her. 'Jacy Robins was always in magazines when she won *Teen Star* – that must have been pretty hectic.'

'Girl, it was *nothing* like this. Half the time Beau was setting up pap action to get Jacy in the press. This time round they're doing it by themselves. We ain't even paying them to follow you.'

Madison sighed and turned to face the front again. She rested her head on Phil's shoulder.

'How much do you think they get for photos of me?'

Phil shrugged. 'Thousands of bucks, probably. You're hot property, little lady, and don't you forget it.'

Madison grinned. Everything was so surreal, and even though she loved being a superstar, she wondered if she really deserved this kind of fame just for winning a talent contest and releasing a number one single. She was the golden girl, and her face sold products like hot cakes. It was why she needed more photos – there was such a demand for her image that publications were having to reuse the same official ones again and again.

As soon as they arrived at the studio, Madison breathed a sigh of relief. The paps weren't allowed in, and for an hour or two she could relax while her hair and make-up were done. This took for ever. It seemed that fifty people were needed every time Madison changed her haircut – should she have bangs? If so, a debate was held on the length, angle, texture and colour – and it was almost a military operation to decide on her make-up. How much glitter was too much? Should fake eyelashes be used? Which was the perfect shade of lipstick? Madison felt exhausted just listening to it, and often remembered how it had sometimes only taken ten minutes to do her make-up at Spotlight. She really didn't see what the big deal was, anyway. As soon as the photos were finished they were always digitally retouched.

'Tilt your head down a little . . . That's right, think Paris Hilton. Now open your mouth slightly, no, not that much, yeah, that's sexy . . .' The photographer was meant to be one of the best, but he was so bossy. So demanding. She'd only been in front of the camera for about an hour, but her whole body ached from holding poses, and her skin prickled under the heat of the lights. Her lips were dry under the lipstick from lack of water, but Madison knew she shouldn't complain. Phil had once told her how photographers never wanted to work with Jacy because of her 'unreasonable demands', and Madison wanted to be liked by everyone. Still, when her cell rang she rushed to answer it. As always, and as she'd hoped, it was Beau.

'Hey, baby,' she said breathlessly.

'How's the shoot coming along?' Beau asked. He sounded calm and relaxed – in boyfriend mode, not manager mode. Madison smiled and squirmed slightly. Even though they lived together whenever Beau was in New York, just hearing his voice still turned her on. 'Really great!' she chirruped happily. 'Marius has done a couple of shots, and he says we've got some really good ones.'

'Tell him to email me over a couple right now so I can take a look . . . And while I wait, tell me what you're wearing. I want a preview of what I'm getting.'

'Um, I'm kinda not wearing too much,' Madison admitted, after she'd passed on the message to Marius. 'They gave me a loose halter-top in cream that shows off my cleavage, and a little floaty mini-skirt.'

'What colour is it?' Beau's voice was neutral down the phone.

'It's cream, too. And my boots are amazing. They've got these really high heels, and they're the softest light-brown colour ever. They're fantastic. I'm gonna keep them.'

Beau was silent for a moment, and Madison wondered if he was pissed that she wanted the boots. Whatever she took from the hundreds of clothes that designers sent for photos, Slate Street paid for.

'And what are you wearing under your skirt?'

Madison went into her dressing room and shut the door.

'A nude thong,' she said slowly.

Beau moaned. 'Leave the shoot and come home, now.'

Madison bit her lip. 'But Beau . . . you said this shoot was totally important, and I had to spend all day getting the photos perfect.'

'I've just seen the ones Marius emailed me, and they'll do. I want you. Now.'

Madison was torn. The crew had spent hours on her hair and make-up, and the set had taken an age to put together, too. Marius had only been shooting for an hour, and they'd all be really angry if she left. They were meant to be shooting until the evening, and it wasn't even lunchtime yet.

But . . . Madison heard the longing in Beau's voice, and she remembered how great the sex had been the night before. They'd rolled around and fallen out of the bed, yet no matter what position Beau put her in, his eyes never left hers, and all night Madison could see her pleasure reflected in the darkness of his irises.

'I'm coming,' Madison said huskily.

Beau laughed. 'You will be.'

Madison walked out of the studio. When you were in love, you put the other person first, no matter what.

Chapter Eight

'Baby, I'm really tired,' Madison said quietly as she lay on their bed. Beau had just finished a conference call to some people in Hollywood about Madison making a guest appearance on the highest-rating teen soap, and even though she knew she was being ungrateful, just the thought of having to do it made her head hurt and her body ache. She was exhausted.

'Have I been wearing you out?' Beau remarked, drinking in Madison's naked body with his eyes and thinking about how much he'd like to fuck her again. 'Or are you moaning about your workload?'

Madison sighed. She couldn't win if she said either, and the reality was that it was both.

'Workload,' she said wearily. In the past three months Madison had performed exclusively at the best bars in the country, posed in a dozen more photo shoots, had been strategically papped at all the best showbiz parties, and had done over two hundred interviews for TV, radio, magazines, newspapers, websites, fansites . . . The list was endless. Madison hadn't known anything like it, and had never realised how hard successful celebs worked. 'I really need a break.'

'Your album's coming out in two months, you need to start prepping for the promotion of that, and then you're on tour for three months. You haven't got time for a break. Tia says you're still struggling with some of her choreography.'

'Beau,' Madison said, her voice sounding thin and brittle, 'I'm at breaking point. I need a vacation. Just a week. I can't do this any more.'

Beau raised his eyebrows as Madison started to cry.

'Come here, baby,' he said with open arms, and even though she went to him, Madison wondered why she was the one who had to walk over to him, rather than the other way round. Wasn't she the one who was working her ass off every day?

'Can we go on vacation, please?' she asked in a small voice. 'I'll work extra hard when we get back. Please?'

Beau dried Madison's tears with his thumb, and considered her thoughtfully. She'd become thin recently, and she didn't have the glow that she'd had when she'd won the TV show. A vacation would give her a tan, and relax her. It would be money well spent, especially if he organised for her to go to a couple of parties when she got back. She'd look sexy in the photos.

'Where do you want to go?' he asked her considerately.

Madison thought about it. She needed space and sunshine.

'Florida maybe? Or California? Anywhere hot would be great.'

Beau laughed. 'You're not vacationing in America, kid. You're a superstar, remember? What about somewhere like Bali, or the Bahamas? How does that sound?'

Madison breathed in deeply. 'It sounds amazing. I'd love to just hang out on a beach with you and relax. We both deserve it.'

Beau looked shocked. 'You expect me to come on vacation with you? You're kidding, right? If we go away together the press will sniff it out in an instant and everyone will know you're my lover.'

Madison hated how he never called her his girlfriend. 'Lover' sounded so tacky, as if their relationship was just about sex.

'We could go undercover. Nobody would know! I want to go on holiday with *you*, Beau. Who else am I gonna go with?'

'One of your girlfriends?' Beau suggested, picking up the remote to the huge plasma screen on his bedroom wall and flicking through the channels. He stopped on *American Idol* and pulled a face, before turning it off.

'I don't have any girlfriends,' Madison snapped, trying not to think about Leesa. She really should have stayed in touch with her, but she'd been so busy, and her life was so frantic . . . Madison pushed the thought out of her mind. 'I don't have any friends at all, really, apart from maybe Phil and Jason. And you don't expect me to go on holiday with my bodyguards, do you?'

Beau looked up sharply. 'You're not going anywhere with other men,' he stated, and even though she was exhausted and upset, Madison felt a little stab of pleasure. He hardly ever got jealous any more.

'Then come with me,' she pleaded. 'Think how awesome it would be. We can lie about in bed all day, eat outside on balmy evenings, drink cocktails, watch sunsets . . .'

Beau sighed. 'I can speak to Richard Branson, see if Necker Island is free. We could hire a private jet out there, and as the island is discreet nobody would ever know we were vacationing together.'

Madison clapped her hands together excitedly. 'Really? You mean it? We can go away together?'

Beau nodded in resignation. He had his doubts about it, but he could do with a break, too. Managing Madison – both in public and out of it – was tough business.

'Let me make a few phone calls, see what I can do. But Madison,' Beau said slowly, 'you owe me for this.'

Madison knew that meant more sex. And as much as she adored Beau, she didn't think she had the energy for a love life any more. She just wanted to sleep for ever.

'I don't know if we can get Necker,' Beau said to Madison a couple of nights later, halfway through her daily workout. 'Apparently some huge hip-hop star – who won't be named to me, but I can guess who it is, the bastard – has hired it for when we want to go. I'm in negotiations at the moment, but if we can't get it, how does Little Dix Bay sound? It's a resort on one of the Virgin Islands.'

Madison looked up from the display on the treadmill, but kept on running. 'Little dicks? Ha, how apt!' she joked, but Beau wasn't in the mood for humour. He jabbed at the treadmill so that it sped up and Madison fell off, hurting her leg.

'Don't ever make a gag like that again,' he hissed.

Madison felt her eyes fill with tears. 'I'm sorry,' she began, but Beau wasn't in the mood to be placated.

'I'm risking a lot going on vacation with you, and don't expect you to be a bitch,' he growled. 'Stop being an ungrateful cow and remember you owe all of this' – he gestured around the apartment – 'to me.'

Madison opened her mouth to speak, but Beau shot her one final glare and stormed out of the room, leaving Madison to sit on the floor and cry openly. She didn't understand how Beau could be loving one moment, and nasty the next. When they were in bed he was so tender, so full of love for her, but then, when they were talking about work or even deciding what food to order in, he was cold and distant. He often acted as though he didn't like her, and sometimes he looked straight through her. Everything she did was for him. Everything. She couldn't bear to have him upset with her. She couldn't lose him.

'Beau, I'm so, so sorry. I wasn't thinking,' Madison pleaded, after she'd tracked him down in his study. 'You know you're not, you know . . .' She didn't want to bring up the name of the resort again in relation to the size of his manhood. She wanted him to forget she ever said it.

'Do I do it for you, Madison?' Beau asked her directly. 'Recently you've not been that enthusiastic about going to bed with me, and I've gotta say it hurts. Is there someone else?'

Madison couldn't believe it. How would she ever have time for anyone else? And didn't Beau know that she adored him? She was so in love with him – he was all she could think about.

'Of course there isn't! I'm just so tired . . . I think you're the hottest guy I've ever seen, and I love being in bed with you. You're just the greatest.' Madison sat on Beau's lap and looked deep into his eyes. 'I'm crazy in love with you, you know. And I always will be.'

Beau gave Madison a long, hard stare, and then he smiled. He believed her.

'Good,' he says. 'You can show me just how much you love me on our vacation. Because you won't be tired when we're away, will you?'

Madison beamed at her boyfriend and kissed him, hard. 'No way,' she said. She was looking forward to the break so much.

They arrived at Necker Island by helicopter just before sunset, and from the sky they could see hundreds of tiny candles lighting up the path to their villa. It was stunning – with an open-air lounge and a private pool with views of the sparkling turquoise sea and the soft white sand of the beach.

Every morning Madison would sit quietly, watching the sun rise over the horizon. The air was sweet with tropical flowers, and in the distance she could hear the call of wild birds. It was heavenly, completely different from Manhattan or Walkertown, and so peaceful, so serene. As they had discovered, a hugely famous hip-hop star *had* booked the Great House, but Beau had managed to get them into one of the five Balinese houses dotted around the island – despite the hip-hop artist's objections. Madison didn't care. She would have been happy in a hut on a beach – just being away from the paps and fans was bliss – but Beau was dissatisfied. When you were Beau Silverman, you generally got what you wanted.

'We should have been allowed to stay in the Great House,' he grumbled whenever he spotted the huge house set above them on the cliff. 'I've stayed there so many times. It's never been a problem.'

Madison didn't understand why he didn't adore their accommodation as she did. Their Bali house had three levels, and was completely open so that they could enjoy the weather and the sound of the sea. They had a stunning panoramic view of the ocean from their luxurious four-poster bed, and their balcony was a suntrap. Madison's skin had already turned a delicious shade of honey. Beau, however, remained pale – despite his dark colouring.

'Why don't you come and sunbathe with me?' Madison called out to Beau from the side of the pool, as he shunned the sun yet again to sit in the shade of the house with his laptop. Madison wore just her sunglasses and tiny bikini bottoms, and as much as she enjoyed the peace of the island and the freshly squeezed peach juice that had just been brought to her, she craved her boyfriend's attention. Though she loathed admitting it, she was slightly bored.

Beau glared at her from the shade of the house, only momentarily glancing up from his spreadsheets.

'No thanks,' he said curtly, and Madison felt her heart drop a little. She knew that Beau found it hard to relax, that he wasn't the type of person who could lie around and do nothing, but she'd hoped that her oiled, sun-kissed body would persuade him to take some time out.

'How about a walk on the beach, then?' Madison suggested, casually walking over to him and looping her arms around his neck. Even though he wasn't sunbathing, Beau was only wearing shorts, and Madison pressed her warm skin against his chest in the hope of persuading him to spend some time with her. It worked.

'Why not,' Beau said with a sigh of resignation.

'You won't regret it,' she whispered, kissing his neck and dragging him to his feet. 'Come on, we can find a private cove somewhere . . .'

As they walked along the beach, Madison thought she'd never been so relaxed — or content — in her life. She was a famous singer, had an amazing, handsome boyfriend, and was vacationing on a paradise island where they had complete privacy, as well as being waited on hand and foot by discreet staff. Life didn't get much better than this.

'Are you happy?' Madison asked Beau shyly, as she squeezed his hand tightly and paddled in the water. She was still topless, but she knew it didn't matter. Nobody could see them.

'Kinda,' Beau muttered non-committally. 'I can think of ways I could be happier, though.'

Madison looked up at him, and was relieved when she saw he had raised one eyebrow flirtatiously. She smiled.

'Oh?'

'I'd be happier if I was kissing you,' Beau commented.

Madison stopped walking and pecked him on the cheek. 'Like this?' she asked innocently.

'You're such a smartass, Madison,' he said. 'No, like this.'

And he grabbed her and kissed her long and hard on the lips, before pushing her to the ground. Madison stretched her body against the soft white sand, and let the gentle waves lap at her toes. It was like a scene in a film.

'I love you,' she whispered, staring deeply into Beau's black eyes. 'I love you so much.'

Beau smiled, and he was just tugging down her bikini bottoms when they heard a noise out at sea. They both looked up, and paled when they saw a speedboat heading towards them. There were men dressed in black on board, and long-lens cameras were trained on them. Paparazzi. And there was no time, and nowhere, for Madison Miller – stark naked and frolicking with her manager on a beach – to hide.

'This is so fucking bad, you have no fucking idea!' Beau shouted at Madison.

They were back at Slate Street in Manhattan, and Beau's desk was piled high with hundreds of press cuttings all carrying the same photos – of Madison completely naked on the beach with Beau.

'My reputation as a manager, as a talent spotter – as a fucking media mogul – is in tatters, and it's all your fucking fault.'

'Can you stop swearing at me?' Madison said shakily, trying not to cry. 'It's not my fault. I didn't tell the paps where we were going to be.' She thought of the swarm of photographers who'd followed their every move since they'd landed back at JFK, and shuddered. They were relentless, and wouldn't leave either of them alone. Phil and Jason were escorting them everywhere, but Madison still felt incredibly unsafe. The burly bodyguards couldn't protect either of them from the paparazzi lenses or from the vicious gossipy articles that had appeared everywhere.

'No, it was that fucking hip-hop guy in the Great House 'cause he was pissed at us being on the island, too!' Beau roared, and Madison shrunk into the chair. She'd never seen anyone so angry before. Ever. 'I fucking told you we couldn't go on holiday together, and you fucking insisted. I could kill you right now.'

Madison took a deep breath and tried to sit up straight.

'My career's on the line, too,' she said as calmly as possible. 'And I'm just as angry as you. But, Beau, it will blow over. It always does.'

Beau slammed his fist on the desk, and Madison jumped.

'Madison, they're investigating *Teen Star*. These aren't stupid little gossip articles about how America's pop princess is dating her manager. They're suggesting we got together before the programme started and we fixed it so you'd win.'

Madison felt the blood drain from her face. 'What?' she whispered. 'They can't do that.'

Beau gave a short little laugh. 'Madison, they can. The phone lines are being investigated, and the network has already started interrogating some of my staff.'

'But why would the network care?'

'Madison, have you actually got a brain in that pretty little head of yours? *Teen Star* is worth four *billion* dollars to Slate Street, and one ad slotted in the show makes the network half a million. If *Teen Star USA* gets taken off the air, they're screwed and we're fucked. It's a global franchise and it will affect us badly. Slate Street could even go under because of this.'

Madison was too stunned to speak. 'Just because we went on vacation?' she whispered.

Beau eyeballed her. 'Yes, just because Madison Miller wanted to go on vacation.'

'But . . . but we didn't fix the programme. You said I had the majority of the votes that came in on the season finale. The network won't find out anything; we're safe,' Madison said with relief. Their relationship might look bad, but they'd not done anything wrong. It was all going to be okay.

Beau ran his hands through his black hair, and sighed. 'I lied. That pretty boy Justin whatshisname got the majority share of the votes.'

'We cheated?' Madison's voice was strained, and she could feel her whole body shaking.

Beau looked her directly in the eye. 'We cheated, and I'm going to have to pay the phone regulators millions to tell the network they made a "mistake" about who won the show.'

'And then will Justin be crowned the *Teen Star* winner?' Madison whispered. That she hadn't actually won the show legitimately really threw her. She was stunned.

'Will he fuck,' Beau said. 'He'd bomb. The network won't admit that anyone made a mistake – Slate Street or the phone regulators – but they will take issue about our relationship.' Beau paused, and Madison felt herself stiffen. Was he going to end it? If he did, it would be more than she could bear. She didn't think she could live without him, even when he was in the worst mood she'd ever seen.

'I've cut a deal with *US Weekly*. We're doing a cover to announce that we're in love and getting married.'

Madison lifted her eyes to meet Beau's. He loved her? And even after this catastrophe he wanted to marry her? Madison broke out into a huge beam, but Beau didn't match it. He grimaced.

'I don't love you. Shit, at the moment I can't stand the sight of you . . . But that's nothing compared to what the good folk of middle America think of you.'

He started flinging newspaper and magazine cuttings at her, and as they whizzed towards her Madison caught sight of headlines that suggested she slept her way to the top, that she was a 'whore' and a 'sex addict' who had worked as a prostitute, and that her career was dead. Beau kept throwing the cuttings at her, but Madison couldn't see what the rest of the headlines said. Her eyes had filled with tears.

'America *hates* you, Madison. You've turned from a good old-fashioned American sweetheart into a "slut" who "stole" *Teen Star* from that Justin kid. The paparazzi that are following us around aren't after pretty pictures that people will fawn over – they want ugly shots that people can stare at as they think about how much they hate you. They want to see you on your way down, because there's nothing America likes more than a fallen idol. They can't get enough of it.'

Madison wanted to put her hands over her ears. She couldn't stand the way Beau was spitting out his words. She couldn't believe that her one source of comfort – the man she thought loved her – could say such terrible things with such relish.

'Personally, I don't give a shit about you, but we've invested far too much money in you for your career to fail. We need to get your album out at the very least, and we need it to sell. An exclusive interview about how we fell in love after the show – and how I proposed so soon so you could remain a virgin for our wedding day – should salvage your squeaky-clean reputation. So how about it, sweetheart?' Beau muttered. 'Want to get hitched?'

Madison opened her mouth in a silent scream and wondered

how it was possible to go from paradise to hell in such a short space of time.

'Ha, don't worry about answering,' Beau said, wryly. 'You're under contract, and you haven't got a choice.'

Chapter Nine

They were still there, Madison realised with a heavy heart. They were still there, and they definitely weren't going anywhere. She pressed her nose to the glass and peered down at the street below. The paparazzi hadn't left the entrance to Beau's apartment block since they'd got back to New York, and rather than getting bored of waiting for her to leave the building – as she'd hoped – there seemed to be even more of them. They were joshing around, laughing, and Madison briefly considered throwing something out of the window down onto them. But she couldn't do that, could she? She was Madison Miller, fallen *Teen Star USA*, and that would make all her negative publicity even worse. Besides, they were waiting for her for a *good* reason. They were waiting to get the first shot of the newly engaged, happy Madison.

But Madison knew she couldn't face them. She didn't know how she'd ever face anyone ever again. It was hard enough just to get out of bed.

Madison felt her legs wobble again, and she leant back against the Italian marble wall of the bedroom. She focused on the gold-embossed leather wall hangings, and told herself to take deep breaths. She'd not eaten anything in days, and her eyes felt raw, her throat scratchy. If she hadn't known better she'd have thought she had a cold, or even the flu, but she wasn't ill.

She was heartbroken.

'Oh, you finally decided to get out of bed.' Madison turned her head to see Beau standing in the doorway of the master bedroom that he no longer shared with her. He assessed her coolly, calculating just how miserable she really was. 'You look like you just stepped out of a swamp. When was the last time you washed?'

Madison shrugged and felt her hair. She'd not washed or brushed it for five days — or was it six? — and it felt like a greasy, knotty mess. Her face was slick with oil, her lips were cracked and dry, and she didn't need to look in a mirror to know that her skin had broken out and she had huge grey bags under her eyes. She was a state.

'If only the American public could see you now,' Beau sneered. 'They'd say you got what you deserved for sleeping with me to win *Teen Star USA*.'

Madison refused to look at her new fiancé. She slumped back into bed, not caring that she'd somehow managed to scuff the 1000-thread-count sheets spun through with 22-carat gold. What was money when you didn't have someone you truly loved to share it with? Besides, Madison thought sadly, these were Beau's sheets in Beau's apartment. She was a superstar, but she didn't have anything of her own.

'I've got a present for you, darling,' Beau said softly, and for a moment Madison felt her heart perform a tiny, almost imperceptible leap. Maybe he felt something for her after all? But when she looked up at him and saw his dark eyes shining with malice she berated herself. Beau Silverman would never change. He was a bastard, pure and simple. And he had never loved her. Never.

He flung a small jewellery box onto the bed. 'It's your engagement ring. Open it up.'

Madison stared at it listlessly, and felt her heart ache. Before the vacation she'd really believed that they'd get married, have kids and be happy together for ever. She never imagined that Beau would turn out to be so nasty, and that she'd be forced into marrying him like this.

'Not interested, Madison? That's unlike you – you're normally so big on romantic gestures. Here, let me help you.' Beau roughly flipped open the box and shoved it in her face. Inside was a stunning solitaire on a simple rose-gold band, and it made Madison feel even worse. It was everything she'd ever wanted.

'Cubic zirconia, of course. Can't be giving you a *real* diamond – you'd start thinking I was in love with you again.' Beau laughed brutally. 'But what the press don't know doesn't hurt them, right, Mads?'

Madison weakly tried to pull the sheets over her head so she could block Beau out, but he was having none of it. He picked up her left hand and viciously shoved the ring on her engagement finger. It fitted perfectly, of course.

'If you remove it you'll kiss your record contract goodbye. How would you like to be working the strip clubs again?' Beau whispered gently, and Madison hated how hot tears flooded her eyes. After the last couple of weeks she didn't think she had any tears left to cry, but this newest insult made her feel as though her chest had been split open and her heart ripped out. She'd never known anything like it – even Kyle breaking up with her had been nothing compared to this.

'I'll be back in a couple of days,' Beau commented with a smirk, looking almost pleased that he'd made her cry again, as though it gave him some perverse pleasure. 'Try to keep out of mischief, won't you, Madison?'

As Beau retreated from the bedroom, slamming the front door

behind him as he left the apartment, Madison felt a wave of burning outrage rush through her. How *dare* he tell her to keep out of trouble? After all she'd been through.

She started angrily punching at her pillow – imagining it was Beau's face – but when that quickly became unsatisfying she flung it at the door. As it crashed into the doorframe it made a gratifying bang, so she picked up another, and another, and soon she was throwing everything she could get her hands on at the wall – ornaments, photo-frames, and a half-full tumbler of water that shattered into glittering shards of glass all over the polished floor.

She was furious, frantically, blindly furious, and the anger that pulsed through her body energised her and spurred her on. It was if the animosity she'd built up had erupted like a volcano, and with the burning explosion of emotion she'd come alive again.

Madison jumped out of bed, flung the 'engagement ring' on the floor, and marched through the apartment – her fingernails ripping at the expensive wallpaper, her incensed steps thudding against the plush cream carpet. She reached Beau's home office, bit her lip nervously, and cautiously pushed the door open. This, she knew, was Beau's inner sanctum. This room *was* Beau . . . and if she had any chance of hurting him as he'd hurt her, of escaping this situation, the clue to working out how to do it would be in here.

It *had* to be.

Madison sat on the swivel chair behind the leather-topped mahogany desk, and took deep breaths. She couldn't stay angry – she had to concentrate, to focus. As she began to cool down, she ran her fingertips against the worn leather of the desk and trailed them down to the top drawer. Disappointingly, there was nothing of interest inside – just household bills, party invitations, and letters of congratulation on their engagement which Beau's PA would deal with.

Nothing incriminating. Nothing that could help her.

Madison turned to the filing cabinet, and when she couldn't find anything in there, either, she rummaged through the shelves, in the safe (of which she knew the password), and even in the garbage. But if Beau had any skeletons in his closet he hadn't been so naive as to leave them lying around. Or not in the usual places, anyway.

Madison sat back down on the swivel chair and surveyed the room. It was typically Beau, a true representation of him. The walls were painted an aristocratic blood-red, and the floor was dark oak. One wall was covered in framed gold discs that Slate Street had earned, and another was lined with floor-to-ceiling shelves full of records. The gold discs represented the professional side of Beau – his commercial musical success – but the record collection was his private joy. Nobody apart from his closest friends knew that Beau loved Kiss, Def Leppard and Poison, and he was determined that nobody ever would. It was his musical hall of shame.

A tiny jolt of electric energy flashed through Madison's body, and, as if in a trance, she stood and walked towards the records. She fingered through them until she found the album that included his favourite Kiss song – 'Forever'. Beau had once sung it to her on a hazy, drunken night, and as Madison pulled the album from the shelves she tried not to think about how in love with her he'd seemed – and how she'd believed every word he'd said. She slipped the black record out of the cardboard sleeve easily, and with it came several official-looking papers and photographs that fluttered to the floor.

This was it, she thought. It had to be.

Madison dropped to her knees and picked up the first photo,

and then one of the documents. This was more than just incriminating, she realised. This was shockingly brilliant.

She'd got him.

'Madison the popstar returns,' Beau remarked wryly as he walked into his apartment several days later. After making her discovery Madison had been spurred on to make herself look human again. There was no point playing the victim, she thought. She had to take a stand and prove to everyone that Beau was the villain – not her.

She'd taken long showers, buffed and bronzed her body, and had even called for an exclusive Manhattan hairdresser to restyle her hair. Madison knew she looked pretty good in her tight, lilac body-con dress. She might have lost her spirit, her hope and her faith in love when Beau had turned out to be a sleaze, but she'd also lost a couple of pounds.

She wasn't about to get fucked around by Beau any more. She was going to take charge of herself and her career again.

'I've more than returned,' Madison said with a smile, and Beau was momentarily thrown. He'd not expected Madison to be so . . . well, normal. It was almost as if she was flirting with him.

'I've been thinking, and I realise I've been a fool,' she admitted, lowering her eyes. 'Getting married is the only thing we can do in this situation to get the public back on side. I don't want my whole career to be thrown into the garbage just because I lost my head on a beach with you,' Madison said quietly. 'So I'll marry you.'

Beau eyed her sceptically. 'I don't love you,' he said bluntly. 'This is purely a business arrangement. You *do* realise that, right?'

Madison nodded. 'The sex was fun and all, but my career is more important to me than anything. I want to make this *work*,

Beau, and if that means marrying you and not being with any other guys for a couple of years I can handle that. After all, I want to be making both of us lots of money from my tour.'

Beau raised his eyebrows. 'You've come round quicker than I thought. Are you sure you're not playing one of your little games? This isn't a strip club where you can lie and tease your way to the top. This is *serious*.'

Madison froze for a second, and prayed that Beau didn't notice it. 'I'm not playing any games,' she said smoothly. 'I just want to be the biggest star on the planet, and I'm not gonna get far hanging out in bed all day, am I?'

Beau seemed satisfied with her answer. 'I'll get the wedding organised for as soon as possible, then,' he said. 'It should be in a couple of weeks – I've got teams of people on it.'

Madison nodded again and smiled. This time her grin was real, not forced. 'I can hardly wait.'

They were married in LA at the mansion Beau had bought to be their new West Coast home. It was a gorgeous day, with perfect blue skies, and a hint of a warm breeze that made Madison's hair dance around her face.

Over four hundred guests came to celebrate their wedding, and as Madison glided across the rolling lawns of the thousand-acre garden, everyone stopped and stared. The boned corset of the exquisite Oscar de la Renta gown pushed her breasts high, and made her already enviable waist no bigger than Beau's hand-span. The full skirt was created from silk and satin panels, dotted with tiny sequins, and draped over one another. Her Indian gold tiara shot minuscule rainbows behind her every time it caught the sun, and her shoes – deliciously high and strappy – made her walk more confidently than she'd ever done before. Everyone was enthralled. She looked like a princess in a movie. She was classy, elegant and utterly perfect.

Madison smiled and sparkled, telling herself that this was the last day she would ever have to act, although it would have to be the greatest show of her life. She knew she looked good – *better* than good – and even when Beau whispered that she 'looked almost as sexy as when she was a stripper', she was determined not to let anything ruin her big day. Who cared that out of the four hundred guests she only knew a handful, and those were from the Slate Street office? And was it *really* a big deal that her parents had chosen not to attend? Beau had insisted they invite her parents to make the wedding appear more legitimate, but when they didn't RSVP to the thick cream invite with gold embossed lettering, he told her to phone them, and to demand they come to LA. Madison made the phone call, but she was nervous throughout the conversation with her mom, who sounded distant and tired.

'I don't think we'd fit in with your showbiz guests, honey,' Jeanie Miller had said sadly, trying not to think about how much the long-distance call was costing her daughter. And how she could easily afford it. 'It's just not us.'

Madison knew her parents were proud of her – they'd given an interview to the *Walkertown Post* shortly after she'd won *Teen Star USA*, in which Madison's mom had said she'd cried tears of happiness when her daughter had won the show – but the physical distance between New York and Ohio, and the emotional distance that had been created by their daughter's fame, was too much for the relationship to take. Madison rarely spoke to her parents, and even during those dark days after Necker Island, she hadn't thought of calling them.

She was a different person, and she was living in a different world.

'We need to dance,' Beau whispered sharply into Madison's ear, interrupting a conversation she'd been having with an elderly man about the weather and real estate prices in LA. Madison fixed a brilliant smile on her face, pecked the cheek of her new husband, and graciously allowed herself to be led to the dance-floor. Beau's hand was warm on the small of her back, and for a moment Madison almost believed in the show they were putting on. A violinist from the Los Angeles Philharmonic started to play Massenet's *Meditation from Thais*, and as the high notes of the violin wove in and out of the piano accompaniment, Madison felt herself glide easily around the room, following Beau's lead. He expertly moved her from corner to corner, and as Madison gave in to his dominance, she began to feel her heart ache again.

A guest at the wedding had told her the story of Thais – whom Athanael lusted after to the point of obsession – and as Madison thought about the opera that their wedding music came from, and the feelings she'd had for Beau, she began to feel tears prickle at her eyes. She pulled Beau closer to her, desperate to control herself, but his warm body and the tragic music only made her feel worse, and she began to shake.

'The magazine's taking photos, so fucking sort it out,' Beau whispered into Madison's ear as though he were smiling sweet nothings to her, and she nodded and concentrated on looking as though she were in love. *US Weekly* had the wedding exclusive, and Madison knew that as soon as the photos were out they'd be syndicated in every newspaper, magazine and website in the world, making them millions and saving her career. Madison had to make her relationship with Beau look like true love, and so far, she thought they'd done okay.

As the final notes of the *Meditation* ended in a whisper, the guests all clapped their congratulations to Mr and Mrs Silverman, and Beau raised Madison's left hand to his lips and kissed it tenderly. The cubic zirconia of the engagement ring and the glittering gold of her wedding band caught the light, and for a moment Madison wished with all her heart that theirs was a real wedding.

But she knew it wasn't real. It couldn't have been.

'That went better than I expected,' Beau said bluntly as he removed his black bow-tie and collapsed onto the four-poster bed in their master bedroom. 'Apart from that little scene on the dance-floor, you managed to pull it off. I'm impressed. We could get you acting gigs on sitcoms when people stop buying your records.'

Madison switched off and stared at herself in the full-length mirror. She really did make a beautiful bride, she thought, and for a moment she wondered why Beau didn't love her. Was she not pretty enough? Not slender enough? Madison felt her eyes fill with tears again, and she angrily blinked them away. Beau was a bastard and she mustn't forget it. She couldn't.

'Apparently I'm Mrs Silverman,' Madison said softly, as if she'd just realised they'd got married. She turned to look at Beau. He was flat out on the bed, his arms and legs spread in exhaustion. He looked like a starfish.

'Yeah, but only in name,' Beau muttered. 'I don't love you – I never have, and I never will.'

Madison laughed. She didn't need Beau to keep telling her this. She'd heard it enough recently. 'Have you ever loved anyone?' she asked curiously, and Beau sat up slowly. His eyes were blank and unreadable.

'I love my work,' he said coldly, as if he was insulted that Madison had the nerve to ask such a personal question. 'Work's always been enough for me . . . And no woman will ever come close. So don't even think about trying to get me to love you.'

Madison leant against the dressing table and took her wedding and engagement rings off. She'd already removed her tiara, veil and satin heels.

'What about Tori Catrino?' Madison asked in her most innocent voice, not looking Beau in the eye. 'Didn't you love her?'

There was a long pause while Beau stared at her, and Madison busied herself by dabbing make-up remover on her eyes. The Slate Street make-up artist had covered her in more mascara and eyeliner than she normally wore, and she'd been desperate to take it off for hours. Since dancing at Spotlight she'd preferred the natural look.

'I've already told you, I've never loved anyone.' Beau's voice was like ice, and in the past Madison would have taken this as a sign to back off, to cool it. This time, however, she was itching to press all the buttons that would make Beau explode.

'That's funny,' Madison remarked idly, watching the make-up remover smear the eyeliner away. 'Because you and Tori got married, didn't you? In secret?' She paused for a second, and then turned back to Beau. 'If you didn't love her, why did you do it?'

Beau jumped up and forced his way close to Madison. She could smell the booze on his breath, and a thrill went through her body. She was scared, but she was also excited. Beau hadn't expected this, and she had him by the balls.

'What. The. Fuck?' Beau hissed.

'You *are* married to Tori, aren't you?' Madison asked, smiling sweetly. 'Or is the marriage certificate I have for you and her a fake?'

Beau didn't say anything, just continued to stare at her, so Madison continued.

'If you and Tori are still married, then, well, it means I'm not Mrs Silverman after all, am I? You can't have *two* wives, can you, Beau? I mean, that's just greedy.'

'How do you know about Tori?' Beau's voice was a whisper now.

Madison shrugged. 'The same way I know about the twins,' she said as breezily as she could. 'You told me that Tori Catrino – the top teen singer in the country, the girl I grew up *idolising* – was dumped from Slate Street for breaking her contract. You didn't mention that you fell in love with her, married her, and then accidentally got her pregnant!'

Beau winced, and for a second Madison could see real pain flash across his face. She'd touched a nerve, and it felt good.

'And she had twins!' Madison said excitedly, as if she were talking about a friend, and not a girl whose image used to be on a poster on her bedroom wall. 'And they look *exactly* like you with black hair and black eyes!'

Beau's hands turned into tight fists, and for a moment Madison wondered if he was going to hit her.

'You went through my record collection,' he said darkly.

Madison nodded. She'd found the marriage certificate to Tori, photos of her twins – who looked so much like Beau it wasn't funny – and copies of their birth certificates in the Kiss album sleeve, and she'd made several copies of each before putting them back. Beau wasn't named as the father of the twins on the birth certificates – that would have been too easy, made her ammunition too powerful – but it would have been obvious to anyone who saw the babies that Beau was their daddy.

Beau let out a long sigh, and sat on the edge of the bed. He ran his hands through his blue-black hair in agitation, but when he looked up at Madison, his face was blank and his voice was neutral.

'She refused to have a termination,' he said simply. 'So we sacked her. Made out to the staff that she'd decided to quit the industry to raise her kids and be a good mom . . .' His voice trailed off.

Madison knew Beau and the industry enough to know that image was everything. Tori could never have got away with being a popstar and a single mother.

'But you married her,' Madison said softly. 'You were in *love* with her. How could you do that to your *wife?*'

'We were drunk, we were in Vegas, and getting married seemed like a good idea at the time,' Beau said sharply. 'I was too busy with Tori's tour to get it annulled, and I've not got around to getting a divorce. I should.'

'But if you're still married to Tori it means we're not really married!' Madison said triumphantly. She was unable to keep the grin off her face.

Beau looked at her and shrugged. Tiredness was etched on his face, and he looked ten years older than he had that morning. 'So what?' he said wearily, as he collapsed back onto the bed. 'Our wedding never meant anything, and what happened with Tori doesn't change that.'

'Everything would change if *US Weekly* – or my fans – found out that you'd tricked me into getting married when you already have a wife and kids.'

Beau sighed and sat up again. 'I hardly tricked you into marrying me,' he said in exasperation, as if he was speaking to a stupid child. 'And why would *US Weekly* ever find out about Tori and the twins? She knows not to go running to the press.'

Madison pretended to consider this for a moment. 'What if I told them?' she asked innocently. 'What if I accidentally let slip that you'd broken my heart by marrying me when you already had a wife?'

Beau's eyes narrowed. 'And why would you do that?' he spat, harshly. 'Your star's on the up again. You're no longer the little slut who was cavorting with the owner of Slate Street to win *Teen Star USA*. You're a married woman who couldn't help but fall in love with a guy she met on the show . . . If you try to fuck this up you're just gonna destroy your career.'

'Not if I play the victim,' Madison said. 'Not if I make you out to be some sexual predator who preys on his teenage pop princesses. America hates sex addicts.'

Beau rolled his eyes again. 'If you do that you're off Slate Street, darling. And if I sack you, no other record label will touch you. Everyone will think you're a loose cannon, a head-case, someone who couldn't handle the pressure. What are you gonna do then? Go back to Smalltown to Mom and Pop? Because they *really* care about you, don't they, Madison? It was *so nice* how they showed at your wedding.' Beau's voice was dripping with sarcasm, and Madison bit her lip. Her plan to show Beau who was boss wasn't going to plan.

'I don't need Slate Street,' she said, trying to sound stronger than she felt. 'I don't need *you*.'

Beau laughed, stretched, and began unbuttoning his shirt. 'That's what Tori said, too, just because I binned her. She cried, she wailed, she even tried to hit me, but nothing worked. She refused to have a termination, so I terminated her contract. End of story.' Beau flung his shirt onto the floor and stood close to Madison. His broad chest looked powerfully strong, and despite herself Madison felt herself begin to get aroused. He really was all man.

'Don't fuck with me like Tori tried to,' Beau said in a low voice. 'Or you'll end up just like her.'

'I'm not scared of you,' Madison said. 'And you know what? When you least expect it I'm gonna speak to the press. It might be in a couple of weeks when we come back from our "honey-moon" and we tell the *New York Post* how in love we are. Or it might be in my pre-tour interviews. But trust me, Beau, *I'm* in charge here, and for as long as you need Madison Miller on your books to do the *Spotlight* tour that's apparently going to make you your billions, you're gonna be living on your nerves. The truth about you and Tori *will* come out.'

Beau stared at Madison for the longest moment. He'd never seen her so riled up, or so determined, and it made him laugh out loud.

'We can always do the *Spotlight* tour without you,' he said in an amused voice. 'It's always been Plan B, and we can still do it . . . I can lock you up in our house and never let you out.'

Madison rolled her eyes. 'I'm the star here, and you can't do Madison Miller's tour without Madison herself. It's impossible.'

Their LA bedroom filled with silence, and Madison could hear the chirruping of hummingbirds outside. Her hands were on her hips, and she knew she'd backed Beau into a corner. He eyed her with slight boredom, and then grabbed a towel before heading to the shower.

'We can, and you know what? I think we will. Game over, darling. I'm gonna show you exactly how Madison Miller Inc can exist without Madison Miller herself . . . You're off the pre-tour parties, and until you sort out your attitude, you're off the radar.'

Chapter Ten

'I can't believe you're getting married!' Poppy squealed as she joined her friend in the Rising Sun. 'Did Matthew get down on one knee? Present you with a ring and tell you he'd love you for ever?'

Jess grimaced, then grinned. 'Keep your voice down, would you?' she giggled. 'We still haven't told anyone at work, and this is the paper's local. Even the barmen trade newspaper gossip.'

Poppy rolled her eyes. 'Whatever. Now show me your hand,' she said bossily, and Jess obeyed, slowly moving her left hand onto the sticky pub table. As their engagement was still a secret in the office, she'd been wearing the ring on a chain around her neck, and even though she wore it on her finger in the evenings and at weekends, it felt awkward and heavy. It was so *grown-up*, and she said as much to her friend.

'Screw "grown-up",' Poppy breathed as she took in the ring, which was a brilliant round diamond set on a platinum band. 'It's stunning. And that diamond's huge! Is it from Tiffany's?'

Jess nodded and stared down at it. 'It *is* beautiful,' she began, but then she stopped and took a long drink of her pint.

'But?' Poppy prompted.

'But . . . I know this is silly, and I sound really ungrateful, but I always imagined that when I got engaged I'd design my own ring. I mean, this is spectacular,' she said, moving her hand so that the diamond glinted in the murky lighting of the pub, 'but it's not really *me*.'

Poppy stared at her in disbelief. 'You're right, you really do sound ungrateful. Matthew Parker of the *Daily World* has just asked you to marry him, and given you a ring that's worth a couple of grand at the very least.'

Jess swallowed. 'And that's another thing. How did he afford this? Shouldn't we have used the money as part of a deposit on a bigger flat? Or at least waited until we've lived with each other a bit longer?'

'You're kidding, right? Where's your sense of romance?'

'In an independent jewellery shop with my fantasy engagement ring designs,' Jess muttered.

Poppy sighed. 'Okay, fine, I give in. What's your dream ring?'

Jess didn't speak for a moment, although she didn't need to think about her answer. She'd always known what she wanted.

'It would be a platinum band, with a pear-shaped pink diamond surrounded by three tear-drop diamonds on each side, so that it looked slightly like a flower. It's kind of hard to describe . . .' Jess trailed her finger through a tiny puddle of beer on the table and drew a pear shape with petals. 'It would look a bit like this. Kind of vintage.'

Poppy looked down at the table and back at Jess. 'But the ring Matthew got you is so beautiful,' she said. 'Are you really disappointed? Really?'

Jess thought about it. 'Kind of,' she admitted. 'It's just the pink diamond ring is the one I always thought I'd wear when I got married. This ring is so . . . *standard*. Everyone has engagement rings like this. Do you know what I mean? It's like Matthew hasn't even thought about me or my tastes – he's just thrown money around in Tiffany's and got me something that I couldn't possibly hate.'

'I'm sure he thought long and hard about what ring to get you,' Poppy said soothingly.

'Do you really think so?'

'I *know* so,' Poppy said. 'Because he loves you. And you love him . . . right?'

Jess tore her eyes away from her ring and thought about Matthew. The more she lived with him, the more she realised she barely knew him at all. He spent an hour in the bathroom every morning before going to work. He was obsessed about his image. Just the other night Jess had tripped over the dumb-bells he kept in the hallway. She was finding it pretty boring having to make conversation with him while he worked out or preened himself in front of the mirror. They'd stopped going out, too – Matthew claimed he was always too tired to go for dinner after work, but he hadn't been like that before she moved in. She just didn't get it.

'Honestly? I'm not sure, I mean we've only been together for just over half a year, and . . .' Jess stopped when she saw Poppy's face fall. 'And maybe we're just going through a bit of an odd patch. You know, it's hard living with someone. Was it difficult for you when you and Joe moved in together?'

Poppy thought about it. 'No, not really. I mean, I got annoyed if Joe wiped his dirty hands on a clean tea-towel, or left the milk out for days on end, but apart from that, I love living with Joe. I love him.' She eyed Jess carefully. 'Don't you feel like that?'

'I don't know,' Jess replied slowly. 'It just seems as if the fizz has gone out of our relationship, and I'm getting to know the real Matthew. I'm going the extra mile to make it special . . . I even let him have sex with me at work last week.'

Poppy's mouth dropped open in shock.

'What can I say? I gave in! Matthew convinced me that my very expensive diamond ring proves he doesn't think of me as a cheap ho, and I wanted to distract myself from all the boring things Faye wants me to do.'

Poppy laughed. 'I wish I worked with Joe so we could flirt at work. Today I ended up eating a Mars Bar outside with all the smokers just so I could get away from my desk.'

Jess grinned and opened a bag of crisps. 'I have to say, I won't do it again. He managed to get a key to the cupboard where all the old supplements are stored, and even though we were locked in, we could hear people walking past. It was more funny than sexy. It cheered him up, though.'

'You know, your relationship sounds normal. It's just pre-wedding jitters, I'm sure of it.'

Jess bit her lip. 'It's a bit early to have those, isn't it? I don't know. Maybe it's the thought of actually getting *married* which makes me feel sick. Is that natural?'

Poppy shrugged. 'I suppose so. But we're all getting married now, so it's clearly the right time to do it. Maybe you're over-thinking it.'

'But I don't *want* to think about it. Shouldn't I be really excited and wedding-obsessed rather than the opposite?'

'Does Matthew talk about the wedding?'

'A bit,' Jess admitted. 'More than me, definitely. But it's so easy for him. All he has to do is turn up. I've got to organise it, and plan my dress, the bridesmaids, the flowers . . . it's over-whelming. To the point where being at work is preferable to thinking about it.'

Poppy raised her eyebrows. 'Okay, maybe you should stop obsessing about the wedding and think about Matthew instead. Pretend you're not engaged – do you love him?'

Jess shut her eyes and pictured her fiancé. She thought about how she loved to run her hands through his light brown hair, how his blue eyes narrowed when he was thinking, how when he bit his lips he could either look vulnerable or cunning. Jess remembered waking up in bed with Matthew that morning. He'd been curled around her, and Jess recalled the smell of his body – how under the biscuity smell of the fake tan she could make out that gorgeous, intoxicating masculine scent that was unique to him. That smell – the tang of Matthew – drove her crazy. It was the very essence of him.

But then . . . he *did* mask it with fake tan and gallons of expensive aftershave. And he plucked his eyebrows! And waxed his back! Jess tried really hard not to be shallow, but being with a man who made more effort on his appearance than she did was worrying – *and* she worked in fashion. Jess tried not to think about these new revelations, and concentrated on the positives.

She imagined Matthew gazing into her eyes as he made love to her, and then her mind went back to how he'd first held her hand in the office, even though their relationship was still in the very early stages and she was just an intern. She remembered how much that had meant to her – Matthew Parker wasn't afraid to tell everyone at work he liked her! – and how he still got jealous if other guys in the newsroom lingered at her desk. She thought about how much he loved her, and how nobody else would ever feel that way about her. Ever.

Poppy was right. Everyone around her – her friends, people she'd been at uni with, people she met randomly – was loved up and part of a couple. If they weren't already married with children on the way, they were at least engaged. And it was time for her to catch up. Jess had always wanted to have a career before she thought about marriage and kids, but she didn't want to end up penniless *and* single. Going for dinner alone when everyone else was in a couple just wasn't any fun.

'I think I love him,' Jess murmured, opening her eyes and looking at Poppy. 'But I just need a bit more time, you know, so I can be sure.'

Poppy smiled with relief. 'Then don't worry about the wedding. You don't have to do it until you're ready.'

Jess smiled and sunk back into her chair. Poppy was right. She was right to have said they should live together, and it was right that she'd got engaged. She would marry Matthew if time proved he was 100 per cent right for her . . . and even though she hated how Matthew belittled her dreams of being a designer she knew she was being petty, and that wasn't reason enough to be single again.

Their wedding would be perfect.

'So you're getting married,' Faye said bluntly, after reading the email Matthew had sent to all their colleagues announcing that Jess had agreed to be his wife. She looked as though she was struggling to be nice. 'Congratulations. Matthew's a lucky guy.'

Jess offered her boss a smile. 'Thanks, that's kind of you,' she said. 'I wanted to tell you sooner, but we agreed not to tell anyone at work until all our friends and family knew. You know, what with Andy being part of my family and all that.'

Faye pursed her lips. 'So when's the wedding? When will you become Mrs Matthew Parker?'

Jess blinked. 'We haven't decided yet. I'd like to wait a bit, think about where we're going to do it, and when, and what I'll wear . . . things like that.'

'You'll be having it in St Bride's, though,' Faye said with a frown.

Jess shrugged. 'I'm not really religious and, um, I've never heard of it.'

Faye let out a little laugh. 'I forget how new you are to this game. Matthew will want to get married in St Bride's on Fleet Street – it's the journalists' church. Has been for hundreds of years, and will be for many more. Everyone who's *anyone* in newspapers goes there. Which may explain why you've never been.'

Jess pointedly ignored the insult. 'We were thinking about doing it abroad, actually,' she lied smoothly. Now that Faye had said it, Matthew had mentioned something about St Bride's, but she hadn't really been listening – every time he mentioned the wedding Jess zoned out. She couldn't help it. She felt as if she'd have a panic attack if she even *thought* about it. 'If we go away we don't have to invite people we don't really like . . . We just want close friends and family.'

'Well, I'm sure you're right. So long as your godfather's there I don't think Matthew will be that bothered,' Faye said, her face flushed and her voice ever so slightly scratchy.

Jess turned away from her boss and back to the congratulatory emails that were flooding her inbox. Even if Faye was jealous of her engagement, there were plenty of people in the office who thought it was the best thing ever. And Jess wanted to concentrate on that.

'Mrs Parker,' Faye called sarcastically after lunch. 'Have you seen this?' She flung a copy of *US Weekly* on Jess's desk. 'It's the Madison Miller and Beau Silverman wedding issue. Thought you'd be interested since you have a wedding to plan quick-smart.'

Jess looked up from her features list. 'The Madison . . . who?' she asked, trying to feign interest and failing.

Faye sighed. 'Madison Miller – you know, that girl who won *Teen Star USA* who was caught frolicking on a beach with her manager? You look a bit like her, actually . . . Don't you remember when the *Daily World* did that huge four-page spread on it?'

'I don't read the showbiz section,' Jess said in a monotone, wishing she could leave work and go and hang out with Poppy. She glanced up at Faye, wondering if she'd gone too far, and when she saw Faye looked more than a little irritated, Jess rushed to smooth things over. 'I mean, I don't read the showbiz section *every* day, anyway. I think it's important to focus on fashion issues first.'

'You should read every page of the paper every day,' Faye parroted, and Jess bit her lip to stop herself from smiling. Faye was famous for never reading the *Daily World* – she often complained that the newsprint got all over her clothes.

'Anyway, I thought you'd like to see it. Seeing as you're getting married in four weeks' time. You must be *very* excited.'

Jess looked at Faye in disbelief. She was getting married in a month? On what planet? 'I told you earlier, we're not getting married for ages. We haven't even set a date yet.'

Faye laughed. 'Oh, really? That's not what Matthew was telling everyone in the Rising Sun this lunchtime. He said St Bride's is booked for four weeks' time, and that we're all invited.' She looked at Jess with a shrewd expression. 'It's no use pretending, *Jessica*. Matthew told us everything.'

'I can't believe you told everyone at work that we're getting married in a month! Without even *consulting* me!' Jess said angrily, the moment Matthew walked through their front door.

'Fucking hell, Jess, I've had a really hardcore day – the PM's up to his usual tricks again and we have to get an exclusive on it or the boss will do his nut. Do we have to talk about this now?'

Jess stamped her foot. 'Yes, we *do* have to talk about this right now. This is my life we're talking about here. What's more important? Me? Or work?'

Matthew sighed and loosened his tie. 'Fine,' he said evenly. 'But I don't see what the problem is. St Bride's had an opening in four weeks, so I booked it. I was going to surprise you with it tonight, but it looks like the rumour mill got to you before me.' He scanned Jess's face. 'I thought you'd be *pleased*.'

'But I don't want to get married in St Bride's. I want to get married on a beach somewhere. In a couple of years. Not in London in four weeks. Are you crazy?'

'Crazy in love.' Matthew raised one perfectly plucked eyebrow. 'Seriously, though, what's the problem? We want to get married, and we can do it in four weeks. What's the point in waiting?'

'There's *so* much point!' Jess practically yelled. 'I'm not *ready* to get married yet! And there's so much to organise! I need to think about our guest list, what I'm going to wear, who my bridesmaids will be, the flowers, the theme, what we're doing for a reception, the catering . . .' She was panicking now. There was no way they could feasibly get married in four weeks. It was impossible.

'Jess, darling, you don't need to worry about any of that. I've got Trudie to sort it all out for us. She offered – she *loves* organising weddings.'

'Who the fuck is Trudie?' Jess's voice was dangerously calm. She was near to exploding.

'Don't be silly, you know who Trudie is. She's the Editor's PA – and she's got loads of experience in St Bride's weddings; she organised the last staff one! Granted, it was a few years ago, but she offered to do it as our wedding present, and I said yes. It was meant to be a surprise for you.'

Jess stared at him. She couldn't believe it. Trudie didn't even know her.

'Sweetheart, you don't look very happy. Give me a smile, go on.'

Jess wanted to throw something at him. 'So, let's get this straight. We're getting married, in less than a month, at St Bride's, and the Editor's PA is organising our wedding for us. Is she going to choose who comes, too? And what dress I'll be wearing?'

'Of *course* not. I've already drawn up a guest list – it's mostly the guys from work, but they're our friends, so that will be fine with you – and as your wedding present I'm buying you a dress.' His eyes sparkled in excitement. '*Daily World* staffers get a discount at Vera Wang! How about that!'

Jess thought she was going to be sick. 'All my life,' she said quietly, as she struggled to keep her voice calm, 'I've wanted to design my own wedding dress. I don't fucking *want* a dress from Vera Wang! And I don't want to get married in four weeks!'

Matthew finally lost his temper. 'For fuck's sake, Jess, what's your problem? Any normal girl would be over the fucking moon to be marrying me in a Vera Wang frock. Are you mental or something? Or do you just not want to marry me?'

A tiny voice in Jess's head defiantly said 'no', and, for once, Jess was forced to listen to it. She *didn't* want to marry Matthew Parker – the more time she spent with him she realised how little she knew him – and she had no idea why she'd said yes when he proposed. She supposed she felt like she had to keep up with all her friends. Poppy was engaged, and it was like everyone around her was in a serious relationship. Part of her felt like it was the right thing to do. And what was she meant to do when Matthew presented that huge rock from Tiffany's? Say 'no thanks'?

She sank onto the sofa, feeling emotionally drained. There

was still time, she reasoned, to get out of this wedding. Four weeks wasn't long, and surely Matthew would understand that she wanted more time to get to know him properly? Their relationship had been so whirlwind, so intense, that she really didn't feel she knew him at all. She knew she was in lust with him, but love? She wasn't sure. She really wasn't sure.

'You don't want to marry me, do you?' Matthew said, sitting next to her and putting his head in his hands. He looked so sad and hurt that Jess felt a terrible pang of guilt. 'I thought you loved me as much as I love you, but you're being so unreasonable about everything that you can't love me. I just don't understand it. Why move in with me, and say yes to my proposal, if you don't love me?' Tears began to slide down his handsome face, and Jess was stunned beyond belief. Who knew that Matthew Parker – who spent his days at work acting as though he were immune to murders and rapes – had the emotional capacity to cry?

'You know how I feel about you,' Jess said softly. 'But I'm not prepared for this. I thought we'd have a long engagement, really spend time getting to know each other, and get married in a couple of years. What's the rush?'

Matthew gazed at her intensely. 'Because I *love* you, and I want you to be Mrs Matthew Parker. The moment I saw you in the newsroom I knew you were the one for me, and that hasn't changed. You feel the same, don't you? So why can't we get married next month? Everyone our age is getting married now – why can't we?'

'I'm just not ready, Matthew,' Jess said as honestly as she could. 'And I want to plan our wedding. I want it to be how we both want it to be.'

Matthew shook his head. 'Jess, we could get married in this living room, dressed in our pyjamas, for all I care. I just want to marry you, and I want to marry you soon, to show the world how much we love each other. I don't care about the trappings – the dress, the flowers and all the rest of that bullshit – and I can't believe you do, too. I didn't think you were that shallow.'

Jess's mouth dropped open. Perma-tanned, super-waxer Matthew Parker thought *she* was being shallow? Really?

'So say you'll marry me next month, Jess Piper. I'm head over heels for you, and I don't think I could stand it if we had to tell everyone the wedding was off.'

Chapter Eleven

Jess stood outside St Bride's and tried to take deep breaths. Breathe, she told herself, just breathe . . . It's only a wedding, just a wedding. A wedding. To Matthew Parker. Breathe, she said to herself, over and over again. Just bloody breathe.

She caught sight of herself in the mirrored windows of the limo she and Andy had arrived in, and had to admit that even though she felt like she was going to throw up, she looked pretty spectacular. In between deep breaths she inspected the Vera Wang dress. It was a soft pink, strapless, A-line tulle gown with bias-cut taffeta bands, layers of silk that fluttered when she walked, and a creamy white corsage at her breast. On her feet were ivory satin stilettos, and woven into her honey-blond hair was a crystal tiara. Jess had to admit it was beautiful, but it was also completely over the top for a London wedding, and if Matthew hadn't insisted on it – saying she was his princess and should look the part – she would have ripped it off.

'You look incredible, Jessie,' Andy said gruffly, with tears in his eyes, as he waited outside the church with her, ready to give her away. 'Like a fairy.'

Momentarily distracted from her nerves, Jess laughed. 'I look like a *fairy*? Really?'

Andy grinned. 'It only seems like a few years ago that you'd have loved to be told that. All right, you look like a supermodel. A princess. Or the most beautiful, elegant bride in the world.'

Jess blushed. 'That's so sweet,' she said. 'And who said you weren't good with words?' She laughed again to stop herself from crying – she was so tense that anything could set her off.

'You're like a daughter to me,' Andy smiled. 'And I'm honoured that you and Matthew asked me to give you away. I know your father was disappointed not to do it – although I hate to bring that up today – but I'm so chuffed you both wanted to involve me in the wedding. I'm delighted you're marrying Matthew. He's a decent guy.'

Jess looked at herself in the limo windows again, then her face began to crumple.

'Hey,' Andy said softly. 'What's wrong?'

Jess shook her head. She couldn't speak for a moment, and if she said what was on her mind, how would Andy react?

'I'm just . . . I'm just wondering if I'm doing the right thing getting married when I feel like this.'

Andy stared at his goddaughter. 'What do you mean?'

'I mean . . . what if Matthew isn't right for me? What if we're just getting married because he proposed and we've got caught up in this whirlwind, but it's not the right thing to do?'

'Of *course* it's the right thing to do, silly,' Andy said gently. 'You and Matthew are really happy together, and this is the natural step to take. Admittedly you've not been together for years and years, but when it's right it's right – you *know* that.'

'But . . . what if I'm not sure?' Jess asked quietly. 'What if I'm having doubts?'

Andy stood very still for a moment. 'What sort of doubts?' he asked, seriously.

'I just don't know if I know who Matthew *is*,' Jess admitted. 'And I don't know if he knows who I really am, either. Since I moved in with Matthew I've found out loads more about him, and he's not the person I thought he was . . .' She trailed off. It was not the best moment to bring this up, but then, Andy knew Matthew almost as well as she did, and now was as good a time as any.

Andy looked at her with concern. 'Go on,' he said kindly.

'I mean, when we're at home he's much more self-centred and obsessed with his image than I thought he would be. He spends *hours* gazing in the mirror making sure he looks as hot as possible. It's like an obsession. And when he's at work he makes jokes about murders and shrugs off famines and terror attacks as if they don't matter. There's a whole other side to him that I wasn't really aware of, and now . . . I just don't know how I feel about him.'

Andy smiled, and Jess stared at him. She didn't see what there was to smile about.

'So he's like me, you mean?' he said.

Jess looked at her godfather blankly.

'You of all people should know how I put on an act for my column. I'm the outspoken, opinionated voice of the people,' Andy continued. 'But that's just me at work. You know I'm not like that at home, and you know that Matthew must put on a front in the newsroom, too. It's the only way to survive. If Matthew let everything bad that happened in the world affect him, he'd not want to get out of bed in the morning. He makes inappropriate jokes because it's how he *copes*. It's how we all cope in the newsroom.'

Jess thought about it for a moment. Andy was right. Matthew's behaviour was how he *had* to be, not who he was. His appearance was his armour. She'd only become aware of it since they'd moved in but it had always been there. She'd been so stupid. How could she not have realised that sooner?

'You're right,' Jess said in relief, casting aside all thoughts about Matthew that she didn't like, and concentrating on the Matthew she liked – the sweet, kind, affectionate man. 'You're absolutely right.'

Andy beamed at her. Crisis averted. 'I always am.'

Jess took Andy's arm, and they slowly walked along the polished black and white flagstones that gleamed under her satin shoes. Even though she hadn't wanted to marry at St Bride's, she had to admit it was beautiful. The white and gold arches led all the way to the stained glass at the far end of the church, and Pachelbel's *Canon in D*, played by the organist, echoed up to the high ceiling. Jess knew the ceremony wasn't really *her*, but the beauty of it made her catch her breath.

The nave was packed with journalists. Everywhere Jess looked she could see colleagues, but apart from Poppy and her parents, there were very few true friends. Faye was there – in a ridiculous, Isabella Blow-style hat that resembled a dead raven – and so were a few of the girls from the features desk that she was friendly with, but that was it. She barely knew everyone else, and for a second she realised this must be what it was like to have a celebrity wedding. There were lots of hangers-on, but not many people who were there because they really liked you.

'A newspaper wedding for a beautiful newspaper girl,' Andy murmured to Jess as they walked towards Matthew and her future. 'Matthew told me that you're going to give up on fashion designing to try and be a fashion writer, and I couldn't be more delighted to have you following in my footsteps.'

Jess felt her body turn to ice, but she kept walking. Matthew had said *what*?

'I really like Matthew, and Jessie, I couldn't be happier that you're going to be a journalist. It's like you're marrying into the *Daily World* family.'

Jess could feel nausea starting to overwhelm her. Just when she thought she'd worked Matthew out – and in the nick of time, too – this had been thrown at her. How could she marry someone who steadfastly refused to accept who she really was and what she wanted to achieve in life? Her legs began to wobble, and she stopped walking. She stared up at Andy.

'But it's not true,' she whispered, her eyes wide. 'You know I'm only at the *Daily World* because I love style and clothes and I want to get involved in the fashion industry.'

Andy took a quick glance at Matthew, who had turned to stare at them, and back at his goddaughter.

'Have you told Matthew this?' he asked urgently.

'Yes! Yes I have! But he just thinks I'm being stupid and that I need to grow up! I *know* I don't! When we were outside I told you that I don't know who the real Matthew is . . . and it's like Matthew *knows* who I am, but refuses to accept it. He just doesn't want to know the real me.

'Think about it,' Jess said, her voice getting higher. The orchestra was still playing, but the guests were looking at Jess and Andy uncertainly, and a low murmur started to sweep the congregation. They couldn't work out what was going on.

'We've been together for less than a year, he hates that I want to be a fashion designer, and doesn't even care if I organise my own wedding or not. That's not *me*, Andy, and you know it.'

Andy ran his hands through his hair, and they both took another look at Matthew. He was furious.

'So what do you want to do?' Andy pressed.

Jess stared at Matthew, who was glaring back at her, and she knew instantly that if Matthew really loved her he'd be looking at her with concern, not anger.

'I don't know,' Jess said, her voice wobbling. 'But I don't want to be here.'

She took a deep breath and stared at Matthew one more time. If he'd looked at her encouragingly, or had smiled, or had shown one inch of concern, she probably would have gone through with it. But as Matthew narrowed his eyes at her, Jess knew what she had to do. She turned on her heels, and, to the shock of all the *Daily World* journalists in the pews, Jess ran out of the church.

'Where are you going? Jess, where the fuck do you think you're going?' Matthew's voice followed her as she fell towards the limo. Jess whipped her head round to face him. His eyes glittered with fury.

'I don't know,' she sobbed as bravely as she could. 'But I can't do this. I can't go through with it.'

'The paper's organised all of this for us . . . it's the perfect wedding. How can you *not* go through with it?' Matthew yelled.

'Exactly!' Jess's voice cracked with frustration. 'It's the perfect wedding for *you*, not me. It's a newspaper wedding and I don't even *like* newspapers. I want to work in *fashion.*'

Matthew looked as though Jess had slapped him. 'You don't like newspapers?' he asked. 'Since when?'

'Since always!' Jess cried. 'You don't listen to me, and you never have. I can't marry you. I just can't.'

Poppy and Andy were standing outside the church now, and they were looking at Jess in concern. Crowds of people on Fleet Street had stopped to see what the commotion was, and Jess was acutely aware that they were the centre of attention. She didn't want that.

'Matthew, I'm sorry,' Jess whispered, as she held her fiancé's gaze. 'We're just not right for each other. And I can't go through with this.'

She tugged at the door handle of the limo, managed to open it, and jumped inside, narrowly avoiding catching her heel on the kerb. As she slid across the soft leather seats her dress became tangled, but she didn't care. She just had to get away.

'Please drive,' Jess begged the chauffeur, who paused uncertainly for a moment. Matthew was banging on the window angrily, telling Jess she had to reconsider, that he loved her. Tears of mascara were dripping down Jess's face. The chauffeur knew that if he drove Jess away from the church, the wedding was definitely off.

'Do it!' Jess yelled. 'Take me to the flat on Brick Lane!'

The chauffeur didn't need to be told twice. He jolted into action, and as the limo screeched away from Fleet Street, Jess gazed out of the window blankly. Today was supposed to be the best day of her life, but as St Bride's and Matthew became smaller and smaller behind her, the tight feeling in her chest loosened, and the pains in her stomach started to ease. Her breathing was still too fast, and she was still panicking, but for the first time in ages Jess became aware of a surge of strength that she'd forgotten she had. It felt good.

'I think he's following you, miss,' the chauffeur said after ten minutes.

Jess turned and stared out of the back window. Sure enough, a black cab was trailing them, and Matthew was inside it. Shit.

'Can you lose him?' she asked worriedly. 'Or take a short cut? I can't face seeing Matthew again, I just can't.'

The driver glanced at Jess in the rear-view mirror and thought for a moment. 'Perhaps you shouldn't return to your flat on Brick Lane. Is there anywhere else you can go?'

Jess picked agitatedly at the soft layers of silk on her dress.

Her first instinct was to go home – to climb into bed and to shut the world out – but she'd not thought it through properly. She *lived* with Matthew, for God's sake. If she ran straight back to his flat he'd be there within minutes. She wouldn't be able to escape him or this sorry mess.

'I want to go to my parents' house in Chelsea,' Jess said, thinking on her feet. She still had loads of her stuff there . . . clothes, make-up and – Jess suddenly felt a rush of excitement – her passport. Thank God there hadn't been time to plan a honeymoon, and that Matthew hadn't wanted to go away until the summer and all the MPs were away too. She could grab her stuff and just go. Getting away from Matthew and the *Daily World* and the wedding was what she desperately needed.

'Turn right here,' Jess demanded, even though it was a one-way street.

The driver looked at her. 'But miss—'

'Just do it!' she yelled, and the limo swerved suddenly down the road. There was no other traffic, so it wasn't dangerous, but Jess knew the cab behind them wouldn't dare do it. 'Now, left here . . . and after a couple of yards there's a turning. Go down here . . .'

Jess continued to give the chauffeur directions until they reached the safety of Chelsea. As they pulled into her parents' road she glanced at her iPhone – there were what seemed to be hundreds of missed calls, but she didn't care – and scrabbled about in her bag for her keys. Yes! She *knew* it had been a good idea not to remove the ones to her parents' front door.

Telling the chauffeur to wait, Jess ran up the stairs to her old bedroom and threw herself on her bed. She burst into tears. Was this really happening to her? Really? Had she *really* been engaged to the 'perfect guy' and had she *really* just run out of their wedding in front of her family and colleagues? The last few hours of her life were a blur – a nightmarish, horrendous blur.

Jess picked herself up and pulled off her wedding dress. There was no mistaking it was gorgeous. But it hadn't been *her*, and the moment it was off and was on the floor Jess began to feel better, and as soon as she yanked on some old, trusted jeans and a comfy jumper she started to feel human again. Like herself. Jess ignored the constant ringing of her iPhone and threw as many clothes as possible into an old suitcase. Knickers? Check. Make-up? Check. Jeans and skirts and tops? Check, check, check. She had everything she'd need, and well, if she'd forgotten anything, she could just buy it. There wasn't enough time to plan for where she was going and what she might need – she just had to take what she could, get back into the limo, and go. She only had a few moments before Matthew or Poppy or her family would track her down, and she couldn't allow herself to see any of them. Jess took one final look in the mirror, and was shocked to see that her wedding make-up was smeared all over her face, and that underneath it she looked pale and desperately tired.

It was time to stop and take stock.

She thought she knew the perfect place to do it.

It was only when Jess hopped in a yellow cab at JFK that she finally stopped crying.

Maybe it had something to do with the way the skyscrapers came into view as she sped along the highway to the city. Or perhaps it was the scent of the air, that intoxicating mix of dirt, hotdogs and money. Whatever it was, Jess always felt that hit of adrenalin as soon as she emerged from JFK and into the hustle and bustle. She may have been a London girl, but she adored Manhattan. And it was the first place she'd thought of going as soon as she'd arrived at Heathrow.

Jess had splashed out on a room at the Bryant Park Hotel, and even though it was the size of a decent walk-in wardrobe, she liked it. If you had to describe a cool New York hotel, this would be it. Jess flopped onto her bed, phoned for room service (trying not to think just how much the fried chicken, fries and beer were costing her), and rested her head against a red leather cushion. Despite feeling exhilarated at being in her favourite city by herself, Jess could still feel the pain of Matthew glaring at her in the church. Matthew. He'd have adored this hotel.

Jess shut her eyes, and forced herself to think about what he'd looked like the last time she'd seen him, and what he said to her. She had to forget about the Matthew she'd had fun with, and had been madly in lust with, and to remember what he was really like. Yes, he was self-obsessed and vain, but that wasn't really the problem. The issue was that he didn't know who she was, and he didn't really care. That, Jess told herself, was reason enough not to marry someone.

'Jess! Where are you? I've been phoning and phoning, and your mobile's been off! Are you okay? Are you in Leeds?' Poppy yelped down the phone, after answering it on the first ring.

'Um, I'm in New York, Pops,' Jess said quietly, as she felt hot, fat tears pressing against her eyes. Just thinking about everything that had happened in London felt like rubbing salt into her wounds, and even speaking to Poppy – whom she loved more than anyone else in the world – still hurt.

'You're in New York?' Poppy asked incredulously. 'New York? Why?'

'Because I had to get away, and this was the first place I thought of. You know how much I love it here . . . and I definitely won't run into Matthew or anyone from the *Daily World*.'

'But what about your job, and all your stuff at Matthew's flat? You can't just walk out on all of that. It's just, you know, like you've completely lost it or something.'

There was a long pause. 'I feel like I have,' Jess said sadly. 'And I don't care about my stupid job or stuff. All that matters to me right now is getting over Matthew and the last few months. As of right now I'm on holiday.'

'You're all by yourself, though!' Poppy exclaimed. 'You should be around your friends and family, around people who really love you and want to take care of you.'

'I know,' Jess said softly, 'but I need to be by myself right now.'

Poppy sighed. 'Babes, I'm always here for you if you need me, but you should let Matthew know where you are. He's worried sick. Are you going to speak to him?'

Jess shook her head. 'No way,' she said. 'At least, not yet. He'll just upset me, and to be honest I'm feeling too fragile to deal with it. I've just got here, and even though I'm jet-lagged and my heart is breaking, I'm going to eat some food and go out and get hammered. After all, I'm in the city that never sleeps.'

'Think Carrie Bradshaw,' Jess said to herself after she said goodbye to Poppy. She emptied her case on the bed and surveyed her clothes through heavy eyes. Eventually, she pulled on a canary-yellow vintage lace top with a deep V-neck – an old favourite – and her tightest, skinniest black jeans. She added some beloved red Louboutins, which she couldn't believe she'd left in Chelsea so she could live with Matthew, and then added a 1960s white leather bomber jacket. It was a kooky, Kate Moss look, and with her blonde hair in a flippy, flirty high ponytail, it worked. She looked cool as. As Jess started her make-up – Urban Decay turquoise liner just under her eyes, and purple liner on top – she realised she may have just run away from her wedding, but she looked like a happy, confident jet-setter. She applied clear lip-gloss and noticed she was smiling. If only getting her life sorted was as easy as making herself look good.

But as soon as Jess got past the bouncer (which really wasn't hard) and stepped into Bungalow 8 – famous from its role in *Sex and the City* – she felt her self-confidence drain away again. She felt alone and lonely, so she turned her mobile on to see if anyone had sent her a text saying they were worried about her. Nobody had, and she guessed Poppy must have told everyone that she was okay and needed some space. She took a deep breath and walked slowly to the bar, hoping she looked as if she'd done this a thousand times before.

'A cosmopolitan, please,' Jess murmured to the barman, taking in the palm trees, the black-and-white-striped banquettes, and the tiny space crammed with New York's beautiful people. As the cocktail slid across the bar and she paid for it – trying not to blanch at the price – Jess wondered what she should do next. She took a sip of her drink, and looked for somewhere to sit. There weren't any spare seats.

'Hey, babe,' a man mumbled in her ear, and Jess turned. He wore a black leather jacket, and expensive-looking sunglasses were perched on top of his slicked-back brown hair. He was just the sleazy type of man she normally avoided but he was some-one to talk to, and Jess was desperate not to look completely friendless.

'Hey!' she said as perkily as she could. 'I'm Jess.'

The man looked her up and down. 'I'm Ramon. I'm a writer.'

Jess tried to look impressed. 'Wow,' she exclaimed as sin-cerely as she possibly could. 'What do you write?'

Ramon took a gulp of his champagne and cleared his throat.

'Novels, mainly. I was a banker, but I got out just before things started to fuck up. You must have read about it in the papers.'

'Um, yeah, of course I did,' Jess bluffed. 'Good for you. What kind of novels do you write?'

Ramon eyed Jess thoughtfully. 'They're sci-fi meets *On the Road*. Trippy stuff.'

'Would I have heard of them?' Jess asked innocently.

Ramon shook his head. 'They've not been published yet. I'm writing my third.'

'Oh . . .' Jess was momentarily lost for words. 'When are they coming out?'

Ramon sighed. 'I'm self-publishing them. I *hate* "writers" who sell out. To me writing's not about money, it's about expression. It's an art form. You know?'

Jess bit her lip. 'Sure,' she said. 'That's really cool.'

'And what do you do? You're a Brit, right?'

'Yep, I'm from London. And I'm kind of a writer, too. For a newspaper.'

Ramon narrowed his eyes. 'Which paper? Would I have heard of it?'

'The *Daily World*? It's one of the biggest in Britain.'

'I *hate* the *Daily World*,' Ramon spat. 'All you do is peddle anti-liberal propaganda.'

Jess started to back away from him. 'I've just seen someone I know . . . If you'll excuse me . . .' She picked up her cosmopolitan, slid away as quietly as she could, and then came face to face with one of the most handsome men she'd ever seen in her life. He was tall and tanned, with a shock of black hair and dark eyes, and Jess loved his sharply cut suit. He was hot, and he knew it.

And then – to Jess's complete surprise – he shot her a slow, lingering, sexy smile.

Jess couldn't help but grin back.

'You escaped him, then?' the man asked, with a nod at Ramon. 'He's been terrorising most of the girls in here all night. I don't know why the management doesn't throw him out. I would.'

They both watched Ramon staring at a girl's rather impressive cleavage, and Jess smiled. 'He's good entertainment, though. I didn't think this bar would be so, you know, quiet.'

'It's all right, sure, but it doesn't really kick off properly until *much* later,' the man said. 'If you stick around you'll start to see some of the Manhattan scenesters. And that's when the party really gets started.'

Jess took a sip of her cocktail. It had been ages since she'd partied all night, and she wasn't sure she had the stamina for it.

'I'm not really a partying kind of girl,' she remarked. 'Been there, done that.'

The man laughed. 'But you're just a kid,' he exclaimed. 'You must be, what, twenty-three?'

'Something like that,' Jess said mysteriously, wanting to play it cool. She had a feeling that this guy was used to girls throwing themselves at him, and she didn't want to be just like everyone else. 'Younger than you, anyway.'

The man grinned. 'I'll pretend I didn't hear that. What are you doing in New York if you're not here to party?'

They slid into a black-and-white-striped booth, and a barman brought over a perfectly chilled bottle of Krug. The man didn't take his eyes from Jess's face to acknowledge it, and she guessed that he was used to great service.

'I just quit my job and am wondering what to do next,' Jess said, and she briefly explained how much she'd hated her job at the *Daily World*, and how she'd come to Manhattan to have some

141

fun. She didn't mention Matthew, or the fact she was a runaway bride. There really didn't seem to be much point.

'I'm kind of feeling that myself,' the man said with a sigh, and he knocked back his glass of Krug in one. 'Work's been pretty shitty for me, too.'

'What do you do?' Jess asked, and for a moment the man didn't speak. He simply stared at her.

'I have my own business,' he remarked finally. 'And I've had a few setbacks. Nothing I can't fix, but it's not been a great couple of months.'

Jess stood up to pour him more champagne, and as she reached over to the stainless-steel ice bucket she felt his gaze on her again. He couldn't take his eyes off her, and she felt empowered. It had been ages since she'd toyed with the idea of being with anyone but Matthew, and even though her ex-fiancé was gorgeous, this man was something else. He truly was one of the best-looking men she'd ever met.

'I'd love my own business,' Jess said. She flopped back onto the banquette and took another sip of champagne. Her cosmopolitan was long gone, and the bubbly was starting to go to her head. 'I've always wanted to be a designer, but to start a label you need money, and I just don't have enough to get going.'

'How much would you need?' The man looked interested.

Jess bit her lip. 'I haven't a clue . . . more than a couple of hundred pounds, which is all I have in my savings account. Working on a paper didn't give me enough to start a nest egg, and everyone knows that fashion jobs are incredibly badly paid. Fashion isn't the only reason girls who work on labels are so skinny – they can barely afford to eat.'

The man smiled, and looked as if he was about to say something when two girls sauntered over and snaked their scrawny bodies into the booth. They both wore tiny white flippy skirts, push-up bras – which raised their silicone breasts even higher up their chests – and little white shirts tied in a knot on their flat stomachs. They were tanned with bleached hair, and their faces were coated in heavy make-up. All the men in the bar were staring at them, and they knew it.

'Hey, baby,' one of them breathed. 'We've missed you recently.'

The man looked at the girls blankly, and Jess noticed that even when one of the girls placed her hand on his thigh, his face remained expressionless.

'Well, I'm back now. But girls, I'm busy making a new friend.'

The girls shot looks of scorn at Jess. 'Don't talk to her, talk to us – she's boring,' one whined.

Jess blinked. 'You know, I can go,' she started to say, but as she stood up the man put his hand gently on her wrist. Despite his light touch she could tell he was strong.

'Don't,' he said to Jess, and he turned to the girls. 'Ladies, I'm afraid that wasn't very nice.' His voice was playful, but his eyes had turned hard. 'Why don't you go and get yourselves some drinks at the bar on my account, and we can party another night?'

The girls pouted and did as he said, but as they crawled out of the booth, one spilled her cocktail over Jess. It was bright red and sticky, and immediately stained her yellow lace top. It was ruined.

'Oops.' The girl giggled and flicked her tatty blonde hair. 'It's a good thing he offered to get me another one, isn't it?' she purred, and the pair teetered off towards the bar.

'I really am going,' Jess said, hoping her voice wouldn't wobble. She was emotionally drained and tired, and wasn't in the mood for bitches. 'I'm not cut out for places – or people – like this, especially not today.'

The man stood up, and even though she was upset, Jess couldn't help but be struck again by just how gorgeous he was. 'Look,' he said, 'why don't we get out of here? My driver's outside and he can take us anywhere you want to go. I know a tiny little dive not far from here – it's almost like an English pub. Would you prefer that?'

Jess desperately wanted to go back to the hotel to climb between the sheets, but the lure of going to a proper pub with a handsome stranger was just too strong. Who needed to dwell on a smart London wedding you'd just run out of when you had hot New Yorkers offering to show you a good time?

'I'd love to,' she said in a small voice. 'That would be great.'

The man smiled. 'I'm Beau Silverman, by the way,' he said. When Jess didn't react to his name, his smile broadened.

'Jess Piper,' she replied, and as she took his hand in a friendly shake, she couldn't help but notice the electricity that passed between them.

Maybe things were starting to look up.

Chapter Twelve

'I need to be honest with you,' Beau said, as Jess finished her third pint and stretched her arms above her head. Despite the stain on her top, she was relaxed and happy. Beau was good company, and they'd bonded over a love of bad jokes and a fondness for 1990s American sitcoms. Now, though, the mood had changed, and Beau suddenly looked serious. He took a deep breath. 'I'm kind of involved with someone at the moment.'

Jess blinked, and forced a smile. Why were the good ones always married or in relationships? 'So you have a girlfriend?' she asked, making sure they were both talking about the same thing.

Beau sighed, and fiddled with his fingers awkwardly. 'No . . . a wife,' he admitted reluctantly, and when Jess started to gather up her white leather jacket and bag, he rushed to continue. 'But our marriage is over. Hell, it was over before it had even begun.'

Jess stared at Beau for a second. 'Right,' she remarked sarcastically. 'She's your best friend but you don't fancy each other any more. You love her like a friend, or a sister. She doesn't understand you, you have "needs", you don't want to hurt her . . . God, men are pathetic.'

Beau drained his glass of beer — which he normally never drank, but which Jess had insisted upon — and shook his head.

'No. I had to marry her to save her career,' he said gloomily.

'And, in a way, to save mine.' Beau bit his lip and took a long hard look at Jess. For the first time that night Jess noticed he looked weary, vulnerable.

'Do you want to talk about it?' she asked, hating herself for being soft as she put her bag back onto the floor. Had Beau actually led her on? He'd not come on to her all night, and he hadn't implied he'd fancied her, had he? The alcohol made it hard to remember, especially since she knew she fancied him. A lot.

Beau stared into Jess's blue eyes. 'Can I trust you?' he said, finally. 'You're not going to extract my life story from me and then file it off to that trashy newspaper back in England?'

Jess smiled. 'If there's one thing you can be certain of,' she said softly, 'it's that I am never going to write for another newspaper again. You have my word.'

Beau signalled to the waitress for another round of drinks, and then, without pausing for breath, he began to tell Jess about how he had met Madison.

'So she blackmailed you?' Jess gasped. She could barely believe what she was hearing. How had Beau Silverman managed to get himself into such a mess?

Beau nodded, and stared down at the table, unable to look Jess in the eye. 'I know I shouldn't have gone to a strip club, but I was drunk and lonely . . . And I just wanted to be around people. Madison was . . . well, she was amazing. She looked unlike any other girl you've ever met. I mean, you've seen pictures of her in magazines – she's stunning. And she's a great actress, too. She told me that she thought there was something special between us, and I believed her. I really did.'

Jess reached across the table to hold Beau's hand – how had

they managed to get so close so quickly? – but Beau put his hands in his lap and continued to look ashamed.

'It wasn't a one-off,' he said, still staring at the table. 'I began to believe that Madison really felt something for me, so I kept going back to that awful strip club to see her. When other men paid her for dances I got jealous, so I spent thousands just so she would dance for me and me alone. I wanted to be her boyfriend, but she said even though she'd love to date me it was against the rules. I didn't know what to do. I was obsessed.'

Beau drained his glass of beer again, and then excused himself to go to the restroom. While he was away Jess felt almost embarrassed by her reaction when he'd told her he had a wife. She was always too quick to judge, too impulsive in her choices.

'It's a terrible story,' Jess began when Beau came back. His dark eyes were glistening, and Jess wondered if he'd excused himself so he could cry in the toilets. Surely a man as burly and self-assured as Beau didn't cry, did he?

'It got to the point where she was my addiction,' Beau continued. 'Some men handle the stress of corporate jobs by drinking too much, or taking drugs, but Madison was what I craved. I started to go to the club every night to see her, and ended up staying there until dawn to make sure she was mine, and mine alone. I spent a fortune in there, hundreds of thousands of dollars – but Madison refused to see how serious I was about her, that I was in love with her and would have paid even more to get her out of there.'

'So what happened?' Jess asked gently.

'Madison found out who I was,' Beau said simply, and for the first time since he'd started telling her his story he looked at Jess directly. 'She found out that I'm Beau Silverman, that I own *Teen Star USA* and Slate Street Records, and that I could make her a star. Madison told me that if I didn't make her famous she'd tell the press I was a sex addict who never stopped going to strip clubs and had spent thousands on her.'

Jess's mouth fell open in shock as she finally realised who she was talking to. Beau and Madison. He was talking about Madison *Miller*, she thought, and he was the manager who'd married her. Jess could have kicked herself for being so stupid. Faye had been right – she really should have read the *Daily World* properly.

'And the stupid thing was it was all true,' Beau continued, seemingly oblivious to Jess's light bulb moment. 'I'd used my credit cards in the club so she had the proof, and, let's face it, my reputation is built on helping America find their next wholesome, squeaky-clean *Teen Star*. I'd have been ruined.'

Beau buried his head in his hands, and Jess moved closer and put her arms around him. He may have been one of the most masculine – and famous – men she'd ever met, but at this moment he was helpless and exposed. And Jess wanted to be there for him.

'I didn't know what to do, so I agreed to put Madison on *Teen Star USA*. I mean, I *own* that programme, and I can do whatever I want. But Madison's demands got worse – she wanted the best outfits, didn't want to live with the other contestants, and told me there'd be hell to pay if she didn't win. Despite her diva behaviour I still loved her, and I really thought we had a chance, so when she won . . . Well. When she won the show, I thought that would be the start of our relationship. She'd be the star, I'd be the manager, and we could live happily ever after. I wanted to tell the press about our relationship straight away, but Madison was insistent that we kept it a secret. She said she didn't want people thinking I'd fixed the show for her, and she had a point. The other directors of the company would have frowned upon it, so we kept it quiet.'

Jess couldn't take her eyes off Beau. It was an incredible story, made even more overwhelming by the fact that the man in front of her was *the* Beau Silverman and he was talking about *the* Madison Miller. It had only been a month ago that Jess had read the piece about their wedding in the paper, and she struggled not to appear starstruck.

'Madison's demands got worse,' Beau continued. His voice had lowered to a dull monotone. 'If we went anywhere she insisted on having the paparazzi follow us. She wouldn't let me kiss her, or even hold her hand in public, and she spoke to me like I was a piece of shit. I know it sounds mad, but I was still so in love with her, and I thought that if I gave her everything she wanted she'd love me, too.'

Tears began welling up in Beau's eyes, and Jess leant towards him and wiped them from his cheek. It was an incredibly intimate thing to do, and had she been sober, Jess probably wouldn't have done it. Beau locked eyes with her for a second, and then kissed her on the cheek.

'You're a kind girl, Jess,' he said, taking a few deep breaths to steady himself. He'd spoken for so long that Jess hadn't been aware of the time, but as she caught sight of Beau's expensive brushed-steel watch, her eyes widened. It was past 4 a.m. Beau noticed her reaction.

'I've bored you enough for one night,' he said quietly.

'It's fine, really – I'm not even tired,' Jess exclaimed, forgetting her jet-lag for the moment. 'So how did you persuade Madison marry you? I saw the photos – it was a beautiful wedding.'

Beau grimaced. 'We got caught out. We were on Necker Island – you know, the one Richard Branson owns – but we were staying in one of the beach houses rather than in the main house. We went for a walk by the ocean, and as punishment for not booking the Great House, Madison whipped off her clothes and began tormenting me. She never really liked me, or even fancied me, but she liked to maintain the sexual power she had over me – and it always worked. I was trying to be strong, and not give in to her, when suddenly the paparazzi appeared and started taking photos of us. Our relationship was suddenly in the press, and the American media was cruel. Madison was accused of being a whore, me of fixing *Teen Star USA*, the whole works. The only way I could see to get out of the situation and salvage our reputations was to marry and act like we were in love. So we did. And now I'm married to a heartless, cold bitch of a girl who only got with me because of what I could do for her.'

Jess didn't know what to say. 'Are you sure she doesn't love you?' she asked tentatively. 'Maybe she does but just doesn't know how to show it. Who knows what she went through when she was a kid if she ended up as a stripper.'

'She hates me,' Beau said bluntly. 'She despises me. She saw me as someone who could make her famous, and now she feels she's stuck with me. I thought getting married would maybe soften her, really prove to her that I love her, but it didn't quite work like that.'

'What do you mean?' Jess asked. She didn't know how Beau could be so matter-of-fact about someone who had clearly hurt him so much. Madison sounded like a nightmare.

'She's going off the rails,' Beau said quietly. There was nobody else in the bar, but he was still being incredibly careful about not being overheard. 'She was always into drink and drugs – it often happens when you work in the sex industry – but she's an addict now. She snorts hundreds of dollars worth of coke a day, she won't listen to me, or anyone else at Slate Street, and I don't know what to do about it. She's on the verge of killing herself with drugs, and if she doesn't sort herself out my whole company's going to go under. We've invested millions of dollars in her, and it's all about to turn to shit.'

Beau's hands were shaking, and Jess grabbed hold of them to try to calm him down. He was in a state.

'I don't know what to do, Jess, I really don't.'

Jess squeezed Beau's hands as gently as she could, and together they watched the sun rise over the grimy streets of Manhattan. Jess was certain that as bad as both their situations were, things could only get better now that they were friends.

Jess woke the next morning with one of the worst hangovers of her life. Her head was pounding, her mouth was dry and tasted disgusting, and her stomach hurt. She cast her mind back to the night before, and tried to tally up what she'd drunk. She'd had a cosmopolitan and some champagne at Bungalow 8, and then Beau had taken her to that pub . . . Jess sat bolt upright. Beau. Beau *Silverman*. Her eyes widened and despite feeling as if she was about to die, she burst out laughing before clasping a hand to her mouth. She'd spent the evening with Beau Silverman! Who was married to Madison Miller! Jess fell back onto her pillow and shut her eyes. She must still be dreaming. She must be.

But she wasn't.

Jess slid her hand across the black lacquered bedside table and reached for her iPhone. Sure enough, the last number she'd saved was Beau's. It was real. She really had spent the evening with Beau Silverman, and, if she remembered correctly, he'd spilled the beans on his sham of a marriage to Madison Miller. Shit, Jess thought. This stuff was dynamite. But poor Beau, Jess reflected, as she rubbed her temples and rummaged in her bag for some painkillers. Madison Miller had fucked him over. She really felt for him. They were *so* similar, she thought, as her mobile rang. Jess's heart skipped a beat – would it be Beau? Already? – but to her disappointment, it wasn't. It was Matthew.

'I take it you're not going to marry me now,' Matthew said bluntly, when, after some hesitation, Jess answered the phone. 'What a crock of shit our relationship turned out to be. Thanks for making a fool of me in front of *all* our colleagues.'

'Why did you look at me like that?' Jess asked as evenly as she could. She wasn't good at keeping her emotions in check – especially with guys – but she knew it was important to stay calm for this phone call. She had to.

'Like what?' Matthew asked tetchily.

'I was speaking to Andy about something important as I was walking down the aisle and you gave me a filthy look,' Jess said quietly.

Matthew laughed as if Jess was stupid. 'You were *late*! The editor would have been furious. I didn't appreciate you dawdling when you should have been walking towards me as fast as you could!'

Jess felt frustration rising up in her. Why didn't he understand? What was wrong with him?

'So what?' she nearly yelled. 'It wasn't the Editor's wedding, it was *ours*.'

Matthew sighed. 'I know it was, sweetheart,' he said, his voice softening. 'You're right. But I still don't understand why you walked out. It can't have been because I may or may not have given you a dirty look in church. I know you wouldn't have thrown all this away over something small like that.'

Jess buried her head in her free hand. He really didn't know her at all.

'Do you love me, Matthew?' she asked. 'Really?'

Matthew let out a bitter little laugh. 'Of course I do,' he said hoarsely. 'I wouldn't be this upset if I didn't.'

'So why don't you want me to be a fashion designer? Why is it so important for you that I start being a writer? Why can't you let me be myself?'

'Jess, we've had this conversation before,' Matthew explained patiently. 'You're a newspaper girl, and newspaper girls should be writing for the paper. Even Andy thinks so.'

'Yeah, I heard you told my godfather that I was quitting designing. How *could* you?'

'It's the natural step for you. I assumed that when we were married you'd grow up and see sense. Was I wrong?'

Jess raged internally. 'Yes, you were wrong! And it's not the natural step for me. I hate newspapers, especially the *Daily World*, and I don't want to work on one ever again!'

'Jesus, chill the fuck out,' Matthew muttered.

'You never loved me for who I was, did you?' Jess retorted. 'You loved the idea of me – a sweet little fashion assistant who happens to be the goddaughter of a columnist on the paper. But you don't even *know* me. And I don't think I know you.'

There was silence at the other end of the phone.

'Maybe you're right,' Matthew said eventually. 'I thought you liked newspapers, and that you liked and accepted me for who I am. I know that you don't like my sense of humour, or who I can be sometimes, but Jess, that's what it's like when you work on a paper. It's high pressure, and everyone needs to let off steam. I thought you accepted that.'

'I accept it, and I could even live with it,' Jess said in a small, sad voice. 'But I could never be with someone who wants – *needs* – me to be someone I'm not.'

'So that's it?' Matthew asked sadly. 'It's over?'

Jess took a deep breath. 'Can you accept that I want to make it as a designer, and that I don't want to work on a newspaper ever again?' Tears rolled down her cheeks. As she waited for Matthew to answer she realised she was holding her breath. She so desperately wanted him to say yes, and for him to tell her he'd support her dreams. If he did, well – she'd be on the first flight back to England to rush into his arms.

'It's a kid's dream, babes,' Matthew sighed impatiently, 'and if you can't see that, and you don't have the same sort of ambition as me to make it on a newspaper, then it really is over.'

Jess didn't think she could hurt any more, but as he said those words she felt as though she was being stabbed through the heart.

'I hope you find what you're looking for in your life,' Matthew continued, his voice breaking. 'And good luck with your fashion designing. I hope you meet someone who wants to help you with that.'

'I'm so sorry I splurged all my emotions on you last night,' Beau said over lunch at the tiny diner he'd taken her to in the Meat-packing District. When he'd phoned and suggested lunch, Jess had briefly flirted with the idea that he'd take her somewhere wildly cool and expensive, but the reality was he didn't want to be seen in public with a girl who wasn't his wife. And Jess could understand that.

'It's not a problem,' she said gently. She guessed everyone saw him as an unbreakable, hard-nosed, successful businessman who couldn't get hurt. The reality – as she'd found out – was completely different. 'You just let me tell you all about my messed-up relationship with Matthew, didn't you?'

Beau nodded, and once again Jess was struck by just how good-looking he was. In the dirty light of the diner his features made her almost breathless.

'So we're even. And you know, if I could help you, I would.'

'I just want to help Madison,' Beau said miserably. 'She needs to get into rehab, and fast, but she refuses. She's got to do her tour, got to do the press . . . If she doesn't, Slate Street is screwed and my neck's on the line with the board members. We may even have to cancel next year's *Teen Star USA*. Who would trust us after this sorry mess?'

'You can't make a drug addict better unless they're ready to help themselves,' Jess remarked quietly, thinking about a friend who'd got into the party scene a little too much at university. She was fine now, but it had taken her longer to see she had a problem than it had for her friends. And her recovery had been long and difficult.

'I suppose not,' Beau said. He sounded depressed.

Jess decided to change the subject. 'How did you get into the music industry?'

Beau cracked a grin over his cup of coffee. 'My dad was in a band called the Jailbaits in the sixties, and when he finished up doing his peace and love shit he started a record label. I kind of followed him into it as an A&R man, and I discovered I had a talent for sniffing out future stars. It led to me setting up Slate Street, and from there it was a matter of time before launching *Teen Star USA* with a guy called Donovan York, who had experience in creating that type of show. We make a *lot* of money. Or we did before this mess . . .'

Jess felt her heart ache for him. It wasn't fair that Madison was screwing up the business that Beau had worked so hard for, and had built from scratch.

'If you *could* get Madison into rehab, would it cause Slate Street problems?' Jess asked. Whatever they talked about, the conversation would always turn back to Madison, and Jess had to resign herself to that.

Beau nodded slowly. 'The part of me that still loves her — because I do, as a friend — desperately wants to help her, but the other side of me, the one that heads up Slate Street, knows we can't afford to cancel this tour. We just can't. We'll go under. If I could get her to go *now* she might be clean in time . . . but there's no way she'll agree to it.'

'It's a shame you can't get a singing waxwork to go on tour instead,' Jess said, hoping that the image of a robotic Madison would make Beau smile. 'Or a lip-synching puppet.'

Beau stared at Jess for such a long time that she began to feel uncomfortable.

'What?' she asked finally. 'What did I say?'

'You know, I wasn't going to say this in case it freaked you out, but one of the reasons I feel so comfortable with you is because you look uncannily like Madison,' Beau murmured. He looked Jess straight in the eye. 'But a better version. It's like she's bad Madison and you're good Madison.'

Jess didn't know what to say.

'Does that bother you?' Beau asked. 'Please say it doesn't – I mean it as a compliment.'

'But I'm blonde. And Madison's brunette. And she's really sexy. She's a babe.'

Beau reached for Jess's hand then. 'And so are you,' he said gently. 'You're more than a babe.'

Jess felt her heart beat faster. What was happening. Was Beau saying he fancied her? How could he? He was a big shot and she was a nobody, just a wannabe fashion designer who'd come to New York on a whim.

'You're kind, you're funny, you're totally hot . . . and you're clever, too. I never would have thought about getting a replacement for Madison in a million years. But it could work. It might work.'

Jess bit her lip. 'I was joking—' she began.

'In fact,' Beau interrupted, 'the more I think about it, the more brilliant it sounds. Would you really do that for me? Really?'

For the first time since she'd met him, Beau looked enthusiastic, and as he gripped her hand tighter, she wondered just what she'd got herself into. Removing her hand from his – or saying no – seemed impossible.

'It would be the most amazing, selfless thing for anybody to do,' Beau went on, seemingly oblivious to Jess's growing discomfort. 'Madison would be able to go to rehab to sort herself out, and when she's clean she can make the tour and her millions of fans wouldn't be disappointed. Everyone would be happy. I can't think of a single reason why we shouldn't do it – you could do all the pre-tour interviews and promotion. It would be *perfect*.'

'It would be a lie,' Jess said quietly. 'We'd be fooling thousands of people across the world, and it wouldn't be fair. I don't know if I could bring myself to do that.'

Beau let go of Jess's hand, and sighed. 'You're right,' he said. His shoulders slumped, and he looked depressed again. 'I suppose we're going to have to let down all of Madison's fans and cancel the tour so we can force her into rehab. And Slate Street will definitely go under,' he continued. 'But it was a nice dream while it lasted. It was genius.'

Tears began to slide from his dull black eyes, and Jess felt her heart break.

'Even though it's morally wrong,' she began, slowly, 'if nobody found out, would it really cause anyone harm?'

Beau shook his head slightly. 'I don't know,' he admitted. 'I can only think it would do good, not bad.'

Jess put her head in her hands and thought, hard. Could she do this, really? Could she step into Madison Miller's shoes? Do press interviews? It was unthinkable. It was unrealistic. It was impossible – wasn't it? They'd never get away with it, not in a million years. They'd get found out . . . wouldn't they?

'I'd give you a million dollars if you would do a month of promotion as Madison Miller,' Beau said quietly.

Jess looked up in shock.

'You could start your fashion label with that, couldn't you?' he added.

They spent the rest of the afternoon sitting in the diner staring at each other. Jess knew she'd only just met him, and that he was asking her to deceive thousands of Madison Miller fans, but the more he spoke about how much Madison needed treatment, and how he feared she'd overdose any day soon, the more Jess realised she had to do this.

If she didn't, she feared it would be too late for Madison Miller to get help.

Chapter Thirteen

'You're going to do what?' Poppy shrieked down the phone. 'You're joking, right?'

Jess paused. She knew what she'd just told Poppy was unbelievable, but it was so exciting. It was amazing!

'Babes, honestly, it's the truth. Beau Silverman wants me – *me*! – to pretend to be Madison Miller for a whole month! I get to do the *Spotlight* pre-tour promotion in place of her – which is interviews with magazines and TV and all sorts. I get to be a famous popstar!'

'Jess, seriously, chill the fuck out. Will you listen to yourself? This is nuts . . . in fact, this is more than nuts.' Poppy was sounding worried now. 'How have you managed to get yourself into such a crazy situation? What if a journalist asks you to sing? You're talking about it like it's a perfectly normal thing to do.'

'That's because I *am* going to do it,' Jess remarked as calmly as her exhilaration would let her. 'He's offering me a million dollars for a month's work, and I can't afford not to. Besides, it will help both Beau and Madison.'

'I can't believe you're on first name terms with Beau Silverman and Madison Miller,' Poppy continued in a stunned voice. 'What are they like? Really?'

Jess grinned and got more comfortable on her hotel bed. She wasn't too keen on Poppy's anxious reaction to her news –

although she could understand it – but talking about Beau was much more fun.

'He's gorgeous,' she said. 'He has the blackest hair I've ever seen, these shiny dark eyes, and he's totally buff, Pops. He's the fittest man I've ever seen.'

'And he's married to Madison, right?' Poppy asked bluntly, although she knew the answer as well as Jess did.

'Yeah, but he doesn't love her,' Jess replied, ignoring Poppy's tone. 'Which is just as well, because I think he might fancy me a little bit. Maybe.'

'Jess, if you're really going to do this, there's no way you can get involved with Beau. No *way*.'

Jess sighed. 'I know. But he's just so hot and clever and funny . . . and vulnerable. Most people just think of him as this amazing businessman – which he is, of course – but he's so much more than that—'

'And what's Madison like?' Poppy interrupted loudly.

'Oh, I've not met her yet. Beau doesn't think it's a good idea for us to meet until we do our handover – which will be in about a month or so.'

Poppy was silent for a moment. 'You're really serious about this, aren't you?'

Jess smiled. 'The day after Beau asked me to do it, I wandered around Central Park for hours, just trying to get my head around it. Pretending to be someone else is hardcore enough, but pretending to be one of the most famous girls on the planet is insane. I was ready to meet Beau and tell him I'd changed my mind, but then I thought about Madison and the bad life she's had, and how if I don't do this she might overdose or something—'

'Madison Miller does drugs?' Poppy sounded shocked.

Jess bit her lip. She'd promised Beau that she wouldn't tell anyone about this, and not only had she told Poppy what she intended to do, she'd also let it slip that Madison was fucked up. It was a good thing that Beau didn't know how indiscreet she could be sometimes, she thought.

'Yes, but you can't tell anyone,' she stressed. 'Like you can't tell anyone about my new job.'

'My lips are sealed. But you can't do this just because you're worried Madison might snort one line too many – can you?'

'It's not just that,' Jess said reluctantly. 'I really like the idea of the money, too. And, let's face it, what else am I going to do?'

'Come. Back. Home,' Poppy pleaded. 'I don't know how many times I've asked you to. Why won't you?'

'Because there's something pretty sad about moving back to my parents' house again. I'm the only one of us from college who hasn't got a job or a flat or a relationship, and I'm sick of feeling like a failure. I can use this month to really turn my life around, and also, Pops, I'm going to experience what it's like to be the most famous person on the planet. It sounds *amazing*.'

'It also sounds scary,' Poppy muttered. 'Look, I don't mean to put a downer on this, I really don't, but you're going to be completely isolated and in a situation that nobody else has ever been in before – frankly, it's going to be a headfuck, and you're not going to have any support over there. Are you ready for it?'

Jess thought about it. 'I don't know,' she said honestly. 'But I do know that with Beau's help I'll be as ready as I can ever be.'

'I've never dyed my hair before,' Jess remarked, as Rhys Symons – one of the most discreet hairdressers in Manhattan (and someone who'd worked with Beau for years) – examined strands of Jess's honey-hued hair.

'It's gorgeous, and in great condition,' Rhys said. 'We're going to be making it a rich chestnut colour – the exact same as

Madison's. You're cool with that, right?' Both he and Jess knew she didn't have a choice in the matter, but Jess thought it was kind that he acted as if she could say no if she wanted to.

As Rhys set to work, Jess flicked through *People*, *Cerise*, *US Weekly* and *Glamour*, and as she started to turn the pages of the magazines her eyes widened. She couldn't get over just how many photos of Madison adorned the pages. She was everywhere Jess looked, and the more Jess examined photos of her – at premieres, at her wedding, on the set of *Teen Star USA*, with Beau at gallery openings, restaurants, or grabbing a coffee at Starbucks – she couldn't see how she could ever look as poised, as beautiful, or as glamorous as Madison Miller. Jess was just a normal girl from London – she'd never be able to pull off Madison's sassy, paparazzi-perfect poise. No way.

But a couple of hours later Jess couldn't help but wonder if she'd been too hasty. With her newly dyed hair she looked *exactly* like Madison Miller – and it unnerved the shit out of her.

'I think you're gonna pull this off,' Rhys commented, as Jess continued to stare at herself in the salon's mirror. For the first time she felt as if she really could step into Madison's shoes – and the thought of it excited and terrified her all at once. She wished Poppy was with her, or that she had a friend in Manhattan to talk to. Beau had told her to call him on his cell any time, but Jess hated interrupting him. She knew how busy and stressed he was over the whole Madison situation, and compared to the problems he had to deal with, her nerves paled into insignificance. No, she had to be brave and deal with this on her own. After all, Beau had already been more than generous with her – and not just with his time.

As soon as Jess had formally agreed to step into Madison Miller's shoes for the duration of the *Spotlight* promotional period, Beau had produced a contract printed on thick, expensive-looking paper. He'd suggested several discreet lawyers Jess could use, and once the contract was signed and deposited in the Slate Street safe, Jess had a quarter of a million dollars in her London bank account, and a heady, intoxicating feeling that life was never going to be the same again.

It wasn't. She had a brand-new apartment in Beau's exclusive block of flats, wardrobes full of designer clothes, and if she ever wanted anything, all she had to do was ask.

'The deal is you can't leave the apartment without my say-so,' Beau said nonchalantly as they ate takeout from Sammy's Noodle Shop one evening.

Jess paused, her chopsticks hovering between the white noodle carton and her mouth. 'What? Not even to go to the shops?'

Beau shook his head and grinned. 'You're not ready yet,' he said, through a mouthful of crispy pork. 'Everyone will think you're Madison, but as soon as you speak, people will know something's up. You still sound *very* British.'

Jess bit her lip awkwardly, hoping Beau wasn't disappointed with her. She'd been working hard. 'I know,' she said quietly, struggling not to sound defensive. 'I'm having another elocution lesson tomorrow, and the tutor is pleased with me so far.'

Beau leant back in his chair. He wore a long-sleeved red T-shirt, and he looked relaxed and happy. 'It's cool,' he said, putting his chopsticks down on the smoked-glass table and assessing her. 'I know you've only just started, and besides, I think your accent's cute. It will be a sad day when you lose it.'

Despite herself, Jess felt a tiny wave of pleasure run through her body. Beau Silverman thought she sounded cute! Coming from the hottest man she'd ever met, that was definitely a compliment. Definitely.

'So how long am I house-bound?' Jess asked. The thought of

not being able to go outside by herself was unnerving, but she had to admit that the flat had everything she needed. The floors were a beautiful dark wood – mahogany? Oak? She wasn't sure – and all the furniture looked as if it came from a Conran-type shop. The silver kitchen gleamed with every high-tech appliance known to man, and twice a day a Vietnamese housekeeper came to clean and even cook if Jess didn't fancy ordering in. Apart from the hard work – the twice-daily trips to the gym to get a popstar's body, the elocution lessons and even an acting class every other day – life was good. Every time she stepped out of the apartment she was ushered into a glossy limo with blacked-out windows, and without fail Jess was struck by how luxurious, glamorous and out of this world her life now was. It was like a film.

'Two more weeks. Then, a few days before the promo stuff kicks off, we're heading out to LA so you can meet Madison.'

The tiny knot of nerves that had taken up residence in Jess's stomach since she'd agreed to stand in for the popstar instantly increased, and, as if on cue, the reality of what she was about to do hit her. She'd been so busy getting into shape that she'd almost forgotten why she was doing it. She was going to be Madison Miller. And she was touring America to promote her tour.

'Does Madison know about me yet?' Jess asked nervously. She couldn't imagine what it would feel like to know someone was learning how to be you. It was like identity fraud, only way more personal and on a much bigger scale.

Beau shook his head. 'I tried to tell her the other night, but she was so out of it I decided not to bother. She's in our LA mansion with a private nurse, who's trying to get her off the drink and drugs. It's not going too well. Even though she knows she's not doing the pre-tour promotion, she might not react too well to you.'

'Aren't you going to tell her that I'm standing in before I meet her?'

Beau grinned. 'If I'm honest with you, I kind of had visions of her opening the front door and freaking out when she saw you standing there looking *just* like her.'

Jess looked less than impressed.

'Obviously I *wouldn't* do that,' he added, 'because that's just cruel, but you can't blame a man for being a little angry. She's put me through hell.'

Beau lowered his head, and Jess immediately felt another wave of sympathy run through her. She knew deep down what they were doing was wrong – millions of fans were going to be tricked by them – but they were doing it for the right reasons. It was all to get Madison Miller back on track, even if she had been a complete cow to Beau.

'Hey, it will be okay, you know,' Jess said softly, and she reached out and touched Beau. Next to his large, masculine hands, hers looked tiny, and when he gripped her hand tightly, she realised just how powerful he was.

'Will it?' Beau asked, and Jess thought he sounded like a little boy. She loved it. One of America's most well-known business-men wasn't afraid to show her his vulnerable side. 'It all seems like such a mess, and I think it might just get a bit messier . . .'

Jess felt her breath catch. Ever since they'd met there had been something between them – a tiny, uncomfortable spark of chemistry – and tonight, over the dinner table, that spark had begun to ignite.

'I don't know what I'd do without you,' Beau said gruffly, gazing deeply into Jess's blue eyes. 'You're not only saving Madison's life, but my business, too.'

'I'm only doing it for the money,' Jess joked. She needed to lighten the mood, and fast, or she'd be in deep trouble.

'I'm serious,' Beau said. 'I think you're incredible.'

Jess shifted in her chair, and focused on their half-eaten takeout. Suddenly she didn't have an appetite any more.

'I think you are, too,' she replied softly, 'but Beau . . .'

'But what?' Beau challenged. He held her gaze, and Jess struggled to look him in the eye.

'This is wrong. This is so wrong.' Jess's voice was barely a whisper, but her face was flushed, and her hands were damp with sweat. 'You're married.'

'Only legally, as you know,' Beau said simply.

'And you're technically my employer.' Jess was looking for something – anything – to stop her from teetering over the edge.

'We both know that's just an excuse.'

Beau and Jess stared at each other for what seemed like an eternity, and then, without another word, Beau threw the Chinese cartons on the floor and dragged Jess onto the glass dining table. As his mouth covered hers, Jess gave in to the temptation that she'd been trying so hard to avoid, and as he carried her into the bedroom, she forgot about her new rule of never mixing business and pleasure again. It may have been wrong, and he may have been married, but it felt so, so right.

'So officially, Madison grew up in Walkertown, Ohio, with a mum and a dad who loved her very much,' Jess said over a glass of velvety red wine as she sat curled up in the living room. She was beginning to love her job – especially since she'd given in to her feelings for Beau. In the nights they'd spent together he'd made her happier than anyone she'd ever known. Matthew and the *Daily World* and London seemed very far away.

Beau – at the other end of the black sofa – nodded, and took a gulp from his wine glass. 'She went to a decent high school, was a cheerleader, and had a boyfriend on the football team. I've forgotten what his name's meant to be. It will be in the files,' he said, nodding at the huge ring-binder on the coffee table. In the flickering candlelight his black hair looked even darker than normal, and he was breathtakingly sexy. Jess knew she had to concentrate tonight – she had to learn all she could about Madison Miller – but it was so tempting to give in to her feelings and kiss Beau. Again. And again.

Jess watched him intently. He was amazing at everything. He was well read, had great taste, and he made her reach dizzying highs in bed that she hadn't known existed. She was hooked.

'And what's the real story?' she asked, desperately hoping that the truth about Madison's past would distract her from her desire. How could *anyone* be around Beau and not want him as much as she did?

'She grew up in Walkertown, Ohio, and was the school slut,' Beau said bluntly. Jess gasped. Even though she knew Madison had been a stripper, she never failed to be shocked that America's number one pop princess wasn't as squeaky clean as everyone thought. 'We've paid thousands of dollars to boys from her high school who wanted to talk . . . we even have a sex tape in the Slate Street safe that would ruin her – and us – if it got out. Mom was an alcoholic, Pop was hardly there, and Madison stole, scammed and screwed her way through high school. She didn't even graduate before she hitched to New York to become a stripper.'

'That's awful,' Jess murmured. She couldn't imagine growing up without loving parents, or enough money to get by.

'She didn't have to turn bad,' Beau commented neutrally, but his eyes flashed with anger. Jess knew he was still hurting from

167

how Madison had treated him. 'But we're getting her sorted out now. And that's the main thing.'

'So what does she like? What does she hate? I need to know everything if I'm going to pull this off.'

Beau considered the question. 'She loves fried chicken and fries. She adores chocolate milkshake. She's a great dancer, a better liar, and she's filthy in bed,' he said flippantly, and even though Jess knew he hadn't meant to be cruel, the words cut through her like a knife.

Was Beau only sleeping with her because she looked like Madison? And did she measure up in bed? She doubted it. How could anyone match a professional like Madison who knew all the moves?

Beau caught the stricken expression on Jess's face. 'I'm sorry,' he said quietly. 'That was stupid of me.'

A long silence hung between them, and Jess couldn't look Beau in the eye. 'Am I as good as her?' she whispered, devastated that tears had filled her eyes. The thought of Beau being with anyone but her was painful enough, but the image of Beau and Madison in bed was too much for her. She'd fallen hard – and quickly – for Beau, and she was jealous. Intensely jealous.

Beau put his wine glass down and moved close to her. He cupped her face in his hands, and forced Jess to look at him. 'You're better than Madison in every way,' he murmured. 'You're gorgeous, funny, clever, sexy and selfless. Not many people would do this for me, and nobody has ever captured my heart the way you have. I've been looking for you all my life . . . and now I've found you I'm not going to let you go.'

Jess swallowed hard. Everything was happening so quickly – her love affair with Beau was the most intense thing she'd ever experienced. And it showed no sign of slowing down. Had they only been sleeping together for less than a week?

'I don't want you to,' Jess admitted. 'But what happens when Madison gets better? Will you decide I'm only second best?' She hated sounding so insecure, so whiny. But she couldn't help it.

Beau shook his head and laughed. 'You're one in a million, Jessica Piper. And if anything, Madison is second best to you.'

'The more I find out about Madison, the more I hate her,' Jess confessed. She knew it wasn't nice, but she couldn't help it.

'Sweetheart, she's ill. She came from trash and survived the only way she could. Deep down she's a good person. And by helping her out like this, you're giving her a chance to find that side of herself.'

Jess squeezed her eyes tightly together. 'I'm just so scared that you're going to fall in love with her again. I can't help it, but I can't bear it. I really can't. I know it's not professional, and that this is a business arrangement and nothing else, but I've fallen so hard for you,' she mumbled. 'I'm crazy about you.'

Beau took Jess's hands in his, and a slow smile spread across his face.

'Then everything's going to work out okay, isn't it?' he said, and despite the relief she experienced, Jess sensed a cold shiver dart up her spine. It was probably nothing, but in the candlelight she could have sworn that Beau's loving smile never reached his eyes.

Chapter Fourteen

Tick. Tick. Tick. Madison stared at the antique mahogany grandfather clock that stood, pride of place, in the drawing room. According to the housekeeper, the clock was over two hundred years old, and although she was slightly awed by something that old and beautiful, Madison hated it. *Hated* it. The steady, relentless ticking never stopped, and it was enough to turn her mad, if she wasn't already.

Madison leapt off her chair and began pacing the room. She'd tried before to stop the clock – she'd opened the casing and fiddled about with the insides – but she didn't know what she was doing, and had no clue how to end the tick-tick-ticking. Even though the clock was gorgeous, with faded tea roses around the face, and intricate silver hands, Madison didn't care if she broke it. In fact, she'd be happy – it was Beau's pride and joy, a pretentious attempt to buy tradition and class, and one of the few things he genuinely cared about.

But she couldn't stop the hands from moving, the pendulum from swinging back and forth.

Phil and Jason – who'd been tasked with keeping Madison inside the mansion's grounds and out of trouble – hadn't been able to stop the ticking, either. So the grandfather clock remained, steadily driving her nuts ever since she and Beau had returned from honeymoon. It was like a ticking bomb waiting to go off, a countdown to the *Spotlight* tour. Beau was still adamant that she wasn't going to do any interviews, but as the promotion of *Spotlight* ramped up – ads in magazines, mentions of it on MTV and all the music programmes – she wondered how it could happen without her. She was Madison Miller. And there was no way that Slate Street could do all the interviews and four pre-tour parties that Beau had lined up without her.

It was impossible. Wasn't it?

'You're not to leave the house,' Beau had barked at her the moment they'd arrived back at the house after their honeymoon. The website and magazine articles that had appeared about their 'romantic, sensual days in the Seychelles' were laughable. The reality was they didn't speak to each other unless the press were around, and the only time they smiled was when there were cameras trained on them. Despite the soft white sand, the shimmering turquoise sea, and the kaleidoscope of colour from the coral reefs surrounding the island of Praslin, their honeymoon was miserable. Madison felt trapped, and she couldn't wait to get back to America and away from Beau.

'Phil and Jason have been ordered not to let you leave the mansion, and if I hear one word that you tried to escape and tell the press about me and Tori, you're finished. Completely.' Beau's voice had been like ice, and as he spat the words at her, Madison had recoiled, tears sliding down her face no matter how hard she'd tried to stop them.

'You can't keep me locked up in this house. It's . . . illegal. I'll be a prisoner.'

Beau had shrugged. 'Have you read your contract?' he'd asked idly, while fiddling with his BlackBerry. According to his emails, ticket sales for the tour were going well, and the number of applicants for the next season of *Teen Star USA* had reached record levels. 'While you're on Slate Street you do *exactly* what we tell you to do. And if we say you're gonna stay out of the spotlight for a bit, that's what happens.'

'And if I don't?' Madison had struggled to sound brave, but she couldn't help her lower lip from trembling. 'I could pick up the phone and call anyone – the *New York Times*, the *Washington Post* . . .'

Beau had eyed Madison thoughtfully. 'I'm impressed that you've memorised a couple of newspaper names,' he'd said. 'When I first met you I had no idea that strippers cared about politics or current affairs.'

'I'm not a stupid little girl!' Madison had cried, but Beau had merely laughed. Madison couldn't believe that she used to find his curt, cruel laugh so sexy.

'Do you really think I'd be so stupid as to leave *phone lines* in the house? There's nothing that can give you contact to the outside world. Nothing. So you'd better get used to listening to the sound of your own voice, sweetheart. Good thing it's so pretty.'

'Why are you doing this to me?' Madison had whimpered.

'Because you tried to fuck with me,' Beau had said simply. 'You're not doing the pre-tour parties because I can't trust you to keep your mouth shut, and I'm not having you fuck up my career and everything I've worked for. If you can keep quiet and be a good girl when the *Spotlight* tour is on, I might let you make another record. You can still make me money, you know, and that's the only thing going for you.'

'Is that all you care about?' Madison had sobbed. 'Money?'

Beau had raised his eyebrows. 'You're finally getting it,' he'd remarked coldly. 'I'm going back to Manhattan to sort out this tour. I'll be back once I have. Be good, Mads – and if you can't be good, be careful.'

As Madison recalled Beau's menacing final remark, she stared at the grandfather clock. It was nearly midday, and according to the Slate Street telegram that had arrived that morning, that was when Beau was due back at the mansion. Madison could hardly wait – she wanted to show him that she could be trusted. She'd been good, hadn't tried to contact anyone or leave the luscious grounds of the mansion, and she hoped – prayed – that because she'd suffered her punishment so well Beau would let her do the pre-tour promotion. She'd do anything to be able to go. She just couldn't stay in this mansion any longer, with the grandfather clock and the otherwise eerie silence that came from being a forgotten person, all alone apart from two bodyguards to keep her company.

Just after the grandfather clock chimed twelve – almost happily, it seemed to Madison – she heard the front door of the mansion open. She stopped pacing, smoothed down her dark-grey Marc Jacobs skirt and white shirt, and took a quick look at her purple Alexander McQueen stilettos. They were her favourite heels, and even though she wore them all the time, they were still impeccable. Beau always appreciated it when she made an effort. Her heart was thudding and her palms were sweaty, but she knew she looked good.

She was ready to face Beau, ready to prove to him that she could be trusted to speak to the press and ramp up the promotion of the tour.

'Madison, I'm back.' Beau's cold voice echoed through the mansion.

Taking a deep breath, Madison flung open the door to the drawing room, and made her way towards the lobby, the McQueen heels giving her tentative walk a sexy edge. As she walked, she thought she could hear a girl's voice. She shook her head slightly. Being trapped in the house for weeks probably *was* sending her mad.

There was no way Beau would bring anyone to the house to see her. Even though the staff at Slate Street clearly knew something was up, he wouldn't have risked bringing even one of his closest colleagues here – let alone a girl.

As Madison turned the corner of the lobby, she gave her biggest, best pop princess smile, but the moment she saw Beau – and the person standing next to him – she froze, dumbstruck.

For standing there, in an almost identical outfit, was a girl who looked just like her. Her mahogany hair hung in shiny sheets from a side parting, her bright blue eyes were wide and clear, and her grin was just like Madison's.

The two girls stared at each other for what seemed a lifetime, but it was only when Beau said, in an amused voice, 'Madison, meet Jess Piper – our brand-new Madison,' that the spell was broken, and Madison fainted, landing in a crumpled heap on the gleaming marble floor.

The last thing she saw, before everything went black, were the purple Alexander McQueen stilettos the girl was wearing.

'I'm doing this to help you, you know,' a British voice said quietly, as Madison began to open her eyes. She lay on her bed, still fully dressed apart from her shoes, and she had a splitting headache. She'd never fainted before, but as she caught sight of the girl who was looking at her intently from the chair next to the bed, she could see why she had. This girl – what was her name? Jess? – looked exactly like her. Apart from winning *Teen Star USA*, seeing Jess for the first time had to be the strangest moment of her life. Nothing could prepare you for coming face to face with your double. Especially not in your own home, when you were expecting something entirely different.

'Beau told me that you're ill, and you're not able to do the promotion before the tour,' Jess began slowly, as if she were trying to be tactful. 'I'm not a singer – or even much of a dancer – but I'm able to answer questions from the media until you've sorted yourself out. I hope I can do you justice.'

Jess's words floated over the bed like bubbles, and as they popped, they shattered like shards of glass all over Madison. He'd done it, she thought. He'd found a foolproof way to promote the tour – *her tour* – without her. It was enough to make Madison start crying all over again.

'Who are you?' she managed to say through her tears, and Jess smiled at her. It wasn't the friendliest smile she'd ever seen, but it was the first real smile she'd received in a long time.

'For the next month I'm you,' Jess said simply. 'And that's all you really need to know. I'm going to be you on the pre-tour promotional trail while you get yourself straightened out and ready to sing your heart out for your tour. Beau's told me everything – the stripping, what happened during *Teen Star USA*, and the fake wedding – and I want to help you. Hopefully by the time the tour starts you'll be back to normal.'

Madison struggled to take in the words. 'What do you mean "back to normal"?' she asked, her voice foggy with sleep and confusion.

Jess reached over and squeezed Madison's hand. It was exactly the same size as hers with the same shade of Chanel nail varnish. Both girls noticed it, and Madison tried not to freak out.

'Let's not talk about it now,' Jess said soothingly. 'When you're feeling a bit better why don't you come downstairs? Beau and I will be waiting for you, and we can tell you what's going to happen next.'

Madison stared at Jess's face, clocking every feature and every angle of her eyes, her nose, her broad, smiling mouth, and wondered if it was possible that she could have a twin, a doppelgänger. But from the first time they'd met, Madison could see something in Jess that was different from her. When Jess mentioned Beau there was pleasure in her eyes – not hate.

Beau stared at the two girls sitting on opposite ends of the antique French sofa, and tried not to leer. They both looked so alike that anyone who didn't know them would assume they were near-identical twins. That Jess looked so like Madison – or that Madison looked so like Jess – was uncanny. And it was perfect for what he needed. What a coup.

'I know this must be strange for you,' Jess began, shooting a look at the grinning Beau, 'but this is the best solution we could come up with to make sure your tour's a success and that all the tickets are sold.'

Madison stared at Jess. 'I don't follow,' she said as crisply as she could, hoping her sharp tone would match the English girl's cut-glass accent. Now she'd recovered fully from her fainting episode, she was tense and alert. She didn't know who Jess was exactly – did she imitate popstars for a living, perhaps? – but there was no way she would let her step into her shoes. No way.

Jess looked awkwardly at Beau, but it was clear he wasn't going to help her out. Not yet. Not while he was enjoying the show.

'Well . . . we want to make sure you get better, and we didn't think you'd be able to cope with the stresses of interviews before the tour,' she said clumsily.

'What's with all this "we" shit?' Madison snapped. 'Who's "we"?'

Jess blinked. 'Beau and myself. Beau told me how ill you are, and, well, it was my idea to get someone to stand in for you.'

'And how convenient that you happen to look *just* like me.' Madison knew she was getting angry, and that she shouldn't start shouting, but she couldn't help it. 'What the fuck's wrong with you?' she spat. 'Are you some freak who likes to dress up like popstars and steal their jobs? Or is it a sex thing? Did you make yourself look like me so you could steal my man?'

To her credit, Jess blushed, and when she didn't immediately answer Madison knew that Jess and Beau were having a relationship. She couldn't believe it.

Madison turned on Beau. 'And what's all this shit about me being ill? What have you been telling her?' she spat.

Beau raised his eyebrows but didn't speak for a minute. 'I told Jess the truth,' he said finally. 'She knows about your drug problem . . . and we want you to use this opportunity to go to rehab to get better.'

Madison was astounded. 'My *what*?' she whispered harshly.

Beau turned to Jess. 'See?' he said knowingly. 'She's in denial. I warned you she would be.'

'But I've never touched drugs!' Madison cried. 'Never!'

'Which is why you could barely stand up when I came home,' Beau muttered.

'I'm not judging you, Madison,' Jess interrupted smoothly, hoping to calm the popstar down. 'Beau told me about your background, and it sounds like you've been to hell and back. It's why I want to *help*.'

Madison buried her head in her hands. 'Jess, could you leave, please?' she asked eventually. 'I want a few moments alone with my manager.'

As Jess walked out of the drawing room, Madison stared at Beau, wishing she could wipe the growing smirk from his face.

'So I'm a drug addict now? Are you kidding me?'

Beau laughed. 'I could hardly tell her the truth, could I, darling?' he said. He sounded as if he was enjoying the situation. 'I had to make her feel sorry for you – it was the only way I could get her to stand in for you and do all the interviews and

177

TV shows we've lined up. She's such an innocent she believed every word I said. Ha, she didn't even know who I was when I met her in New York.'

'I don't believe you,' Madison said simply.

Beau shrugged. 'Believe what you like. I must have found one of the only girls on the planet who doesn't care about the Madison and Beau show. But I twisted Jess's arm and she's up for being you for a bit. You should hear her American accent – it's faultless. I've struck gold.'

'So what do you plan to do with me while Jess is on *my* promo tour?' Madison asked. She knew there was no way out of this situation now. Beau would never let her do the *Spotlight* promotion now – not while he had a pliable Madison lookalike to take her place. God, what if she could sing? Then she really *would* be in trouble . . .

'I'm telling Jess you're going to rehab in Arizona but what you do is up to you. You can stay here for all I care, or one of my other places. Wherever you choose to go you'll be in isolation. Can't risk you running off to the press, can we?'

The ticking of the grandfather clock suddenly seemed louder then, and Madison knew that if she had to stay in the LA mansion she really would go off the rails.

'I can't stay here,' she whispered, tears filling her eyes. 'Please don't make me. Please. I beg you.'

Beau assessed her thoughtfully. 'I think you're right,' he said finally. 'If you're here I can't use the house – I certainly don't want to be dealing with you and Jess at the same time. It could get confusing. I have a ranch in Oklahoma that I've not been to for a couple of years – you could go there.'

Madison wiped the tears from her eyes. 'Has it got a grandfather clock?' she asked quietly, and Beau looked at her as if she really were mad. He chose to ignore her question.

'Jason and Phil are going to be Jess's bodyguards while she does the parties, so I've drafted in Jared from the LA security team to be your bodyguard. He is aware of the whole situation, and he knows not to let you have any contact with the outside world. He'll be the only person – apart from me, if I can be bothered – you'll be allowed to talk to until the tour kicks off, so you'd better be nice to him. You're gonna be on the ranch with him for quite a few weeks.'

Madison stared at him. 'What if I don't want to go to Oklahoma?' she asked. 'Or what if I escape?'

Beau smiled again, and stretched his arms behind his head. He looked relaxed, happy and perfectly in control.

'Then we've got Jess. She's great at lip-synching, you know. We could, quite plausibly, do the *Spotlight* tour with her, and leave you in Oklahoma for ever.'

Madison paled.

'But if you're good, then I might consider giving you your life back. But Madison, you're definitely going to Oklahoma. You've got no choice – you never had.'

Chapter Fifteen

'That went better than I expected,' Beau remarked to Jess that night as they lay in the master bedroom of the LA mansion. A warm breeze made the organza curtains flutter gently, and the sweet smell of orchids drifted through the window. Jess propped herself up on one arm. She stared down at him quizzically.

'Are you saying I'm a bad lay?' she asked indignantly, desperately praying that he wasn't referring to what they'd been getting up to only ten minutes earlier.

'I was talking about Madison and her agreeing to go to rehab,' he replied, with a smile. 'But yeah, you were pretty hot tonight, too.'

Jess slapped Beau playfully on the cheek and lay back down, resting her head on his broad, hairy chest. When she was in bed with Beau everything seemed so perfect, so right. She couldn't believe she'd met someone so amazing so soon after breaking up with Matthew, but she had. He was real. And he was hers . . . even if he was officially married to Madison.

'She's more fucked up than I thought she would be,' Jess began quietly, disliking that they were talking about Madison in bed, but knowing they had to discuss her at some point. 'I mean, she didn't even seem to remember that you'd told her about me.'

Beau stroked Jess's hair. They hadn't known each other for long, but they'd become close quickly. Jess supposed that if you were planning on doing something so surreal, becoming intimate was almost inevitable.

'It's the drugs,' Beau said simply. 'She's out of it most of the time, and when she's not . . . well, you saw what she's like. She's tearful, irrationally angry, a fireball. She's better off in rehab, and when she's come through it she'll be thanking you for helping her out.' He kissed Jess's forehead.

'I hope so,' she said, trying not to think about the forlorn figure Madison had cut when she got in the limo that was driving her to rehab. It was the last either she or Beau would see of Madison for a while, and Jess prayed that the popstar would come out of rehab a happier, healthier person. Jess's job would be almost pointless if she didn't.

'Are you prepared for tomorrow?' Beau asked, changing the subject. He seemed uncomfortable talking about Madison in bed, too, and Jess was glad. She didn't want the shadow of Madison hanging over their private life as well as their professional one.

'I think so,' Jess replied. 'But I'm so nervous. What if I fuck up?'

Beau smiled. 'You won't. It's a ten-minute interview with the *LA Times*, and then the first pre-tour party in the evening. You'll be fine.'

'Not if I muck up my accent,' Jess said sadly. Even though her elocution teacher said her Midwestern twang was pitch-perfect, Jess was nervous about doing it in front of anyone but Beau.

'You won't,' Beau reassured her soothingly, and he held her closer to him. His body was warm and hard against hers, and as Beau began to stroke her shoulders, Jess could feel herself relax again. This was the last night of being herself before she had to start acting like Madison, she thought, and she was bloody well going to enjoy it.

She struggled free from Beau's arms and stared at him with a sexy grin. 'You're gorgeous, you know that?' she said in her concise English accent. 'But you know how you could look even sexier?'

Beau shook his head slowly.

'You'd be on top of me.'

Beau stared at Jess for a long moment, and then he flipped her onto her back and began kissing her. After tonight nothing would be normal again . . . and even though Jess was excited about starting her month of being a popstar, she wanted to be herself with Beau – completely and utterly – one last time.

Jess and Bailey – who handled the PR for most of the bigger acts on Slate Street – walked into the Avalon Hotel on West Olympic Boulevard a little after 10 a.m. They were meeting Maxwell Fletcher from the *LA Times*, and as soon as Jess caught sight of the journalist sipping a cup of coffee by the figure-of-eight swimming pool, her heart began to thud loudly.

'I'm a little nervous,' she whispered to Bailey.

'But you've done a trillion interviews before,' Bailey chuckled, poking her in the ribs. 'What's so different about this dude? I mean, he's only a freelancer. Just answer his questions, smile, and we're outta here.'

Jess bit her lip. Bailey hadn't seemed to realise that the girl she was looking after wasn't Madison Miller, but Jessica Piper – an unemployed fashion designer from London who'd never done an interview in her life.

'But what if I mess it up?' Jess asked quietly.

The PR girl looked at her in bewilderment. 'When have you ever screwed up an interview? This is just pre-tour nerves, right?' she said, not waiting for an answer. 'Here, put some of this lip-gloss on . . . you've chewed most of yours off.'

Bailey handed Jess a raspberry-coloured Juicy Tube, and Jess smeared it on her lips nervously.

'Do I look all right?' she asked Bailey, who could have passed for a model without even trying. Her buttery blonde hair trailed down her back, and even though she was a born and bred New Yorker, she'd totally nailed the LA look in a tight vest, short shorts, and Havaiana flip-flops. Jess was wearing Jimmy Choos and a fussy Diane von Furstenberg Margo print dress, and the silk clung to her skin uncomfortably. She'd have given anything to be in a scruffy vest and shorts, too . . . so long as she'd had the chance to customise them and make them rock.

'Totally gorgeous as always, sweetie,' Bailey said distractedly.

Maxwell Fletcher had spotted them from the other side of the pool and was standing, ready to greet them.

'Now fix your smile to your face, and act cute. You're Madison Miller, remember?'

Despite her nerves Jess had to grin. Bailey may not have known that she wasn't Madison, but she'd said exactly the right thing.

'Hey there,' Jess said in her Madison-perfect American accent. 'I'm Madison, and it's *so* great to meet you.'

Jess had seen enough interviews with Madison on MTV to know that whoever she was meeting, and whatever situation she was in, Madison played the part of perky cheerleader. It was an attitude a thousand miles away from Jess's sedate London cool, but she wasn't getting paid a million dollars to be herself. She had to be Madison exactly. And the first step in that was fooling this journalist.

'Hi, Madison,' Maxwell replied nervously. He was clearly flustered at meeting America's most talked about pop princess, but was trying hard not to show it. He was also failing. 'Can I get you a drink? Coffee? Water?'

'Water would be good, thanks,' Jess replied, smoothing down her dress and sitting down. Both Bailey and Maxwell did the same. She was in charge. It was amazing, she thought. Absolutely amazing. 'How long have you been working at the *LA Times*?'

Maxwell looked at Madison in shock. In the years he'd been interviewing celebs, not a single one had asked him a question about himself — much preferring to talk about themselves and their careers endlessly.

'Um, about six months,' he replied. 'I've worked all over, on *Vanity Fair* and the *Washington Post* . . . I love LA, though. It's a great place to hang out.'

'I totally agree,' Jess said, with a huge grin. 'I love New York, but LA's something else.'

'You grew up in Ohio, didn't you?' Maxwell began, pressing 'record' on his Dictaphone and putting it on the table in front of them.

'Yeah, I did, and I loved it. I had a great childhood, and I miss Walkertown and my mom and dad,' Jess said smoothly. When she'd woken up that morning she'd worried that she'd never remember all the different facts about Madison that she'd need, but now she'd started the interview they were all coming back to her. Being treated like she was someone special was kind of fun!

'So what made you move to New York?' Maxwell asked.

'I'd always dreamt of being a singer, and I'm the type of person who follows their dreams. I auditioned for *Teen Star USA* and when I got through the first round I couldn't believe it! I worked hard, and I think if you work hard you really can make your dreams come true.'

Inwardly Jess marvelled at herself. With her pitch-perfect accent and American pep talk, she really did sound like Madison. Maybe she was going to get away with this after all. She suddenly smiled then, and it was a real one — a real *Jess* smile — rather than her phoney Madison one. Being natural felt good.

'And now you're about to start your first tour. Tell me about that.'

Jess beamed. 'It's so exciting. It's called the *Spotlight* tour, and I'm doing forty dates in twenty states. It's gonna be hard work, but I can't wait to give something back to all my fans who voted for me on *Teen Star*!'

'And what message would you send to the fans who think you only won the show because of your relationship with *Teen Star* owner Beau Silverman?' Maxwell asked. He'd warmed Jess up nicely, and now he was going in for the kill.

But Madison hadn't answered any questions about the debacle since it happened, and Bailey wasn't going to allow it now.

'Madison won't be answering that question, Maxwell,' she interrupted smoothly.

'It's okay,' Jess said, gently touching Bailey's arm. 'I'll answer it.'

She turned to Maxwell and took a deep breath.

'I know that lots of magazines and websites wrote malicious things about me when they found out I was in love with Beau, and they hurt. They really hurt. But you can't help who you fall in love with, and I only fell in love with Beau after the show finished. I didn't do anything wrong. Beau and I are married now, and we're happy, and I really want to use the tour to give back to everyone. I want to make it up to my fans who were fooled by the media, and I hope they'll allow me to do that.'

'Nicely done,' Bailey muttered under her breath, and Jess smiled. Under her silk dress she was sweating madly, but she knew she hadn't messed up. Beau would still be proud of her.

'And what's next for you after the tour?' Maxwell said, disappointed he hadn't got a controversial quote. He hadn't really expected one – she was far too slick a media machine to make a mistake – but it was always worth a shot.

Jess laughed. 'I'm going to have a couple of weeks off and then I'm going to start recording my second album. And even though I can't wait to start the tour I'm even more excited about getting back into the studio and writing some new songs. It's my passion,' she said, thinking of the tiny boutique shop she wanted to open on the King's Road. It was going to be fantastic.

Maxwell clicked his Dictaphone off, and after a couple more pleasantries and an autograph for his niece – a perfect copy of Madison's signature – Jess and Bailey walked out of the hotel. Everyone was staring at them and whispering. It was Madison Miller! In LA!

'So how did I do?' Jess asked excitedly as soon as they were back in the Slate Street limo. 'Was that okay?'

Bailey rolled her eyes. 'Since when have you cared so much?' she replied. 'But since you ask, it was good. Fine. It will be a nice bit of PR for the LA gig of the tour once it's written up. What are you doing for the rest of the day? Wanna hit the stores with me?'

Jess shook her head. 'I'd love to, but I need to get ready for the party tonight at the Viper Room on Sunset – are you coming?'

'Miss the first *Spotlight* promo party? Are you kidding me? It's my *job* to be there – after all, I put together the guest list . . . Be prepared to schmooze journos, models, actresses and directors, babe – tonight's your night to shine.'

Jess smiled. Beau had been banging on about how Jess had to make a good impression at the party – and the three others they were holding in three other major cities – and she'd been worried that she wouldn't be able to pull off her Madison impression in front of all the other Slate Street employees. But if Bailey – and

Maxwell Fletcher – had been fooled, she might be able to let her hair down. Just a bit.

The sidewalk outside the Viper Room was *heaving*. Even though the *Spotlight* party was invite only, there seemed to be thousands of wannabes hanging out on the Sunset Strip, with a queue outside the club snaking its way down the road. Jess was so in awe of the scene that when she climbed out of the gleaming Slate Street limo she completely forgot why she was there – and who she was meant to be. It was only when she paused and someone yelled, 'It's Madison! Madison Miller's *here!*' that it all came back to her. She wasn't anonymous, she wasn't like everyone else, and she was hot property.

She was the reason for the party and the crowds.

Flashes from the paparazzi cameras blinded her, and suddenly hordes of people circled her, all screaming and whistling and yelling. Jess was truly frightened for her life. How was she meant to deal with this? How did Madison deal with this every day of her life?

Phil and Jason – the scary-looking security guards who used to protect Madison but were now looking after her – suddenly appeared out of nowhere, and began pushing people out of the way to create a path to the entrance of the club. Under the feet of all Madison's fans was a red carpet, laid out especially for her, and seeing that snapped Jess into action. She straightened her shiny black Herve Leger mini-dress, took a deep breath, and grinned her best Madison Miller smile. That was what Beau had told her to do if she ever got stuck in a situation where she felt freaked out. She had to smile, wave, and look cool and confident.

It was easier said than done. And the pressure didn't stop after Jess entered the club and came face to face with journalists, hangers-on and LA's professional party people.

'Madison! I just *loved* your first single. You're amazing!'

'Madison! You're looking hot tonight, babe! Come party with us later, yeah?'

'Hey, Madison! Madison Miller! You're the *best*. I think you're the greatest singer I've ever heard. We should hook up and get some dinner when this is over!'

'Madison! We want you on the cover of the next edition of *Hollywood Insider*. You up for it?'

'Madison, can I get a few words for my blog? I'll totally rate your party if you can just give me a few words . . . Madison! Hey, Madison!'

Jess worked the crowds for two hours as soon as she stepped into the Viper Room. She gave pithy sound bites for magazines, posed for photos that would be uploaded to the web in a matter of minutes, and charmed everyone as best she could. It was only when Bailey rescued her that she could finally stop talking and take a sip of champagne. She was parched.

'Big crowd tonight, huh?' Bailey remarked, watching Jess slowly take a couple of deep breaths. 'Everyone's going crazy for you! This party's the hottest ticket in town and you're the star of the show, showgirl.'

'It's fucking ridiculous!' Jess exclaimed. 'Who *are* all these people?'

Bailey grinned. 'The people outside or the people in here? I don't know who the people are outside – who cares? They're not important enough to be invited so they're nobodies. Wannabes. Did you catch that girl who was wearing the see-through dress? Like *that's* gonna convince me to put her on the guest list. And as for the people you've been talking to, well, they're the cream of the LA media scene. They work for the best papers, mags and websites, and I can guarantee that you'll be plastered over everything tomorrow. Good job, pop princess.'

Jess allowed herself a smile. Beau was in the club somewhere, and she was pleased Bailey thought she'd done well. Beau would have been watching her, too, and she wanted him to be satisfied with how she'd performed tonight.

'But what about everyone else? Not *everyone* here can be press, can they?'

'No way,' Bailey laughed, and she gestured to the dark corners of the Viper Room. 'Over there is the usual party crowd: Lauren Conrad, Lindsay Lohan, Jessica Simpson, Pepper Rose, blah blah blah. They're gonna be fighting over you later to claim you as their "new best friend".'

'Me?' Jess breathed, before taking a long, hard sip of champagne. 'They want to be best friends with *me*?'

Bailey shot Jess an odd look. 'Sure they do, honey. Starlets want column inches, and you're America's sweetheart. Being friends with you guarantees success. I'd steer clear of Pepper Rose, though,' she advised, under her breath. 'I hear that girl is trouble.'

Jess strained her eyes in the dimly lit club. She'd vaguely heard of Pepper Rose from her time at the *Daily World* – was she an actress? – but couldn't remember what she looked like.

'I can't see her,' she said to Bailey, who was smiling at all the journalists and editors. Now they'd had their piece of her, they were too respectful to come over and interrupt. 'Madison' was officially off duty.

Bailey sighed. 'She's over there, looking surly.'

Jess followed Bailey's gaze. Pepper Rose was drinking clear liquid from a highball glass. She was bathed in red light, and with her dyed black hair, white skin, huge doll-like eyes and Cupid-bow mouth, she looked like a younger, trashier, skinnier Dita Von Teese.

'What's her story?' Jess asked.

Bailey turned to her incredulously. 'Are you kidding me? You're kidding me, right?'

Jess shook her head. 'I've been in a *Teen Star* bubble for months, and before that I never really read the gossip columns,' she lied. She didn't think telling the truth – that she couldn't be bothered with the showbiz pages when she worked for a newspaper – would go down too well with Bailey. Or Beau, for that matter.

Bailey laughed. 'I always forget you're such an innocent. Pepper's famous for being *desperate* to be famous. She says she's a movie star but she totally can't act. I mean, she's never even been in a film. She was on a reality show called *Bunk'd Up*, and she used it to strip off and make an ass of herself.'

Jess stared at Pepper Rose, and wondered why she was at her party. It was the free booze, probably, but something about her drew Jess in. Maybe it was because she was dark and bewitching compared to all the Californian blondes in the room, or maybe because she was so obviously tortured like the real Madison, but Jess couldn't take her eyes off her. She looked like the girls who hung out in Hoxton. 'I'm gonna go chat to her,' she said to Bailey, refusing to catch her eye, and marched across the room.

'Hey there, I'm Madison,' Jess said awkwardly, holding out her hand to Pepper, who looked at it with a smirk. Eventually she took it, and Jess was struck by its coolness, despite the heat of the club.

'Yeah, I know,' Pepper said, knocking back her vodka. 'It's your party, right?'

Jess bit her lip. What was she *doing*? Why was she trying to talk to some fucked-up girl who'd be bad for Madison's career?

'Are you enjoying it?' she asked awkwardly. 'The party, I mean?' Now she was in front of Pepper Rose she didn't know what to say. What were you meant to say to someone who wanted to be famous when you were the most famous person in the world at the moment? Maybe Pepper thought she was rubbing her nose in it.

Pepper Rose shrugged. 'Sure. It's a party, right?' She knocked back her highball glass of whatever she was drinking – straight vodka or gin? It most definitely wasn't water.

Jess grabbed a champagne flute from a passing waiter and did the same. 'It's a party full of fakers,' she muttered, and immediately regretted it. Maybe it was because she'd never encountered LA media people before, or maybe it was because she wasn't used to being on the receiving end of what journalists were like when they were out of the newsroom and on celebrity assignments, but the fawning and worshipping of 'Madison' was starting to leave her cold.

Pepper eyed Jess thoughtfully. 'And there I was thinking you were one,' she drawled.

Jess blushed. It was the first time since she'd started pretending to be Madison that someone had implied she was faking, and it was a shock.

'It's okay, though,' Pepper continued. 'I'll let you into a secret.'

Jess stared at Pepper curiously.

'I'm a faker, too. In fact, I think we're pretty similar, you and me, lying to the press—'

'Madison,' Bailey interrupted smoothly. 'I'm gonna have to break up your little party.' She shot Pepper Rose a dirty look, and dragged Madison away.

'What was that about?' Jess asked, as soon as they were out of earshot.

'Beau doesn't want you anywhere near that piece of trash,' Bailey said. 'I told you she was trouble, and Beau agrees. If anyone takes a photo of you with her tonight it will be totally bad for your career. You are who your friends are, after all.'

'But we're not friends – we were just talking,' Jess said. Pepper Rose was the first person Jess had met all night who hadn't fawned all over her. It was refreshing.

'You were talking to a drunk ho, yeah,' Bailey replied.

'It's a party! People are meant to drink . . . and besides, she didn't *seem* drunk.'

Bailey rolled her eyes. 'Pop princess, alcoholics rarely do. Now, I think your husband wants a couple of words.'

Jess turned, and spotted Beau sitting at a table, surrounded by empty bottles of champagne. He was staring at her, and as soon as Jess caught his eye she felt trapped by his gaze. He was so sexy in his black suit, white shirt and black tie that Jess almost didn't know where to look. The sexual chemistry between them must have been obvious to everyone. Despite all the people desperate to talk to 'Madison', Jess only had eyes for Beau. And the whole room knew it.

'You look fucking sexy tonight,' Beau whispered to her, as he pulled Jess onto his lap. She could feel he was hard underneath her, and it turned her on. She wondered how much longer they had to stay at the party. She felt she'd worked the room for long enough, and she wanted to be alone with Beau.

'But, Jessica,' Beau continued, his breath hot on the back of her neck, 'if I ever catch you talking to people Bailey's warned you against, I will chuck you out onto the streets without a penny. I can always find someone else to play the part of Madison. And fast, too. You're not irreplaceable, you know.'

Jess was so shocked by the cold, callous tone of his voice that she froze. Was this Beau talking to her? Really?

'Every minute of every day people are watching you. I'm

watching you. And if you step out of line one more time I *will* fire you.'

Jess turned so she was facing her boyfriend, and when she looked into his black eyes, she could see they were completely expressionless.

'I won't mess up again,' she said softly, hoping she wouldn't cry. Had Beau drunk too much? Taken drugs? This wasn't the Beau she knew. What had happened to him?

'I know you won't,' Beau whispered. 'And I forgive you.'

He kissed Jess so gently then, and trailed his fingers along her bare arms so erotically, that Jess wondered if she'd just imagined what he had said to her . . . and if he'd ever spoken to Madison like that.

Chapter Sixteen

When they first arrived at the ranch in the middle of the night Madison had practically ignored Jared. She'd spent so much time with Phil and Jason – her previous bodyguards – that when they'd followed Beau's orders and deserted her to protect Jess, she felt abandoned. Looking back, Madison understood that Phil and Jason were on the Slate Street payroll and that being friendly wasn't the same as being friends, but their quick dismissal of her hurt. Still hurt. And Madison wasn't about to make the same mistake with Jared. He was her bodyguard, plain and simple. He wasn't her friend. He was employed to make sure she didn't come to harm, didn't get hassled by fans, and – most importantly to Beau – didn't escape the ranch. Jared was her captor.

Like Phil and Jason, Jared fitted the bodyguard mould. He had sandy blonde hair, a nose that looked as though it had been broken in several places several times, and thin lips that seemed always to be set in a straight line. He was the strong, silent type, and when he didn't speak to Madison in the limo on the way to the airport, on Beau's private jet, or in the jeep on the way to the ranch, Madison had pointedly acted as if she didn't care. If they didn't speak for the entire time they were in Oklahoma, that was fine with her.

She was through with trusting people and then getting fucked over by them, and she wanted to be left alone.

After a couple of days living side by side in silence, Jared started catching her eye and initiating the beginnings of conversations. No matter where Madison went on the ranch, she couldn't seem to get away from him or his intense, blue-eyed stare, and she prickled uncomfortably at the feeling that she was being constantly watched.

There was something about Jared that seemed so straightforward and *normal* compared with Beau, that Madison almost wanted to chat to him. But that scared her. She didn't want to get close to anyone again: she'd been let down by Kyle, Leesa and Beau, and that was enough hurt for anyone. She decided she was going to play the ice queen until she could leave Oklahoma and start the *Spotlight* tour. It was the only option.

'What's with the attitude?' Jared said to her one day as he unpacked the groceries. He went to the closest stores every day – the only time when she was truly by herself – and he spent his evenings cooking elaborate meals for her. Madison ate them, and politely thanked him, but that was as far as her gratitude went. He was being *employed* to look after her. She wasn't about to gush just because he'd spent a couple hours at the stove.

Madison shrugged. 'No attitude,' she said simply, and stared at Jared's strong back as he put the groceries away in a cupboard.

'You're quite the diva,' he commented.

Madison was immediately infuriated. 'Just because I don't talk to the Slate Street staff like they're my best friends doesn't mean I have *attitude*,' she remarked defensively. 'I know the score. Beau's employed you to make sure I don't run off and blab to the press. I get it. You don't have to pretend you're here for anything else.'

Jared turned and looked at her for a moment. 'Are you like this with everyone or is it just me?' he asked, his eyes not able to hide his disbelief. 'I heard you were pretty down to earth, but that clearly isn't the case. Guess all your friends at the label were wrong.'

Madison shrugged again. Just thinking about everyone at Slate Street – and how they'd no doubt bowed to Beau's dollars rather than being there for her – felt like a hit in the stomach. The music industry was two-faced and fake, and Madison had learnt that now. Maybe Jared didn't get it, or maybe he was as naive as she'd been.

'Guess they were,' Madison said as lightly as she could, and then, after picking up an apple and taking a loud, crunchy bite, she walked out of the kitchen.

For days Madison and Jared followed the same routine. Madison would make the coffee in the morning, they'd both grab something separate for lunch, and in the evenings they'd sit down together in silence and eat whatever Jared had made them for their supper. After the meal Madison would retreat into her bedroom to read or watch TV, and Jared would sit on the veranda watching the stars, wondering why he couldn't get Madison out of his mind. He couldn't understand why she wouldn't open up to him. She'd clearly been pretty hurt in the past but he was different. And he wanted to prove it to her.

'How about a board game?' Jared suggested one night after dinner. 'I found Scrabble in a cupboard in the living room.'

Madison shook her head. 'No thanks,' she said politely, collecting up their plates and stacking them in the dishwasher.

'I love Scrabble, though . . .' Jared said, his voice trailing off, as Madison walked out of the kitchen and into the hall. He followed her.

'Just one game?' he asked hopefully.

Madison turned to face him. She couldn't ignore the pleading in his voice.

'I'm no good at games like that,' she said. 'I'm no good at words.'

'Cards, then? I found a pack. Poker? Rummy?'

Madison shook her head again.

Jared stared at her. 'Clue? Monopoly? There's a whole stack of games . . . there must be one you like.'

Madison thought briefly of how she used to love Clue when she was little, and how she'd always begged her parents to play it with her on Sunday nights so she could get away with not doing her homework. Walkertown, and her childhood, seemed a very long way away.

'I hate board games,' she said bluntly, and she walked away from Jared and up to her room where she closed her door firmly. She didn't open it for the rest of the night.

Several days later Jared tried again.

'I've got a bottle of red,' he said, not meeting Madison's eyes. 'It would be lovely if you'd sit outside with me and have a glass.'

Madison hesitated. She'd not had a drink since she and Beau had been on Necker, and even though she wasn't a big drinker, there was something appealing about having a glass of wine. She'd not been sleeping well – having someone impersonate you across the country didn't make for feeling relaxed – and suddenly a glass of wine seemed a great idea.

'Just one?' Jared looked up and held her gaze. He seemed so open, and, despite his size, almost vulnerable. Madison hadn't felt guilty for spurning his attempts at being friendly until that point, but now she felt terrible. He was just trying to be kind, and make a bad situation a little better.

'I'd love a glass,' she admitted, and saw Jared smile for the first time. It lit up his whole face.

From that evening, Madison and Jared shared a bottle of wine every night. At first they barely spoke – Jared didn't want to scare Madison off, and Madison was too petrified of opening up and getting close to someone again – but slowly, and definitely, they started to become friends. Madison told Jared about her childhood in Walkertown, how she'd always wanted to be a singer, and Jared shared his background, too. He was a born and bred Californian. After a stint in the army he'd moved back to the West Coast for the sunshine, his friends and his family. He loved his life.

'So why security stuff?' Madison asked. 'And, more importantly, why Slate Street?'

Jared grinned. 'It pays well, and out of all the labels, Slate Street pays the best. It also has an LA office, which means that whenever Slate Street's artists are on the West Coast I get to meet them. You're probably totally used to it, but I love meeting celebs.'

Madison smiled. It was refreshing to talk to someone who wasn't jaded by the music industry. 'Who've you met?' she asked.

Jared reeled off a list of some of Slate Street's most famous acts, finishing with Tori Catrino.

Madison paused. 'You met Tori?'

'Sure I did,' Jared said easily. 'She was a sweet girl. I sometimes wonder what happened to her. She didn't seem that happy.'

'I know the feeling,' Madison said in a soft voice, and Jared fixed her with a warm gaze. It made her want to open up to him.

'Did you know that Beau and Tori had an affair?' she asked. She was desperate to know the answer.

Jared nodded easily. 'Everyone does,' he replied. 'Well, everyone who works at Slate Street, anyway. It was common knowledge to all of us, although the press never got hold of it. How they kept it a secret from *them*, I don't know.' He shook his head in disbelief.

'Why do you say that?' Madison asked in curiosity. Until they'd been sprung on Necker, the press hadn't a clue about her and Beau, either – and keeping it private hadn't been that hard.

'Because Beau and Tori were, like, always all over each other. You'd walk into a room and there was this intense connection between them. They'd only have to look at each other to know what the other was thinking. It was pretty passionate. They just couldn't help themselves, even if other people were around. And we *always* saw them making out.'

Madison's mouth dropped open. 'Beau kissed her in front of you?'

Jared shrugged. 'Sure,' he replied easily. 'In front of all the staff. They were like kids in love, and they could never take their hands off each other. If there was an excuse to touch, they'd do it.'

Madison turned her gaze up to the night sky. The stars were sparkling with an intensity she'd not seen outside of Oklahoma, and the evening air was warm on her skin.

'He was never like that with me,' Madison whispered in a voice so tiny that Jared wasn't sure she'd said anything at first. 'He told me he adored me, but he never acted as if he did. Not really.'

Jared considered this for a moment. 'Maybe he did love you. When Beau and Tori split, he was pretty cut up. Rumour has it he didn't do any work for weeks . . . and you know how unlike Beau that is.'

Madison laughed. She didn't believe it.

'All I'm saying is that maybe Beau was just too scared to get close to you, after what happened with Tori. Maybe he *did* love you, but couldn't show it. I wouldn't be surprised.'

Madison considered what Jared had said, but dismissed it straight away. She knew Beau hadn't loved her – he'd told her enough times after the Necker Island debacle. And, looking back, she could see it was all about power and sex for him. Nothing else.

'What happened with him and Tori?' she asked, changing the direction of the conversation. She knew she must be one of a very small number of people who knew the pair had married and had twins.

'We don't know,' Jared admitted. 'Beau went on her tour, everything seemed great, and then one day – bam. They'd split. Tori was suddenly off Slate Street, and then she disappeared. It's a shame, but it seems that's how it goes . . . one day you're a Billboard number one, and the next day you're history.'

Madison took a long swig of her wine and laughed. 'Don't I know it,' she grinned. 'Here I am, cast aside in no-man's-land until my tour starts. That's if Beau *lets* me do my tour. I'm still not sure if he's going to.'

'He's got another girl pretending to be you, hasn't he?' Jared asked matter-of-factly.

Madison paled. How many people knew about Jessica Piper? 'It's only for the promotional stuff,' she managed to say, although she started to feel choked up when she saw Jared was looking at her with pity. 'How do you know about her?'

'Those who need to know about her do,' Jared said as simply as he could. 'I know because, well . . . can you imagine what I'd do if I saw you – I mean *Jess* – on TV promoting your tour? I'd freak out and start wondering what the fuck was going on. I'm pretty sure Phil and Jason know, too, but that's about it. Like I said, it's on a need-to-know basis. Beau wants it as quiet as possible.'

Madison buried her head in her hands. She couldn't bear to think about Jess going around America pretending to be her, but she felt even worse knowing that other people were in on the secret. What if Phil and Jason thought Jess did a better version of Madison than she did? It would be the worst thing in the world to find out they preferred Jess to her.

'Madison,' Jared began gently, 'why *are* you here? I know Beau doesn't want you to talk to anybody while you're out here – and especially not the press – but why? It doesn't make sense to me.'

He seemed so awkward sitting on the veranda that Madison suddenly felt sorry for him. Jared was employed to protect her, and to make sure she didn't run off and blab to anyone – but he didn't know the whole story. He didn't know why he was here with her, looking out for her.

'I can't tell you,' she said finally. 'I'm sorry. It's just too difficult.'

She longed to tell someone – anyone – what she'd found out about Beau and Tori, and Jared seemed the perfect person to confide in, but Madison wasn't about to make another mistake. Jared seemed friendly, but he could have been spying on her for Beau. She wouldn't put it past him, and she wasn't about to take the risk.

If she told Jared what she knew, and he told Beau, her career – or what was left of it – would be over for good.

'So I thought I'd bring over a cake and greet y'all.'

Madison was lying on her stomach under her bed, but she still managed to hear the woman's voice drifting through her open window. Her palms were sweaty, and her heart was pounding.

But it was just a woman standing on the veranda. A neighbour. Wasn't it?

'We don't often see new folk in this part of Great Plains Country,' the voice continued, 'so I thought I'd come over and say hi.'

'Hi there.' Madison marvelled at how easy-going and collected Jared sounded. Only moments before he'd thrown her out of the pool and into the house, where she'd run to the first place she could think of to hide: under her bed. It was as if she was seven again and scared of monsters, she thought. She was petrified by the thought that someone had nearly discovered she was on a ranch in Oklahoma, and not in whichever city the TV was reporting today. One false move and her career was finished.

'It's great to meet you, and thank you *so* much for this cake.'

'Well, you know, I'm on the farm just over there,' she said, 'and as I'm your closest neighbour I thought I'd stop by and welcome y'all. I've been seeing your jeep, and it's been a while since anyone was on this ranch . . .' The woman's voice trailed off, but Jared didn't try to rescue her from an awkward, nosy situation.

'Is it just you and your wife?' the woman asked eventually. 'Or have you little ones as well?'

Jared paused. 'Just my wife and me,' he said, finally. 'No kids. Not yet.'

'Is she home? Your wife?'

Madison held her breath.

'She's out of town visiting her mother,' he said. 'And I'm in the middle of some work . . . so if you'll excuse me?'

The woman was obviously too well mannered to say anything else. She said goodbye, then Madison heard the truck drive away.

A few minutes later Jared walked into her bedroom and told her it was safe for her to come out. She crawled out from under her bed and started shaking uncontrollably. She felt as though she couldn't breathe. The woman hadn't been a journalist, a paparazzo, or even Beau, but she could have been . . .

'Hey, it's okay,' Jared exclaimed, sitting on the bed beside her. Tears were pouring down her face, and she was agitatedly rubbing her bare arms with her hands as though to keep herself warm. She still wore just her bikini, and despite the heat, there were goosebumps all over her.

'What if we'd been found out?' Madison whispered, her blue eyes wide with fear. 'I'd have lost my career, my identity, everything . . .'

Jared put his arms around her, and under the weight of them, Madison felt herself begin to relax. Unexpectedly she flung herself onto Jared's lap, and began crying hard.

'If you hadn't have spotted her . . . if you hadn't have got me out of the pool . . .'

Jared began to rock her gently. 'I'm just doing my job,' he said quietly into her shiny brown hair. It smelt of coconuts and chlorine. 'Although it wasn't on my job description to become your friend,' he joked. He desperately wanted Madison to stop crying. It *had* been close, but he'd spotted the truck from a distance, and he'd got Madison out of sight before the neighbour had seen her.

Madison suddenly went very still, and then she looked up at him. 'Are you my friend? Really?' she asked him quietly. She was calmer, less frantic now.

'Of course I'm your friend,' Jared replied. He didn't take his eyes off hers, and before either of them knew what they were doing they were kissing, passionately. Jared's hands began to move over Madison's body, and with every touch her goosebumps disappeared and her anxiety began to be replaced by a different kind of tension. She hadn't realised it before, but Jared was possibly the sexiest, manliest man she'd ever met. And he'd just saved her career.

'Do you want this?' Jared whispered, pausing, but not taking his eyes away from hers. Not for a second.

'More than you could know,' Madison replied, and without another word he swept her off her bed and into his bedroom, where he slammed the door behind him and only opened it the next afternoon.

Madison sat on the veranda with her back to the ranch. The scorching sun beat down on the yellow grass and the green-blue lake, but in spite of the beautiful turquoise sky and the peaceful silence, Madison yearned for a breeze and some distraction. She was sitting in the shade, dressed in just a bikini and sarong, yet she felt as though her skin was blistering in the heat.

Madison cast her gaze over the red soil of the ranch, the dirt tracks that the neighbour's truck had left the day before, and let her fingers trail along her face. Her cheeks and chin felt as though they'd been rubbed raw, her lips were tender and swollen, and – and most surprisingly, especially as she felt as though she'd done ten rounds in a boxing ring – she couldn't stop smiling.

She forced the corners of her lips down with her hands and wondered if she dared go back into the house yet. She didn't think she could stand sitting out here in the late afternoon sun, but she wasn't sure it was safe to go back inside. Regardless of the state-of-the-art air conditioning, it was almost hotter inside . . . and much, much more dangerous.

'So this is where you got to.' A deep, male drawl made Madison jump, and her whole body tensed with anticipation as she heard heavy footsteps behind her on the wooden decking. She didn't need to turn around to know who it was. He was her protector – and now he was her . . . her what? Madison hadn't a clue. And she wasn't in the right frame of mind to try to work it out.

'Please leave me alone,' she whispered, refusing to look at him. She couldn't bear to, and she knew if she caught his blue eyes she'd be gone again. 'What we did last night was wrong, and I want to forget it. Make like it never happened.'

There was a pause, and then Madison felt herself being lifted up from her simple wooden chair. Jared was strong, and when he picked her up he did so effortlessly. He wasn't wearing a shirt with his shorts, and as Madison felt herself crushed against his sturdy chest and held in his muscular arms she knew she was helpless. He overpowered her – physically, mentally and emotionally. And even if she wanted to run away, she couldn't.

There was nowhere to go.

'What are you scared of, Madison? That I'm going to hurt you like Beau did?' He took her inside, put her down on a sofa and handed her a glass of iced water. She drank it gratefully. 'Because I'm not going to hurt you. I'd never do that.'

'How do you know Beau hurt me?' she asked defiantly.

Jared ran his eyes over Madison's face. Her eyes were so open and innocent, yet she wore an expression of a woman who'd been in a battle and had lost.

'Because you wouldn't be here if he hadn't,' Jared said finally. He didn't mention that every time he mentioned Beau's name Madison flinched, or that he frequently noticed her gazing into the distance. She could only have been thinking about Beau Silverman. That much was certain.

Madison shrugged, and pulled a throw over her shoulders as if she needed to be comforted.

'It just seems like every time I get close to someone they hurt me, or let me down,' she said in a small voice. 'I'm a magnet for it.'

'I'm not going to hurt you,' Jared repeated again, and the way he said it – so simply, so strongly – made Madison's eyes well up.

'How do I know that?' she asked.

'Because it's my job to protect you,' he said, smiling. 'And even if I weren't being paid to be here with you, I'd want to be. I think you're the most amazing girl I've ever met.'

Madison didn't speak for a second. 'That's what Beau used to say, too,' she said finally.

'But Madison, I'm *not* Beau.'

Madison looked at him. Physically he was bigger than Beau, with a smattering of blond hair on his chest and powerful legs. His hair was mussed up from the time they'd spent in bed the night before. He was as opposite to Beau in appearance as could be, yet he was a man, and he wanted to be close to her. That scared her.

'It doesn't matter,' Madison muttered. 'Everyone lets me down in the end.'

Jared sat next to her and sighed. 'Sounds like you've been hurt, kid. Who else has done a job on you?'

Madison shook her head. 'Nobody, really . . . well . . . I had a friend, Leesa, and she got addicted to drink and drugs when we were in New York, and instead of being pleased for me when I met Beau, she freaked out. We just stopped speaking.'

'So she was jealous?'

Madison shrugged again. 'I guess,' she said. 'But if some acting agent had approached her, I'd have been so happy for her.'

'People react to success in different ways. You *know* that.'

Madison bit her lip. 'Yeah, but we were so close. We were like sisters. Or so I thought.'

'You still in touch with her?'

Madison shook her head. 'She won't be in the same apartment any more, I've no way of phoning her, and I know she's not at the Spotlight club any more. She was my best friend and I got so carried away with being a *popstar* that I forgot all about her.'

Jared squeezed her hand tightly in his. It comforted her and turned her on all at once.

'I thought I was so cool, you know?' she continued. 'I was suddenly the most famous person in the world, had an amazing boyfriend who I thought loved me like I loved him, and I threw away a proper friendship with Leesa for *that*. How stupid am I? I can't believe I fell for Beau's bullshit.'

'Plenty of people have,' Jared murmured quietly. 'It's how he's so successful. He pulls people's strings like they're puppets, and he knows which buttons to press to get people to do what he wants. I wouldn't be surprised if he pulled some number on that Jess girl to get her to pretend to be you. Made out that it would be for your benefit or something.'

Madison didn't speak for the longest time, but began turning over the conversation she'd had with Jessica Piper back in LA. Madison knew Beau had told Jess she was going to 'rehab' – was Jess the kind of altruistic person who thought she'd be doing good by stepping into her shoes? Jess had said that she was doing this to help her out, that she'd be doing the promo interviews and parties for the tour while she straightened herself out.

'Jess thinks I'm in rehab and that I'm a drug addict,' Madison told Jared. 'But she wouldn't *just* pretend to be me for a month on that alone, would she?'

Jared shook her head. 'I heard she's getting paid, too,' he remarked quietly, but after he said it he regretted it. Madison looked furious.

'Are you kidding me? So all that stuff she said about wanting to help me was a load of shit!' she cried. 'So not only is she pretending to be me, and screwing my ex, she's getting paid loads of money, too?'

'She's having a relationship with Beau?' Jared interrupted. 'Are you sure?'

'Yeah, I'm sure,' Madison said bitterly. 'Jess even blushed when I suggested it.'

Jared let out a long sigh. 'Man, that's messed up.'

'Tell me about it. He's found some girl that looks just like me, and not only is she pretending to be me at press conferences and stuff, she's pretending to be me in bed.'

'So Beau could be pulling the old "I love you" stuff on her, too?' Jared suggested.

Madison nodded. 'Possibly. Probably. Who knows? Beau will stop at nothing to get what he wants. We both know that.'

They were silent for a moment, then Jared looked intently at Madison.

'But does Jess?' he asked.

Madison bit her lip. As much as she hated Jess for pretending to be her – both in public and in Beau's bed – she didn't wish Beau on anyone. He was rich, powerful and manipulative, and once you crossed him there was no going back.

'I don't know,' she whispered. 'But if you'll help me, I'd really like to find out.'

Chapter Seventeen

Jess may have hated plastic LA, but she was in love with Chicago. Despite knowing New York inside out, she'd never been to any other part of America, and she was surprised at just how much she loved the Windy City. She had her picture taken by fans outside the Auditorium Building, signed endless copies of Madison's CD in Macy's on State Street, and was papped everywhere: on a beach by Lake Michigan, at Lincoln Park Zoo, on top of the Sears Tower Skydeck, and even outside the Peninsula Hotel – which was where she, Bailey and Beau were staying.

'It's kinda unusual for Beau to join his acts on a pre-tour promotional trip like this,' Bailey began, as she and Jess had breakfast on their third day in the city. They were spending a whole week in Chicago – where Madison would play several nights at the United Center as part of the tour – and Jess's job was to charm the city. Beau wanted all three nights to be sold out before they left, and the way things were going, ticket sales were looking good. Everyone loved 'Madison'.

'He's not done it since Tori Catrino's tour, and that was years ago. Normally he just leaves me to it,' Bailey continued, the slight whine in her normally confident voice a sure sign that she wasn't ecstatic to be accompanied by the managing director of the record label. 'It's kind of freaking me out a little.'

'It's only because he loves me and can't stand to be away from me,' Jess said happily as she tucked into an egg-white omelette. She'd have preferred a chocolate croissant, but she was playing the part of a celebrity, and didn't want to gain any weight. She'd treat herself when it was over, when she stopped being Madison and could be Jess again. 'He's not checking up on you, I promise.'

Bailey grinned and took a sip of her coffee. Jess knew her well enough now to know that Bailey drank about ten cups of coffee a day before switching to champagne or vodka in the evening. She didn't know how she didn't start twitching on all the stimulants.

'Yeah, he's certainly crazy about you,' Bailey commented wryly, as she wiped a tiny smudge of lipstick from the coffee cup. She'd not seen her boss so besotted in ages, and just the thought of Beau and Madison together made her want to roll her eyes. They were sickening.

Every morning Jess would open the door to their suite – the Peninsula Suite, the best in the hotel – and would be greeted by a hundred red roses, which were placed in vases on every square inch available. There were roses in the master bedroom, roses in the master bathroom, roses in the exercise room, living room, dining room, study, and even beside the jacuzzi on the outside terrace. Jess was totally and utterly overwhelmed, and when she tried to express her gratitude – and her feelings – to Beau, he'd simply smirk.

'It's only because I adore you,' he'd say, before dragging her back to bed for an hour or two. Every second with Beau was bliss, and Jess had never been so happy. He showered her with gifts and compliments, and when he took her head in his large hands and told her how beautiful she was, Jess knew – without a fraction of a doubt – that he really meant it. He was in love with her, and he was perfect . . . just like Madison's life.

Apart from the hangers-on, and the press people who always

told Jess how much they *loved* her work, how *amazing* she was, and how *fabulous* her singing voice was even though they clearly preferred indie or rock to Madison's perfect, punchy pop – Jess loved being a popstar. Loved it!

She adored meeting Madison's fans – who were genuinely mesmerised at meeting their heroine – and when young girls were actually struck dumb, or, even better, had tears in their eyes, believing that this was the best moment of their lives, Jess felt a lump in her throat that wouldn't go away.

She'd never felt breathless at the thought of popstars or actresses when she was a teenager, but she imagined she'd be speechless and shaking if she met Alexander McQueen or Tom Ford, and she guessed it was the same for the hundreds of screaming fans who followed her. Madison was everything to them – and everything they wanted to be. Being Madison was spine-tingling, exciting and exhilarating.

But it was also exhausting – both physically and emotionally.

Late at night, as she lay in bed, trying to commit her surreal days to memory, Jess would start to feel guilty that she wasn't actually Madison.

'Is what we're doing wrong?' she'd whisper to Beau in the pitch-black room, and Beau would always roll over, hold her close to him, and squeeze her tight.

'We've been through this,' he'd stress patiently, even though he had to tell Jess the same thing every night. 'We're doing this so Madison can get better and do her tour.'

'But what about the fans?' Jess would ask, feeling wretched that for the rest of their lives the teenage girls she encountered would always talk about the day they met Madison, even though they really hadn't.

'They're meeting the spectacle of Madison – that's the same thing as Madison herself, babe.'

Jess wondered if this really was true. Every time she signed an autograph she felt as though she was cheating the person she gave it to. And every time she posed for a photo she wondered if her smile was a little too bright.

The freebies, on the other hand, Jess didn't feel guilty about at all, especially the clothes. Every day, huge boxes of designer clothes would turn up – ranging from high-end couture creations to T-shirts and sweats created by wannabe designers – and Jess loved them all. She'd never been so close to so many designer labels before, and if she'd had the time she would have spent hours trying everything on. She was sent Chanel suits, Balenciaga gowns, Chloe skirts, Missoni maxi-dresses, Ossie Clark wide-leg trousers . . . the list went on and on, and she still hadn't unpacked everything from all the layers of gold tissue paper that hid even more delights.

And then there were the bags. She squealed over the blue Bottega Veneta casual bag, swooned over the delicious Mulberry Poppy bag – which made her yearn for Poppy back in London, but Beau had insisted she talk to no friends and had even confiscated her mobile – and practically fainted at the beauty of the black lamb leather Chloe shopper. Especially when she saw how well it went with the Christian Louboutin Neuron shoes that Beau had forbidden her to wear, as they were 'scandalously sexy and not right for Madison's image'.

But even though she *loved* the designer clothes, Jess appreciated the street-smart, cool pieces that aspiring designers sent her even more. She could see the sweat and tears that had gone into an intricate silk vest with layers of smocking over it, and fell in love with a pink houndstooth and leather biker jacket that she wished she'd designed herself. Seeing those pieces made her yearn for her sewing machine, but she knew she was being ridiculous. She barely had time to eat, let alone think about designing clothes. It would have to wait until she got home . . . and she'd have to make do with what she was sent for now. Not that she was allowed to wear any of it.

When Jess had received her first package of clothes from Miu Miu, Beau had smiled distractedly and told her they had to stay in the closet. She had to stick to the fresh, preppy style that the Slate Street team had so carefully created for Madison, which was jeans, vests and heels for meeting her fans; and classy, not overtly sexual dresses for interviews and evening events. Secretly Jess thought it was dull and uninspiring – especially when such amazing clothes were sent for free – but she understood why she had to look approachable. Madison was who everyone wanted to be. And she dressed like every teen in America could.

'You know,' Beau said slowly one afternoon, as he watched Jess shriek in delight when she spotted a beautiful Temperley skirt that she'd wanted for ages, 'when all this is over I might hire you to design some clothes for Madison and some of our other artists. What do you think?'

Jess turned to Beau, the skirt still in her hands. 'Really? You mean that?'

Beau laughed, but his black eyes were unnervingly blank. 'I always mean what I say,' he replied. 'Haven't you worked that out yet, Jessica?'

Jess couldn't read his tone, but she refused to think he was being sarcastic or cruel. Beau just *wasn't* like that, and even though the night at the Viper Room kept haunting her when she was off her guard, she reminded herself that the way he spoke to her then was just a one-off. Beau was lovely. There was nothing else to it.

'That would be *amazing*,' Jess breathed, as she thought of all the different artists on Slate Street. 'Thank you so much.'

Beau raised his eyebrows. Every time he did that, Jess felt her heart tug. He was so gorgeous. 'Thank you for being such a great Madison so far. You're doing really well. Now, are you ready for the party tonight? We've hired the whole of Club Royale and invited Chicago's prettiest people.'

Jess grinned and put the skirt carefully back on its tissue paper. She'd try it on before she got ready tonight, even if she couldn't wear it until she was back in London. If she went back to London, that was. She wasn't sure she could stand to be away from Beau.

'I can't wait,' she said, then hesitated. She didn't want to piss Beau off, but she had to ask. 'Will there be press at the club, too?'

Beau didn't speak for a moment, and Jess wondered if she'd crossed the line. She hadn't *complained* about all the interviews she'd been doing, but Beau could tell she was getting tired of it. The problem was they still had two more cities to go.

'Your job is to speak to the press, pose for pictures, and make sure we get as much coverage for the party as possible. Have you got a problem with that?'

His tone was neutral, but Jess knew he was annoyed. If their roles had been reversed she probably would have been, too, but she spent every day with the press, with paparazzi, with PRs and record people and hangers-on who all wanted a piece of her, and she would have loved to kick back at a party, not work even harder.

'No problem at all,' Jess replied lightly, not catching Beau's eye. She bit her lip, and started to mentally prepare herself for even more schmoozing and charming. After a couple of hours, she'd insist on having some fun with Beau. Even he couldn't say no to a little dancing and drinking to celebrate how well Chicago had gone, could he?

And, she thought, as she let her gaze trail over the collection of new designer pieces hanging in the wardrobe, if she wore the sexy white Yves Saint Laurent number, Beau wouldn't be able to resist her.

Sod the rules, she thought, with a reckless abandon that made her feel free and happy. She was going to dress up, have fun, and make Beau fall for her even more.

He'd love it. She knew he would.

'What the fuck do you think you're wearing?' Beau hissed as Jess made her entrance at the club. The scene was becoming familiar: hundreds of people stood outside the club, hoping to bypass the exclusive guest list, and there were three or four members of the press to every celebrity. It was, as Bailey had commented upon seeing the setting, 'exactly what they wanted', but Jess couldn't care less about who was standing at the bar or sitting on the brown leather sofas. She just wanted to wow Beau.

'Don't you like it?' Jess said playfully as she gave a little twirl. The white dress was cut close to her curves, and while it didn't display any cleavage it was almost scandalously short, showing off Jess's long, tanned legs – made to look even longer by Yves Saint Laurent platform sandals. Jess had always loved the 1960s look, and, with heavy eyeliner and her hair in a jaunty ponytail, she embodied it. She knew she looked more than good – she looked amazing.

'You don't look like Madison,' Beau said flatly, grabbing her roughly by her arm and dragging her into a corner so they could be as far away from prying press eyes as possible. 'You look like Jess.'

Jess rolled her eyes. 'Bollocks,' she said. 'I look *just* like Madison. Only I don't look like a born-again virgin, which is how you want her to look. I can guarantee Madison would be happy with this outfit tonight. It's sexy. Fun. It's perfect.'

'And you know *all* about Madison Miller, don't you, Jessica?' Beau's voice was like ice. 'Right down to every last detail.'

Jess's confidence was wavering, but she refused to lie down and let Beau walk all over her. So what that he was Madison's manager? He was also her boyfriend, and she knew he couldn't fail to be won over by how sexy she looked.

'So you don't like it?' she asked again, biting her lip and refusing to answer Beau's question. She was *sure* that in a second he'd give up his hardball manager act and shoot her a rueful, sexy grin. He was bound to.

'I fucking hate it,' Beau finally said, his lip curling as he struggled not to lose his temper. 'This is your last warning. If you ever break any of my rules again you're out.'

Jess watched Beau's back as he stormed off to talk to some high-level record execs, and for the first time since they'd met, she felt completely alone. She had no friends and no family in America, and even though she loved the city, she barely knew Chicago. Jess could feel her eyes prickle with the tell-tale sign of tears that she couldn't control, so desperate for some respite from the press, who were starting to inch towards her now she was standing by herself, she began to hunt for the restroom.

What was *wrong* with him? Jess could feel the eyes of hundreds of men all over her body as she walked across the dance-floor, but the only man she wanted to impress – the only man in the whole club that she gave a damn about – had just walked away from her, purely because her dress didn't touch her knees. Jesus, she thought angrily, as she pushed open the door to the VIP restroom. It was like being at school again. Next Beau would be issuing detention because she'd rolled a skirt up at the waist to make it look and fit better.

Why did he have to control *everything*? Why couldn't he let go and live a little?

Jess turned to the mirror and began dabbing at her face when she heard vomiting in one of the cubicles. Someone had clearly drunk too much. But just before Jess could offer help, the toilet flushed and a pale face appeared in front of her.

'You took your time,' Pepper Rose drawled, her eyes blood-shot, a glass of clear liquid in one hand. She put the glass down, rummaged in her handbag, took out a couple of pills, and popped them in her mouth, along with a swing of her drink. She was so nonchalant about it that Jess barely even realised what she'd just done.

'I'm not supposed to talk to you,' Jess hissed. 'If Beau catches me I'll be in so much shit.' She wondered what would be safer – locking herself in a cubicle until the girl went away, or daring to go back on the dance-floor with tears rolling down her face. Neither option appealed.

'Honey, it's a restroom. Guys can't come in here,' Pepper said in her smartass tone, and Jess wondered why she'd even bothered to approach the girl at the last party. Bailey was right. She looked like trouble because she *was*.

'What are you doing here, anyway? Following me around the country and crashing all my parties?' Jess had stopped crying now, but she didn't want to go back into the club just yet.

'I wanted to talk to you,' Pepper sighed. 'But I can tell this isn't a good time.' She stared at the tear-stains on Jess's face, and then, surprisingly, reached out a hand to comfort her.

'Talk to me about what?' Jess backed away, suddenly a little scared. Had Madison got herself into something with Pepper Rose that Beau and Bailey didn't know about? Or maybe they *did* know about it, and that was why they were so intent on keeping her away. Jess rubbed her temples gently. Being Madison was fun, but it was a headfuck, too.

Pepper shook her head. 'It can keep.' She handed Jess a card

217

with a New York address and cell phone number on it. 'When you're through with all of this,' she said, 'give me a ring. You and I have more in common than you think. *Madison*.'

Jess winced. Instinctively, she knew she'd been rumbled. Whoever Pepper was – and however she knew Madison – she'd cottoned on that Jess wasn't who she said she was. Jess just didn't know why.

Pepper staggered out of the restroom – she really did drink too much, Jess thought, and she was far too skinny – and as soon as she left Jess locked herself in a cubicle and buried her head in her hands. She had to get herself together, and she had to go out there and put on a brilliant show of being Madison. She was being paid a million dollars to party with the press, and if she didn't do it, well . . . she could wave goodbye to her fashion label, and most probably Beau, too.

Jess couldn't work out which would break her heart the most.

She'd been working the club for a couple of hours – breezing across the dance-floor from one group of people to the next – but Beau was nowhere to be seen. She'd done shots with about ten journalists from the *Chicago Tribune*, sipped champagne delicately with staff from the *Chicago Sun-Times*, and had got on famously with the guys from the *Daily Herald*. Jess had not stopped grinning, talking or laughing for three hours, and even though she had a slight headache from all the booze and the relentless camera flashes, she had to admit the Chicago party was a success. Bailey was ecstatic.

'You know, I don't think we've ever had a party *this* good before,' she announced, raising her champagne flute to Jess. 'This beats your LA party hands down for a totally cool vibe, and it's even better than the legendary ones that Tori Catrino did a couple of years ago.'

'You mentioned her the other day and I completely forgot to speak to you about it. Was Tori on Slate Street?' Jess asked in surprise. Although she didn't care about celebs and gossip, even *she* had heard of Tori. She wondered what had happened to her. One day she'd been the biggest star on the planet and then she just ceased to exist.

Bailey shot her an odd look. 'Drink a lot tonight?'

Jess considered the question and realised that if she couldn't remember, she probably had.

Bailey laughed at her confused expression. 'No problem. It's a party, right? And we're getting paid to have fun!'

Jess tried hard to smile, but Bailey's remark was wide of the mark. She'd give anything to be back in her bedroom at her parents' place in Chelsea, doing nothing but sipping cocoa and watching *Hollyoaks*. God, she missed London. If only she could move Beau out there. Life really would be perfect. Which reminded her . . .

'Have you seen Beau?' she asked Bailey in an urgent tone. She hadn't seen him for hours, and wasn't sure he was even still in the club. Had she pissed him off so much that he'd left the party?

Bailey shrugged. 'Last I saw him he was heading to the VIP room with a couple of execs and told me he didn't want to be disturbed.'

'Not even by me?' Jess knew as soon as she'd spoken the words that she sounded distinctly unlike Madison. She had to act like a popstar and remember that Bailey worked for her. If she wanted to go into the VIP room at her own party, not a soul would stop her. Not even Beau.

'Honey, I'm sure that doesn't include you,' Bailey replied, giving Jess an odd look again.

'I'm going to find him,' Jess announced, and without waiting for a reply she spun on her heel and found the VIP room. The door was closed and the silence from the room was foreboding. If Beau wasn't in there, where was he?

Jess opened the door, not expecting to find anyone – after all, she was the most VIP of all the VIPs in the club, and if anyone should be in there, she should be – and was surprised to find the lights turned off. She was about to leave – clearly nobody had used the room all night – when she heard a sigh. And without thinking about what she was doing, or what she might see, she fumbled against the wall for a light switch.

And then she saw Beau sitting with his trousers around his ankles, and a bottle-blonde teenage girl giving him head.

Beau opened his eyes and stared at Jess, slowly taking in her stricken expression and her wide blue eyes that were filling with tears. He smirked, and when the girl on her knees stopped pleasuring him, he raised his eyebrows, sighed, and gestured for the blonde to join him on the sofa.

Jess was about to turn and run out of the room, the club, and maybe even Chicago, when Beau raised his hand to stop her.

'Don't pull that one with me, *Madison*,' he said, his lips curling into a wide grin. 'And don't act like you've got a problem with this. You know as well as I do that this industry's all about the casting couch, and little Marinka here might well be our new pop sensation. She's certainly good with her mouth . . . although I'm not sure about her voice yet.'

Jess gathered up as much of her strength as she possibly could. She couldn't leave without having the last word. She just couldn't. A lump had appeared in her throat, and her sight was blurry through her tears, but she told herself to get a grip. She had to. If there was ever a time to be strong it was now.

'How could you do this to me?' she asked quietly.

But Beau was unashamed. It was almost as though he was

enjoying the situation, and the girl with him – Marinka – was grinning, too. What a bitch.

'I *told* you not to wear that dress,' Beau said idly, running his hands over Marinka's arms as she sat next to him on the leather banquette. A tiny girl, she had a weasel-like face and looked in need of a good meal. There was no way on earth she was pretty enough to be a popstar, and Jess thought she was going to throw up.

'But you . . .' Her voice cracked with the effort of trying not to cry. 'You said you *loved* me.'

Beau burst out laughing. 'Darling, we say all sorts in the music industry. How many people have told you they love you tonight? Hmm? Hundreds, I bet. Did you believe them?'

'Of course not, but I haven't slept with them!' Jess cried. 'It's their job to tell me they love me so they get good copy out of me! I'm not that stupid!'

Beau sighed impatiently, as if Jess was thick. 'No?' he replied. 'Then maybe I told you I loved you because it was my job, too.'

Jess had heard enough. Without bothering to think of a retort, she let out a little whimper and made her way out of the club as quietly as she could.

Being Madison wasn't as much fun as she thought it would be, and she didn't know how she was going to manage the last two cities of the tour knowing Beau had just been using her.

It was devastating.

Chapter Eighteen

Jess stood on the upper deck of the yacht and looked down at the choppy waters of Galveston Bay. The sky was an inky blue, and if she turned her head she could see the orange lights of Houston just behind her. From what she'd seen of the city – including the Grand 1894 Opera House, and the Toyota Center, where Madison was due to perform on her *Spotlight* tour – she loved it. She just disliked everything else in her life at the moment. Including Beau.

'Smile for the cameras, Madison,' Beau whispered, as he approached her from behind and looped his arms around her body. Despite knowing she had to put on a performance, she couldn't help but tense up. Had it only been a few days ago that she'd caught Beau cheating on her in Chicago? And how could he act as if nothing had happened now they were in Houston? She didn't understand him but she knew the show had to go on.

The photographers called to her and Beau, directing them in what felt like a million poses, and Jess kept her smile frozen throughout. She'd managed to avoid Beau in Chicago after he'd told her he was only pretending to love her, and when they'd arrived in Houston she'd made sure their hotel suite had a camp bed that she'd dragged into the living room so she didn't have to share a bedroom with him. But now, in front of the cameras, she had to make out that she and Beau were madly in love and happily married. It was one of the hardest things she'd ever had to do.

'How about giving your husband a kiss, Madison?' yelled out one of the snappers, and Jess felt her heart drop. She couldn't do it. She just couldn't.

'Come on, Madison, don't be shy,' Beau whispered, and before she could protest, she felt his lips on hers. He gave her a long, lingering kiss, and Jess knew that if she pulled away the photographers would file the photos straight to their newspapers. She couldn't afford to start 'trouble in paradise' rumours for Madison.

'The photocall's over, guys,' Jess said, the minute Beau ended the kiss. She knew it was rude to cut the session short, but she couldn't bear to stand next to Beau for a moment longer. 'I wanna go mingle with everyone. But thanks for taking the time. It was great.'

Jess slowly walked off the deck and onto the dance-floor. A local band was playing some of Madison's tunes from the CD, and as soon as Jess grabbed a glass of champagne from a waiter, Bailey came rushing over.

'How about getting up on that bandstand and singing along?' she suggested excitedly, her blonde ponytail bobbing up and down. 'It would be *so* cool. And it would definitely give the journalists something amazing to write about.'

Jess paled. The last thing she wanted to do was sing. As soon as she opened her mouth the game would be up.

'Um, my singing coach told me I had to rest my voice before the tour,' Jess said quickly, thinking on the spot and wondering if Bailey would believe her.

'Oh come *on*, Madison. I bet you sing in the shower every morning . . . one little song won't hurt.' Bailey pouted. She didn't get Madison sometimes. Most popstars wanted to be the centre of attention *all* the time, but in the last couple of days Madison had wanted to be left alone. Maybe she was getting tired of the promo stuff. She hoped not – it didn't bode well for her energy levels on the tour.

'Really,' Jess said as firmly as she could. She smoothed down her light pink Ralph Lauren dress – which sat just above her knees so as not to antagonise Beau – and stared back at Bailey. 'I don't think it's a good idea, and Beau will agree with me on this one.' If nothing else, she knew Beau would come to her rescue on this. She'd once sung for him, and he agreed she was as tone-deaf as some of the early, laughable applicants on *Teen Star USA*.

Bailey sighed. 'Fine,' she said reluctantly. 'But you'll have to charm everyone here to make up for it.'

So Jess did just that. She spent hours with reporters from the *Houston Chronicle*, chatted into the microphones of some of the local radio stations – spending particular time with KSEV and KNTH, just as she'd been briefed – and even spent a few minutes wowing the students who ran the *Daily Cougar* for the University of Houston. She knew she was doing a great job when Bailey dragged her away from some freelance journalists and told her she could relax.

'This is the third city in a row that's fallen in love with you!' Bailey yelled over the jaunty song the band was playing. 'Why don't you let your hair down and have a dance with me? From this moment you're off duty!'

If Jess hadn't been on a yacht she'd have made her excuses and left for the hotel, but they weren't due to dock for another hour, and there was nothing she could do but dance with her PR girl.

As Jess began to lose herself in the music and the booze, she slowly felt herself start to shake off the numb feeling that had been consuming her since she realised what a snake Beau was. She and Bailey had the time of their lives taking centre stage on the dance-floor, and everyone watching them commented how great it was that Madison and her PR were such good friends.

Jess overheard one such conversation, and as she watched Bailey wiggling her hips, she wished so much that they really *were* friends. She was desperate to tell someone about how much Beau had hurt her . . . but the only person she could really talk to was Poppy, who was a million miles away in London and had thought that pretending to be Madison was a bad idea from the start. Jess knew Poppy wouldn't say that she told her so, but still – she had too much pride to admit that living a popstar's life wasn't all it was cracked up to be.

Bailey shimmied over to her and flung her sweaty body onto hers, wrapping her arms around her neck to give her a hug. Jess hugged her back – God, she was drunk – but she was consumed with sadness. Her friendship with Bailey wasn't real. Nothing was real.

And it was then that she remembered Pepper Rose. Apart from Beau, she was the only person who knew she wasn't really Madison, and that was enough. As she continued to dance with Bailey and some of the drunker journalists, Jess smiled. To-morrow, at least, she could stop the charade of being Madison – even if it was just for one phone call.

'Yeah?' an unfriendly voice slurred at the other end of the phone, and Jess instantly wondered if ringing Pepper Rose was such a good idea. She'd grabbed the phone on the bedside table as soon as Beau had gone downstairs for breakfast – the sham of hundreds of red roses and breakfast in bed had stopped as soon as Jess had sprung him and the girl in Chicago – and although she didn't know Beau's schedule for the day, she knew she wouldn't have many opportunities to make a phone call in private again. Jess – like Madison – always had teams of people around her. They were her entourage, and no popstar was complete without one.

'Um, hi, this is Madison Miller,' Jess said in her best American accent. Was she about to make a terrible mistake? She'd dialled the number a couple of times before hanging up and panicking.

'Where are you?' Pepper snapped.

Jess hesitated. This wasn't the reaction she'd been hoping for. 'Houston, Texas . . .' she began, and heard a long sigh at the other end of the phone.

'Well, I'm visiting friends in LA and you're two hours ahead of me. It's eight in the morning here. You woke me up.'

Jess bit her lip. She'd forgotten how big America was. 'God, I'm so sorry,' she stuttered down the phone. 'I can call back?'

She heard Pepper sigh again, and then a match strike and a deep breath. She was having a cigarette.

'It's cool. I've been waiting for you to phone me, and I don't want to risk you not phoning again.'

There was an awkward pause as both girls remained silent. Jess didn't know what to say next. She'd been hoping Pepper would take the lead, but clearly this wasn't going to happen.

'I was wondering,' Jess began, 'why you came to my party in LA, and then in Chicago. You weren't on the invite list for either, but you managed to crash it. You must have wanted to see me pretty badly.'

Pepper let out a little laugh. It was sweet and girly, and at odds with her harsh, overtly sexy exterior. It briefly reminded Jess of Poppy, and she felt a rush of longing for London. Home.

'I wanted to see Madison, for sure – but you're not Madison, are you?'

Pepper had got straight to the point, and even though it unnerved her, Jess had to respect her for it.

'What makes you think that?'

'Because Madison and I know each other inside out, and honey, you're nothing like her. Sure, you look a *lot* like her, but there's no way you're Madison. You don't even sound like her.'

It was the truth, but it still stung to hear Pepper say it out loud.

'Okay, you got me,' Jess said slowly. 'But if you're such good friends with Madison, why doesn't anyone on Slate Street know that you're pals? Madison's PR hates you because of your reputation . . . not because you're friends with her.'

Pepper snorted. 'You remember when I told you I was faking it, too? Well, I haven't seen Madison in a while, and certainly not since I got famous. We both hung out in New York before Madison met that guy in the strip joint and made it big.'

'So you were a stripper, too?' Jess asked. That made sense. Pepper Rose was trashy and could definitely have worked the crowds in a lap-dancing club. There was no question about that.

'Yeah, I was a stripper,' Pepper said, and she took a long drag on her cigarette. 'But I knew Madison before that, too. We were at school together. We were both even on the cheerleading squad.'

Jess's eyes widened at this. Why hadn't Beau or Bailey mentioned that Pepper Rose had been to school with Madison?

'Does Beau Silverman know that?' she asked distractedly, as she heard a bang from the corridor outside the hotel room. She tried to ignore it and concentrate on the phone call. If word got out that Madison and Pepper Rose were old friends, Madison's career would be over. Madison's image was squeaky clean, and any association with Pepper Rose – especially if coupled with the photos of Madison and Beau getting down and dirty on that beach on Necker – would probably ruin her. Her reputation was still fragile, and Jess wanted to make sure it stayed intact.

'Ha, hardly,' Pepper drawled. 'But I met Beau Silverman. He

came to Spotlight once – that was the name of the strip club, by the way; must be his little joke to name Madison's first tour after it – and I chatted to him. He didn't have time for me, though. He just wanted to meet Madison and get her the hell out of there.'

Jess's mind was spinning. She had so many questions for Pepper, and she didn't know where to start first.

'He only went to Spotlight once? Are you sure?'

'Honey, of course I'm sure. He said he found out about her from some singing teacher, came to the club, had a chat with Madison and then they left. She never came back to the club after that – and Beau definitely didn't.'

'But . . .' Jess's brain was starting to hurt. 'But Beau told me that he went to the strip club every night, and that Madison found out who he was and started blackmailing him.'

Pepper laughed. 'What? Are you kidding me?'

'And that the only reason he made her a star was because she had loads of proof that he was addicted to strip clubs and . . .' Jess's voice trailed off as she remembered what Beau had told her. That Madison had made Beau spent thousands of dollars on her. That he'd been desperately in love with her but that she'd treated him like a dog . . . Suddenly Jess realised it had probably been the other way round.

'Shit, girl, you've been fed quite a few lines, haven't you?' Pepper remarked.

Jess's eyes began to well up with tears. She'd been so stupid! She couldn't believe that she'd been so naive as to assume Beau had been telling her the truth when they'd first met. He'd clearly spotted her in Bungalow 8, noticed she looked just like Madison Miller, and had been spinning her a web of lies from that point on to make her take the job of covering for Madison while she went to rehab – if Madison really *was* in rehab.

228

'Pepper,' Jess said urgently. 'Did Madison ever do drugs when you were friends? Or drink a lot?'

Pepper Rose started laughing again, only this time she sounded a little sad. 'You *really* don't know Madison, do you? She's totally anti-drugs, and she doesn't even like drinking much. She likes to be in control.'

Jess paused. 'So, if I told you Madison was in rehab right now because she's an addict, what would you say?'

'I'd say either you were lying, or you've been told a very big fib and you're dumb enough to believe it.' Pepper suddenly sounded serious and alert.

'I think I'm going to have to admit I've been pretty stupid,' Jess began. 'But if she's not in rehab, where the hell is she?'

Pepper groaned. 'Who knows?' she said. 'When are you meant to stop being Madison – or is this job for ever and ever?'

'I'm only doing it until the *Spotlight* tour starts,' Jess said. 'And then Madison can be Madison again. Beau said that by the time the tour started, she'd be out of rehab and clean.'

She remembered how Madison had reacted when they'd met in LA, how she'd vehemently denied taking drugs. Beau had said she was in denial. But now Jess knew she'd been telling the truth. She remembered Madison's pale face, and how despondently she'd got into the limo. Jess felt terrible.

'You know Madison,' she said. 'Why do you think Beau wanted her out of the way so badly?'

Pepper thought about this for a moment. 'I haven't a clue,' she said finally. 'But Madison's a good girl, you know? She doesn't go on TV to make an ass out of herself like me. She's always kept her nose clean, and she'd never do anything to hurt anyone. She wouldn't have married Beau, either, unless she was really in love with him. Regardless of what she's done, she wouldn't have deserved *this*.'

'Maybe I should try to find her,' Jess began, but Pepper cut her off.

'And risk fucking off Beau? Girl, I don't know what Beau's up to, but I really wouldn't cross him. You don't know what will happen.'

'So what am I meant to do?' Jess asked desperately. She felt awful, and her head hurt with the realisation that she'd been Beau's accomplice in removing Madison from her own life and career. It was despicable.

'I'd do nothing,' Pepper said finally. 'Act like you haven't spoken to me, act like you still think Madison's been off her head on drugs and that rehab's the best place for her. Then, when the tour's about to start, she can come back, you can disappear, and that should be the end of it.'

'And what are you going to do?' Jess wondered in a small voice. She was abruptly aware that she'd been incredibly indiscreet on the phone to a stranger – and a stranger that Slate Street had no time for, too.

'I'm gonna sit tight and wait for Madison to reappear, too. We've got lots of catching up to do . . . I really need to see her. Maybe I can grab her when she's on her tour. Maybe. Or if you see her, could you tell her I was looking for her? Give her my number and address?'

Jess smiled. Even though she knew she couldn't trust anyone but herself any more, Pepper had told her the truth about Madison, and she was more grateful than Pepper could know.

'Of course I could. I'd be happy to. Um . . . you promise you won't go to the press with all of this?' Jess hated to ask it, but she knew she had to. From what she'd heard about Pepper, the girl was determined to become famous – and there was always the risk that she'd use this story to propel herself in the papers.

'Girl, Madison was my best friend at school, and I'd never do anything to hurt her or risk messing up her career, and to be honest, I have enough on my plate without any more media attention. I think we're the same like that, right?'

'Right,' Jess agreed. Despite what Bailey had said about Pepper Rose, she seemed nice. Friendly. Normal. And even though they barely knew each other, it gave Jess a warm feeling to know that someone else in America knew her for who she was, and not just as Madison. 'Can I phone you again, do you think? If I hear anything about Madison?'

Jess could sense Pepper's grin. 'Sure,' she said. 'But honey, you really should tell me your name – your *real* name, I mean. I can't keep calling you "girl", and I'm definitely not calling you Madison.'

Jess smiled. 'I'm Jess. Jessica Piper,' she said in her British accent.

'And I,' Pepper said, 'am not really called Pepper Rose at all. I mean, that's just my stage name. When I'm not on set – or stupid reality TV shows that have been edited to make me look like a slut – I'm Leesa Harland.'

Coming back to New York was like coming home, Jess thought, as the Slate Street private jet circled over the Hamptons before landing on a tiny airfield. Manhattan was the final stop on the promo tour, and the one Jess was looking forward to the most. Now she was in New York she could go back to her apartment – well, the one Beau had rented for her in his building – and start to relax. Yes, she had a million interviews and a couple of parties to go to, but she *knew* New York, and she wasn't going to be trapped in a hotel with Beau or Bailey. She would have her own space again, which was exactly what she needed.

During the flight from Houston, Jess had done nothing but think about Madison and their brief meeting. It seemed such a long time ago, and after speaking to Pepper – or Leesa, as she reminded herself – she'd realised how immature and foolish she'd been. Madison must hate her for what she'd done, she thought. She hated herself.

What kind of girl, she asked herself with uncomfortable honesty, broke up with her fiancé on the phone, and then suddenly decided not to go back to London? And what kind of girl, she thought angrily, would meet a man in a bar, and, just because he was friendly, would believe his lies and end up agreeing to 'stand in' for the most famous popstar on the planet?

As Jess considered how irresponsible and thoughtless she'd been, hot, angry tears ran down her face. She'd turned to look out of the window so nobody would spot her crying, but even if they had, nobody would have said anything. Everyone on the plane – apart from Beau – thought Jess was Madison Miller, and nobody would dare be so disrespectful as to ask her what was wrong. Not many popstars would confide in 'the staff', and Jess was pretty sure Madison was no different.

The worst thing of all, Jess realised, as she tormented herself during the three-hour flight, was that not only had she fallen for Beau's lies – which, the more she thought about them, had been pretty incredulous – but she'd fallen for Beau himself. Even now, as she looked across at him, she could see why she'd been so attracted to him. His black hair and black eyes looked even darker set against his tan, and his expensive suits gave off the scent of success. But it wasn't just about his looks. He was so powerful, so sexual, that she hadn't been able to resist him. Beau knew how to play women, and Jess hadn't been aware that she was a bit part in his wider game.

She was just the stand-in, just someone who could help him make money. That he'd been sleeping with her – well, that was a bit of fun on the side for him, and nothing more.

'*Madison*,' Bailey said, in a way that so reminded her of Faye at the *Daily World* that she jumped, 'I asked did you want to take the helicopter to Manhattan with Beau, or the limo with me?'

Jess turned to the PR girl, who was looking at her intently, and smiled. It was time to stop thinking like Jess for the moment and to turn back into Madison.

'Limo,' she said easily, with a grin. 'I've had enough of being in the air for one day, and I'd like to go over the interview schedule for tomorrow with you. That okay with you, Beau?' She shot Beau a sexy smile, and he mirrored her expression, playing along.

'No problem, Madison,' he said. 'See you back at the apartment later?'

Jess nodded, but they both knew Jess would be going back to her own apartment that night, and not his. That side of their arrangement was well and truly over.

Chapter Nineteen

Despite the slow news day, and rumours of budget cuts and redundancy, the newsroom was electric with excitement. Even though celebrities dropped by the paper all the time – Jessica Simpson, David Letterman and Russell Brand had all been to the newsroom to do in-house interviews and photos in recent weeks – today was different. Everyone, from the messengers in the mailroom to the senior editors, kept looking up from their work to see if she'd arrived yet, and when they couldn't see her, they went back to what they were doing, disappointed. Everyone knew she was coming in, and nobody could stand it for much longer.

When she did walk in, she all but silenced the idle chatter, and let the hundreds of pairs of eyes take her in with a gracious smile. Jess knew that a decent celeb visiting a newsroom was the high-light of a bored journalist's day – God, it hadn't been so long ago that she'd been the one desperate for distraction – and as the men stared at her body with lust, and the girls envied her clothes, Jess couldn't help but feel a million dollars.

She was wearing a cobalt-blue Alice Temperley dress cinched in with a black patent belt, and even though it covered her up and nearly touched her knees – as per Beau's controlling require-ments – there was no denying she was still sexy as hell. Her dark blue Jimmy Choo stilettos made her legs look even longer, and her brunette hair swung in shiny waves onto her shoulders. She was effortlessly gorgeous, and the stares confirmed it. If ever there was a moment she'd remember from playing the part of Madison Miller, it was this.

'And this is our newsdesk,' stuttered the work experience girl – who'd been told to collect 'Madison', Bailey, Phil and Jason from reception. 'And over here is our showbiz section. Giles is the showbiz editor. As you probably know . . .'

Her voice trailed off as she delivered Jess to Giles's office. Unlike everyone else in the huge *New York Star* newsroom, he was the only person who wasn't paying attention to her. He was on the phone, and he was annoyed.

'Look,' he said, his English accent making his tone both polite and crisp, 'if we can't stand the story up we're not going to run it. It's that simple.'

There was a pause, while Giles listened to the person on the other end of the receiver. He sighed and jiggled his foot. Jess liked his shoes – they were John Lobb.

'The PR and I go way back, and if she says the story isn't true, it isn't true. I don't care if the *Sun* or the *Mail* in the UK are running it. I'm not prepared to annoy people and get *us* sued.'

Jess stood in Giles's doorway, holding the copy of the paper she'd been reading in reception. It had been ages since she'd been in a newsroom, and standing in the showbiz section of the *New York Star* got her heart racing again. She remembered just how much she hated the yelling, the adrenalin, and the rush to meet daily deadlines.

Giles caught her eye, smiled, and then concentrated on his call again. Whatever the person on the other end of the phone was saying, it was starting to rile him.

'Take it to the *Post* then,' Giles said evenly. 'Get them sued. And while you're at it, don't bother trying to sell us stories again.

The *Star* isn't prepared to risk a lot of money on something like this. I have *integrity*. Oh, and a word of advice? If you're going to get quotes from people, make sure they don't email me in advance saying you paid them to make the interview up.'

He put the phone down, took a deep breath, and ran his hands through his hair. Like Matthew Parker, his hair was light brown, but it had more reddish tones than blonde. And like Matthew, he was well built. His shirt strained slightly as he put his hands behind his head, and despite telling herself not to look, Jess couldn't help but catch sight of the muscles of his torso outlined under the thin cotton.

'Hi there, I'm Giles Tavener. Great to meet you,' he said, standing up and apparently forgetting all about the phone call. Jess took his hand in his and felt an electric shock. If Giles felt it, too, he didn't react.

'Everyone at the *New York Star*'s a massive fan of yours, Madison. We supported you on *Teen Star*, and, hey, even the sports department got in on the act. I don't know if you can see their desks over there,' Giles continued, walking out of his office a few steps ahead of Jess, 'but they have several posters of you up. You're the office babe of the year.'

He spun round to look at her, and grinned when he saw she'd blushed. He assumed it was because Madison Miller was touched to have her poster up in the newsroom of one of the biggest dailies in America, but actually it was because she'd been checking out his ass, and when he'd turned round, her eyes had accidentally lingered on his groin. Hopefully he hadn't noticed. It wouldn't do for Madison – the biggest popstar on the planet, who was also 'happily married' – to be checking out journalists, even if they were cute.

'And I'm Bailey, Slate Street's head of PR,' Bailey said smoothly. 'It's *so* great to finally meet you, Giles.'

Giles shook her manicured hand. 'The famous Bailey Brinton, in the flesh,' he commented. 'I can't believe we've never met before, considering all the showbiz bashes we both go to in the city.'

'I know, it's so stupid,' Bailey agreed. She'd adopted a breathy, girly voice, and she was still holding Giles's hand. 'But you know, if we *had* ever been to the same party, I'm sure I'd have recognised you.'

Jess watched Bailey in amusement. She'd not taken her eyes off Giles, and even though she'd finally let go of his hand, she was still standing incredibly close to him. Bailey flirted all the time, but not normally on this level. She obviously thought Giles was cute, too.

'And I you,' Giles said smoothly. 'After all, you're a celeb PR legend.'

Bailey beamed. 'And how's your girlfriend back in England?' she asked.

Jess tried not to smile. For a PR, Bailey was *so* indiscreet.

'Oh, she's fine, thanks for asking. She's currently buggered off to France to her parents' place for a holiday. Would have loved to join her, but I only get eleven days off a year. It sucks.'

Bailey patted his arm. 'But what you lose in vacation time you make up for by being in the best city in the world. *And* you get an exclusive interview with Madison Miller.'

Giles narrowed his eyes. 'Isn't New York the last stop on a travelling promo junket before Madison does her tour?' he said. 'How's this interview exclusive?'

Bailey laughed. 'It's the only one she's doing this morning.'

Giles smiled, before turning back to Jess. He'd had enough of the small talk.

'How about you and I go into a meeting room – without your entourage?' he asked.

Jess shot Bailey a concerned look, but she needn't have worried. Bailey was focusing hard on trying not to look like she cared.

'Madison, if it's cool with you it's cool with me,' she said as flippantly as she could. 'I've got tons of errands to catch up on, so you'd be doing me a favour. I can take Phil and Jason with me – so long as you don't want them?'

'The *New York Star* has watertight security,' Giles interrupted. 'I don't see anyone papping or pestering you up here, Madison.'

He was right. They were on the twenty-ninth floor of a skyscraper, and security guards were walking around, as well as guarding the various different entrances on the ground floor.

'Yeah, it's cool,' Jess said, concentrating carefully on her American accent. It had been a while since she'd spoken to anyone English, and she didn't want to accidentally mimic Giles. 'See you in an hour?'

Bailey nodded, and Giles led Jess down several corridors into a wood-panelled room with plush cream carpets. A butler stood patiently outside the door. There were oil portraits on the walls, cut-glass tumblers next to bottles of water, and fresh flowers in expensive-looking vases. The room was so different from the newsroom that Jess fell silent as she took it all in. Giles misread her silence for awe.

'Interesting room, isn't it?' he asked her.

Jess looked around. The skyscraper seemed new – and had probably been built in the 1980s – but this room had been created to suggest it was old and traditional. Jess hated it. She knew it was hypocritical, given she was pretending to be Madison Miller, but she couldn't stand pretence.

'It certainly is,' she remarked softly. 'And are those old guys there the proprietors?' She nodded at two paintings that hung under lights on the far wall. They looked as though Rolf Harris had painted them.

'Yep,' Giles said, leaning against the table in the middle of the room and staring at them. 'They like to say they don't interfere editorially, but they do. They can't help it.' He turned to Jess. 'And I would, too, if I were them. You can't blame them. Their little newspaper is a toy.'

Jess smiled and sat down. 'Newspapers aren't toys,' she said. 'And they can ruin people's lives.'

Instantly, she regretted what she'd just said. Being at the *New York Star* had reminded her of her time at the *Daily World* – and how Matthew and the other news journalists had seen victims of gruesome crimes merely as names on newsprint rather than real people – but she *had* to remember she was Madison Miller, and not Jessica Piper, former journalist on a British newspaper.

It was hard.

Giles raised his eyebrow. 'You mean they help *make* people's lives,' he said. 'I'm not saying we won *Teen Star* for you because you're an incredible singer, but you wouldn't have done it without all the press coverage. You'd have been a nobody on a TV programme.'

Jess bit her lip. She wanted to argue with the man in front of her, but there was no way Madison would have done that. She'd have smiled sweetly and thanked him for all the coverage. She probably would have gushed.

'What?' Giles challenged, as he caught her expression. 'Are you going to say that the media exposure didn't make a bit of difference?'

'Of course it helped,' Jess replied, instantly riled. 'But just as the media has power to make people stars it has the power to take stardom away, too. Just on a whim.'

Giles shrugged. 'So?' he asked. He'd not pressed record on his

Dictaphone yet, so everything they'd said so far was off the record, but Madison Miller clearly wasn't quite what he'd expected.

Jess took a deep breath. She had to stop behaving like this right now, and she had to cut the attitude. She didn't understand it. She'd spoken to hundreds of journalists on this press tour, and it hadn't bothered her at all. But now she was in a newspaper office, with Giles Tavener in front of her, she just couldn't seem to help herself.

'So I don't think it's nice, is all,' she said. 'It seems like celebrity is now only about how much media coverage you can get, and less about actual talent. And the gossip columns – like yours, like those blogs – only make it worse. A photo of someone flashing their breasts gets more interest than someone doing something for a good cause, and I think that's wrong.'

'But it's the real world,' Giles said bluntly. 'Sex and scandal sells.'

Jess shrugged. 'And so, it seems, does ruining a person's career.' She put the copy of the *New York Star* on the table between them. She'd kept it open at Giles's column ever since she'd read it in the foyer.

'Why are you picking on Pepper Rose?' she demanded. 'I'm asking because this piece about her is kind of brutal, and the only thing she seems to have done is fallen out of a club in LA and been papped.'

Giles looked at her incredulously. 'You can't be serious,' he said. 'You of all people should know how much America hates a good villain. It wasn't so long ago that the whole country hated you just because you were having an affair with your manager.'

Jess flushed. She'd briefly forgotten about how Madison and Beau had been caught out. 'Exactly,' she said, hurrying to make it look as though that's why she was so annoyed. 'I'd not done anything wrong but the press was baying for my blood.'

Giles crossed his arms. 'Because the people were. We're the voice of the people.'

Jess stood up. 'No, you're *not*,' she said angrily. 'You use that as an excuse. You trash people – like Pepper Rose here – for no good reason other than you like to be bitchy, because you think it gives people a good laugh. Well, it's not funny. Pepper's a decent girl, and she doesn't deserve this kind of treatment.' Her voice had started to wobble, and she was sure her American accent wasn't holding up too well, but she was so annoyed she didn't care.

Giles laughed. 'I'm assuming that because I've not turned on my Dictaphone this is all off the record?' he asked, clearly not quite able to believe what had just happened. The most famous girl on the planet – who was touring America to charm the media so she could have a sell-out tour – had just stood in the *New York Star*'s boardroom, and slated the press and the temple of celebrity. Nobody would believe it in a million years.

'Damn right it's off the record,' Jess murmured. 'Or are you going to try and ruin my career, too?'

Giles laughed again. He'd been prepared to write Madison Miller off as another air-brained celeb who was only interested in herself, fashion and other celebrities – in that order. But the girl in front of him, although spiky, clearly had some depth. And she was the first famous person who'd interested him on a personal level as well as a professional one for a long time.

'I'm going to give you the greatest coverage in the world,' Giles said easily, standing up and gazing into her eyes. 'But only if you come for dinner with me tonight and then give me a proper interview tomorrow. What do you think?'

Jess was so confused that she didn't know what to say. Was he hitting on her? He had a girlfriend in England, didn't he?

'You can come to my party at Chromosome X and interview me then,' she said, finally. He was annoying, so why did she kind of want to go for dinner with him? In any case, she couldn't. She was Madison Miller and she was *married*.

'I was coming to that anyway. I'm VIP. Bailey made sure of it,' Giles remarked with a smile, and Jess was infuriated again. He really thought he was someone special.

'Well, you're not coming as one of Slate Street's VIP guests any more,' she snapped. 'You're coming as a jobbing journo, and if you're nice, and if you're polite, I might give you and your newspaper five minutes of my time. Have a nice day, okay?' she said as civilly as she could, and with that she marched out of the boardroom, out of the newspaper's offices, and waited in the reception area on the ground floor for Phil and Jason to collect her.

As she waited, all she could think about were Giles's laughing brown eyes, and how infuriating all journalists could be.

Chromosome X was *the* coolest club in Manhattan. It was so exclusive that only a handful of New Yorkers had heard of it, although, after tonight, that was going to change. By hosting Madison Miller's final pre-tour party, it had been guaranteed hundreds of column inches in all the gossip magazines, and to celebrate bagging one of the hottest parties of the year, the club had pulled out all the stops. Life-size posters of Madison plastered every wall, well-known magazine models walked around the dance-floor with glasses of champagne and caviar canapés, a DJ from Ibiza had been flown in for the night, and if you were into drugs, they were available, too. Slate Street wanted to make sure everyone had a *really* good time.

All the major Slate Street stars were hanging out and entertaining the guests, and it seemed as if every Manhattan celebrity – from Sarah Jessica Parker to Mariah Carey to David Blane – was there, chewing the fat and having a blast.

Jess slowly walked around the dance-floor and tried to look blasé. Ever since she'd stepped into Madison's life she'd been overwhelmed by what she'd experienced – especially the designer clothes and the Slate Street private jet. Whatever Jess wanted, she got – but this party, all in aid of her – well, *Madison*, she reminded herself – was something else.

It was exclusive, it was expensive and it was hers. It was amazing.

'This is some party,' an English accent muttered in her ear, and Jess turned. It was Giles. He was still dressed for the office in a black suit and white shirt, but the effect was effortlessly good-looking and classical. Jess tried not to check him out. What would be the point? She couldn't date anyone while she was still 'Madison', and even if she could, she wouldn't go near Giles. Not only did he have a girlfriend, but he was a journalist, too. Jess would never date either type of man again.

'Can I get you a drink?' Giles smiled at her easily, and immediately Jess was riled. He clearly knew he was good-looking and charming, and it only turned her off. And who did he think he was, flirting with Madison Miller? She was totally out of his league.

'I'm good, thanks,' Jess said as coldly as she could, and turned her back to him. There were hundreds of people in the room – most of them celebrities – and she hoped that Giles would leave to try and wheedle some titbits out of them for his column.

'Are you sure?' he pressed on. 'I could get you some champagne, or something a bit more interesting . . . like whisky? Or tequila?'

Jess tried not to roll her eyes. 'Really, I'm fine. But help yourself,' she said.

'Maybe I'll have some champagne,' he remarked, as he took a flute from a tray carried by one of the most gorgeous girls Jess had ever seen. She was far too pretty to be a waitress. 'I don't drink tequila any more,' Giles said conversationally, not even noticing the waitress, who was gazing at him from under her long eyelashes. 'It's how I ended up on a plane to New York in the first place.'

Jess signed and turned to him. 'What do you mean?' she said, finally. She had to admit Giles was good. He'd got her interested.

'I lost a drinking game with my editor,' he explained, 'and the consolation prize was to come and work here. Turned out all right in the end, though. I love New York, and I get to meet very pretty popstars like you.'

Despite herself, Jess couldn't help but smile. 'Which paper did you work on in London?' she asked.

Giles raised his eyebrows. 'Don't tell me you're an American singer who actually knows about papers in England?' he asked in mock horror. 'I bet you couldn't even name three.'

Jess looked at him sweetly. 'Why, how many newspapers are there in Britain?'

Giles thought about it for a moment. 'Why don't you tell me?' he said finally, with a cunning look in his eyes. He'd been hoping to put Madison Miller in her place since she'd walked out of the newsroom and his interview, and now was a great time to do it. Popstars liked to think they knew everything.

'And what if I can tell you all of them?' Jess asked lightly. 'What do I win?' She was aware that Bailey was watching them, and that she could only really spend a few moments with each journalist if she was to speak to all of them, but she couldn't help it. Everything about Giles Tavener annoyed her. He was cocksure and smarmy, and she wanted to show him up.

Giles caught her gaze and held it. 'Whatever you want,' he said in a low voice, and despite herself, Jess felt a shiver run through her body. He knew Madison was the biggest star on the planet, and that she was married to Beau Silverman, but he still couldn't help himself.

'Good,' she commented briskly, and paused. 'There are about twenty, I think,' she said, and reeled off the names of all the national papers in the UK, from the *Star* to the *Guardian*.

Giles looked dumbfounded.

'I think that's all of them, isn't it?' she remarked coolly. 'Unless you'd like me to name the Scottish and Welsh ones, too?'

Giles managed to shake his head, and Jess beamed at him.

'Cool. Well, I'll think about what prize I want for that, and I'll let you know what I've decided,' she said. 'It will have to be a *big* one, though,' she remarked, with a quick look at his groin, and then she spun on her heel and walked away, silently thanking Matthew Parker for his obsession and non-stop chatter about the British nationals.

'Ladies and gents, may I have your attention, please?' Beau was standing on the club's stage, microphone in hand. His black hair and eyes gleamed under the violet lights of the stage, and he was everything all American businessmen aspired to be: powerful, well groomed and clearly a hit with the ladies.

'Tonight we're here to celebrate Slate Street's newest and most sensational star, Madison Miller.' Beau's eyes caught Jess's, and he nodded, ever so slightly. That was her cue. As everyone clapped, Jess slowly climbed the stairs to the top of the stage and took her place next to Beau. He was wearing a black suit with a gold tie, and she knew that, in her shimmering bronze maxi-dress, she looked good next to him, that they looked sensational together. He was large, almost bear-like, and she was tiny and delicate. They were the ultimate in how to be a celebrity couple: savvier than Posh and Becks; more wholesome than Brad and Angelina; more *normal* than Tom Cruise and Katie Holmes. They had everything other celeb couples wanted but couldn't get. They were – apparently – *credible*.

As the cameras flashed, Jess automatically shot the crowd her best Madison Miller smile, and once again performed her heart out. Little did anyone know that inside she was cringing. Thank God the promo tour was nearly over, Jess thought, as her eyes sparkled at the journalists gawping up at her. She'd loved being a famous popstar at the beginning of her job but she hated it now. It was just too hard.

'I first came across Madison when she applied to be on Slate Street's prime-time show, *Teen Star USA*,' Beau continued, blithely unaware of Jess's discomfort. 'And the moment she started to sing I knew she was more than just one of the most gorgeous girls I'd ever seen. Madison has – and I think you'll agree – one of the most special singing voices of her generation. No other female singer in the country can match her.'

The applause that had greeted Jess as she'd climbed onto the stage returned, only louder. Beau raised his voice and leant into the microphone.

'Of course,' he said, with a wry grin, 'when it comes to Madison's talents I'm biased. Not only am I lucky enough to have Madison signed to Slate Street, but I'm also lucky enough to call her my wife.' He reached over to Jess and kissed her passionately on the lips, and Jess felt her whole body go limp. If there was ever a time to pretend to be Madison – the Madison who was madly in love with her husband – it was now. She kissed Beau back, and afterwards they gazed into each other's eyes. Everyone watching was spellbound. Madison and Beau truly were the most captivating couple, and the cheers grew louder in celebration of their partnership.

Bailey took another sip of her champagne as she watched Giles Tavener from the *New York Star* push through the crowds to get to the back of the club. She sighed. For some reason or another Madison's interview with him hadn't happened, and it didn't look as if he was going to hang around tonight to get a few words out of her. It was too bad, she thought. Her eyes followed him to the silver double doors that led into the foyer, then lingered on a couple that had just arrived. The woman had flame-red hair, and she was staring up at the stage with a hand over her mouth. The large man standing next to her was gripping onto her arm tightly, but before Bailey could get a proper look at them, Beau and Madison were leaving the stage, and it suddenly seemed as though a hundred journalists wanted her attention. She turned to the most insistent one and flashed a practised smile.

She put the couple – and Giles Tavener – out of her mind. They were nobodies.

Chapter Twenty

Jess stared at the *New York Star* in disbelief. Instead of a glittering, gushing article about the Madison Miller New York party — as there was in all the other newspapers and magazines — there, taking up most of the showbiz section, was a large photo of Pepper Rose looking super-skinny and out of it. A scathing piece about her drug-taking accompanied the picture. Giles Tavener had written it, of course, and he looked smarmier than ever in his byline photo. Jess scanned the rest of the spread, looking for a mention of the party. There was nothing. They'd been ignored.

Jess was annoyed. 'How dare he?' she complained, as Bailey walked into the Slate Street office where Jess had been reading the press coverage. 'How can he completely snub our party? And how can he do this to Pepper Rose *again*? He's totally on her case.'

Bailey raised her eyebrows and took a sip of her latte. 'What do you care about Pepper Rose?' she asked casually, casting her eye over the piece. Like all good PRs, she'd read the party coverage before even getting out of bed. She never came to the office without being 100 per cent prepared. 'If the stupid girl wants to take drugs and sleep around publicly, let her. It's the only way she'll get in the paper, although she's not going to get sympathy from anyone. She's not pretty enough.'

Jess was silenced for a moment. Think like Madison, she

248

thought. Think like Madison and act like Madison. 'It's just mean, that's all,' she said finally. 'I hated it when the press did this shit to me and Beau, and I don't think it's fair that they're doing it to Pepper Rose.'

Bailey shrugged, and pushed her blonde hair away from her face. 'She's asking for it. You should be more pissed that there's nothing in there about you. What happened to our great piece that Giles guaranteed me?' Bailey raised her eyebrows, and for the first time since she'd been playing the part of Madison Miller, Jess realised she'd messed up.

'We didn't do the interview . . .' she began slowly. 'And then we didn't really get to talk properly at the party. You know, apart from small talk.' Jess remembered how obviously she'd flirted with the journalist and struggled not to blush. She shouldn't have done that. 'I was ready to be interviewed, but I think Giles left early.'

'Well, when Beau sees this he's not gonna be happy. Lucky for you your favourite PR wonder-woman is on the ball. Giles has agreed to a lunch, today, with you. You're to give the best interview of your life, and he's gonna run it as soon as.'

Jess bit her lip. 'Today was meant to be a day off,' she said. 'We've been working so hard for weeks, and I was hoping to do a bit of shopping, maybe go to a spa . . .' She just wanted to be left alone so she could read English *Vogue* and chill out, but she trailed off when she saw Bailey's expression.

'You need to sort this out, Madison,' Bailey said. 'And you need to do it pronto. When Beau reads the *New York Star* and sees there's nothing in there, we're gonna have to say it's because they're running a special on you – and you need to be with Giles sorting it out when he asks. But hey, it's your career, not mine.'

Jess felt terrible. So what if she was exhausted? She'd agreed to be the custodian of Madison's career, and she wasn't doing it properly. After how Madison had been treated by Beau, putting on a good performance in an interview was the very least she could do.

'Of course I'll do it,' Jess said, and she smiled, although her heart was sinking. She didn't want to come face to face with Giles Tavener again. The attraction between them was just too dangerous.

'I didn't know if you liked sushi, but I figured that as you're a popstar you'll eat anything low-fat,' Giles said, sticking out his hand to shake Jess's. She'd just climbed out of the Slate Street limo alone – she'd managed to convince Bailey she didn't need bodyguards today – and was immediately offended. She reluctantly took Giles's hand, shook it once, and then dropped it as though it was on fire.

Because despite being annoying, self-satisfied and arrogant, Jess begrudgingly admitted to herself that Giles Tavener was one of the best-looking men she'd ever met. He was tall, fit and handsome . . . and clearly knew his stuff. Jess allowed herself to run her eyes over his face – because he was quite obviously clocking *her* in her peach Herve Leger bandage dress – and the more she took in, the more she was attracted to him. He was everything Beau was not. His face was warm and friendly, and when he smiled, tiny crinkles appeared around his brown eyes. He had a smattering of freckles on his slightly lopsided nose – which diluted his sexiness with cuteness – and he was freshly shaven. He was, without question, traditionally handsome, and just the sort of man Jess told everyone she didn't go for.

So why, she asked herself in a tiny voice, was she so attracted to him?

'I love sushi,' Jess said, struggling to pull her eyes away from his. 'It's one of my favourite foods.'

'Did you eat a lot of it in Ohio when you were growing up? It doesn't strike me as the sort of place that would have hundreds of sushi restaurants,' Giles said, holding open the door to the restaurant. He had good manners, Jess thought. She had to give him that.

'We mainly ate proper American food back home,' Jess said, thinking on her feet. 'You know, burgers and corn on the cob . . . the usual stuff.'

'So when did you get into sushi?' Giles asked, once they'd been seated in a corner, under a ceiling of bamboo rods.

Jess was about to say 'in Leeds' and caught herself in time. 'Um . . . when I moved to New York just after winning *Teen Star*.' She noticed Giles had put a Dictaphone on the table between them, and had pressed 'record'. They were rolling. Time to move into interview mode. 'New York is such an amazing city,' she continued, in a perky voice. 'It's really opened my eyes to so many cultures and possibilities.'

'Like sushi,' Giles remarked dryly.

'Yes, like sushi,' she continued, ignoring his tone. 'And culture. New York's brimming with it, and I love the museums and art galleries.' She prayed he wouldn't ask which ones. Jess hadn't had the time to play the tourist. She'd been too busy being Madison Miller, international popstar.

Giles ordered for both of them – a selection of sushi and sashimi that glistened on the square plates – and then he raised a glass of sake to her. 'To culture, then,' he said, before taking a sip. Jess reluctantly did the same. She'd been drinking almost non-stop because of all the parties, and she desperately wanted a few days off alcohol.

'So what's this interview about? What's the angle?' she asked conversationally, as they began eating.

'The public *still* can't get enough of your rags to riches story,'

Giles said. 'So I thought we'd do more of the same. You'll tell me about your childhood and how you desperately wanted to become a popstar, and then through hard graft on *Teen Star USA* and the coincidental pairing of you and the Slate Street MD, you found your fairytale happy ending.'

On the surface nothing that Giles had said was offensive, but Jess was infuriated. He made it sound so *easy*. Of course, Giles didn't know anything about the stripping, and how Beau had manipulated her – and God forbid he found out – but it still riled. It wasn't like that.

'So it's going to be a nice piece?' Jess asked, with wide innocent eyes. 'Not like what you did to Pepper Rose this morning?'

Giles sighed. 'Are we back here again?' he asked.

Jess leant over and turned the Dictaphone off. 'I just don't get it. What's your problem with her? Why are you ruining her career?'

Giles laughed. 'What career? Her reality TV fame? Sweetheart, even *you* know that if she wasn't papped without her knickers she'd be history. It's the only thing keeping her famous.'

Jess shook her head in disbelief. 'Maybe she's doing other things, like acting. Maybe you're just not giving her a chance. But I know for a fact that no girl wants to be in the papers showing her private parts.'

'You're still such the innocent, despite being one of the most famous girls on the planet,' Giles said teasingly. 'Pepper knows what she's doing, and she wants the exposure, if you excuse the pun. It's what she lives for – male attention. She was a stripper, after all.'

'You know about that?' Jess asked in a tiny whisper. 'How do you know about that?'

252

Giles rolled his eyes. 'Madison, I'm a *journalist*. Finding out about people is what I do. Now, can we get off the subject of Pepper Rose and back to you? Or have you got some stupid moral issue about us running a piece on you in the *Star*?'

Jess struggled to keep her temper. 'Of course not,' she said haughtily.

'Well then,' Giles said in a satisfied tone. 'You're happy enough for us to run a fawning piece about the Madison Miller machine, just as Pepper Rose is happy for us to run pieces about the fact she hates wearing knickers.' He clicked the Dictaphone on again, but Jess wasn't about to let his last remark go.

'You talk as if ruining a girl's life is just part of the job to you. I think it's disgusting.' Jess was aware that her voice was wobbling, and she was about to stand up and leave – sod the interview, she'd tell Beau that Giles had made a pass at her or something – when she noticed two girls standing by their table. They were trembling with excitement.

'Can we . . . can we get your autograph?' The first girl brandished a piece of paper, and Jess took it and wrote Madison's signature with a flourish.

'It's nice to meet you, girls,' she said, snapping out of her mood and into the slick, Madison professional she hoped she was. 'Are you coming to my tour?'

The second girl nodded. She was so thrilled she could barely speak. 'We're coming to two nights . . . it's all we could get tickets for.'

Jess beamed. 'And what's your favourite song? Let me know and I'll dedicate it to you.'

The first girl blushed bright red and named a couple of Madison's better-known songs. 'That would be awesome, thanks so much.'

Just then, several more girls appeared, and Giles and Jess were completely surrounded. 'Um, girls, it's been lovely talking to you, but I'm in the middle of an interview,' Jess said as kindly as she could. 'Perhaps if you could give us some space we can chat afterwards?'

One of the girls started to speak, but was interrupted by a scuffle near the door. Suddenly there were camera flashes everywhere. They were being papped, and they were trapped.

'Shit,' Giles said. 'I'll get rid of them, and then we should get out of here.' He flung some money onto the table to pay for the meal, and after ten minutes of coaxing and negotiating, the paparazzi agreed to stand on the sidewalk to give them some breathing space. The girls all looked awestruck. Not only had they just met Madison Miller – in the flesh! – but they'd been there when she was papped! Maybe they'd be in some of the photos when they made it onto the web.

'Where are we going to go?' Jess asked Giles nervously, as they negotiated their way out of the restaurant and into the waiting limo. The paparazzi were following them, and as the limo sped out of the East Village into the direction of Gramercy, Giles peered out of the blacked-out windows, thinking hard.

'Let's just stay in here,' he said finally. He lowered the screen to separate them from the driver, and as they drove around Manhattan with the paparazzi on their tail, they breathed sighs of relief. They were away from prying lenses. The photographers had no way of snapping either of them so long as they remained in the plush leather seats of the car.

'Thank you for rescuing me,' Jess said softly, and looked up at Giles. He'd been watching the paps, but turned back to face her. They were so close that suddenly both of them were aware just how private their setting was. Nobody could see or hear them, and the small space made their surroundings even more intimate.

'Not a problem,' Giles said, after a pause. 'I worked with some paps back in England, and I know the drill. They're just doing their jobs – as I am – but sometimes they push it just a little too far. You've got to know how to handle them.'

'Well, you handled it really well,' Jess said. She was impressed. Beau would have got some heavies to sort the photographers out, but Giles had reasoned with them.

'As a reward, will you let me do this bloody interview? Finally?' Giles asked, cracking a grin.

Jess leant back in her seat. 'As if I could deny my knight in shining armour his livelihood,' she teased.

She took the Dictaphone from Giles's hands, turned it on, and then spent the next half an hour answering his questions. It wasn't a probing interview, but there was something about it that made it . . . intense. Jess really felt that Giles was genuinely interested in Madison Miller, that he wasn't just asking run-of-the-mill questions because he had to get decent copy out of her. She felt his eyes run over her face as she spoke, and for the first time since she'd been interviewing as Madison, she felt as though the interviewer cared. It unnerved her.

'But what about you?' Jess asked Giles, as he finished the interview and turned the Dictaphone off. 'You know everything there is to know about Madison Miller, but I know hardly anything about you.'

Giles smiled. Again, Jess was struck by how open his face was when he was being genuine.

'There's not much to know,' he said. 'I moved to Manhattan a while ago, but I cut my teeth on some English newspapers.'

'We never did establish which ones, and that reminds me – you owe me on that bet.'

'Damn, I hoped you'd forgotten about that,' Giles said, teasingly. 'What can I give you?'

His words hung in the air between them, and suddenly the

sexual tension was cranked up a notch. Sitting in a blacked-out car – away from the world and real life – was surprisingly sexy. They could say anything or do anything, and nobody would be any the wiser. For Jess – who'd spent the last few weeks in the spotlight – the idea was intoxicating.

'What's on offer?' she asked huskily, and Giles stared at her for a moment, as if he couldn't quite believe that the biggest popstar on the planet was flirting with him. Actresses and models often pretended to adore him to get decent press coverage, but this was different. The girl in front of him didn't seem to want anything from him . . . apart from him. He didn't know what to do.

'You're happily married, aren't you?' Giles said finally, break-ing the spell. 'What's it like being married to your manager?'

'I thought the interview was over,' Jess said softly. She didn't want to think about Beau, or that Giles thought she was Madison. She just wanted to be herself again, and to lose herself in Giles.

'A good journalist's always working,' Giles said lightly, as he pressed the intercom and asked the driver to take them back to the Slate Street office.

Jess almost laughed out loud. That was exactly what Matthew used to say to her when she complained about him always being on duty.

'Well, I'm clearly not a good popstar,' she said, 'because at the moment I'm just being me.'

Giles eyed her. 'And who are you?' he asked quietly.

Jess thought about the question. Who was she? She didn't know any more. She used to be Jess Piper – wannabe fashion designer who loved London, always saw the good in people, and thought that to achieve your dreams you had to work hard, rather than play hard. But recently, well, she wasn't sure she was still the same girl. She still wanted to be a designer – her heart ached when she thought about it – but the money Beau had promised her had turned her world, and maybe even her morals, upside down. She was a girl who was living a lie for cold hard cash. And she wasn't sure she liked the Jess that she'd become.

The car gently pulled to a stop outside Slate Street.

'I'm Madison Miller, aren't I?' Jess replied sadly, and before she could stop herself, tears began to well up in her big blue eyes.

Giles reached over and wiped one away, and suddenly, instinctively, they were kissing, hard, and the Dictaphone had fallen to the floor. When it landed with a bang, Jess pulled away, and stared at Giles. His expression was unreadable, but she knew without doubt that what they had done was the start of something uncontrollable and perilous.

She opened the car door and fled into the skyscraper. She was on Slate Street soil, and she was safe.

'What the fuck is the meaning of this?' Beau bellowed, crashing into her bedroom.

Jess had forgotten that he had a set of keys to her apartment, and as she struggled to open her eyes and focus on Beau, she felt a shiver of fear running through her. They got on fine so long as they were around other people, but she hated being alone with him. She hated it even more when he was in a bad mood.

She sat up and gazed at the newspaper that he'd flung heavily onto the silk sheets of her bed.

'What's the meaning of what?' she said sleepily, determined to show Beau that he didn't intimidate her.

'Page six,' he said curtly. 'The blind item.'

Jess's hands were trembling so much that she fumbled with the paper. Beau sighed impatiently and snatched it from her.

'Which pop starlet,' he read in a slow, angry voice, 'who's no stranger to keeping out of the shadows, got down and dirty with a certain celebrity interviewer earlier this week? The run-of-the-mill singer has turned her attention from her beautiful man to a guy from the press pack.'

He threw the paper back on the bed and began pacing the room.

'It's so obviously you – or *Madison* – that it isn't even funny. But is it true? Is it?' Beau eyed Jess with such loathing that she felt herself involuntarily shrink back into the pillows.

'Of course it isn't true,' she said, when she was able to speak. 'I'd never go with a journalist. Who do you think I am?'

'Jessica, don't treat me like I'm dumb. You lived with a journalist in London, or have you forgotten you told me everything about yourself when we first met?'

'And for that reason I'd never do it again,' Jess said nervously. 'I'm not stupid, Beau.' She tried to make her voice placating, but it wasn't having the desired effect.

'How could you be so idiotic? Your contract's nearly up – and I fully regret ever hiring you, by the way, don't think I'm happy with how you've behaved – and at the last minute you fuck it up spectacularly. The PR office has been fielding phone calls for hours while you've been getting your beauty sleep, and Bailey is practically pulling her hair out.'

Jess was silent. Don't cry, she told herself. Whatever you do, don't cry.

'I haven't done anything wrong,' she said in a small voice. 'And I don't know what the item is about. I'd never do anything to hurt Madison's career, I promise you.'

Beau stopped pacing and sat down on the edge of the bed. For the first time since she'd known him, Jess thought he looked defeated.

'We're so close to the tour I can almost taste it. It's nearly time to get Madison's ass back over here, and nearly time to get shot of you. Why the fuck did you have to do it?' He sounded tired, and Jess realised that as exhausting as it had been for her to pretend to be Madison, it must have been hard on Beau, too. She'd never even thought about it.

'Beau, I *promise* you, I've not done anything.'

'Who is it?' Beau's voice was calm and neutral. 'What man are they talking about?'

'The only interview I've done in the past couple of days was with the man from the *New York Star*,' Jess said. 'But nothing happened. We went for lunch, got chased out of the restaurant by the paparazzi, and then we got a limo to Slate Street. That was the last time I saw him. I promise.' She pushed the memory of the kiss out of her head. She didn't want to think about that now. Besides, she'd given it enough thought recently.

Beau turned to her, and examined her carefully. His black eyes, as usual these days, were expressionless and cold.

'Then I shall sue,' he said. 'I shall speak to this journalist, I shall get the story from him, and I shall sue. What's his name?' Beau asked coldly, and when Jess paused, his eyes flashed with anger. 'What is his fucking name?' he roared, and Jess started shaking. Properly this time.

'Giles Tavener,' she said softly, and Beau's eyes narrowed.

'The English one you were flirting with at the New York party. I see. Well, Jessica, there's never any smoke without fire, is there?' he snapped.

Jess swallowed hard. She was done for.

'What's his number?'

Jess shook her head. 'I don't know. I've never phoned him.'

'I don't believe you!' he yelled. He was out of control, and being irrational. 'No doubt you've managed to get a cell phone from somewhere and have been phoning him secretly. Sending sexy little texts and photos of yourself, too, I bet. Where is it?'

He pulled the silk sheet from off the bed and left Jess exposed in just knickers and a vest. 'Where's the fucking phone?'

'Beau, I'm telling you, I don't have a phone. You never said I could have one, so I didn't get one!' She'd jumped off the bed now, and was standing in the corner of the ornate room. Beau was acting crazy, and there was no telling what he'd do.

'Did you have an affair with him?' Beau shouted, and as he began to approach her, Jess genuinely began to feel scared. Would he punch her? Knock her out? She was fast on her feet, but Beau was so large, so powerful, there was no way around him. She truly was trapped. He began to inch towards her slowly, his face twisted with menace. When Jess didn't answer him – for she was too terrified to make a sound – he walked even closer towards her, until he was towering over her.

'I asked,' he said in the quietest, most threatening tone Jess had ever heard, 'if you fucked him. So did you?'

Beau's face was so close to hers that she could smell the stale coffee on his breath, and just as his fist crashed into her face, a voice came from the doorway to the bedroom.

'Like you fuck all the artists on your label, Beau?'

Standing there – looking cool, composed and together – was Madison. Jess could have cried with relief.

Chapter Twenty-One

'Madison . . .'

For a moment Beau was speechless, but he quickly composed himself. He looked from Jess – who lay in a crumpled heap on the floor, her hands covering her face – and back to the popstar in the doorway. He smirked.

'You escaped from the ranch, then. I have to say, I thought I'd be angry, but your timing is impeccable. There's no way this stupid English bitch could do a photo shoot in a couple of days, so you can stand in for her. I'm not about to fork out hundreds of dollars on make-up to cover up that bruise.'

Madison stared at Beau. It felt as if she hadn't seen him in a lifetime, but she wasn't surprised he hadn't changed. He still believed he ruled the world. She wasn't going to put up with it ever again.

'I'm not standing in for anyone,' Madison said coldly. Her eyes flickered to Jess, who was now crying softly, and then she turned her focus back to Beau, her face hard with anger. '*I'm* Madison, not her. I'm not standing in for myself.'

Beau glowered. 'Do you want to go back to Oklahoma? Because with one phone call I can get a car here and send you away for good.'

Madison remained silent.

'No? I thought not. Since I've had good reports about you for the past month, I'm willing to overlook the fact you left the ranch without my say-so, but there are some conditions to you being in New York.'

'I'm listening.'

'One, you're not Madison yet, *Madison*; Jess is. You need to have a handover to find out what's been going on in your life. You can only be Madison again when I'm satisfied you're up to speed.'

Madison crossed her arms across her pink Coco Ribbon dress. 'Fine with me. What else?'

'Two, you're to sign a new contract that specifically states you're not to open your mouth. You're not authorised to speak to anyone – be it Mom and Pop back in Ohio, or even Bailey – without my permission. Do it, and your career's over for good.'

Madison shrugged. 'I'll sign whatever you want,' she said.

'And third,' Beau continued, 'you're not allowed any boy-friends. To the outside world you're still my wife, Madison, and that's how you're going to behave.'

Through her tears Jess noticed a tiny flicker of something pass across Madison's face, but she doubted Beau would have spotted it. He was too busy pacing the room.

'Good for me,' Madison said. 'It's all about my career from now on. You may be surprised to hear this, Beau, but you've put me off men for good.'

Beau laughed, and moved closer to Madison. 'I'll get Tia to work some lesbian moves into the tour choreography, then. If you're very good, not only will I let you do the tour, but I'll let you do some girl-on-girl moves on stage – just like you did at Spotlight.'

Madison didn't even blink. 'Whatever you want, Beau,' she said neutrally. 'I just want my life and my career back, and I want to do the tour.'

'Sort out this stupid cow,' he remarked, with a nod to Jess, 'and I'll see how I feel.'

He swept out of the apartment, and left Madison and Jess alone with each other for the first time since they'd met in LA.

'You need to keep this cold pack on your face for a couple of hours,' Madison said matter-of-factly as she passed a bag of frozen hotdogs in a tea towel to Jess, who was sitting at the kitchen table. Madison moved so confidently around the kitchen that it was as if she'd never gone away. But she had . . . and Jess was racked with guilt.

'It will help with the swelling, but you're still not going to be able to go out in public for a while.'

Jess took the home-made ice pack gratefully, and pressed it against her face. The coolness of it helped ease the pain and the relentless throbbing. She'd been so engrossed in watching Beau and Madison together that she hadn't realised how much it hurt. It must have been the shock, she thought.

'How do you know about first aid?' Jess asked, not daring to talk about anything serious, but not wanting Madison to leave the kitchen. If she and Madison could make small talk . . . well, it might be a way to build some sort of relationship with her. Above all else, Jess was deeply sorry for stepping into Madison's shoes, and she wanted the opportunity to tell her that.

Madison shrugged. 'My boyfriend in high school was on the football team. He got black eyes sometimes, and I played nurse.'

'That was Kyle, wasn't it? Kyle Brockway.'

Madison didn't speak for a moment. 'Even though I've thought about you pretending to be me for every second of every day, I still forget you know pretty much everything about me. It's fucked up. What's my favourite colour?'

Jess lowered her eyes, hating that she knew the answer. 'Indigo.'

'And my favourite food?'

'Hamburgers.'

'What was I wearing when I won *Teen Star*?'

'Gold Manolo Blahnik heels that you'd worn on another performance, a wispy cream baby-doll dress, and a fresh peony corsage. You were wearing Chanel perfume, MAC make-up, and you'd been sprayed with subtle silver glitter.'

Madison was silent. 'You know, it's unnerving how much you know about me, and how you look *exactly* like me.'

Jess lifted her head and pulled the ice pack away. 'It freaks me out as well, you know,' she said softly, but Madison shook her head angrily.

'It's not the same. Do you have any idea how trippy it was to have someone who looks *just like you* – who's even wearing the exact same heels as you – standing over your bed and telling you that you're ill and that they're going to be taking over your life? Can you imagine what that did to my head?'

Tears began to fall from Jess's blue eyes, and for a moment she couldn't speak. She felt wretched.

'Beau told me you were an addict, that you were taking drugs. I thought I was *helping* you. He manipulated me. I didn't realise . . .'

'You didn't realise what? That what you were doing was wrong? That didn't cross your mind when you were in bed with Beau? When you were in public with Beau acting as though you were in love? Or when you were doing interviews pretending to be *me*?' Madison's voice cracked, and, despite herself, she began to cry, too.

'I'm so sorry,' Jess whispered. 'I'm so, so sorry. I said I'd be you because I genuinely thought I was helping you, and as for

Beau . . .' Her voice trailed off, but she gathered enough strength to tell the truth. 'I thought I'd fallen in love with him,' she admitted. 'He told me that your relationship was over. That you'd blackmailed him to get a career, that you never loved him. I knew you were his wife, but I thought it was in name only.'

Madison held Jess's gaze. 'I'm not his wife,' she said simply. 'I never have been.'

'What do you mean?' Jess asked.

Madison thought for a moment. If she told Jess everything she knew about Beau and Tori Catrino, and Jess blabbed, that would be it for her. Her career – or what was left of it – would most definitely be over.

But then, Madison believed Jess now hated Beau as much as she did.

'I know you're a Brit, but have you heard of Tori Catrino?' Madison began tentatively.

Jess smiled. 'We *do* have music over there, you know. Yeah, I've heard of her. I'm not really into pop, but she was massive. And then one day she just disappeared. She was on Slate Street, wasn't she?'

'She was . . . but then she made the mistake of having a relationship with Beau, and . . .' Madison stopped. Could she really trust Jess? Really? Her career – and her whole life – depended on keeping this secret, and she wasn't so sure she could really trust a girl who'd *stolen* her life. Could she?

'And what?'

'Look, Beau sent me away to make sure I didn't tell *anyone*. When I threatened to tell the press about him and Tori, he lost it, and to make sure I didn't, he sent me to a ranch in Oklahoma. Oklahoma of all places! He was *that* pissed with me!'

'But I won't tell him I know whatever it is you're trying to tell me. I don't love him any more, I hate him,' Jess pleaded. 'It's over between us. It was all over when I caught him with another girl. I despise him.'

Madison gave her a wry smile. 'It didn't look like that to me when I saw you at the party at Chromosome X. You both looked very much in love.'

'You were there?'

'In a red wig. But I *saw* you, Jessica. I saw how in love you were with Beau, and how he felt about you. Not that it's excusable, but I can see him hitting you if he thought you'd been cheating on him.'

'But I wasn't cheating on him! And we weren't in love. It was for the cameras. I was pretending to be *you*, remember? I was pretending to be the Madison Miller who's madly in love with her husband!'

'You did a good job of it,' Madison muttered. 'You had me convinced.'

'Honestly,' Jess stressed, 'there's nothing going on with me and Beau any more. Nothing. He's . . . he's horrible. He's devious and controlling, and I didn't realise it until very recently. It wasn't until I spoke to Pepper that I realised Beau fed me a load of lines to get me to pretend to be you. You *have* to believe me. I'm telling the truth.'

'Pepper?' Madison asked curiously. 'Who's Pepper?'

Jess put her icepack on the table very slowly. Leesa. She'd completely forgotten about her.

'Madison,' she said urgently. 'Do you know who Pepper Rose is?'

Madison thought for a moment. 'The name rings a bell. Is she some slutty wannabe who's always in the papers? I don't think I've ever seen a picture of her, though. Why?'

Jess took a deep breath. 'Because I met her a couple of times at some pre-tour parties, and it turns out her real name's Leesa

Harland. She's been trying to get in touch with you. I've got her phone number and address.'

Madison's eyes widened, and it was at that moment she decided to throw caution to the wind and let Jess in on everything. She knew *Leesa*. This girl could put her in touch with her oldest friend.

'Find her details for me, and I'll fill you in on the Tori situation,' she urged, and as Jess rummaged through her bedroom, Madison told her all about how she'd met Beau in Spotlight, how devastated she'd been when she found out he'd never really loved her, and what she'd said to Beau when she found out about his marriage to Tori and the children they'd had.

'Fucking hell,' Jess said finally, once Madison had finished talking and she'd found Leesa's phone number and address. 'That's hardcore. So he basically makes wannabe popstars play the casting-couch game, and then has affairs with them when they become stars so he can control their every move? He *should* be reported to the press, or maybe the police. That *can't* be legal.'

Madison grinned wryly. 'I think Beau's above the law, but not the press. It's the one thing he's scared of, because he can't control it. You have to understand that Beau's all about his image. Can you imagine the outrage there'd be if people found out he'd been having sex with Tori, married her, and then ruined her career because she accidentally got pregnant and refused to get rid of her babies when he told her to? She may not be in the charts now, but she was, like, the biggest star America's had since Britney. Beau would be lynched.'

'But where's Tori now?'

Madison shook her head. 'I don't know,' she said. 'But I think that being away from Beau has got to be better than being in his life. It sounds like she had an awful time, but she's out of it now, which is more than can be said for us.'

'We're going to get through this, you know,' Jess said with determination, and Madison gazed at her thoughtfully. The expression on the English girl's face mirrored her own — a mixture of grit and resolve — and in that moment Madison knew she'd been right to trust her. They could do this. They had to. They were both in it together, and even though they didn't really know each other, or even like each other, they both wanted the same thing: to be free of Beau and the situation they were in.

'Agreed,' Madison said at last. 'Beau found it hard to deal with one Madison Miller, and he's going to find it even tougher dealing with two. First stop, Leesa Harland, second stop, sorting out Beau once and for all.'

The Slate Street limo pulled up outside a run-down apartment block on Avenue D in the East Village. The street was home to a cheap-looking deli and over-filled trashcans.

'I've never been to Alphabet City,' Jess murmured, as Madison adjusted her Ray-Bans so they hid her eyes. 'It's not really on the tourist trail . . .'

Madison took a deep breath. 'Well, at least this building looks clean on the outside, which is better than the apartment Leesa had in Harlem when she first moved here.'

She pressed the intercom to speak to the driver. 'Can you please wait here? We won't be long . . . and, as I said before, if Beau Silverman gets in touch, *please* don't tell him that I'm with Jess, and that we've left the apartment.'

'Whatever you say, miss,' the driver said neutrally, and Jess glanced at him. Both she and Madison knew that if it came to it, the driver would respect Beau's wishes over theirs every time. But it was a risk they had to take. There was no way they could have got a cab here.

Madison pressed the buzzer on Leesa's apartment, and took a

deep breath. How long had it been since she'd seen Leesa? Even though they'd been best friends at high school, she was still nervous about seeing her again. So much had happened since then – to both of them.

A muffled voice came through the intercom. 'Madison? Is that you?'

Despite not knowing what nightmare they were about to walk into, Madison grinned. It was so good to hear Leesa's voice. 'Sure is, babe, and Jess is with me. Buzz us up?'

The girls walked up the three flights of concrete stairs to Leesa's apartment, where she was standing in the doorway waiting for them. She looked terrible – gaunt and pale, with dark circles under her eyes, and dry hair.

'I'm in the paper again. The *Star*, this time,' she said, as a form of greeting, and it instantly put Madison at ease. Even though they'd not seen each other in what felt like a lifetime, Leesa was acting as though they'd only seen each other the night before.

'Apparently I'm addicted to crack. That's what they're saying, anyway.' Leesa held up the paper so both Jess and Madison could see the story. Jess swallowed hard when she saw the picture of Giles as part of his byline. He was clever and sexy as hell, but there was no way anything could ever happen between them. Ever.

'Forget about that stupid rag,' Madison said bossily. 'It's so good to see you!' She enveloped Leesa in a big hug, and tried to hide her shock at how thin Leesa was, and how fragile her body felt.

'You too,' Leesa whispered, pressing her cheek to Madison's. 'You have no idea how much I need a real friend at the moment.'

The girls walked into Leesa's apartment, and both Jess and Madison tried hard not to look shocked. Clothes littered the threadbare carpet, old newspapers were stacked up on every available surface, and dirty bowls and plates were strewn all over place . . . on top of the old TV, on the window sill, on the shabby sofa.

'You know, it's totally weird seeing you two together at the same time. Like you're twins,' Leesa said.

Madison smiled faintly. 'You're telling me,' she said softly. 'When I first met Jess I thought I was going out of my mind.'

'And even though I was prepared for it,' Jess continued, 'it was really strange seeing her in person for the first time. I didn't believe in doppelgängers until I met Madison.'

'But you're getting along okay?' Leesa said again, lighting a cigarette. 'And Jess, you've split up with Beau?'

Jess nodded. 'After I spoke to you I realised what a wanker he was,' she said, and Leesa and Madison grinned at her British accent and slang. 'We're totally over. And it was Beau who gave me this shiner.' She gestured at her black eye, and sighed.

'All men are bastards,' Leesa remarked bluntly, and she raised her eyebrows when Madison started shaking her head again.

'Not all men . . .' she began, and both girls stared at her.

'Who isn't?' Jess asked, and when Madison started to blush she knew there was something that the popstar wasn't telling them.

'Do we have to talk about this?' Madison groaned. 'Can't we just catch up like normal people?'

Leesa laughed. 'Normal? So, since I saw you last, Madison, you've become an internationally successful popstar and been sent away to Oklahoma while a British girl pretended to be you. I gave up stripping, went on a bad reality show, and am now in a mess. That's hardly normal – and besides, what's there to say?'

Madison shrugged. 'But do we have to talk about Jared?'

'Who's Jared?' Jess squealed, and for perhaps the first time since they'd arrived, Leesa's face lit up.

'Yes, who's Jared?' she echoed.

Madison flushed again. 'He was my bodyguard on the ranch in Oklahoma. And, well, he's the most amazing man I've ever met,' she whispered.

'And?' Jess pressed.

'And . . . he's just . . . he's just the complete opposite of Beau. He's physically really strong, as you can imagine – I mean, he is a bodyguard – and he's blonde, really thoughtful, quiet and can totally read my mind.'

An image popped into Jess's mind, and she burst out laughing. 'Like Kevin Costner in *The Bodyguard*?'

'Huh?' Madison looked perplexed.

'You *know*, the film with Whitney Houston where she has a bodyguard to protect her and they fall in love? Madison Miller, you're such a cliché!' she teased.

'Oh, well, maybe! It does sound like that. He's just so hot. He makes Beau look scrawny.'

Jess thought of Giles, and how he made Beau seem such a sleaze.

'Sounds like you're in love! So when are you going to see him next?' Leesa asked.

'It's really hard,' Madison said, and suddenly she looked deflated. 'I'm not allowed boyfriends, and if I wanted to be with Jared I'd have to give up the singing, the fame, everything. I don't think I'd be able to. We only spent a month together in Oklahoma, but I've been sneaking off to see him in his apartment whenever I can. I feel as though he's my best friend. And you know, I've not had one of those in a while . . .'

Leesa looked downcast. 'What about you, Jess?' she asked, changing the subject. 'Any hotties hitting on you? What about that guy you're meant to be having an affair with? Any truth in that?'

Jess paused for a moment. 'Not really. He's a journalist called Giles, and he flirted with me a couple of times, but nothing really happened,' she said, trying not to think about how Giles had kissed her in the limo. And how she'd felt. 'And that's about it. I mean, how could anything have happened? He thought I was Madison.'

'So do you think he liked me – Madison – or was it you he fell for, the British girl pretending to be me?' Madison asked.

Jess bit her lip. 'Who knows? He was attracted to me, and we had this *connection* that I can't really describe, but what if it was the idea of *you* he really liked, and not me – the girl behind your image? I don't think he's the type of person to only want to be with someone because they're famous, but what if he really is that shallow? I'm not going to see him again, so I'm not going to find out. I suppose I'll always wonder, though. He's going on the what-if pile,' she said wistfully.

Leesa looked up from the paper and straight at Jess. 'Giles Tavener? From the *Star*?'

'Um, yes . . .' Jess began.

Leesa stood up and threw the paper on the floor. 'That son of a bitch is making my life hell. I don't need it. I hate him.'

'I tried to stop him,' Jess said in a small voice, 'but he says you like the attention. That you're . . .' She stopped, not wanting to upset Leesa any further.

'That I'm *what*?' Leesa demanded.

Jess looked nervously at Madison, and back at Leesa. 'That . . . that you lap up any press attention because you're so desperate to be famous.'

'That's bullshit,' Leesa said, and there were tears of frustration in her eyes. 'Okay, so I courted them when I went on *Bunk'd Up*, but that was a reality show – I was *trying* to be famous. But now I'm getting papped when I leave the apartment or go to the stores, and every time my photo appears in the paper it's with a bunch of lies. I'm *not* doing drugs, and I'm *not* drinking.'

Madison exchanged a look with Jess, and sat next to Leesa. 'I only just found out you went on a TV show,' she said gently. 'Why did you do that?'

'The same reason you went on *Teen Star*, I guess,' Leesa said. 'I wanted to be famous – I didn't want to be a stripper any more. I wanted to be like *you*.'

Madison couldn't speak for a moment. 'But *Bunk'd Up*? That's basically a show where people live in a house and have sex with each other live on TV.'

Leesa shrugged. 'Yeah. I know. It was the first show that would take me, and I thought if I went in with a fake name – Pepper Rose – it would protect me from any shit that happened afterwards. You know what it's like, girls go in there, and come out expecting to be famous and loved, but really they're hated. Somehow I thought I'd be different. That people would really like me for being me, and then I could get auditions for real shows – shows where I could do real acting.'

'I'm sure people don't hate you,' Jess said gently.

Leesa laughed. 'They do, you know,' she said sadly. 'They really do. I just wish the press would stop making up lies about me, and that the paparazzi would stop hounding me. I'm not using. Not any more . . . And I wish they'd stop saying I am. It doesn't *help*,' she said in a strangled little voice.

Madison looked around the apartment, and then finally dared to look at Leesa again. When they'd first met, Leesa had long strawberry-blonde hair, flawless skin and awesome curves, but now she was super-skinny, her hair was breaking near the roots, and her skin looked terrible. Simply, she was a mess, and she'd aged dramatically.

'Then you could sue,' Jess said. 'If the newspapers are printing lies about you, you can get a lawyer and you can sue them.'

Leesa looked up at her, and then at Madison. 'Do you think I could?' she asked.

Madison shrugged. 'Jess knows more about this stuff than I do – she used to be a journalist on an English newspaper.'

'It would take a lot of time and money,' Jess continued, 'but if you really think you have a case, it would be worth it. You could be awarded quite a lot in damages. Thousands, probably.'

Leesa's eyes lit up for a moment, but then they filled with tears. 'I haven't got any time or money,' she said quietly. 'And I don't want any lawyer prying into my personal life. It's out of the question.'

'But why?' Madison pressed. 'I could lend you the money if you needed it. I could help you.'

Leesa laughed. 'Yeah, I can just see Beau Silverman letting you use your pocket money on me. He hates me – well, he hates Pepper Rose. You'd never be able to do it.'

'I could,' Madison said. 'And if it helps, I will.' She was practically pleading with Leesa. But her friend remained quiet. Eventually she spoke.

'Mads, I do need your help, and it kind of involves cash.'

'What's happened?' Madison asked.

Leesa looked down at the floor, and Jess could see she was choosing her words carefully.

'Do I have to tell you?' she asked eventually, in a tiny voice. 'I don't want you to be upset. Can't you just trust me?'

'Leesa,' Madison began evenly, 'if you need money for booze and drugs I'm not going to give it to you. If you want to go into rehab I'm happy to help you, if it's something you're ready to do.'

Leesa's eyes widened. 'You believe the papers?' she asked

tearfully. 'You think I'm on drugs? That I'm drinking? Look around this apartment – can you see any empty bottles? Any wraps? Fuck, Madison, I thought you knew me better than that.'

'But Leesa, look at you. Look at the state of your apartment, of your life. If you're not using, how could you let your life get like this?'

'And how could you let your life get how it is, too?' Leesa retorted furiously. 'Do you think it's normal to be sent away and to have another person pretend to be you in public? Your life is more fucked up than mine. Just because the press isn't reporting on Jess pretending to be you doesn't make it any less of a situation. And you know it.'

Madison stood up angrily. She already *knew* things were bad, but Leesa didn't understand how manipulative Beau was.

'If you're going to be like this I'm leaving,' she said, her voice shaking. 'Come on, Jess.'

Leesa curled up in a ball on the sofa and tried hard not to cry. 'Don't go,' she whispered, wrapping her arms around her knees. 'Please don't go.'

Madison and Jess stopped in their tracks, and stared at her.

'Okay,' Madison said after a pause, 'what's wrong?'

Leesa looked up at both of them, and her face crumpled.

'I'm not an addict,' she murmured. 'I just can't stop making myself sick . . . I think I have bulimia.'

Chapter Twenty-Two

Madison and Jess sat back down on the couch. Leesa was crying properly now.

'You don't know what it's like,' she sobbed. 'I came to New York to make something of myself, and instead of getting cast in a commercial, or a show, or *anything*, people just criticised me. I wasn't pretty enough, I wasn't slim enough, and according to all the casting directors I couldn't *act*. Madison, I *hated* stripping, *hated* it when guys pretended they were in love with me. They didn't even know me, they just wanted to get laid. Loads of girls like Erika and Mona said they got validation from men when they got hit on, but I never felt that. It just made me feel worthless, like a piece of trash. And when I bombed on *Bunk'd Up*, it sent me over the edge. Instead of being loved I was hated, and I felt the only way I could have some control was to control my eating.'

Leesa's eyes were wide, and she looked depressed and scared. 'I know I've got a problem,' she whispered, 'but I can't stop it, I can't stop myself. Every time there's an ugly photo of myself in the papers it starts all over again. I need help. I desperately need help.'

There was a silence, and then Madison reached over and gave Leesa a big bear hug. She felt excruciatingly thin through her clothes.

'We'll get you through this,' she said as comfortingly as she could, although her heart was sinking. 'The hardest part of getting better is admitting you have a problem, and you've already acknowledged that. I can help you get through this. I can, and I will.'

'And we can put a stop to these articles in the papers,' Jess added. 'I can ask Giles to stop running these stories. If he knows you're ill – and not drunk or on drugs – he'll definitely stop writing them,' she said confidently.

'You mustn't tell him I've got an eating disorder,' Leesa begged. 'I can't have people knowing about this. I just *can't*. I know I haven't got much of a career – shit, I'm well aware everyone thinks I'm some party-loving slut, I'm not stupid – but I don't want to be known as "the girl with bulimia".'

Jess thought about it for a moment. 'But . . . it would be an end to all the door-stopping and nasty articles, and people would know the truth. You could inform other girls about the dangers of eating disorders. It could be a *good* thing.'

Leesa shook her head. 'I don't think I could do it. Isn't there another way?'

'Okay, I understand – but convincing Giles to leave you alone isn't going to be easy without telling him the truth.'

Jess eyed Leesa thoughtfully. 'You know, I hate to sound callous, but this is the sort of thing that would make people see you in a different light. The girl behind the reputation, that sort of thing . . .'

'Jess!' Madison said, looking shocked. 'Leesa has a serious disorder. This isn't some kind of stunt to make her popular, this is *real*.'

'I know,' Jess said. 'But . . .' She caught the expression on Madison's face and realised she was about to overstep the mark. But she didn't care – this was for Leesa's own good. 'Leesa, listen, will you have a think about it at least? You could sell your story, make some money so you can go to a clinic, change your reputation – and the paparazzi would leave you alone, I'm sure.'

Leesa ran her fingers through her white-blonde hair. She looked exhausted. 'If it means making enough money to pay for treatment, what choice do I have?' she said in a resigned voice. 'I just don't want anyone giving me false sympathy, or accusing me of making it up.'

'If we handle it properly, nobody would do that,' Jess assured. 'I promise.'

'And you mustn't worry about money for some initial treat-ment,' Madison said, making a mental note to talk to Jess about Giles – and how Leesa should approach him – when they were back at the apartment. 'I don't have much, but what I have got I can give to you, Lees. We need to make sure you're well.'

'I don't know what I'd do without you guys,' Leesa said, and she turned to Madison. 'I know we fell out after you met Beau, and I'm sorry I was such a bitch. I was just so jealous – it was like a knight in shining armour had come along and rescued you, and I was being left in the gutter. I should have been pleased for you.'

Madison gave her friend another hug. 'It's cool, it's forgotten,' she said. 'What's important now is sorting this out, and getting us all back on track.'

She looked at Leesa and Jess, and instead of feeling exhausted about the mountains they all had to climb, she felt energised.

'We can do this, you know,' she continued. 'It can't get any worse, not for any of us.'

'God, I wasn't expecting that,' Madison said to Jess in a whisper as they stood outside Leesa's front door. 'I can't believe she has an eating disorder . . . no wonder she was so desperate to see us. She really needs some help, and soon.'

'It's awful,' Jess agreed, as they made their way down the concrete stairs. 'But it kind of puts our problems in perspective, too. At least we have our health.'

At the bottom of the stairs Jess pulled open the door to the street, and as the girls stepped out onto the sidewalk, camera flashes blinded them. They froze in fear – they'd been so caught up in Leesa's problem that they'd forgotten to wear their sunglasses. They'd been busted.

'Madison, Madison, over here!'

'Madison! How do you know Pepper Rose?'

'Madison, who's your double? Something you want to tell us?'

'Girls, this way! That's right, this way!'

'Madison, who's your twin? And why has she got a black eye?'

'Hey! Madison! Who's been hitting your pal?'

'Madison, has Pepper Rose been beating up your twin?'

Madison and Jess gripped each other's hands tightly. They were trapped. A wall of paparazzi blocked them from their limo, and there was no way out. It was like they were in a nightmare, with looming men in black circling them . . . And then, for a split second, in between the camera flashes, Jess saw him. It was Giles Tavener, door-stepping Pepper Rose for another story, but coming face to face with her and Madison instead.

'Giles,' Jess croaked. 'You promised . . .'

Giles looked from Jess to Madison, and then back to Jess again. Confusion was written all over his face, and for a second Jess wanted to rush to him, put her arms around him, and tell him everything. But she knew she couldn't. He was *press*. And whatever their connection, she just couldn't trust him not to run a story on her, on Madison, or on Pepper.

'Madison! Crack us a smile, will you?'

'Madison, what's with the twin thing? Why've you kept it a secret?'

'Madison! Madison! Madison!'

People were stopping in the street to watch the spectacle, and Madison's name rang out all the way down Avenue D.

Giles continued to stare at Jess, who held his gaze. She knew she looked like shit, that her face was swollen and her eye was bruised, but she didn't care.

'Don't do anything with these photos,' she begged him over the noise of the paparazzi who were still screaming Madison's name. 'Please don't do anything until I can talk to you about it. Please.'

And then suddenly the cameras and the yells stopped, and there was silence as the paparazzi huddled around Giles, who was saying something to them.

The girls didn't need another chance. They jumped into the Slate Street limo, and it sped off towards their apartment, the tyres screeching as they left a mark on the road.

'So, what's the story?' Giles asked Jess as they sat in the wood-panelled meeting room where he had first tried to interview her. Jess was sensibly dressed in Acne jeans and a Sonia Rykiel jumper, but she still felt exposed and vulnerable, especially as Giles was looking sharp in a suit, and they were on his turf.

Jess buried her head in her hands. 'I don't know how to explain it to you,' she said quietly in her American accent. 'I *can't* tell you. If I say anything my career's definitely over.'

Giles stared at her. 'Okay, so what about your black eye? Can you tell me about that? I hate the thought of anyone touching you. I mean, where were your bodyguards, for fuck's sake?'

Jess shook her head again and didn't make eye contact. 'I can't tell you that, either . . .' She knew she was in trouble. How would Giles react if she told him that Beau had punched her because of him?

Giles sighed and crossed his arms. 'Let's get this straight. I catch you and a girl that looks just like you leaving Pepper Rose's apartment, *and* you have a black eye, and you can't tell me anything?'

Jess looked at him desperately. 'I can't,' she stressed. 'I wish I could, but I can't.'

Giles sighed again. 'This is all off the record, you know. I'm your friend. You can trust me.'

'Then you should be able to trust me when I say I *can't* tell you! But please, please, please, don't publish those photos. Please.' Jess knew she was begging, but she had to. She absolutely had to. The pictures of her and Madison may not have been published yet, but the photographers were sure to tell everyone that they'd caught two Madisons coming out of Pepper Rose's apartment. It was only a matter of time before Beau found out. She felt sick to her stomach – for her, for Madison and for Leesa.

'Lucky for you all the photographers were from the *New York Star*, but my editor's already seen them and he's going to ask questions about why we're not running them. What am I meant to say? Jesus, Madison, I know you're worried about your career, but you're putting mine on the line here, too.'

Jess wanted to cry, but she knew it would do no good. She had to stay in control.

'But why were you even *there*?' she asked. 'Why were you door-stepping Pepper Rose again?'

'My guy got a tip-off that you were visiting Pepper, and the photo opportunity was too good to miss. Plus, you gave me so much grief about the stories I've been running about her I wanted to see if you really were friends. Are you?'

Jess was silent for a moment. Saying Madison was friends with Pepper wouldn't be great for Madison's image, but who cared that Leesa had a bad reputation? They *were* friends and that was all that mattered. Friends came before everything.

'I am friends with Pepper,' she said proudly, 'and not only that, I've told her that you and I are friends, and she'd like to give you an exclusive.'

Giles snorted. 'Like anything she does is exclusive. Who has she shagged this time? Some Z-lister? If it's another kiss-and-tell, we're not interested.'

Jess faced Giles square on. She knew she had Pepper's permission to tell him that she was ill, and that she wanted to sell her story to him and the *Star*, but she still felt nervous at spilling the news. This wasn't a kiss-and-tell, or a bikini body story, or something light-hearted and fun. This was serious and a big responsibility. This was Leesa's life.

'It's nothing like that,' Jess said, biting her lip. 'But if I tell you what it is, and you agree it's something you want to run, do you promise you won't print those pictures of us . . . of me and, um, the girl that looks like me?'

'Madison, you know I can't promise anything like that,' Giles said softly. 'Look, I don't know what situation you've got yourself in, or why you're being so protective of being caught with this girl that looks *just* like you, but I can buy you some time, if that helps. I want to help you, you know. I . . . well, I like you. You know I do.'

'I'd really appreciate that,' Jess said, trying to swallow back her tears. 'And you really should consider the interview that Pepper wants to give to you. I think it's important.'

Giles raised one eyebrow. 'So what's it about if it's not a kiss-and-tell?' he asked.

Jess paused for dramatic effect. 'Pepper's not doing drugs, or drinking too much,' she began. 'And her real name isn't Pepper; that's just her stage name. Her real name is Leesa, and we were at high school together. That's how I know her. And the thing is . . . Leesa's ill. She's got an eating disorder. All the time you've been running stories about her being drunk and on drugs, well, you were wrong. And every time you publish another article about her, it makes it worse. It sends her over the edge. I'm the first person she told, but now she's ready to tell you, and America, why chasing fame can damage your self-esteem and your health.'

Giles's eyes lit up, and Jess recognised that look from working at the *Daily World* – she'd seen it enough when journalists got hold of an amazing, exclusive story. There was no doubt that the interview would run, that Leesa would be able to get proper treatment with the money she made out of the *Star* exclusive, and that, for once, the American public would see her doing something worthwhile.

When the interview with Leesa appeared in the *New York Star* – alongside beautifully shot photos of her without her usual make-up and trashy clothes – New York, and America, fell in love with her.

Giles had written the double-page interview as a public apology to Leesa, saying he'd been wrong to report she'd been taking drugs and sleeping around, and instead of being castigated for being so vicious in the not-so-distant past, he was applauded for admitting his mistakes and for trying to right them now.

Leesa told her story simply, how she'd moved to New York with hopes of being an actress, but had fallen into stripping. She described how she felt as if she'd run out of options, and how she had hoped that being on *Bunk'd Up* would be a way out of the sex industry and into proper acting. She admitted she'd been naive, and that America's hatred of her had led to her partying to take her mind off it.

'It got to be a vicious circle,' she commented. 'I drank and partied to forget the negative publicity, but that only brought about more. I couldn't win. When it got really bad I started making myself sick . . . if everyone was saying I was trash maybe I really *was* that bad, and purging myself was the only way I could feel clean. My appearance went downhill, and to cover for it I pretended nothing had happened, and that I was still drinking, still taking drugs, still off my head . . .

'But I wasn't. I was scared and alone, and to make it worse the papers ran horrible copy about me every day. Photographers wouldn't leave me alone, and it got so I was scared to leave my apartment. Can you imagine having to deal self-loathing, and having it validated by the press? I couldn't do it any more, and that's why I'm coming clean now. I want to be honest with people.'

Leesa immediately became someone the public admired for her frankness, and eating disorder charities contacted her, not only to ask her to represent them, but to help her, too. A Pepper Rose fan started a website asking for donations, and in a very short amount of time, Leesa had enough money for her treatment, her rent, and a little extra to treat herself. For the first time since she'd left school she'd found self-respect, and she knew she was extremely lucky. She had the whole country behind her in her fight for health, and she felt blessed.

'I couldn't have done this without you,' Leesa said to Jess.

They were sitting in her apartment, and for the first time in a long time, Leesa was no longer scared of being door-stepped. The press had said they'd leave her alone, and her apartment no longer felt like a prison.

'I was so scared of everything, but you showed me that by being honest I could save myself,' she continued. 'I owe it all to you.'

Jess smiled weakly. 'Don't be silly,' she said. She was delighted that Leesa was so calm and serene, but inside her stomach was a ball of knots. Giles had promised not to run the pictures of her and Madison yet, but there was still every chance that Beau would find out about them. He'd left Jess alone while Madison began rehearsals for the tour, but the fear was always there.

'Giles called me today, you know,' Leesa continued. 'He says he's been trying to contact the PR department at Slate Street, but Bailey's refusing to let him speak to you, or even pass on a message.'

Jess grimaced. 'I'm not surprised. Ever since that piece about me – or Madison – having an affair, Giles is blacklisted. If I had a phone he could get in touch, but it's strictly forbidden. Even Madison had to cover for me today just to come and see you. If Beau found out, I'd be done for.'

'Giles wants to see you again,' Leesa continued. 'I told him I was meeting you today, and he wants to talk to you tonight. He's booked a room at the Plaza.'

'He's crazy. I can't just go to the Plaza! And why has he booked a room?' Jess was outraged. Who did Giles think he was?

'I don't think he's expecting anything, honey,' Leesa said. 'I think he just got a room so you could have some privacy. You know, so you could chat away from prying eyes.'

'Yeah, right. He just wants to know what's going on with Madison and me, and he thinks he can get it out of me by putting a hotel room on his expense account. God, journalists are all the same.'

Leesa considered this for a moment. 'But didn't you say there was a connection between you two? And that you really liked him?'

'Of course I do,' Jess blustered. 'But I'd never tell him about my arrangement with Beau, never. And don't forget, I know how journalists operate. This is all a ploy to get me to spill the beans. I just know it.'

Leesa grinned. 'Jess,' she began gently, 'I've hated Giles Tavener for a long time, but I also know that when I met him, and got to know him, I liked him very much. Yeah, he's a journalist, but he's also a decent guy. I think you should meet him tonight, you know.'

Jess glared at her. 'And what time am I meant to be at this hotel room?' she asked, annoyed.

'Eight o'clock, in time for dinner.'

Jess rolled her eyes. 'As if I'd even go. Giles Tavener is going to be waiting a long time for me to appear tonight.'

Jess hadn't been to the Plaza before, but as soon as she walked into the lobby she knew the hotel would live up to her expectations. It was like walking into a slice of history, with shimmering cream floors, glistening gold practically everywhere, and beautiful crystal chandeliers hanging from the ornate ceiling. It screamed class and celebrity, and Jess was glad she'd worn huge sunglasses and a trilby to go with her silk Manoush mini-dress. It seemed discreet enough, but Jess knew you could never be too careful. If anyone got wind of Madison Miller making an appearance at the Plaza – or worse, going up to a room booked by a journalist – that would be it. Just the thought of it put her on

286

edge, and her blue eyes darted from one end of the lobby to the other. She had to get up to Giles's room, and fast.

But as Jess was led there by a butler, she began to doubt herself. What was she doing? Hadn't she been adamant that she wasn't going to come? What if Giles was trying to trick her into telling him what was going on? What if she'd only imagined their connection because she was so crazy about him? What if he was just playing her?

She started to back away from the door when suddenly it opened, and Giles was there. He was barefoot, in light blue jeans and a fitted navy T-shirt, and he looked hot. So, so hot.

'Madison,' he said, smiling. 'You came.'

Jess nodded. 'I did.' She pulled her sunglasses from her face and stared at him. He couldn't take his eyes off her.

'Would you like to come in?' he asked. 'I'd really like to talk to you.'

Jess silently walked into the room, and saw that he'd booked a suite. It was massive.

'I didn't realise you had a suite here,' she said. 'I thought . . .'

'You thought I'd booked a room and had lured you here to sleep with you? Or pump you for information?' He grinned. 'I wouldn't be so presumptuous . . . although, if you're offering sex . . .'

Jess laughed, and wandered around the living room, trailing her hands over the marble fireplaces, the heavy curtains, the polished mahogany desk and the plush blue and white sofas.

'It's the Vanderbilt Suite,' Giles began. 'Not only does it have this living room and dining room, there's also a kitchen and three bedrooms. And a jacuzzi.'

'It's beautiful,' Jess breathed, and she walked towards a window and gazed down at Fifth Avenue. 'And the paper doesn't mind you putting something like this on expenses? You're a lucky boy, Tavener.'

Giles looked puzzled. 'You think this is a work thing?'

Jess looked at him. 'Isn't it? I just assumed that you wanted to meet me to talk about the photos . . .'

Giles shrugged. 'I'm desperate to know about the photos, and who that girl is, but that's not what I wanted to talk to you about.' He looked nervous for a second, but managed to compose himself. 'Would you like some champagne? I have some Tattinger on ice . . . or maybe you'd like some orange juice? Or a cocktail?'

'Champagne would be lovely,' Jess said, and she sat down in an armchair that was as comfortable as it looked. 'So what was it that you wanted to talk to me about, if it's not a work thing?'

Giles was busying himself with the champagne bottle, so she surreptitiously looked around the room to see if there were any Dictaphones or video cameras planted anywhere. She couldn't see any, but they might be hidden.

'It's personal,' Giles began. He handed her a glass of champagne and took a deep breath. 'I wanted to thank you for sending Leesa my way. That exclusive was fantastic – thank you so much. It really raised my profile in the industry, and I've had loads of people trying to poach me. Even editors in London are phoning me up and making me offers – one for a deputy editor's job.'

'Giles, that's brilliant!' Jess exclaimed. 'Are you thinking of going back to England?'

Giles gazed into the distance for a moment. 'Maybe,' he said, taking a sip of champagne. 'But, well, there's something I need to find out first. It's why I wanted to, well . . .' Jess was amazed to see him shifting uneasily on the sofa. He actually looked racked with nerves.

'What?' Jess said. 'What is it?'

Giles paused for the longest moment, and then his words came rushing out.

'I don't know how to say this, so I'm just going to say it. Madison, I can't get you out of my head. I know it's ridiculous, and that you're married, but you're all I can think about. You're so amazing. You're beautiful and talented and funny, and you're refreshing. I've never met anyone like you, and certainly no celebrity I've ever met is as honest and down to earth as you.' He flushed red, and refused to meet her eyes.

'Quite simply, you're my dream girl, and I know that you could never go for a journalist like me, but, well, I'm falling for you, big time. And I had to tell you. I had to.'

Giles stopped speaking, and Jess gazed at him. He'd said the words she'd been desperate to hear since that day in the limo, and she wanted to embrace him and kiss him and tell him that she felt the same way, too, and that she couldn't stop thinking about him, either. But she couldn't. How could she?

'I . . . I don't know what to say,' Jess murmured, aware of the uneasy silence that had filled the room. 'I'm flattered . . . but don't you have a girlfriend?'

Giles shook his head. 'After *that* kiss I knew I had to break it off with her. Long-distance relationships don't work at the best of times, and after that day I knew I was crazy for you. It wouldn't have been fair on her.'

Jess swallowed hard. Giles was being so honest. Would it really be such a bad thing if she was honest in return? She may not have been able to have a relationship with him now, but once Madison began the *Spotlight* tour and Jess was no longer pretending to be her, well – couldn't she do it then?

'Giles, I have to tell you something, too,' Jess said slowly, as her mind raced. Did she dare? Could she?

'I've got feelings for you, too,' she admitted. 'I've never felt like this before, about anyone, and if my life wasn't so complicated right now I think we'd be the happiest people in the world. You make me feel so sexy, but so comfortable at the same time. I can be myself with you,' she said, before giving a little laugh. How ironic it was that she felt completely herself with him, given that Giles didn't know her true identity.

'But why is it so complicated?' Giles pressed. 'I know you're married to Beau, and that he's your manager, but you're not happy with him, are you? I know you're not!'

'I'm not, but we have to keep up our marriage for appearances' sake. It might all be for the camera, but it's also for my career. I wouldn't want anything to harm that, not when it was such a struggle to get where I am now.' Jess paused, and realised that she was still feeding Giles lies. She hated herself for doing it. She wasn't Madison Miller, so why was she still pretending to be her? She supposed she still didn't really know if Giles liked her for who she was, or who Madison was, and it hurt so, so much.

'Tell me again why you like me so much, Giles,' she asked. She needed to know if it was Madison he was in love with, or her. Everything depended on what he said next.

'I like you because you're one of the few people who isn't afraid to speak their mind to me; because you're funny; because you constantly surprise me; because you're fascinating, sexy, clever and your own person; because you don't seem to be afraid of anyone or anything. And mostly, because you're *you*.'

Tears formed in Jess's eyes, and she blinked them away. 'But I'm not me,' she whispered, and she took a deep breath. She wanted Giles so much it was killing her, and she was so close to the end of being Madison that she was willing to risk telling him who she really was.

'Giles, I'm not really Madison Miller. My name's Jessica Piper. I used to be a journalist at the *Daily World* back in London, and, well . . . Beau sent Madison away some time ago. I've been standing in for her ever since.'

Giles went white and dropped his champagne glass on the floor.

Chapter Twenty-Three

'I can't believe you told him!' Madison's face was taut with anger, and her hands were shaking. How had Jess been so *stupid*? To run straight to Giles – one of the leading showbiz journalists in the country – and tell him that she wasn't really Madison was potentially disastrous . . . If Giles told *anyone* what Jess had blurted out, her whole career would be over in a shot. She'd never be taken seriously again.

'Leesa said you thought it was a trap to get you to spill all, and that you weren't even going to *go* to the Plaza, let alone tell Giles everything. I can't believe you've done this to me. And to us!'

Jess buried her head in her arms. They were in the living room of the apartment, and she'd been crying for twenty-four hours straight. Her head pounded, her eyes were raw and red, and there was a darkness in her heart that she couldn't shake. She'd taken a risk and told Giles who she really was, and he'd rejected her. He'd been disgusted with her. He told her that she was a fake and a liar and definitely not the type of girl he'd ever want to be with. Jess remembered how his face had been like thunder – hurt thunder, if that was possible – as he slammed the door to the suite behind her, and how she'd dropped to her knees in anguish. She was inconsolable. She wished she'd never met Giles Tavener, had never fallen for him, and had certainly never told him the truth.

'I don't know what I was thinking,' Jess mumbled, desperately wanting some comfort from Madison rather than this anger. But Madison wasn't Poppy, was she? They weren't even proper friends – just two people caught up in a nasty situation – and she couldn't expect anything more from Madison than hurt and resentment. How could she?

'Tell me again *exactly* what you said to him,' Madison demanded, as she paced the room. 'I need to know, word for word, to see if there's any way out of this. Fucking *hell*, Jess.'

As Jess painfully recounted her short evening with Giles the night before, Madison stopped pacing and sat down beside her. It was hard not to feel for her. Jess had made a really stupid mistake, admittedly, but she wasn't the first girl to mess up over a man, and she certainly wouldn't be the last. She sighed.

'Do you think he'll expose us?' Madison asked eventually.

Jess bit her lip. 'I don't know. Technically there's no reason for him not to. He's disgusted with me, *and* he has the photos of us. He could if he wanted to. But he also told me that he loved me . . . pretty much . . . and I believe him. I just don't think you could do that to someone you feel that strongly for, regardless of what they've done or said.'

'Well, if he does, that's it. I'll have lost my career, and you'll have blown everything.' Madison was shocked at how angry she sounded, but she couldn't help it. Jess had played with fire, and Madison was the one who would get burned.

'I know,' Jess said quietly. 'And Madison, I'm so, *so* sorry. I never meant to tell him, and honestly, I'd never do anything to harm you. I've always been in this to help you . . . I just made a mistake.'

For the first time that evening she looked Madison in the eye, and once again her breath was taken away by their similarity. It really was like having a twin. They looked the same, they sounded the same, and they were living the same life with the same problems . . . with the same threat of Beau hanging over them.

'Honestly, I don't think Giles will do a piece on us,' Jess said sincerely. 'We just need to be careful that Beau doesn't find out I told him. If he does, that really *will* be the end of us.'

At that moment they heard a bang outside the living room door. They both froze and stared at it, and then, as if on cue, Beau walked in with a malicious smile on his face.

'It certainly *is* the end of you,' he said triumphantly. 'Both of you. Game over, girls. Madison, as of this moment, your career is history.'

Jess stood up. 'But she hasn't done anything wrong,' she pleaded, hoping Beau wouldn't notice the wobble in her voice, or that she was intimidated by him. 'If anyone's at fault it's me. Sack *me*, cancel my contract, don't give me a dime. Just don't punish Madison for my mistake.'

Beau narrowed his eyes. 'And what mistake would that be, Jessica?' he asked her coldly.

Jess quickly looked at Madison, whose blue eyes were as wide as hers.

'I . . . I . . .' Jess was lost for words. He did *know* that she'd told Giles Tavener everything, didn't he? Or, shit, had she just landed them both in it?

'You're such a stupid little girl,' Beau spat. 'I liked that about you when we first met. It meant I could feed you a pack of lies and you'd eat them straight up – but the dumb blonde act is tiresome, Jessica. Why don't you stop pretending and tell me exactly what's been going on?'

'Nothing's been going on!' Jess said defensively. 'Nothing at all.'

Beau stared at her. 'So your mistake was . . . ?'

Jess looked to Madison for help. Shit. Shit. Shit.

'Jess told someone that I'm from Walkertown, North Carolina, rather than Walkertown, Ohio,' Madison said quickly. 'It was a stupid mistake, and she's really sorry for it.'

Beau looked at Jess. 'Is this true?' he asked her, his voice like ice.

Jess nodded. There would be hell to pay for this kind of error, but if Beau knew what her real mistake was, well – it didn't bear thinking about.

Beau sat down in an armchair and surveyed the girls thoughtfully. 'So Jessica fucked up on a basic Madison fact, did she?' he clarified.

Both girls nodded.

'I see. And you think that will be it for you now?' he asked, as if trying to get his head around it. 'You think I'd end Madison's career for *that*?'

'Yes,' Madison said. She could see Jess quivering out of the corner of her eye, and she felt a pang of sympathy for her. What a shitty couple of days she'd had – not only had Beau punched her, but she'd lost Giles, too.

Beau laughed. 'Well, you're right about me ending Madison's career, but you're wrong about why. Do you *really* think I believe your stupid little lie? Really?'

He gazed at both of them, and in the same instant both Madison and Jess could see why they'd been attracted to him. He was so powerful, so commanding.

'I know everything you've been getting up to recently,' Beau continued in a bored tone. 'From your little trips to see Leesa the hooker, to Madison sneaking off to see that dumb-ass jock Jared, to Jess seeing Giles last night at the Plaza.'

Madison and Jess froze in shock. They thought they'd got away with it, and Beau smirked at their shocked expressions.

'Girls, girls, girls. You must think I'm completely stupid. As if Madison could simply walk back into the apartment "unexpectedly" and I'd just "disappear" for a few days. Do you *really* think I'd leave the two of you alone together without keeping a *very* close eye on you . . . Or that you'd be allowed to leave this building without my say-so? You forget that I *own* both of you, and, quite simply, I decided to let you dig your own graves. Madison may be bankable, but without the backing of Slate Street she's worth nothing. And besides, I've got a new *Teen Star* on the rise who can make me even more money.'

Beau leant back in his chair and allowed himself a private, tiny smile. 'She's a minx in bed, too – far better than either of you, and with *much* better tricks.'

Madison leapt up and rushed towards him, but Jess managed to grab her before she could punch him.

Beau simply laughed. 'What's the matter, Madison? Annoyed your little stripper moves weren't that good after all?'

'You bastard,' Madison said in a low, menacing voice that neither Beau nor Jess had heard before. 'You can't do this to me. You can't *end* my career just like that.'

'Oh, I can,' Beau remarked easily. 'And I have. I may not allow you internet access, but if I did you'd see that your website has announced that the tour's off. We've got ads running in all the major newspapers and magazines this week saying the same thing, and we're refunding all your pathetic schoolgirl fans tomorrow.'

'No!' Madison cried out. 'You can't! You haven't!'

Beau sneered. 'I have. I need people on the books who I can *trust*, Madison, and I can't trust you.'

"But . . . you've spent so much *money* on this. You spent a fortune building my brand, on getting Jess to pretend to be me, on the parties, the pre-tour promotion. You can't just do this to me, to us!" Madison tried to reason with Beau, even though she knew it was no good. He may not care about her, but he cared about money.

Beau dismissed Madison with a wave of his hand. 'I have plenty of money set aside for little setbacks like this. And like I said, I have a new pop sensation who's going to make it up for me. If you're trying to appeal to my business side, Madison, you've no chance. My accountants have sorted it all out.'

Madison bit her lip anxiously. Desperate times called for desperate measures. 'Then I'll go to the press! I'll go to Giles Tavener and I'll tell him all about you and Tori!'

Beau shrugged. 'Like that sack of shit journalist will believe anything you or Jessica say to him now.'

'He will!' Madison yelled. 'You got Tori *pregnant* and then dumped her because she wouldn't have a termination, and you tricked me into having a relationship with you just so I would be pliable. You even did it to Jess! You didn't love any of us! Apart from Tori—'

'That's enough!' Beau said sharply. 'Don't mention Tori to me ever again. And as for you going running along to the papers to tell them that I seduced you, so what? Millions of men fuck girls they don't like to get what they want, and millions of girls do the same thing to men. I'm no exception. It's been happening since the beginning of time, and it's not going to change.'

'The press *will* care,' Jess said in a quiet voice. 'You're all public figures, and Beau, you paint your girls as whiter than white while deceiving them and fucking them and making money out of them. You're practically a pimp. If that isn't scandal, I don't know what is – and if people know what you're really like, your little empire will come crumbling down.'

Beau sighed. 'Oh, Jessica. I have to say that I honestly was attracted to your naivety when we met, and I still think it's touching now. But you need to grow up and stop being a child. This is the music business – it's sex, drugs and rock 'n' roll, and nobody is going to be shocked by a CEO having sex with his acts. Everyone's at it, and it's a non-story.'

'So why were you so outraged when I threatened to go to the press about Tori?' Madison said. 'Why was it such a big deal then, but not now?'

'You really are pathetic, Madison, you know that? You're almost as pitiable as Jess. I never was worried about you running to the press with your little stories about Tori and me. Why would that bother me? But doing it just before we launched your tour and jeopardising the money I stood to make from it? That would have made me pissed. But as we've cancelled the tour and won't be working with you again, I really couldn't give a shit. My new girl is dynamite, and since I'm making sure I get a divorce before we launch her career – and I'm not going to get caught with her being my lover – this "scandal" of yours really won't touch me. It's hardly a big deal.'

The girls looked at each other in panic. Going to the press and exposing Beau had always been their fallback plan. And if Beau really didn't care, they were in serious trouble.

'I don't need to remind you that even though Slate Street will no longer be working with you, we still control everything you do for the next ten years. You're both to disappear from the spotlight, just like Tori did. And if you don't make yourself scarce, well . . . you don't want to know what will happen to you.'

Beau's face was twisted and hard, and neither Jess nor Madison doubted he meant business.

'You're both to leave this apartment tomorrow. I never want to hear from or about either of you ever again. And don't forget, girls, if you breathe a word of this to anyone you'll live to regret it.'

*

The girls' new apartment in Murray Hill on East 36th Street was beautiful, like something out of *Sex and the City*. It was pre-war, with a long entry foyer, a large living room with a wood-burning fireplace, hardwood floors throughout, and high-beamed ceilings that made the west-facing apartment bright and sunny. It was expensive, admittedly, but they needed a proper home after everything they'd been through.

The girls had decided to move in with Leesa on the spur of the moment, while they worked out what they were going to do next. Madison had considered moving back to Ohio, and Jess had thought about going home to London, but both realised they wanted to stay in Manhattan for the time being. They wanted closure on the last few months – and they knew running away wouldn't help them resolve their feelings about Beau and how he'd treated them.

'You know, it's a shame there's not a fourth bedroom,' Leesa said to the girls, as she sank onto the squishy cream leather sofa. 'We could invite Tori Catrino over for a We Hate Beau slumber party.'

Madison stopped unpacking one of the boxes and excitedly looked up at Leesa, and then at Jess.

'That's it!' she exclaimed, pushing her hair off her face and leaving a smudge of dust on her cheek. 'We need to get hold of Tori and find out what the story was with her and Beau! If we know what Beau did to her, then we might be able to get our own back somehow!'

Jess looked sceptical. 'But we *know* what Beau did to her. He did exactly the same thing to her as he did to you – built her up as an American sweetheart, and then, when she was the most famous person in the whole world, married her, got her pregnant, and dumped her.'

'But what if there's more to it than that?' Madison pressed. 'What if something else happened that we don't know about? I mean, we don't know for *sure* that's what happened – we're only guessing from what I managed to piece together. What if he did something else?'

'Like what?' Jess asked curiously.

Madison shrugged. 'I don't know,' she said. 'But it's worth finding out.'

Giles was warily nursing a latte in Kaffee und Kuchen when Leesa breezed in and dumped her coat on the chair next to him. He looked like shit. His normally immaculately pressed suit was creased, he had a week's worth of stubble, and his eyes were tired. Leesa felt a stab of sympathy for him. It wasn't just Jess who was hurting.

'Do you want another?' she asked him, as she made her way to the counter to order a decaf cappuccino.

Giles shook his head, took a bite of his lemon cake, and chewed it thoughtfully. Even though he'd told her that he didn't want her in his life any more, Madison – well, *Jess* – still dominated his thoughts. He'd read all about the cancellation of Madison's tour, how Slate Street stood to lose millions, and how Beau Silverman didn't seem to care. Everyone was asking why Madison would cancel her tour. Was she ill? Pregnant? Had something terrible happened to her? Giles knew he was one of a handful of people who knew the truth, and the reality sickened him. He just wanted nothing more to do with it.

'So what's up?' he asked Leesa, as she sat down and took a sip of her too-hot coffee. 'How are you feeling?'

'I'm all right,' Leesa said soberly. 'Taking each day as it comes, you know? But that's not why I needed to see you, despite wanting to thank you yet again for that piece you ran.'

'Let me guess, you just missed my handsome face,' Giles suggested wryly.

Leesa laughed. 'Well, there is that, although you're not looking too pretty at the moment. But no, I need your help. That is . . . Madison and Jess need your help.'

Just the mention of her name was like a kick in the stomach, and Giles frowned. 'I told Jess I didn't want anything to do with her, and I meant it. And besides, I don't know how I could help them. Beau Silverman is one of the most powerful men in the entertainment business, and I'm just a showbiz editor.'

'We're trying to track down Tori Catrino,' Leesa announced quietly. 'We think she can help the girls find some sort of closure on everything . . . And Giles, they really need it. They're in limbo. You could help.'

'I don't know where Tori is,' Giles said, surprised. 'Why would I?'

Leesa rolled her eyes. 'You may not know where she is *now*, but you're a journalist, aren't you? Don't you investigate things? Besides, Jess said there's some sort of system at newspapers that allow journalists to search for people, like a phone book.'

Giles stared at Leesa. 'There is, but I don't see why I should help either of them,' he said eventually. 'After the lies Jess told me, why should I? Why should I trust anything she says?'

There was silence while Leesa considered her answer. Giles had a point, but unless they spent thousands on a private detective, he was their only hope.

'Because Jess was just doing her job. I know it's a despicable truth, but despite the act she put on, Jess never meant to hurt you. How many times have you justified trashing someone's reputation in that paper of yours because it's your job? You didn't trash me because you hated me, but because it's your job to help sell papers, and at the time, that was the quickest and easiest way to do it.'

Leesa looked Giles in the eye and held his gaze. It was uncomfortable, but she knew she was right.

'I'm not asking you to do something that's going to take up a lot of your time, or harm you in any way . . . I'm just asking you to help two of my friends as they've helped me, and to consider that maybe Jess hated having to lie to you. But Giles, Jess came clean in the end because it was the decent thing to do. And maybe you can help her and Madison make things right by finding out where Tori Catrino is.'

Giles sighed, and drained his coffee cup. He could see he didn't really have a choice.

Chapter Twenty-Four

'God, it's different from flying on the Slate Street private jet, isn't it?' Jess remarked to Madison, as they settled into their American Airlines flight to Boston. They were sitting at the back of the plane, and trying to be as inconspicuous as possible, but it wasn't easy considering just how famous Madison was.

Madison wore her best disguise for the occasion – an auburn wig and baseball cap – and she'd decided to slum it on the flight in jogging bottoms, sneakers and a tight T-shirt.

Jess, on the other hand, was dressing as herself again, and her newly blonde hair shimmered down the back of her bleached, too-small denim jacket over a black Helmut Lang cotton mini-dress. She yawned and stretched her feet out in the aisles to admire her beloved red Louboutins. They were high, but they were also her favourite shoes, and just wearing her own clothes – and dressing in her own style – made her feel good about herself again. Nobody who caught sight of Madison and Jess together would ever confuse them for the same person again.

'It's different, but I definitely prefer it,' Madison said, as she looked around the cabin. The seats were tiny, but she genuinely didn't care. If it was a choice between flying economy with Jess or flying private with Beau, she knew which she preferred.

'You *do* have Tori's address, right?' Jess asked.

Madison rolled her eyes. 'Jess, you've asked me that, like, a million times since we left the apartment. Yeah, I do. She's in Telegraph Hill. It will be a cinch to get to in a cab.'

'And then what?'

'And then,' Madison said patiently, even though they'd already gone through the plans before they left Manhattan, 'we wait.'

Madison and Jess dumped their bags in the room they were sharing at the Copley Square Hotel, and got a cab straight to Tori's house in Telegraph Hill. They stood outside it for a moment, and took in the unassuming surroundings. It was a world away from the glitz and glamour that they – and Tori – were used to, but it was a nice neighbourhood. Madison tentatively rang the bell on the side of the wooden-clad house, and when nobody answered they sat on the step outside the front door and waited, wondering what Tori would be like now, and what her reaction would be when she finally came home.

Several hours later Jess and Madison were roused out of their boredom when a station wagon pulled up outside the house. A small, slender girl got out of the driving seat and shot them a friendly smile. It was, without question, Tori Catrino.

'Tori?' Madison asked.

Tori nodded and lost her smile.

'My name's Madison Miller, and this is Jessica Piper. I hope you don't mind us crashing your home like this, but we really want to talk to you about Beau. Beau Silverman.'

A dark cloud passed over Tori's face, but it didn't detract from her prettiness. She may not have looked as young and fresh as when she'd hit the charts, but she was still cheerleader perfect, with bouncy blonde curls, penetrating green eyes, and gorgeous wide lips.

'I have nothing to say about Beau, or that part of my life,'

Tori said neutrally, and she turned her back on the girls to get her daughters out of the car. The twins.

'We're not here on behalf of Beau, or anything like that.' Jess hurried to the car to help Tori. 'He's . . . well, he's ruined our lives. Madison's especially.'

'I know all about Madison Miller,' Tori said, and her eyes flashed with something Jess couldn't decipher. 'I may not be in New York or LA any more, but I do watch TV, and I do listen to music.' She turned to Madison and stared at her. 'You cancelled your tour, didn't you? It certainly made headlines, but I guess you and Beau know what you're doing. It's for extra promotion, right? He wanted to pull that trick when I was on the label, but luckily for me he didn't.'

'I'm off the tour, and off Slate Street for good,' Madison said, but her eyes were on the twins, who were in their car seats. With their black hair and dark eyes, they looked so like Beau that she couldn't stop staring at them.

Tori looked at Madison quizzically. 'So why do you want to see me? I don't get it.'

Jess gently touched Tori's arm. 'Because we need some help, and we think you're the person to assist us. Could we please come inside so we can tell you our story?'

Some time later, after Madison and Jess had filled Tori in on exactly what had happened to them, they were surprised to see Tori's green eyes fill with tears.

'I can't believe Beau would be so cruel and devious,' she said, wiping her cheeks. Madison and Jess exchanged a glance. She *was* married to the same Beau Silverman that they knew, wasn't she?

'I mean, I *can* believe it, I guess . . . I just didn't realise he was capable of behaving just so badly.'

'What do you mean?' Madison asked gently. 'Didn't he do the same thing to you? Did he build you up to be a superstar and then dump you when he got bored?'

Tori was silent for a moment, and Madison and Jess were on the edge of their seats waiting for her response.

'You know what? He really didn't . . . not in the way you think, anyway. He plucked me from obscurity, sure, but we worked together on my career, and fell in love. We were so happy, and for a while he was the perfect boyfriend – attentive, affectionate. He was always buying me presents and checking I was okay and not tiring myself out. He was good to me.'

'But, I don't understand . . .' Madison said. 'You got married, got pregnant, and then that was the end of your career, wasn't it?'

'Yes, but more happened before then. You have to remember that I was so *young* when Beau and I got together, and he was a big influence on me. Whatever Beau said I took as gospel, and if he'd told me the sky was yellow instead of blue I'd have believed him and scorned anyone who said anything different. Beau and my career were my life, and I kind of became isolated from the rest of the world.'

'That happened to me, too,' Madison whispered. 'Apart from Beau and singing, there was nothing else. It was all about Slate Street.'

'So you know what it's like,' Tori continued. 'But as I started to grow up I began to see that Beau wasn't as perfect as I thought he was. He made silly mistakes with regard to my tour, like wanting to "cancel" it to generate more interest – I mean, what the fuck? – and I started to see he wasn't all that.

'Anyway, I guess you could say I started to rebel, and when I began to question him professionally I also started to wonder if he really was at an "industry dinner", for example, or at late night meetings with record producers. I started snooping, read his texts and emails, and found out he was having affairs – lots and lots of affairs, especially in his office with the door locked. I'm not ashamed to admit that it devastated me. Even though I was starting to lose respect for him, I still loved him.'

'What did you do next?' Jess asked. She and Madison were on tenterhooks.

'I confronted him. I told him I'd seen his emails and that I knew he was having affairs, and I gave him an ultimatum. He committed to me, or we were over. As you can imagine, I was making Slate Street a lot of money at the time, and Beau didn't want to let me go . . . but, in his own way, he loved me, too. I know he did. You can't fake stuff like that.'

To prove he loved her, Beau and Tori got married in secret, and for a couple of months, things were great. But as Tori's career went supersonic, Beau became more distant again, and he began being cagey about the meetings he had at hotels in the daytime, and about who he'd been with when he came home late at night and jumped straight in the shower. Once again Tori went through Beau's phone and emails, and realised he was never going to change. He was a cheater, and always would be.

'But this time I didn't let on,' Tori continued. 'If I'd messed things up with Beau I'd have jeopardised my livelihood.'

Jess's eyes widened. 'So you put up with it for the sake of your career?' she asked.

'Sort of,' Tori said, and a small smile spread across her face. 'I stayed with Beau – I mean, we *were* married – but I began to fall in love with someone else, and even though I'm totally against cheating and everything it stands for, I started having an affair, too. It wasn't puppy love, like it was with Beau, but the real thing. I met someone who loved me for *who* I was, not for what I was – a famous, sexy popstar – and I was blissfully happy.'

'I don't understand,' Madison said, as she digested this information. 'I know what it's like to be Beau's famous female act, and he doesn't let you out of the Slate Street bubble. How did you manage to have an affair?'

Tori laughed. 'Because I was having an affair with Beau's business partner, Donovan York. When I fell pregnant I wasn't sure whose it was, and I knew it was crunch time. I told Beau the truth, Donovan and I were sacked from Slate Street, and that was the end of my career.'

Silence filled Tori's living room, as Madison and Jess digested this news. Suddenly it provided a reason as to why Beau behaved the way he did. It wasn't an excuse, but they understood why he didn't trust women, and kept his superstar female acts completely under his control.

Madison was the first to speak, her mouth dry. 'So apart from having affairs, Beau didn't actually do anything wrong?' she asked.

Tori shook her head. 'Having affairs is bad enough, though, don't you think?'

Madison looked at Jess, who was staring down at the carpet. She knew instinctively they were both thinking the same thing. 'It's terrible, but . . . I don't think that's going to help us,' she admitted, as she gazed over at the twins, who were playing together. They were undeniably cute.

'And the girls? *Are* they Beau's kids?'

Tori nodded. 'They look just like him, don't you think? Luckily Donovan loves them like they're his own.'

'And what's Donovan doing now?' Jess asked Tori. She and Madison had spent hours quizzing Tori about her life with Beau, and she was desperate to change the subject, to talk about something – anything! – normal.

'Well, he originally set up *Teen Star USA* with Beau, so now he's been working on a new talent show with a bit more integrity. You know, one that isn't so heavily influenced by Beau. He did a pilot, and showed it to a few networks who are interested, but nobody will air it while *Teen Star* is still so popular . . . Not only would it get Beau pissed, but it probably wouldn't get the audience it deserved.'

Madison gazed at Tori in interest. '*Teen Star* is a massive source of income for Beau, isn't it?' she said, almost to herself.

'He makes money from the music business, sure,' Tori said, nodding, 'but everyone knows it's getting harder and harder to make money from records. Without *Teen Star* he'd be in the shit. Slate Street could even go under.'

Jess and Madison stared at each other, their eyes wide. Once again, they were thinking the same thing. If they could get *Teen Star* off the air, not only would Beau and Slate Street be in tatters, it would mean Beau wouldn't have the opportunity to manipulate any more budding starlets.

'So if *Teen Star* was cancelled, because, I don't know, someone could prove the phone votes don't count because it's fixed from the start, Donovan's new show would have a chance?'

Tori nodded. 'But how would anyone be able to prove that *Teen Star* is fixed?'

Jess stared at Madison, who was shaking slightly.

'I'll tell them,' she said, swallowing hard. 'I'll tell the world that *Teen Star USA* is all a big con, that the phone votes are just a source of revenue and aren't even counted, and that I entered the contest knowing I was going to win before all the auditions had even started.'

Tori looked worried. 'I know you hate Beau, and with good reason, but nobody's ever taken him on and won. Are you sure you want to do this?'

Madison's eyes narrowed. 'Nothing would stop me.'

By the end of the week Madison's exclusive interview with Giles was out, and her words spread across the world like wildfire, burning Beau Silverman, *Teen Star USA*, and the music industry as a whole.

'I'll admit it,' she said, 'the whole *Teen Star USA* concept is a con. Supposedly the show is open to all – right from the audition process to the live final – but what the millions of viewers don't know is that it's a fix. I was working in a strip club when Beau Silverman approached me and said he'd heard I was a good singer. I cut a demo for him, and he liked it enough to tell me that not only was he putting me forward to be on *Teen Star*, but that I was going to win it, too.

'When the votes were counted during the live final, I didn't get the most – Justin Lewis did. But I knew I was going to win because I'd already recorded my winner's album, and work had started on my next few singles. I felt terrible about that, but Beau Silverman assured me that this was how all TV shows work – that this was what the "real world" was like. I know now that he was wrong, and he manipulated me.

'My marriage to Beau was a sham. I truly loved him, and believed he loved me, but he was only pretending so he could have complete control over me. When we were caught on Necker Island, Beau showed me what he really was, and insisted on a sham marriage to make America like me again. My huge diamond engagement ring turned out to be cubic zirconia and I was left heartbroken.

'I began to feel incredibly uneasy about the whole *Teen Star* situation. I didn't feel comfortable about doing a tour for my fans knowing I hadn't really won the show. When I tried to approach Beau about it he told me I had two choices: I could do the tour and shut up, or he'd cancel not only that, but my singing contract, too. I chose the latter, and that's why my tour was cancelled. I'm extremely sorry that I was involved in such a situation, and that I deceived my fans for so long. I can only apologise from the bottom of my heart, and hope that one day people will be able to forgive me.'

Within hours of publication, the viewers of *Teen Star USA* began revolting on the internet. Hundreds of Facebook groups were created calling for *Teen Star* to be taken off the air, the terms 'Madison' and '*Teen Star*' became trending topics on Twitter, with hundreds of thousands of people castigating Beau Silverman, declaring that they'd never watch *Teen Star* ever again, and offering sympathy to Madison, now seen as a victim of the show.

When the TV network got wind of the story they called a crisis meeting. They'd never encountered anything so damning. The executives of the network immediately issued a statement saying they were going to investigate Madison's claims, but by then the wounds were so deep that there was little they could do to salvage the situation. There was negative publicity, and then there was this. There was no way out of it.

The *Teen Star USA* sponsor pulled out of the next series, stating they no longer wanted their brand to be associated with such a fraudulent show, and quickly afterwards advertisers began to cancel their spots. The network was losing millions of dollars every hour, and without even consulting Beau, the network made a call: they cancelled the show.

Teen Star USA was no longer going to be on the air – and no other network would touch it.

Beau tried to get his company to carry out damage control, telling Bailey to leak to the press that Madison was a pathological liar, and that she needed to go to rehab, but it was no good. Nobody would listen to them, and the journalists that did take

Bailey's tearful calls told her to go to hell. Not a single person wanted to be associated with Slate Street, and most of the artists on the record label hired lawyers to get them out of their contracts and onto whichever other label would take them.

Several staff members also resigned that day – Bailey included – saying they could no longer work for a company with such low moral standards and with a bigamist at the helm. Beau flew into a rage every single time a resignation email landed in his inbox, and he only just managed to pull himself together to go to the American Phonographic Industry Awards. Slate Street wasn't up for any awards, but, as he did every year, Beau had reserved a table. It had always been important that he and his key staffers were seen at the right events, and this year it was vital. Beau was determined to put on a good show, and to pretend Madison's interview hadn't bothered him in the slightest.

'I'm sorry, sir, but we're not going to be able to let you in,' the bouncer said, when Beau arrived at the venue. He stood on the red carpet, clutching his invitation, and the paparazzi were all over him, their cameras flashing against the dark night sky.

'I'm Beau Silverman, and I have a table,' Beau said neutrally, giving the cameras a strained smile.

'I know that, sir, but we're still not going to be able to admit you. The organisers had a change of mind about your attendance.'

Despite the rage that engulfed him, Beau knew better than to make a scene, and the paparazzi gleefully trained their cameras on him as he walked quietly away, their flashes stabbing him like knives.

He had only one thought: he wanted to find Madison and that stupid little Brit Jess, and kill them.

*

'Here's to you, Madison Miller,' Jess said, as she raised a flute of champagne in Madison's direction.

'Yes, here's to you,' echoed Leesa. 'You did a very brave – and honest – thing today, and you should be proud of yourself.'

Madison gave her friends a wobbly smile. 'Do you think so? Really?'

'Of *course* we do!' Jess spluttered. 'You told the whole world that *Teen Star USA* was a sham, and that Beau manipulated you right from the beginning. But you also said that you were walking away from it because you wanted to do the right thing, and that's the bravest thing you could have done.'

Madison looked down at the table they were sitting around. 'I'm not brave,' she said. 'Not like Leesa. Giving a newspaper interview's nothing like dealing with an eating disorder, is it?'

Leesa reached across and took Madison's hand. 'Mads, it *was* brave,' she said softly. 'And I'm so impressed that you stood up for yourself like that. It took a lot of guts.'

Leesa and Jess both beamed at her, but instead of smiling back, big fat tears began to fall from Madison's face onto the tablecloth.

'I've ruined my career, though, haven't I?' she said quietly. 'I may have broken Beau, but I've ruined my integrity, too. After this nobody will buy anything I release again. My days of being a popstar are over.'

Both girls were silent for a moment, and then Jess spoke.

'Madison, I don't know you very well, but I *did* live your life for a bit, and . . . it seemed to me that the whole world you lived in was a nasty and shallow place. Is that *really* what you want? To spend the rest of your life trying to make it in a cut-throat business where nothing is as it seems?'

Madison was just about to open her mouth to answer when there was a huge crash at their front door. The girls looked at each other in terror, and then, without any warning, Beau was in their living room.

'You *fucking* whore. You *fucking, fucking bitch*. How *dare* you do this to me? How *dare* you?' he yelled. His shirt was dirty and sweaty, and he had an expression on his face neither girl had ever seen before. Beau was engulfed in absolute rage, and he was determined to make someone pay for the devastation they'd caused to his company.

Madison stood up, but before she could get out of the way, or before Jess or Leesa could stop him, Beau began punching and kicking her, and he didn't stop, didn't ease up . . . not even when Madison lay still and bleeding on the floor.

'Beau!' Jess screamed. 'Stop it!' She jumped on his back, and just managed to pull him away from Madison when he turned on her. He narrowed his eyes.

'You think you're special, don't you, Jessica,' he snarled, inching his way towards her. 'But let me tell you, you're not the sweet little runaway bride you make yourself out to be. You're as dark inside as I am. You had to be, to pretend to be Madison for so long.'

Jess shook her head. 'I'm not,' she whispered. She was so terrified she was barely able to speak. 'I'm nothing like you.'

Beau began to close in. He was like a feral animal, and he towered over her, petrifying Jess to her very core 'You may be wondering how I knew where you lived. Well, let me tell you,' he spat, 'I've had you and Madison trailed by my bodyguards. Yet again you've been a stupid little girl. As *if* I'd just wave goodbye to you and Madison and trust you not to get up to no good . . . As *if*.'

He was so close to her now that Jess could smell the booze on his breath. Leesa was screaming something at them, but all Jess could focus on was Beau, and where his fist was going to land.

She prayed it wouldn't hurt, but she knew it would. It had hurt the last time.

'You're a *fucking* piece of shit, Jessica Piper. I know you persuaded Madison to go to your little newspaper boyfriend, and that it was all your idea for her to expose me. Well, now you're going to pay the price.'

He raised his fist up in the air, and just as it made contact with her lip she heard a scuffle, and Phil and Jason, Madison's former bodyguards, were pulling Beau off her, and pushing him to the floor.

'Phone the police,' Jason barked at Leesa, 'and get an ambulance here, quick.'

Leesa didn't stop to think what two huge guys were doing in her living room. She dialled 911 with shaky hands, and just about managed to give their address to the operator before rushing back to Madison, who still lay in a crumpled heap on the floor.

Jess was bending over her, holding her bleeding face, and sobbing hard. 'She's not moving!' she screamed, her tears sliding off her cheeks and falling onto Madison's blood-covered body. 'She's not fucking moving! Someone do something. Someone, please, please do something,' she howled.

But all Leesa could do was take Jess in her arms while Beau looked on, and the night became a blur of ambulance sirens, police reports and a lot of pain for everyone.

Epilogue

Jess couldn't take her eyes off the ivory wedding gown hanging in front of her. It was exquisite. The fitted, strapless bodice was adorned with tiny pink crystals sewn with gold thread, and the full, floor-length skirt made of cream duchesse satin and silk taffeta was just the right length so that it would pool luxuriously at the feet. It was classy, sexy and understated. Jess didn't think she'd ever seen anything so beautiful in her life, and just gazing at it made her feel breathless.

Even though it had taken months and months of work to perfect, she still couldn't believe she'd made it. It was an achievement beyond her wildest dreams.

'That dress sure is stunning,' Leesa said, as she examined it. 'Are those *real* pearls?' she said, taking a closer look at the bodice. 'And is that *antique* lace?'

Jess nodded.

Leesa whistled. 'It must have cost you a fortune to make this dress.'

Jess laughed. 'It did, but if you're going to wear something on the happiest day of your life, it should be mind-blowing.'

The girls both stared at the dress again, marvelling at Jess's handiwork. Neither girl could quite believe that Jess had designed and hand-stitched the entire dress all by herself.

'I wish Madison was here to see it,' Leesa said softly. 'It doesn't seem right to be visiting you in London without her.'

Jess gave Leesa a little hug. 'I know what you mean,' she said as brightly as she could. 'But now the wedding dress is done we need to concentrate on getting your bridesmaid dress finished. Are you ready for your final fitting?'

After Beau's attack on the girls, Jess decided it was time to move back to London so she could start to put the last few months behind her. Fortunately for her, Beau had been told that if he didn't give her the money he owed her, she could sue for even more, so he did, and quickly. Jess left Manhattan with a hefty bank balance, and days after getting back to London, she rented a warehouse conversion flat near London Bridge, and started work on her fashion label.

At first, it was tough. She had her family around her, and she spent all her free time with Poppy and Joe, but it was hard to talk about her experiences in America without hurting, so she tried not to. In the middle of the night Jess would wake up with a jolt, not knowing where she was, but she supposed that, given time, the trauma of the previous months would leave her.

To help her sleep, Jess would think of Giles, and wonder what he was doing in New York. Was he okay? Did he ever think about her? She remembered their kiss in the limo, how he'd told her he was falling for her at the Plaza, and those snapshots of happiness felt almost unreal – like a fantasy she was creating to make herself happy. She had to keep telling herself that they *had* happened, and that Giles really had loved her at one point.

Jess just wished he loved her now. It was so hard to get through everything, and without Giles and Madison, it seemed harder. She wished so much that she had Madison by her side . . . Madison, her American twin. Jess missed her so much.

Slowly though, Jess's label – Piper's Dreams – began to take off. Despite everything, Jess still had the knack for creating zeitgeisty pieces and repeatedly pipped the high street to the post when it came to making clothes that girls wanted to wear *right now*. At first she began selling her collection on eBay and Etsy, but as the orders started flooding in, she asked an old friend from college to set her up with a website, and before long she was in business. She even had to take on three assistants to help her design the clothes, which ranged from ripped T-shirts and skin-tight jeans, to textured mini-skirts and sequinned jackets.

When she wasn't working, or out with Poppy, Jess spent most of her time on the internet, catching up on the latest news on Beau and Slate Street. She was obsessed with it, and would often to go bed at two or three in morning because she couldn't leave the web alone.

'It's not healthy, you know,' Poppy said to her one night over a pint of beer, and salt and vinegar crisps, as Jess checked the internet on her iPhone for the sixth time that night. 'You need to try to forget about Beau and all of that.'

Jess smiled weakly. She knew Poppy was right, but she couldn't seem to help it. She'd been fascinated at his attempt to worm his way out of how he'd hit her and Madison, and glad that justice had been served for his bloody attack on Madison. He'd been sent to jail for a couple of years, and was financially ruined.

'I'm trying to, you know,' Jess said, gulping her beer, and concentrating on looking as normal as possible. 'But it's hard. Being part of all of that – Beau, Slate Street, Madison, Leesa – was my *life*, and even though I came back for a fresh start, I can't just pretend that it never happened. And I can't forget about the people I got to know. Does that make sense?'

Poppy sighed. 'It does but, babes, it's all over now. Everything's good again, right?'

'Everything's great!' Jess said, as lightly as she could. She didn't dare tell Poppy that she'd just read on the *Media Guardian* website that Giles Tavener had accepted a job as deputy editor at the *Daily World* in London, because she didn't dare think about the fact that soon he would be in London, working with her godfather and ex-fiancé, and ignoring her from even less of a distance. Everything *was* good again, it was true, and she just had to concentrate on that.

As soon as Beau had been convicted, Slate Street went under, and to make matters worse for Beau, Donovan and Tori's new show – *America's Hits* – had taken the *Teen Star USA* slot, and was an instant success, with a worldwide audience of 100 million that eclipsed anything Beau had achieved with *Teen Star*.

Jess supposed she should be pleased for Tori, and she was, but really, it was nothing to do with her. She wasn't involved. It was as if it was happening to someone she didn't even know.

'Jess, I *love* it!' Leesa said, as she twirled around. Her bridesmaid dress fitted perfectly, and the pale pink silk shot with gold made her strawberry-blonde hair and huge blue eyes stand out even more. She was conquering her bulimia, had put on weight, and looked beautiful.

Jess crossed her arms and grinned. 'You *make* the dress, Lees . . . it really suits you.'

'I might even catch the attention of the best man,' Leesa smiled. 'Do you know what he's like?'

Jess shook her head. 'No idea. Now, what else do we need to do before the wedding?'

'Er, find you a date?' Leesa said, teasingly.

An image of Giles flashed in front of Jess's eyes, and she angrily pushed it away. She wished she could forget about him. But she couldn't.

'I'm fine on my own,' she said neutrally.

Leesa looked at her carefully. 'You don't have to be alone, you know,' she said. 'I know you've been through hell and back, but the next man you like won't reject you as Giles did. He'll understand why you stood in for Madison.'

Jess smiled. 'I made a promise to Madison that I'd never tell anyone about that, and even though it's all over now, I still won't.' She bit her lip. 'It kind of leaves me in a difficult position. I can't seem to let go of it, and if I *did* meet someone I liked – which is doubtful, by the way – I couldn't tell him about it. It was such a big part of my life that it would be like lying, and I'm so over deceiving people.'

Leesa looked at Jess sympathetically. 'It will get better, you know. When I thought death was around the corner I almost gave up, and without you and the support of my friends I probably would have . . . but I didn't, and life's great again. I have my eating disorder charity, and I'm open to having a proper relationship with someone *normal*. I'm leaving D-listers alone for ever! But Jess, I wish it was great for you, too.'

Jess forced a smile. 'It will be, in time. I'm just being melodramatic.' She took one final look at the dress on Leesa and concluded that it was perfect. There was nothing more to do than sew it up properly. 'Now, let's forget about all of that for the moment and concentrate on this wedding – and how we're going to be the best bridesmaids in the world.'

It was a beautiful evening for a wedding in Long Island. The sun was starting to set over the lush green vines that were dotted with pink and purple grapes, and the reds and oranges of the sky cast a rosy glow over the vibrant colours of the vineyard.

'Is everything set?' Leesa asked Jess worriedly, and Jess smiled. It wasn't so long ago that people had thought that she and Madison looked identical, but today, in their pink bridesmaids dresses, and with their blonde hair and blue eyes, she and Leesa matched perfectly. They both dazzled.

'I'm normally the one who worries,' Jess said, breezily, 'but everything's perfect. It couldn't be better.'

And it was true. The girls were standing by the lake that glistened with the changing colours of the sunset, and to their left was a strip of pure white carpet that led all the way to a silver lectern. On either side of it were fifty white chairs tied with pink satin ribbons, and they were filled with guests chatting happily among themselves. At the front were two men clad in smart black suits and ties. Both were fidgeting nervously, although the best man did keep shooting interested looks at Leesa.

'Then I guess we're ready to go,' Leesa said, with excitement shining in her eyes. She pulled herself together and gave the harpist an authoritative nod, and music filled the vineyard. Everything felt magical. Huge white candles flickered in the gentle breeze, and purple lanterns were strung up around the vines. The air was fragrant with the jasmine and honeysuckle that surrounded the mansion just behind them, and everything was still. It was time.

Jess and Leesa turned around, and immediately both of them felt tears pushing at their eyes. The father of the bride was walking slowly towards them, and gliding next to him, with only the slightest hint of a limp from Beau's attack, was Madison, wearing Jess's stunning wedding dress. She looked incredible.

'My second wedding in two years!' Madison whispered to them, as they paused for a moment. Jess quickly checked that Madison's dress was okay, and Leesa handed her a bouquet of creamy, pale pink roses. 'Except this one's real, and I'm blissfully happy.'

Leesa and Jess struggled hard not to let their tears fall as they beamed at her. Madison had had a hell of a ride since the night that Beau attacked her, and had spent a month in hospital recovering from her injuries. For a few days it was touch and go whether she'd pull through, but the doctors underestimated her strength. Two months later she signed up to present *America's Hits*, and now, a year later, she had fully recovered and was America's darling again. She was the successful, sexy presenter of the biggest TV show on the planet, and she was a star.

Madison began the walk down the aisle towards Jared, who gazed at her with such love in his eyes that Jess had to look away. She felt as if she was intruding on a gorgeous, private moment, and seeing him look at Madison like that made her remember Giles. She took a deep breath and followed Madison down the aisle carefully, with Leesa beside her. She wasn't going to think about Giles today. She wasn't going to let anything ruin this happy moment.

As they reached the lectern, and the wedding began, Jess took a moment to survey the guests, who were all watching Madison and Jared intently. On Madison's side were her mother and father, and in the next row were Tori and Donovan, and Phil and Jason, the former Slate Street bodyguards, with their girlfriends. Tori shot Jess a quick grin, before casting her eyes back to Madison and Jared. The other guests had mostly flown in from Manhattan, Walkertown and Jared's hometown in California.

Just then, there was a movement at the back of the ceremony, and Jess almost dropped her bouquet in shock. Madison had invited Giles Tavener to the wedding, and he was taking a seat at the back. He caught Jess's eye, and a slow smile spread across his face. It took a moment, but when she saw how Giles was looking at her — as though she was the sexiest, cleverest and funniest woman he'd ever seen – she began to smile back, and all the stress and nervous energy that had enveloped her body for months slowly began to disappear.

It really was going to be an incredible wedding.